Ulm, AR 72170

A Nasty Way to Die

A Nasty Way to Die

A Randy Lassiter & Leslie Carlisle Mystery

Joe David Rice

ISBN (paperback): 978-1-7362391-3-1
ISBN (ebook): 978-1-7362391-2-4

Copyediting: Ali Welky

Cover and book design: H. K. Stewart

Printed in the United States of America

This book is printed on archival-quality paper that meets requirements of the American National Standard for Information Sciences, Permanence of Paper, Printed Library Materials, ANSI Z39.48-1984.

To **Clovita Rice,** my mother
A fine artist, wonderful poet, and loving parent

~ ONE ~

I knew something was wrong half a block before I reached J.J.'s house. While my best friend could make no claim as a master gardener, he'd always maintained his property in good shape if for no other reason than to mollify a nearby pair of widows with too much time on their hands. But there were enough fallen limbs and branches on his front lawn to fill a wheelbarrow many times over. A severe spring thunderstorm had hammered Little Rock a couple of days earlier and wreaked havoc throughout the city. Only one yard on the entire block still showed ill effects: J.J.'s.

I pulled my pickup to the curb, got out, and stopped in my tracks. Up close, it looked even worse. The zoysia grass stood about shin-deep, the flowerbed bordering his driveway needed a major overhaul, and his privet hedge seemed to have been fertilized with anabolic steroids.

Picking up two candy wrappers and a crumpled cigarette pack from the sidewalk, I made my way to the deep front porch running the width of his house. As I climbed the worn concrete steps, anxious thoughts filtered through my mind. The house appeared vacant. A wrinkled and yellowed flyer from a commercial window-washing outfit hung from the doorknob. After ringing the doorbell, I peeked in the mailbox. Empty. I rang again and eyed the porch. It hadn't been swept in a while. The sole tracks in the gritty dust ended at my feet.

Unless he'd left in a big hurry, J.J. would have called. That's what I told myself as I cupped hands around my face and gazed through the picture window. The dark living room appeared unchanged—a floor-to-ceiling bookcase on the far wall, stone fireplace to the right, and massive leather sofa opposite. J.J.'s antique roll-top desk and a companion captain's chair completed the furnishings. Except for a potted ficus tree next to the window, I saw no signs of life. And even it looked unhealthy; an assortment of withered leaves lay scattered on the hardwood floor beneath the plant.

Like a peripatetic peeping Tom, I circled the house and peered into every window displaying the slightest hint of a crack in the curtains. Nothing seemed out of the ordinary.

The rear half of the property mirrored the front, desperate for attention. After depositing the handful of trash I'd collected into J.J.'s otherwise empty garbage can, I stood, dumbfounded, and stared across the expansive backyard. The overgrown lawn resembled a pasture, soggy leaves and pine needles filled both birdbaths, and at least a bushel of pine cones blanketed the driveway leading to the detached garage.

When I turned to leave, my addled brain began to function again and I remembered a key stashed deep in the recesses of the glove box in my truck. We had exchanged house keys years earlier, soon after J.J.'s move to Little Rock. He checked on my home during those rare occasions when I traveled on extended trips, and I did the same for him. A crash course on houseplant stewardship and aquarium maintenance had been part of the arrangement.

With his house key gripped in a sweaty palm, I returned from my Toyota and climbed the grimy steps to the back stoop. The key slid into the lock and the kitchen door swung open. Inside, I immediately noticed the smell. Musty. As if the place had been abandoned for days.

"Anybody home?" I eased down the long hallway and flipped lights on at every chance, stopping first at J.J.'s bedroom. The bed had been made, more or less, and there were no dirty clothes to be seen. A thin layer of dust covered his nightstand and dresser, but everything looked in order, much to my relief. The same was true for the rest of the house. No jimmied windows or doors, no ransacked rooms or closets, no bloodstains. But no J.J. Newell either.

I walked back to the den, drawn by the gentle gurgle of J.J.'s aquarium, a 50-gallon tank of tropical waters far removed from coral reefs and mangrove bights. A slimy film of algae coated much of its glass walls, but what I could manage to see was unnerving. The fish population had been reduced by three-fourths, and the few survivors looked weak. I searched without success for J.J.'s pair of prized angelfish. Several flimsy skeletons littered the sandy bottom, picked clean. A miniature saltwater catfish, the sole scavenger of the lot, provided the only healthy exception to this dismal picture. He swam about with vigor and stirred up tiny clouds of sediment while nosing among the brittle bones. I sprinkled some food onto the water and watched as the remaining fish darted back and forth like frenzied piranhas.

Pulling myself from the aquarium, I made another pass through J.J.'s home, hoping I might have overlooked something. A faint but peculiar smell in the hallway teased my nostrils. I followed my nose into the laundry room where a large load of damp towels had soured in the washer. I tossed a cup of detergent on top and started the machine. What could have caused J.J. to have left his laundry unfinished?

For half an hour, I tended to my friend's houseplants. Some had wilted and would recover, but others had already given up the ghost. I then treated and added two gallons of water to the aquarium and was about to leave the den when my eyes locked on a guitar propped against the sofa. What's that doing here? I wondered. To the best of my knowledge, J.J.'s musical talents were pretty much equal to mine. Non-existent. But it was a handsome thing, and the brand—Gibson—was one I recognized. A beginner's guidebook to chords lay on a nearby end table, all but hidden under a small stack of sheet music. The piece on top—Dylan's "Knockin' on Heaven's Door"—caused me to momentarily freeze.

Baffled, I returned to the kitchen. A swarm of gnats circled above a bowl of mushy apples. I tossed the fruit into the backyard, figuring the squirrels and birds would solve that dilemma. I then examined the refrigerator, and my nose again recognized a problem. A dull layer of mold hid what remained of a pint of raspberries. Those disappeared down the disposal, but the subtle smell didn't go away. I rechecked every shelf and drawer and soon discovered an expired carton of milk stored in a compartment on the refrigerator door. About to gag, I poured the thick, lumpy liquid down the drain and then backtracked to the laundry room where I heaved the load of towels into the dryer.

The unexpected jangling of the telephone made me jump. I lifted the receiver on the third ring, took a deep breath, and said, "Hello." My pulse raced.

After a brief hesitation, a timid female voice asked, "J.J., is that you?" The woman sounded nervous. Maybe frightened.

"No, it's—"

The line went dead. I stared at the phone, the same land line that had gone unanswered time and again when I'd called over the past two weeks. I wished J.J. owned an answering machine or one of those caller ID gadgets. But my independent friend had never been one to embrace technology. More than once I had kidded J.J. that he was the last man in America without a cell phone.

"And I sure don't want Fritter or Spacebook," he'd said earlier this spring.

"That's Twitter and Facebook, not—"

"I don't need them either," he had replied with a dismissive wave of his hand.

My heart still pounding, I spotted a remote control for the garage door, one of J.J.'s few concessions to technical innovations. I stepped onto the back porch, pushed the button, and watched as the large door lifted. Before it reached the halfway point, I realized that J.J.'s classic Jaguar convertible was gone. I fingered the device once more to close the garage and was about to step outside and lock the house when the ringing of the telephone again startled me.

"Hello," I said.

"Professor Newell." Another female voice. "I'm Natalie Yee at—"

"Excuse me," I said, interrupting. "This is Randy Lassiter, one of J.J.'s friends. He's ... uh ... unavailable right now."

There was silence at the other end of the line.

"May I take a message?" I asked.

"Yes," she said. "Thank you very much. J.J. missed his last appointment with us and he's scheduled to be here late this afternoon. I'm calling to confirm."

I paused a moment and tried to collect my wits. "You may have to fill me in a bit," I finally said.

"I'm with the Neonatal Intensive Care Unit at Arkansas Children's Hospital," she said. "We have a program called Child Life where adults volunteer to hold infants—and J.J. has always been one of our most dedicated and reliable participants."

"Hold infants? What do you mean?"

Ms. Yee shared a light chuckle. "You're by no means the first to ask. Our hospital screens and trains adults to hold newborn babies, providing them with warmth and comfort and soothing voices. The results have been nothing short of miraculous."

"And J.J. does this?"

"Oh yes! He's one of our original volunteers—we call them 'the cuddlers'—and he's never missed one of his sessions. Until week before last, that is."

An image of a tiny baby nestled in J.J.'s brawny arms filled my mind. I'd known him half my life and had no idea he participated in such a program. Were there other secrets to be uncovered?

"Mr. Lassiter, are you still there? Can you pass my message along to J.J.?"

I had to clear my throat. "Yes, I'm still here. And ... uh ... when I see J.J., I'll tell him you called."

"Do you think we can count on him later today?"

It was a question I didn't want to answer. "I'm afraid not," I said. "I don't believe I can reach him in time."

"I understand, but thanks for your help. And please give me a call if you'd like to volunteer. We need more folks like J.J. Newell to get these precious newborns out of bassinets and into human arms. As I'm sure you know, he's a very special man."

"He is that," I said with a sniff. "A very special man."

"Goodbye."

I placed the phone's receiver in its cradle, leaned against the kitchen counter, and wiped away a tear trickling down my cheek.

* * *

J.J. had bought the craftsman-style bungalow half a dozen years ago after moving to the city from Baton Rouge. He must have inspected 25 houses before a desperate seller accepted his low-ball offer on what his weary agent charitably called an "extreme fixer-upper." Ever the perfectionist, J.J. had devoted most of his first summer in Little Rock to a steady stream of do-it-yourself home improvement projects. He jokingly claimed to be on a first-name basis with the entire staff at Home Depot. He scraped and sanded layers of old paint, cut and laid tile, replaced siding, glazed and caulked windows, and even built a deck. Repainted in beige—or antique champagne, to use real estate jargon—with a rich burgundy trim, the house was a showplace. Or at least used to be.

On the way back to my truck, I encountered a young man on the sidewalk. "It looks like you need some professional help," he said.

I stopped and looked him hard in the eyes. "I beg your pardon."

He met my stare with a practiced smile and then handed me a business card. "Your yard," he said. "My lawn service company is the best in town." He gestured over his shoulder to an extended-cab pickup with a trailer full of mowers, blowers, and edgers parked in front of my Toyota. Two tanned college-age young men leaned against the hood. "My men and I can make this property sparkle. Guaranteed."

Following a quick round of negotiations, I shook the youthful entrepreneur's hand and gave him one of my cards. "Please send the bill to this address."

"You bet."

I turned and stared at J.J.'s empty house. When I shut my eyes, I recalled the tour he had given me the day the deal had closed.

Located in the city's old but chic Hillcrest neighborhood, his home occupied a large corner lot a few blocks north of War Memorial Stadium. "Perfect for the Arkansas-LSU football games," he'd said before we reached the front door. It was also near enough that we sat on the front porch and eavesdropped on concerts on occasion, including a standing-room-only performance by the Rolling Stones in the same stadium earlier in the spring. The acoustics were lousy, but parking spaces were guaranteed and J.J.'s beer selection couldn't be beat. And I never had to wait in line for his restroom.

The roar of a two-cycle engine brought me back to reality. I sidestepped a roiling cloud of bluish-gray smoke, gave my new friend behind the lawn mower a nod, and climbed into the truck. I wished for enough time to check with some of J.J.'s neighbors, but a moody, high-maintenance client was scheduled to arrive at my ad agency in fifteen minutes. Punctuality was one of her few good traits. That and she paid her bills on time.

I'd known James Joseph Newell—called J.J. by everybody—for years, and we'd been close—almost brothers—after his move to Little Rock. We often talked by phone and saw each other a couple of times a month. He had never left town for any length of time without letting me know.

My mind searched for a reasonable explanation. But my heart knew otherwise.

* * *

On the drive back to my office, a flurry of random, disjointed thoughts fought for recognition. As I remembered a pivotal conversation J.J. and I'd had years earlier, a smile worked its way across my face. I had just set up shop as Lassiter & Associates, the newest addition to Arkansas's already overcrowded advertising scene. J.J. resided in Baton Rouge at the time, wrapping up his Ph.D. in zoology. While he'd gone to Louisiana State University for graduate work following our days together at the University of Arkansas in Fayetteville, I had settled in Little Rock to undertake a less formalized continuing education program of my own design. Hopping from one ad agency

13

to another every six months, I filed away a wealth of experiences—good, bad, and awful—and somehow managed to survive the 70-hour weeks expected of junior employees. After two long but memorable years in the trenches, I submitted my final resignation.

I then threw caution and common sense to the wind, acquired a ragtag collection of secondhand office furniture, and opened my own agency. Located on the wrong end of a semi-fashionable street near the city's Amtrak station, my quiet two-room workspace overlooked a world of winos and wannabes. I didn't have a single client, but I could claim a spiffy logo, a fancy telephone, and an irrepressible urge to be my own boss.

The first call on my new phone came from Baton Rouge. "Randy, I've got some good news," J.J. said.

Something was up. Always before he had called me at home in the evenings to take advantage of cheaper rates. "Let me guess … Your tests from the Health Department came back negative?"

"Go to hell," he said with a laugh. "It's official. I got the degree and—"

"Congratulations!" I interrupted. "Shall I address you as … Dr. Newell?"

"How does Professor Newell sound? I've accepted a faculty appointment."

This sounded serious. I slid my crossword puzzle to the side, certain that I had the rest of the week to work on it. "Don't tell me you'll be in a position to influence the lives of young, impressionable students?"

"It's a full-time job."

I noticed a hint of excitement in his voice. "Let's hear the sordid details," I said.

"The biology department is small, but it's in an up-and-coming institution."

"And where might that be?"

"The University of Arkansas Little Rock." He paused for a moment. "I'm scheduled to move next week."

14

~ TWO ~

My last visit with J.J. had been a good one. Desperate to discover a clue—any hint of a clue—that might explain his disappearance, I replayed it in my mind countless times, trying to recall every gesture, every comment, and every expression he'd made that afternoon.

He had arrived at my house for a May Day cookout carrying a dozen roses. I met him at the front door and led him to the kitchen, the refrigerator to be specific. Like me, he'd dressed casually, wearing a coral polo shirt, khaki shorts, and scuffed, size 14 deck shoes. Once he selected his craft beer of choice, we walked through the house toward the back door. The bottle of pale ale in his left hand balanced the flowers in the right.

I'd invited him over to meet Leslie Carlisle, my beautiful and talented fiancée, who'd moved to Little Rock days earlier. I had planned to introduce them months ago when she scheduled one of her infrequent trips to Arkansas. But our first tentative get-together fell through after one of J.J.'s colleagues had taken ill, forcing J.J. to rush to a national conference in St. Louis as a last-minute speaker replacement. The second collapsed when an unexpected assignment from a frantic photo editor caused Leslie to cancel a weekend visit. I had high hopes our luck would change with the third try.

"Things already look better," J.J. said and pointed to a bright new throw and matching pillows on the sofa in the den. "It must be the feminine touch." He stopped for a moment and studied the room. "But where's your ping pong table?"

15

"We … er … decided to give it to the Boys & Girls Club."

J.J. slapped me on the back. "Ah, a concession to cohabitation. But that classic rocking chair is a perfect addition to this room."

"It's an heirloom from Leslie's grandmother."

My two-story Victorian house, located in the city's historic Quapaw Quarter District, had indeed become much more of a home with Leslie's arrival. Besides, I could claim a tax deduction for my Boys & Girls Club donation along with several similar contributions—including six large boxes of priceless Dallas Cowboys memorabilia—I'd made in recent weeks to other charitable organizations.

"J.J. Newell, meet Leslie Carlisle," I said as he and I walked down the back steps and across the patio to the picnic table.

Leslie, who'd returned from her Saturday afternoon aerobics class half an hour earlier, had changed into a short linen sundress complementing her deep green eyes and accentuating her long, tanned legs. Strappy leather sandals and crimson toenails completed her eye-catching spring fashion statement. She placed the last of five plates on the red-and-white checkered tablecloth, then extended her hand and flashed J.J. a warm smile, highlighted by dimples. He set his beer on the table, brushed her arm aside, and enveloped her in a big hug. The flicker of surprise in her eyes made me grin.

J.J. backed off, but kept one arm around her shoulders. The other hand still held the roses. "Handshakes are for strangers, Leslie. Since you're the focus of every conversation I've had with Randy during the past six months, it seems like I already know you." She laughed as he gave her another squeeze. I couldn't help but notice she hugged back.

As he stepped away, J.J. brought a hand to his chin and gave Leslie an exaggerated inspection, followed by a low whistle. "You weren't kidding about one thing, Randy. This Leslie Carlisle chick is a real babe. A genuine hottie." He arched his eyebrows and shared another wide grin before quickly handing her the roses.

"These are lovely," Leslie said. She then punched him on the arm. "But don't push your luck."

"Couldn't you have done better than this burned-out, washed-up, over-the-hill adman?" J.J. asked. He shot a wink my way.

Leslie came to my defense. Sort of. "I think he's cute." She swung her free arm around my neck and kissed my cheek.

At six two and tipping the scales at 185, I'm within 10—okay, 15—pounds of my college weight. While no Adonis, I have a full head of brown hair, my own teeth, and—I'm told—a good smile. In my mind I'd always pictured myself as marginally handsome and … well … virile. But cute?

"The single major flaw I've observed so far," Leslie said with a sparkle in her eyes, "seems to be his selection of friends."

"Ouch!" J.J. grimaced as his shoulders slumped. "Not only is she attractive and brilliant, she's got a rapier wit. Randy, you could be in real trouble."

"I have no fear," Leslie said, "that he's up to the challenge." She patted J.J. on his broad back and then stepped inside to find a vase for the roses.

J.J. followed me across the patio where I wiped down the grill and lit the mound of lump charcoal. Leslie rejoined us moments later and we moved our lawn chairs upwind under the shade of a massive white oak.

A large hand wrapped around his bottle of beer, J.J. held it high. "Let me start over," he said to Leslie. "Welcome to Little Rock. You've been here a week, right?"

"Almost. It took a little longer than expected to get the last of my furniture and clothing packed and moved."

"Didn't what's-his-name help?" J.J. leaned his bottle in my direction.

"Just like I drove your U-Haul truck from Baton Rouge," I said. "Sometimes I think I should have been a teamster."

"Even that would be a big improvement over your purported profession of advertising," J.J. said. The gleam in Leslie's eyes told me she'd found a kindred spirit. I pretended to ignore them both.

A pair of fox squirrels playing tag in the limbs high overhead interrupted our conversation. After they vanished in the branches, J.J. looked back to Leslie. "Think you'll miss Austin?"

"It's gotten too big and the traffic is horrible." She tipped her beer to her mouth. "Little Rock's a nice town, much more my speed."

"I'm liking you better all the time," he said. J.J. was in the middle of a healthy swig when a loud "Anybody home?" caught our attention.

The gate in the fence swung open and woman well into her pregnancy stepped into the yard followed by a man with an ice chest balanced on his shoulder. Ellen Yarberry, my younger sister, and her husband Gib had arrived.

Her manners much better than ours, Leslie stood and greeted them with hugs. In a feeble effort to avoid appearing like lazy and loutish slugs, J.J. and I followed suit. Reluctantly.

Their arrival was my cue to put a platter of catfish fillets on the grill.

"You're looking more radiant every day," Leslie said to Ellen.

Hands draped across her abdomen, she smiled. "Another six weeks and you can call me Mom."

"And I'll be that lucky child's uncle," I added as I dropped the last of the fillets into place.

"That's not a very comforting thought," my brother-in-law said, shaking his head.

J.J. gave Gib a gentle slap on the back. "Have you killed anybody this month?" Gib—short for Gibson, an old family name—is one of the city's top plastic surgeons. As expected, he wore a cell phone on his belt.

"Not yet," he said with a shrug. "But there's still plenty of time. After all, it's only the first."

Gib was also a notorious and unrepentant punster. Wondering when his first alleged witticism would strike, I reached for my beer.

Gib opened the ice chest and removed the bowl of boiled shrimp they'd offered to bring as an appetizer. It must have tilted on the way over; all the little crustaceans had slid to one side. He observed the mess for a moment and shrugged. "This looks … shrimply awful." Gib dipped one into the cocktail sauce and then slipped it into his mouth. "But the spice is right!"

I couldn't stand it any longer and returned to the grill where I basted and flipped the fillets. Leslie and I then stepped inside and brought out the rest of the meal—rolls, green salad, corn-on-the-cob, and fresh strawberries. When she announced "chow time," I retrieved the catfish.

We were about ten minutes into the meal when J.J. waved his fork to get our attention. "I've never heard the complete story behind this unusual long-distance courtship between Leslie and Randy. Can somebody explain it to me?"

"I'll take full credit," Ellen said as she patted Leslie's hand. "Last October I more or less forced Gib and Randy to go on a camping trip together in the Ozarks—and that's when my brother met his wonderful fiancée."

"Truth be told, I dreaded the expedition," I said. "Gib and I had never gotten along—"

"Randy's not coming clean," Gib said. "The fact is, he couldn't tolerate looking at me, much less being in my company."

J.J. turned his gaze to me, his eyebrows raised.

"That's pretty accurate," I said with a nod. "In fact, with Gib sharing one of his obnoxious puns every ten miles or so, I wasn't sure I could survive the drive up. But when we hit the trail, I tried to stay far enough ahead so I wouldn't have to listen to his incessant chatter."

"And there I was on a magazine assignment out in the middle of nowhere, photographing the spectacular fall foliage, when these two guys came stumbling along," Leslie said. "My first thought was something straight out of *Deliverance*."

"Next thing we know, we're somehow involved in some tricky business with a desperate drug-runner and his hired thugs," I said.

"So, the three of us hightailed it through the Ozark wilderness, fleeing for our lives. Meanwhile, some serious chemistry had developed between those two," said Gib, pointing at Leslie and me.

"You can learn a lot about a person when times are tense," Leslie said. "And I liked what I saw in Randy." She leaned over and kissed me on the cheek. "Even more now."

Gib had cut into his fourth serving of grilled catfish when the cell phone rang. He asked a couple of questions and listened a few seconds before he gave a series of precise instructions. "I'll meet you at the hospital in 30 minutes," he said and snapped the phone shut.

"Sorry," he said, "but I'm on call this weekend."

"I'm going to let Gib drop me off at home on the way to the hospital," Ellen said. "I can feel a major nap coming on."

"No problem," I said. "We'll get together again soon."

After a hurried round of hugs, Gib and Ellen gathered their supplies and waved goodbye.

J.J., Leslie, and I nibbled on the remaining food, exchanged opinions on various local and world events, and drank another beer or two as we relaxed on the warm, lazy afternoon. I was on the verge of dozing off when J.J. rapped his knuckles on the table. "If it's permissible, I'd like to offer a toast." He raised his beer and ours followed. "To Leslie Carlisle and Randy Lassiter. May the gods favor you both."

"I like that," Leslie said, and I echoed her thought.

"When's the big date?" asked J.J.

"Sometime this fall," Leslie said. "We're thinking mid-October."

J.J. cringed and reached for his wallet. "Jesus! The Razorbacks and Tigers will be playing then." He pulled a small card from his billfold and studied it.

Leslie gazed at me, her bright eyes full of questions.

"He's looking at a Razorback football schedule," I said. "J.J. hasn't missed an Arkansas-LSU game in years."

The fact was, I hadn't either. After graduating from the University of Arkansas, J.J. and I established a tradition of attending the annual gridiron battle between the bitter rivals. Whether in Baton Rouge, Fayetteville, or Little Rock, we always enjoyed a memorable weekend, with time set aside to include excursions to the local brewpubs. Now and then we even saw some good football.

"Damn right! And I'm not going to start now, ei[...]
I winked at Leslie.

"It's the second Saturday in October," said J.J. "[...] Rouge." He snapped his fingers. "Here's an idea. You could [...] ried down there. Bring in a Cajun band. Make it a tailgate pa[...]

Leslie almost choked on her beer.

"I'm not suggesting you live in Baton Rouge," he said, spearin[g] another strawberry. "A couple of days would be plenty. You know, a quaint little ceremony and the honeymoon routine."

"Thanks, J.J. We'll take care of all the arrangements," I said. "But your schedule will be handy. We need your help with the date."

J.J. looked at Leslie and then to me, his fork stopped in mid-air. "What?"

"I'd like you to be my best man."

As he lowered the fork to his plate, a smile eased over J.J.'s face. "Me? Your best man?"

"We'll work around the game."

He turned to Leslie, his mouth gaping.

She grinned, then said, "Randy's counting on you."

I tossed him another bottle. "What's your answer?"

"Hell, yes! I'm always ready for a good celebration."

"You'll have to wear a tuxedo."

"I'll be the tallest penguin in Arkansas."

But a handsome penguin, I thought. At six feet six with his solid build and ready smile, J.J. would look damn good in a tux.

I was still chuckling when Leslie's gaze shifted. "Are we expecting another guest?" she asked. She stared over my shoulder, her eyes fixed on the gate.

~THREE ~

I glanced toward the gate and saw a diminutive figure weaving across the lawn in our direction. Leslie must have heard my involuntary gasp.

"Who is it?" she asked, her voice low.

With my eyes squeezed shut, I prayed that I'd experienced a mirage, a bad dream, or even a mild hallucination. I took a chance and peeked. No such luck.

J.J. snorted. "You're in for a unique experience," he whispered. "It's Booker Arrison, Randy's screwball uncle. One of the strangest people on the face of this earth."

And J.J. was being kind.

As was his custom during daylight hours, Booker hid almost every square inch of his gaunt body from the sun. Wearing baggy cotton slacks, a loose-fitting long-sleeved shirt buttoned to the collar, and a wide-brimmed Panama hat, he gave us an anemic wave as he neared the table. Except for shiny black leather boots, a matching belt, and a fuchsia scarf wrapped around his skinny neck, he presented a study in white.

Twenty feet away, he stopped and lifted what appeared to be some sort of high-tech camera to his pale face. "Continue with your trivial and inane conversation," he said in his low, breathless voice. "I'm producing a documentary on the American middle class."

We stared at him.

22

"Please humor me," he insisted. "I'm in possession of the latest digital camera and must ascertain its capabilities." He moved closer to the picnic table, panned the compact device across the food, and provided a dry, nasal commentary as he filmed. "Here we observe a favorite American pastime: carnivores consuming the flesh of innocent animals in a quaint outdoor environment." He leaned over and recorded what remained of the platter of fillets. "Today's offering was, let me guess, a piscatorial sacrifice?" He swung the camera to my face, the lens mere inches away.

"Catfish," I said, and nodded at my distorted reflection in the glass. "Would you care for a piece?"

My vegan uncle ignored the question and aimed his camera at the bottle in J.J.'s hand. "And here," he said, "we have a typical American consumer in the never-ending quest to escape his drab and dismal existence." J.J. winked at Booker, brought the beer to his lips, drained it in a couple of deep gulps, and then wiped a hairy forearm across his mouth. Booker, of course, had been a teetotaler his entire life.

Circling the table, my uncle slid in next to Leslie, his face pressed against the camera's view finder. "And whom do we have here?" He moved the camera up her body, slowed for a moment at the scooped neckline of her dress, and stopped when he drew even with her face. "Does the charming lady have a comment for Booker's *Lifestyles of the Average and Unknown*?" Leslie stared into the lens, sharing the slightest trace of a smile, but made no reply. He zoomed in for an extreme close-up. "Such an exquisite goddess. An oasis of beauty in a den of despair. Do you have plans this evening?"

"Big plans," she said and her smile deepened. "Very big plans." Under the table, her bare toes tickled my calf.

Booker got to his feet and panned the camera one last time across the picnic table. "That's the report from Little Rock on this most festive of occasions, May Day." As soon as he removed his face from the eyepiece, he slipped on a pair of opaque, wraparound sunglasses, the colorful frame matching his silk scarf. His nose and sunken cheeks had been swabbed with zinc oxide. "I will request a serving of mineral water, dear nephew," he said. "French, of course. But first, I demand an introduction to this refreshing bit of humanity."

"Leslie Carlisle, this is my uncle, Booker Arrison."

Leslie rose and extended her hand. Booker took it and lifted her fingers to his lips. "An extraordinary pleasure indeed. I do worry about your choice of companions, however. Given your association with my disreputable nephew and his Bunyanesque compatriot, I fear I have already formed certain forceful opinions about your judgment." He released her hand with a flourish. "Rather negative, I should add." He settled into a lawn chair next to J.J.

Leslie didn't know what to say. Or maybe she was just being polite. She somehow found a smile, sat down, and reached for her drink.

J.J. patted Booker on the back. "I haven't seen you in months. Are you still the poster boy for Reprobates Anonymous?"

Booker pretended not to hear him and waggled a delicate hand at me. "Water. I'm beyond parched. Oh, yes. The motivation of this visit is to return your binoculars." He slipped his hand into an oversized shirt pocket and handed me a leather case. "They proved quite handy." He pulled a tube of balm from another pocket and applied a generous treatment to his narrow, colorless lips. Extracting a tiny container from yet a different pocket, he spread a thick lotion across the tops of his small, pasty hands and rubbed it into his skin. Organic sunscreen, I supposed.

When I pushed back from the table and stood, Leslie did the same. "I'll help," she volunteered. Booker and J.J. had begun a debate about the history of May Day as we left for the kitchen.

"Is that character really your uncle?" she asked once we were out of earshot. I sensed that second thoughts about our engage-ment—not to mention my genetic material—might be swirling through her head.

"My mother's younger brother. He's not as bad as you think." Truth be told, he was far more eccentric than Leslie could have imagined. I'd hoped to avoid any mention of Booker, much less a face-to-face introduction, for many years … if not longer.

Neither malicious nor evil, Booker was, well, bizarre. A complete surprise to my grandparents, Booker arrived after his sole sibling, my mother, had entered high school. Tiny at birth, he remained small through adolescence and topped out at maybe an inch or two over five feet. Uterine fatigue, I've heard. While his size precluded participation in organized sports, he hit his studies hard, earning the "Booker" sobriquet and a host of academic honors. His given name of Gerald went by the wayside, recognized only by a few officious bureaucrats.

Booker accepted a full academic scholarship to Houston's Rice University where he majored in electrical engineering. Within three years he had earned his degree and signed on with an up-and-coming computer company in California. After an initial posting to Europe, he spent a decade in Asia. Booker retired on his 40th birthday and returned to Little Rock, fixed for life on royalties from an obscure invention that, the best I could determine, had something to do with fiber optics. His interest in cutting-edge gadgets and gizmos never waned, making today's episode with the new camera a bit of an embarrassment but not uncommon. I figured his May Day video would soon join the lengthy collection of his previous works on YouTube.

The one thing Booker pursued with more gusto than technology was women, and he was successful if marriages are the measuring stick. Despite his effeminate nature, or maybe because of it, he brought out the nurturing instinct in certain unfortunate members of the opposite sex. He's partial to blondes—natural or otherwise—who possess generous figures. I believe it was my father who years ago said Uncle Booker had a predilection for women "who are clearly mammals." My theory attributes this interest to his stature; he's often at eye-level with their breasts.

I could vividly recall when Booker introduced a new trophy wife to the relatives one Thanksgiving, then showed up with a newer consort over the Christmas holidays. At last count, Booker had said

"I do" at least six times, and that number may be low since his activities during a two-year stint in France remain unknown to the family. Outside of a raft of titillating anecdotes, the unions have produced nothing more than a steady series of divorce decrees.

Inside the kitchen, Leslie opened a cabinet and removed a glass.

"That won't do," I said. "Uncle Booker is very particular about his water." I searched the pantry, found the empty Evian bottle I'd set aside for these occasions, and handed it to Leslie. "Fill 'er up."

She gave me that arched eyebrow look I find so appealing. After locating a clean goblet, I shrugged. "I've done this for years. He's never said anything."

Leslie removed the cap and held the bottle under the kitchen faucet. "Can I assume Booker is a birdwatcher?"

"Not that I know."

She pointed to the compact leather case I'd placed on the kitchen counter. "But the binoculars—"

"He said something weeks ago about keeping an eye on a neighbor."

"So, he's one of those citizen activists, a neighborhood guardian?"

"Not quite," I said. "I believe 'voyeur' is more appropriate in his case."

Leslie raised her eyebrows again as she twisted the Evian cap into place. "Is there anything *else* about Uncle Booker you should tell me?"

"Did I mention that he's on my payroll?"

Her eyes went wide. "You've got to be kidding!"

As I searched for a suitable serving tray, I told her how Booker ended up at the agency. Soon after Lassiter & Associates opened for business, I ran into a rather major and unexpected cash flow problem. Never mentioning collateral, which was fine by me since assets were scarce, Booker extended a $10,000 loan. Interest free. I repaid it within a year but felt obligated to agree when he asked to kill some time by doing odd jobs around the agency. I consented and have paid him a modest monthly retainer ever since.

A decade later, he's my senior employee, a curmudgeon more often than not but committed to the agency's success. While Booker has always refused a title and disdains business cards, I'd describe him as my director of technical services. Avoiding normal working hours, he shows up almost every night except weekends and tinkers with everything from electric pencil sharpeners to color copiers. Computers and their peripherals, I explained to Leslie, are his forte.

I found a tray and wiped it clean. "Any other questions?" I asked as we started to the door. That was a mistake.

Leslie took a few steps before stopping. "Yes, there is one." She paused for a moment. "I'm not sure how to ask this, but is your Uncle Booker … Does he lead, shall we say, an alternative lifestyle?"

I knew she'd ask sooner or later. I rubbed my chin, then took a deep breath. "Booker has an unusual sexual—"

"That's okay," Leslie said. "I have a lot of gay friends."

"He's not gay."

Leslie stared at me as if I'd lapsed into an unknown tongue.

"The old goat's about as heterosexual as you'll find."

"What?"

"He's had … er … several wives over the years. Several more than several, in fact, although I believe he's unattached at the present."

Leslie stared at me, her mouth open.

I cleared my throat, took another deep breath, and said, "He enjoys costumes."

"Costumes? Like for Halloween? I still don't understand."

"Booker is a drag performer."

Leslie gave me a long sideways look as she ran a hand through her silky hair. "He wears women's clothing?"

"Evening gowns, for the most part. With hose, high heels, cosmetics, the works. And wigs, of course. Dozens of wigs. There's a private club in town with pageants every Saturday night. Booker—whose stage name is Monique Monét—is a crowd favorite."

She stared at me for what seemed like half a minute before an impish grin inched across her face. "Just don't tell me you're his booking agent."

"I've heard he even gets fan mail. His Facebook friends number in the thousands."

"Is this common knowledge at your office?"

I shook my head. "Booker's discreet. Most of the staff barely know him since he's seldom around during normal business hours. And when he does show up, people keep their distance. Booker's not one to chitchat around the water cooler."

"But this … interest of his …" She sighed heavily. "Aren't we in the Bible Belt?"

"The festivities begin at midnight if you'd care to go," I said. "It's a fascinating experience. Great music, boisterous crowds, and—"

"Maybe another time."

As Leslie carried the tray with the Evian bottle and goblet to the picnic table, Booker jumped to his feet. He filled the glass, raised it toward the heavens, and said, "A toast to the gracious gods for allowing such beauty in our midst." As Leslie and I exchanged surreptitious winks, he took a slow sip, then again held the water skyward. "*A la France, pour cet eau merveilleux des Alpes.*"

While J.J. and I swapped puzzled looks, Leslie lifted her beer to the heavens. "*Et a vous, monsieur, pour votre gout discriminatoire.*"

Booker lowered his sunglasses and gazed at Leslie with a dreamy smile as he returned to his seat. It was anything but an avuncular appraisal.

"Enough," I said. "I believe the Louisiana Purchase made English the local language."

"Your Uncle Booker thanked the French for the wonderful spring water from the Alps," Leslie said. "And, in turn, I toasted the distinguished gentleman with discriminating taste."

Booker slid his designer sunglasses back in place, but they did nothing to hide his smug look of satisfaction. J.J., however, was not through with the salutations. "To you, Booker, for blessing us with a visit. I haven't seen you in months."

"Blame the nephew. Every night without fail you'll find me at Lassiter & Associates, dragging his barbaric staff into the twenty-first century."

"Every night?" I asked.

Booker shot me one of his rare grins before glancing at his watch. "Saturday evenings are the exceptions. Thank God." He finished his water. "While you melanoma misfits scorch your skin, I must return home. I can feel the ultraviolet rays eviscerating my epidermis."

"Did you repair the fax?" I asked.

"I took the liberty of affixing a rather advanced component, giving me reason to believe it's now the fastest facsimile in the South." He rose and tucked the camera under his arm. "Also, I installed and debugged the new electronic mail system we discussed earlier. It's far superior to what the dolts deserve."

My uncle has little patience with the varying levels of technical sophistication at Lassiter & Associates. For one slow learner, Booker left—anonymously, of course, although no one ever questioned its source—a set of homemade flash cards on the man's desk. Each labeled in large print, one showed an electrical outlet, another a keyboard, a third a monitor, and so on. Booker more or less confessed to the crime a week after the man resigned but showed no remorse. "Let him take his anachronistic attitudes to another agency" was his sole comment.

"Booker, before you go, I need to ask you for a favor," J.J. said. "I've assigned a graduate assistant in my department to upgrade our computers. Any chance you could give her some help?"

"Did you say 'her'?"

"I did indeed. She's quite charming and very intelligent. One of my top students."

"Does she have a love interest?"

J.J. shrugged. "I believe she broke up with her boyfriend not too long ago."

"So, this young woman is vulnerable," Booker said. "Just the way I like them."

Under the table, Leslie's foot delivered a sharp blow to my shin.

"Is she properly curvaceous?"

"Uncle Booker!" Leslie's cheeks had turned red. "That is no way to talk about a woman you've never even met. You are incorrigible."

Booker responded with a smile, his second in the past few minutes and no doubt a record. "Yes, my dear. I often describe myself as 'irresistibly incorrigible.'"

"I'll call you soon with her name and phone number," J.J. said, "but I want you to treat her right."

"I accept telephonic messages after the noon hour." After he'd taken a few steps toward the gate, Booker stopped and peered back at Leslie. "We must visit again, dear, when time's not so precious. Are you new to the nephew's neighborhood?"

There was a slight hesitation in her reply, but she met his gaze. "I'm Randy's fiancée."

Booker's eyebrows peeked above the sunglasses for a moment and fell back in place as he made a series of peculiar clucking noises. "If that's the case, perhaps you, too, should give me a call. The nephew has the number." He pivoted on his heels and left before any of us could wave.

Over the next half hour, while munching on plump fresh strawberries, we selected the third Saturday in October as the wedding date. Although J.J. recalled agreeing to moderate a panel for a conservation group sometime that weekend, he felt a replacement could be found with little trouble. As Leslie and I escorted him toward his car, he promised to get back with us soon and confirm the date.

"One more thing," J.J. said. He paused and shared a self-conscious grin. "I have a special female friend I'd like you both to meet."

"Is she ... properly curvaceous?" Leslie asked. She forced a smile and batted her eyelashes at me. "I hope you'll excuse my earlier outburst."

"I'm sorry that Booker's so ... well ... weird," I said. "He has a good heart. For the most part."

"Unless you're a 'vulnerable' young woman." Leslie made quote marks in the air with her hands when she said it.

"I promise to give my associate a fair warning about Booker," J.J. said. "Full and complete disclosure."

"Tell us about your new friend," I said. After a long-term engagement had fallen apart a couple of years ago, J.J. had all but dropped out of circulation.

"We met in the university library," he said. "Pure serendipity. She plans to make a career change and is working on her master's degree. You'll like her; she's a lot of fun."

"Let's get together first chance we can," Leslie said. "The sooner, the better."

"I'd hoped she could join us today," J.J. said, "but she'd already committed to attend a friend's bridal shower."

We walked J.J. to the curb, where he gave Leslie a peck on the cheek and me his routine bone-cracking handshake. He then folded his big frame into his prized 1971 Jaguar XKE, its top down, and slipped on a pair of sunglasses. He reached for the ignition and the 12-cylinder engine sprang to life, its throaty rumble muffled under the long, gleaming hood. With a smile highlighting every laugh line in his handsome face, he flashed us a hearty thumbs up and pulled the convertible into the street.

J.J. twisted in his seat and looked back to give us a final wave as he turned the corner on that perfect Saturday afternoon in May. It's an image that will be forever etched in my memory. I haven't seen him since.

~ FOUR ~

At the office on Monday morning following the cookout, I checked my e-mails first thing. I'd received yet another exasperating message from Clifford, my head copywriter and newest employee. A bright and energetic young man who came to us with glowing references, he'd been on board less than a month and had already established himself as a productive member of the Lassiter team. That was the good news. The bad news wasn't that he planned to write motivational books in his spare time, but that he insisted on testing my reactions to his tentative titles. Every other day or so he e-mailed me the latest name for his yet-to-be-penned business bestseller and asked for my thoughts. Today's was *Machiavelli for Morons*. In my brief reply, I again advised that he first draft a detailed outline and next get to work on the manuscript itself, one chapter at a time—on his personal computer at home. He could worry over a title much, much later in the creative process. And recalling that last week's titular submission had been *Managing an Epidemic of Morons*, I suggested that perhaps the word "moron" carried certain undesirable connotations.

My challenging relationship with Clifford was an ever-present reminder of a fundamental tenet of the American workplace: being boss involves a lot of unexpected responsibilities. Yet another thing instructors don't bother to mention in college.

As I sat behind the desk and tried to get morons off my mind, a framed photograph on the credenza caught my eye, an all-smiles shot taken of J.J. and me several Octobers ago in New Orleans. We'd driven down to the Crescent City after the Arkansas/LSU football game in Baton Rouge and had enjoyed a good time. Not too good, mind you, but an exceptional combination of food and drink and companionship with an agreeable bit of music in the mix somewhere. And maybe a hog call or two to celebrate the Razorbacks' victory. We'd given up out-and-out debauchery years earlier.

The last time J.J. Newell had visited the agency was a few months ago when he stopped by to return a pair of Emmylou Harris CDs he'd borrowed. He stood with me in a safe corner and watched the office hubbub, his eyes wide and his chin halfway to his chest. Two dozen of us rub shoulders in cramped quarters on West Third Street, half a mile from the downtown skyscrapers but still a vast improvement over my first location. It's an interesting and often chaotic assortment of egos and personalities. For some reason things were a bit rowdy when J.J. arrived. I think the staff was in the initial throes of developing an inspired pitch for a prospective client with lots of potential. Also, it was a Friday afternoon, a time when things get a bit more, shall we say, "loose."

"Welcome to the real world," I said. "No ivory-tower views from here."

Only half joking, J.J. claimed that Lassiter & Associates was Little Rock's version of a Madison Avenue sweatshop. I ignored him. According to the prestigious and expensive West Coast consultants I'd hired late last year, a close workplace environment encourages creativity and contributes to a sense of esprit de corps. These experts had spent five days getting acquainted with the agency staff and observing interactions and activities before they reorganized our physical layout over a hectic weekend. The resulting array of desks, files, conference tables, and workstations may look like hell, but it produces. For Dilbert disciples, let me assure you we have no cubicles. Nor does Lassiter & Associates have policies on pantyhose, neckties, or office decor.

Before J.J. left for his campus office, I showed him a five-figure check, made payable to the Arkansas Department of Finance &

Administration, that we'd place in the mail later in the day. "This, my friend," I said, "is our quarterly contribution to the state's coffers. No doubt a portion of it will be used by the Department of Higher Education, and some of these dollars may go to the University of Arkansas Little Rock to cover your salary."

J.J. grinned, patted me on the back, and said, "Perhaps my initial comments were a bit hasty. UA Little Rock needs and appreciates your help. Keep those checks coming!"

Those memories of J.J.'s visit to my office made me smile. And I was delighted, but not surprised, that he and Leslie had hit it off so well the previous weekend. Like me, Leslie felt J.J. would be a perfect best man.

* * *

Ten days after our May 1st cookout, I telephoned J.J.'s office to verify he'd been able to work the wedding into his October schedule. I should have called earlier, but Leslie and I had traveled to Texas for a couple of days to visit her family in Fort Worth and then on to Austin to attend the wedding of one of her sorority sisters.

After eight rings, a secretary picked up the phone and informed me, between weird smacking noises, that Professor Newell wasn't available. When I asked if she'd take a message, she agreed, grudgingly, and put me on hold as she searched for paper. She placed me on hold again while she located a pen.

"Professor Newell," she explained a full minute later, "has already turned in his grades for the spring semester and isn't scheduled to teach during the summer sessions." After reluctantly taking my name and number, she hung up.

A late morning call to his home went unanswered. After lunch, I tried again with the same result. Most of the remainder of the afternoon slipped away as I hosted a group of visiting business executives from one of those republics carved from what used to be the Soviet Union. Sort of a "people to people" exchange, the event was organized by the State Department and U.S. Chamber of Commerce. After introducing these guests to my colleagues, I spent an hour explaining the ins and outs of the ad agency business and answering their questions. No doubt their queries were better than my responses, but I enjoyed the change of pace. Not only that, the spokesman presented me with a large bottle of premium vodka on the way out. They may yet catch on to this free-enterprise way of making a living.

Ready to call it a day, I was summoned to the telephone one more time. It was Mom, calling to thank me for the Mother's Day lunch Leslie and I had treated her and Dad to the previous Sunday.

"One more thing," she said. "Is J.J. okay?"

Her question both surprised and worried me. "What makes you ask?"

"Well, you know he's sent me a beautiful vase of roses every Mother's Day for years," she said. After his parents' deaths, J.J. had more or less adopted mine. Or maybe it was the other way around. "But this year the flowers never came. Perhaps he's been too busy with his classes …" She sounded crestfallen.

"I'm sure he didn't forget. My guess is that J.J.'s out of town and will deliver a big bouquet when he gets back."

"I hope you're right."

I hoped I was, too.

* * *

Involved in finalizing a complex presentation for a prospective out-of-state client, I forgot about calling J.J. again until Leslie asked several evenings later if I'd heard from him.

"Not yet," I said and reached for the telephone. Still, no answer.

Leslie bit her lip as I replaced the receiver. The consummate organizer, she wanted to get on the minister's calendar, reserve a reception hall, and order invitations. Then there were arrangements to be made with florists, caterers, and—of course—a photographer. And a dress to buy.

"He'd have called if problems arose," I said. "Let's lock in the October 16 date."

"Good," she said with a big smile. She took my hands in hers and led me to the couch. "It's a special date. Very special."

I wrapped an arm around her shoulders and whispered into her ear. "Why is October 16 so special?"

"You know," she whispered back. "Or you'd better know."

"Well, it marks a certain random encounter deep in an Ozark wilderness."

"A random encounter leading to our eventual engagement," Leslie said. "But just how much did fate play a role in our chance meeting? We've never talked about that."

"It's a miracle Gib and I even got out of town together. As you know, we didn't hit it off when we first met. Quite the opposite in fact."

"You felt he wasn't good enough for your sister."

"Yeah, and I'm still not sure he is," I said. "He always seemed so dang arrogant—and those puns came close to driving me crazy. I didn't want to be anywhere in his vicinity."

"So, Ellen's solution was to force you to spend time together? Thinking you two could set aside your differences and develop a friendship?"

"Right. She finagled things around so I had no choice but to include him in my annual backpacking expedition, a trip I'd always made alone. Gib and I began planning the expedition months out, and our calendars both happened to be clear that week of October."

"I take it Gib had little camping experience?"

"I don't think he'd ever been off a paved road until our drive to the trailhead," I said. "I helped him pick out boots, socks, flashlights—you name it. He didn't even know how to place batteries in his flashlights."

"So, on that fateful day, you and Gib drive up from Little Rock, begin your hike, and stumble upon me while I'm photographing fall foliage deep in the heart of an isolated 12,000-acre wilderness." Leslie shook her head in disbelief. "What are the odds that we'd even run into each other?"

"Too small to imagine," I said. "Had we arrived an hour earlier or an hour later, you and I wouldn't be here right now."

"Or if I'd picked another place to shoot at that particular time. I had four or five potential shot locations on my list for the day." Leslie took my hand in hers. "And there's something else I've never mentioned to you."

"What's that?"

"When I told my editor at *Southern Living* a few months ago that we were getting engaged and I'd be moving to Little Rock, she confessed there was an aspect to our story even I didn't know. She originally had another free-lancer scheduled to shoot the Ozarks."

"You're kidding!"

"Her plans called for me to photograph Williamsburg that very same week. You know, the historic town in Virginia. The guy given the Ozark assignment had to cancel because of an emergency appendectomy. The fall colors wouldn't wait so she sent me instead."

"So, fate did play a role." I leaned over and planted a kiss on Leslie's cheek.

"Either that or we got real lucky." She turned and our lips touched. Several times, in fact.

I gently pulled Leslie from the sofa and led her toward the stairs. "What would you think about getting lucky again?"

"That, my dear, is a most excellent idea." She followed me to our bedroom.

* * *

Leslie proceeded with our wedding plans, and I continued to call J.J.'s home number—without success. Returning from a meeting after another week had passed, I yielded to an impulse and made a quick detour to J.J.'s house in the city's Hillcrest neighborhood. That's when I made the gut-wrenching discovery. My best friend was missing.

~ FIVE ~

"There's got to be an explanation," Leslie said when I arrived home and related my inspection of J.J.'s house. "Maybe J.J. got called away on a family emergency."

"That's just it. He doesn't have any family."

Her mouth opened a bit and she blinked her eyes several times. "No one?"

"He has no siblings, and his folks died in a car wreck 15 or more years ago. An elderly second or third cousin living somewhere in Florida is his sole kin. And they don't keep in touch."

"Perhaps J.J. ran off with the woman he mentioned. The one he wanted us to meet."

"That's not like J.J.," I said, shaking my head. "He would have called."

Leslie took me by the hand and led me into the kitchen. "Let's fix supper. A good meal will make us feel better."

"Let me ask you something first. Have you ever been caught off guard—maybe even stunned—by some unexpected revelation regarding a close friend?"

"Does this have anything to do with J.J.'s disappearance?"

"Sort of."

Leslie rubbed her hands together and stared out the kitchen window. "I can recall one similar situation during the spring semester of my senior year in college. Four of us girls shared an apartment, and I found out later one of my room-mates wasn't even enrolled that term. She studied, went to the library, appeared to be writing papers, and—we thought—attended classes. You know, the whole nine yards. But it was all a sham."

She turned and looked to me.

"While I inspected J.J.'s house, his phone rang twice. The first caller hung up, but the second wanted to confirm J.J.'s appointment at Arkansas Children's Hospital."

"Children's Hospital?"

"They have an innovative program in the Neonatal Unit where adult volunteers come in on a regular basis and hold infants. They're all screened and trained, of course."

"Are you telling me J.J. Newell, the biggest man I've ever met, gives comfort to little babies?"

"I had no idea until today. He's never mentioned it to me."

Leslie sniffed, her mouth quivered, and then a tear trickled down her cheek. She took a step forward, wrapped her arms around my waist, and pulled me close. "That's one of the sweetest things I've ever heard."

* * *

While Leslie cooked fettuccine and set the table, I washed spinach, diced tomatoes, sliced cucumbers, and assembled a salad. The kitchen was quiet. Too quiet.

"How's my favorite photographer?" I asked, hopeful for some comforting conversation.

When her eyes lit up, so did my spirits.

"Much better, thank you. The official papers arrived in today's mail. My business is now a legal entity in Arkansas. A subchapter S corporation, to be exact."

"Which means?"

She waggled her eyebrows at me. "Let's just say your chances for a dowry have improved."

"It sounds like a celebration is in order."

"If you know what's good for you!"

I popped the cork on a bottle of Champagne that I'd stuck in the refrigerator a few days earlier. Leslie found a pair of flutes and placed them on the countertop.

"There's more," she said.

I watched as a smile etched its way across her cheeks. "Oh?"

"The Southern Living editor really liked my photos of the Buffalo River country. She's given me two more assignments."

I laughed. "Don't tell me they're going to use one of those shots you took of Gib and me sitting around a campfire."

She shrugged and tried to hide another grin. "We'll know when the magazine comes out."

"To continued successes," I offered and we clinked our glasses together. "You mentioned other jobs?"

"One's to cover the Big Thicket area in southeastern Texas." She hesitated while a glint of suspense flickered in her eyes. She outwaited me.

"The second?"

"Would you have any interest in assisting me for a month in the Out Islands of the Bahamas?"

My jaw dropped. "A full month? In the Caribbean?"

"We'll need to check out the coral reefs, sample the fresh seafood—"

"Count me in," I interrupted. "When?"

"Sometime following the wedding," she said. "Maybe we could make it a delayed honeymoon." She winked.

"Pin the dates down and I'll block them out." I felt a wave of guilt wash over me as I thought of J.J.

Leslie noticed and patted my shoulder. "Let's eat."

Once we were seated, she said, "Back to our professor friend. Have you talked with his neighbors?"

I shook my head. "I'll take tomorrow morning off and try to get some answers. J.J. and I have at least one good friend in common, and I'll give her a call, too."

"You could also check with the university."

"That's a possibility. He might have signed up for a summer sabbatical," I said, adding pasta to my plate. "I've heard it's a common practice within the academic community, although I can't recall him ever taking one."

"Maybe your Uncle Booker heard from J.J. after our May Day picnic. I remember them talking about a computer project of some sort."

"I'd forgotten about their discussion. I'll call Booker and ask if they've visited in recent days."

That led to a conversation on my exasperating afternoon at the ad agency.

"Not having to supervise any subordinates is a real blessing," I said. "You're lucky."

"*Au contraire,*" she said. "Supervising oneself is the most difficult assignment of all. Playing computer games, reading the mail, surfing the Internet, browsing for bargains on eBay, updating your Facebook page, checking out movie reviews, doing anything to postpone that next assignment ... The temptations are enormous."

I cleared the table on that note and reached for the bottle of bubbly. "Speaking of temptations ..."

Leslie held out her goblet.

"Do they have Champagne in the Bahamas?" I asked.

"More likely rum."

"And deserted beaches?"

"Miles and miles of 'em."

"Have I ever asked for your opinion on tan lines?"

"From a photographer's perspective," she said, "they're distracting."

"And personally?"

"I'm not planning on coming back with any."

"Do you have any left from last year?"

"Maybe you should check."

We took the rest of the bottle upstairs.

* * *

After a quick telephone call to the office first thing the next morning, I made a return visit to J.J.'s neighborhood. It was Friday, May 21st. I hadn't seen my close friend in almost three weeks.

An estate sale across the street from his house had drawn a large crowd. Weaving through near gridlock conditions, I parked my pickup in J.J.'s driveway like I owned the place and eased into the bevy of bargain hunters. A snowy-haired woman sat behind a card table on the front porch and seemed to be in charge. Her left arm rested none too casually atop a cash box.

I introduced myself as a close friend of Dr. Newell's and asked if she knew when he'd be back. She paused and put a fleshy hand to her uppermost chin as her eyes darted across the throng inside the entrance. Before she could answer, a skinny man in overalls approached her with a cardboard box of paperbacks under his arm. I stepped aside as he slid the collection onto the table. There must have been 30 books altogether, most of which seemed to be mysteries.

"How 'bout five dollars for the lot?" he asked.

She ran her eyes over the box. "I'll take ten."

Once they'd compromised halfway in between, the woman looked back to me. "Now that you mention it, I haven't seen Dr. Newell in a couple of weeks."

She sold a gaudy chartreuse vase for a dollar, then glanced over my shoulder to his house. "I'm sure J.J.'s back, though. His lawn is so nice and tidy. And there's a truck parked in his driveway. He must have company."

I bit my tongue, thanked her for her time, and walked back across the street and knocked at the house of J.J.'s next-door neighbor. I'd already given up and started for my pickup when the door opened and a young woman stepped onto the porch. Stifling a yawn, she cinched a belt wrapped around her bathrobe. After apologizing for waking her, I asked about J.J.

"We've said hello a time or two, but I can't say we really know each other," she said, rubbing the sleep from her eyes. "I've lived here about two months and, since I work the late shift at Baptist Hospital, I haven't had much chance to be a good neighbor."

I handed her one of my cards. "If you see anything, maybe you could give me a call?"

"Sorry I couldn't be more help," she said as she eased back into her house.

I turned to walk to my truck and nearly collided with the postman, a handsome black man with a graying beard. His worn leather satchel overflowed with flyers and circulars.

"Morning," I said. "I'm a buddy of Professor Newell's and am trying to track him down."

The mailman scratched his chin. "Haven't seen Doc Newell in some time. He put a hold on his service."

"Are you sure?" The news hit me like a punch to the gut. "He stopped his mail?"

Quietly efficient, he sorted through the stack for his next stop. "Ten days ago at least, maybe two weeks now," he said, examining a thick envelope. With a casual wave he moved down the sidewalk, skipping J.J.'s house as if it didn't exist.

Half an hour later found me on the UA Little Rock complex in the south-central part of the city. Serving over 10,000 students, most of them commuters, the campus is a haphazard assortment of undistinguished structures erected by a succession of low-bid contractors. I seldom went to J.J.'s office and had forgotten where the Science Building was. A maintenance man pointed out the uninspiring building, and the directory indicated that the Biology Department occupied the entire third floor. When I got off the elevator, the main office stood straight across the hall.

"I'm here concerning Dr. Newell," I said to a skinny young receptionist. I assumed she was the one I'd talked to earlier. She gave me a slight nod, but kept her sunken eyes on a computer screen.

As I stared at a gold ring affixed to her left nostril, a large pink bubble emerged between her thin lips. It added some color and dimension to her anorexic frame. After it popped, she sighed and gave me a blank expression. "He's not teaching this summer," she said in the same uninterested voice I'd heard over the phone.

"Maybe I could talk with someone who might know where he is."

Like a cow chewing its cud, she pushed the wad of gum from one side of her mouth to the other with her tongue. Her bony hands frozen on the computer keyboard, she concentrated on birthing another pink sphere. Something told me she didn't belong to Mensa.

"Huh?"

"I'd hoped to visit with some of his associates."

"You mean other instructors?"

I nodded eagerly.

A bubble the size of a ping-pong ball blossomed between her lips and she played with it, twisting the pink glob with her twiggy fingers. It slipped back into her mouth.

"Let me think," she said, and I had to stop myself from replying with something rude. Instead, I rocked on my heels while she closed her eyes. Two gaudy deposits of purple eye shadow stared back at me.

"Most of 'em are gone for the first summer term," she said, her eyes still shut. They opened to watch another bubble emerge and then vanish. "But Dr. Ackerman should be around next week."

"If I leave a message, could you make sure Dr. Ackerman gets it?"

She mulled it over for a long moment. "No problem."

After scribbling a brief note on the back of a business card, I fled for the elevator. Walking toward my truck, I spied the Administration Building across a brick courtyard and decided to take a chance. A young man at an information desk fiddled with his cell phone, apparently playing a game of some sort. After I finally got his attention, he directed me to the second floor where I found the office I sought. The sign on the door read: *Dean, College of Arts and Sciences—Dr. Rankin Campbell*. Unless I was mistaken, the dean would be J.J.'s boss.

I walked in, glad I happened to be wearing a tie and sport coat. The reception area reminded me of a prosperous law office. A series of framed English hunting scenes hung from the walls. A closer inspection revealed that the paneling wasn't a cheap veneer but individual boards of solid oak. A trio of leather armchairs occupied a sumptuous

44

Persian rug. Beyond sat an antique oak desk. So, I thought, this was where my tax dollars for higher education were going.

"May I help you?" An attractive middle-aged woman wearing a tailored suit looked up from behind the costly desk. I checked for a nose ring or bubblegum, but all I got was a warm smile.

"I'd like to see Dean Campbell, please."

"Do you have an appoint—"

A door behind her opened and a short, thick man carrying a leather briefcase backed into the room, unaware that he had a visitor. "Doris," he said, interrupting her. "I'm off to the club." He locked the door and spun around, his bushy eyebrows lifting a notch as I entered his field of vision. Round-faced with thinning brown hair, he gazed at me indifferently through tortoiseshell glasses. The initials of a fashionable designer were visible on the frame.

"Dr. Campbell, this is ..."

"Randy Lassiter." I stepped in front of the dean, my hand extended. A natty dresser in his mid-fifties, he wore a well-cut navy pinstripe suit, complete with a pressed silk handkerchief placed in the breast pocket and a burgundy and charcoal bow tie. The white monogrammed shirt contained enough starch to make me itch, but the heavy gold cufflinks appeared quite comfortable. His tasseled shoes were Italian and expensive and complemented the alligator belt. Counting the briefcase, his outfit had to be pushing $3,000. Maybe more. And that didn't include the hint of a pricy cologne wafting past me.

"Umm ... hello," he said, fumbling with an elegant pocket watch after we shook hands. "I'm afraid I'm running quite late for ... uh ... a meeting." I figured the vintage timepiece added another couple hundred dollars to the total.

"Perhaps we can walk out together," I said. "It won't take but a minute." I suspected his appointment involved chasing a little white ball from one hole to the next.

Realizing he had no graceful alternative, he gave his assistant an indifferent nod while I held the door.

"What can I do for you?" he asked as we strode to the elevator.

"I'm trying to find Dr. J.J. Newell."

He stopped and looked me in the eye. "Are you a student?"

"A longtime friend. I'm worried about him." I pressed the *Down* button.

He hesitated a moment before swinging his gaze to the floor. "I haven't seen James in several weeks."

I flinched. I had never heard J.J. called James in my entire life, at least not by anybody who knew him.

A bell chimed and I stepped behind Campbell into the elevator.

"I'm curious if Dr. Newell might have had summer plans," I said as we descended. "Maybe an off-campus sabbatical. Or perhaps a teaching assignment at another school."

The door opened on the ground floor. Campbell seemed preoccupied as we dodged a trio of boisterous students and walked through the lobby and out the main entrance. Stepping into the bright noonday sun, we stopped in the middle of a pleasant brick-paved plaza. Campbell propped his briefcase against the base of a large concrete planter before he reached into his suit jacket and pulled out a pipe. He extracted a packet of tobacco and went through the predictable routine before bringing a classic Zippo lighter to the bowl with a grunt of satisfaction.

"It's been a hectic spring, one of the busiest I can recall." Campbell returned the lighter to a pants pocket. "But I don't remember James mentioning any unusual plans for the summer."

I cringed again and followed that with a shrug. "Things just don't add up. His house has been vacant for weeks."

Campbell exhaled a cloud of pungent smoke to the side. "I have half a dozen department heads reporting to me, plus even more committee chairs." He made a feeble effort at eye contact before his gaze locked on the pavement.

I faked a sympathetic expression, anticipating his next comment.

"As you can imagine, it's difficult to keep up with all the programs, much less the individuals," he said, taking another long drag from the pipe. "The very nature of an academic institution encourages autonomy." Campbell flipped open his pocket watch and studied the dial. I concluded it was a less-than-subtle signal that our conversation was ending. "He enjoys traveling. I suspect that James has taken a trip."

We shook hands again and I left one of my business cards in his possession. Then Campbell grabbed his briefcase and went one direction and I went in another. Maybe it was the heat, but his palm felt clammy.

~ SIX ~

I left the campus, driving north on University Avenue, and used my cell phone to call Booker at home.

"Did you and J.J. ever get together to resolve that computer situation in his office?"

"Interesting you should bring that up, lad," he said. "For better than a fortnight now, I've attempted without success to initiate a conversation with our professorial acquaintance. If you remember, he also promised to introduce me to an attractive young lass in his department. Will you be so kind as to volunteer as an intermediary?"

"I can't find him either."

"It's getting so bloody hot," he said. I realized Booker must have gotten back on his English movie kick. "Perhaps Dr. Newell has fled our city, joining a festive group of traveling minstrels in search of warm-hearted strumpets."

"If you talk to him," I said, "please let me know." Thank God my uncle had given up on his infatuation with operas. Earlier this spring, he'd been so enamored with arias I had to quit taking his calls.

"At once, dear nephew. Cheerio."

Rather than returning to the agency, I followed a chancy impulse and drove to the Brady Post Office, the branch station serving J.J.'s Hillcrest neighborhood. I sat in the truck for minutes, wondering if I had the guts to follow through with the wild scheme that my brain had just concocted. Muttering to myself, I took a deep breath, stepped from the cab, and headed for the entrance.

48

My palms damp with sweat, I walked past a wall of post office boxes and into the service area. The absence of a line surprised me. A young clerk eyed me as I approached the counter. His name badge read: *Dennison*.

"What can I do for you?" he asked with a smile.

The man's friendliness caught me off guard. Something about my personality often brings out the worst in public servants, especially those employed by the federal government. I inhaled, put on my warmest adman smile, and tried to ignore the line of Wanted posters suspended from the wall to the right. My pulse quickened as my eyes caught the words "Mail Fraud" in big type across the top sheet. I grabbed the countertop to steady my shaking hands.

"Good morning, Mr. Dennison. I'm … uh … J.J. Newell," I said and cleared my throat. "I live on North Beechwood and need to pick up my mail." I took in another gulp of air. "It's been held the past few weeks."

"Newell?" he asked as he rose from his stool.

"J.J. Newell. 447 North Beechwood."

He disappeared behind a partition, and I began to worry as the minutes added up. Half a dozen other customers had fallen in line behind me. Another postal employee grudgingly stepped to the counter and began selling stamps at the adjacent window.

Dennison rounded the corner a minute or two later, whistling as he walked. He carried an armload of mail. Rubber bands held the bundles together.

"I'll need to see some identification please," he said, placing the stack on the countertop.

I felt the blood drain from my face. "I … uh … left my wallet in the truck," I said, patting my pants pocket. "Let me go get it." I shrugged and started for the door.

Dennison noticed the line of customers behind me and then took a glance at the pile of mail. "Dr. Newell, huh? I suspect you're an honest man." He shoved the heap to me. "Here you go," he said.

As I reached for J.J.'s mail, Dennison said, "I had a class under a Professor Newell at UA Little Rock a couple of years ago. The best instructor I ever had. Maybe you two are related?"

"I've met him," I said, feeling the sweat trickle down my back, "but we come from different families."

"Anything else?"

I started to go, then decided to press my luck. "There is one other matter." I felt the glare of impatient eyes on my neck. Paid by the hour, Dennison wasn't troubled. "Things remain a bit unsettled. I may have to ask that you hold my mail a little longer."

Dennison nodded as he fiddled with a tape dispenser.

I shrugged again. "The problem is, I can't remember when I asked delivery to be resumed. Any chance you could check?"

As Dennison pivoted, I heard a grumble behind me. I ignored it. Back within seconds, he held a bright yellow card in his hands.

"This expires next week," he said.

"May I see it?"

He hesitated a moment before handing me the form. Slightly larger than a standard index card, it had the U.S. Postal Service's stylized eagle in the upper left corner and adjacent to that were the words, **Authorization to Hold Mail**. Scanning the card, I noticed the order went into effect on May 8, a week after J.J. had joined Leslie and me for the picnic. Two-thirds of the way down the form, my eyes stopped at the space reserved for the customer's signature. As I stared at the inky endorsement, a chill invaded my spine, spreading over my entire body.

"Thanks ... very much," I said and returned the card. "I'll get another to you when my schedule's finalized."

As Dennison said "Next," I scooped up the pile and angled toward the exit on unsteady legs. Head down and lost in anxious thoughts, I'd made it halfway across the lobby when a loud and somewhat familiar female voice shouted, "Randy Lassiter!" As the sound waves reverberated through the room, I looked up and saw Jamie Epperson, a former neighbor. She stood between me and the entrance, her arms outspread. Pretending not to see her was out of the question.

I glanced over my shoulder, expecting to spot Dennison reaching for the phone or conferring with a supervisor. Busy with the next customer, he either hadn't heard her outburst or didn't care.

Jamie had always reminded me of a golden retriever. Large and affectionate with thick reddish hair, she craved attention. "Randy," she said, waddling to me. "It's so good to see you." I could feel every eye in the building on my back.

"What a surprise!" I barely recognized my own voice. "What's it been? Four, five years?"

With her immense bosom pressed against my chest, she wrapped her squabby arms around me and kissed the air beside my cheek. "Did you ever talk to anyone with Johnny's estate?" she asked, her voice low. Jamie is the consummate Johnny Cash groupie, and has pestered me since we first met nearly a decade ago to use Cash as a spokesman for one of the agency's clients. I'd been in her home a couple of times, always amazed with the Johnny Cash shrine in her living room. She had posters, coffee mugs, pocket knives, books, concert programs, and even a pair of bobblehead dolls in his likeness, not to mention dozens of albums and CDs. Her framed collection of Johnny Cash autographs filled most of a wall. "They're using old film clips of John Wayne and Elvis Presley all the time," she had said at our last visit. "You can do the same with Johnny!" When I replied that purchasing the rights would cost far more than our budget for the entire production, she'd had a ready answer. "But he's from Arkansas. I'm sure they'd work a deal." Yeah, right.

I extricated myself from her embrace and, gently holding her elbow with my free hand, guided us to a far corner of the lobby. "It's best we not block the door," I said and took a step back. "You're looking great." Maybe it was the light, but I could hardly see her mustache.

"You advertising gurus always know what to say," she said. Leaning closer, she whispered, "Back to Johnny. Any luck?"

"My producer's still working on it. You know how it is dealing with celebrity estates and their lawyers."

"Maybe I can help. Did I ever tell I went to grade school with his second cousin?"

I nodded, taking a few sliding steps closer to the door. "We're waiting on the right situation before playing our aces."

"Promise you won't forget me." Like a beauty queen on parade, she waved her pudgy, cupped hand.

"I promise." It was probably the most truthful thing I'd uttered in days.

Outside at last, I trudged to the Toyota, heaved J.J.'s mail onto the passenger seat, and climbed into the hot cab, where I slumped behind the steering wheel. I gave up trying to slide the key into the ignition and clenched my trembling fists.

Eyes shut, I visualized the signature on the postal form. Written in fine penmanship, it slanted upward from left to right in a classic, textbook script. But ever since our freshman year in college, I've known my friend J.J. Newell was a messy left-hander.

~ SEVEN ~

After my eventful stop at the post office, I went straight home, somewhat surprised to discover that Leslie was gone. And then I remembered she had scheduled an appointment with my sister Ellen.

Ellen had worked for me at Lassiter & Associates following her graduation—in marketing, with honors—from Southern Methodist University in Dallas. I'd hired her with more than a bit of apprehension, worried about supervising a sibling known for her rigid and independent views, a trait that seems to run in the family. My fears proved to be unfounded. Within a few months, she'd earned her promotion to the agency's creative director slot. In addition to being among the most imaginative people I'd ever met, Ellen had an unsurpassed work ethic that spurred the rest of us on to new heights. She also introduced me to a career-changing quote from Italian designer Massimo Vignelli that I'd taped to the top of my computer monitor: "It is better to starve than get a bad client."

Ellen's original accounts included the Arkansas Arts Center. That's where she met Dr. Gibson Lamar Yarberry, one of the organization's board members and a regular on Little Rock's list of most eligible bachelors. Their initial encounter led to a dinner date that very evening and they were soon inseparable. The wedding took place just over a year ago.

Meanwhile, Ellen had grown restless in her job, eager for new challenges. With my reluctant encouragement, she accepted a similar position with the state's largest ad agency—a firm with far bigger clients and their matching media budgets. Although disappointed to lose her to a semi-worthy competitor, I knew it was the right thing for her career. At least that's what I kept telling myself.

The good news was that she and Leslie—soon to be sisters-in-law—had become great friends. Given her interest in Leslie's photography, there was a strong chance they would develop a business relationship as well.

* * *

I dumped the load from the post office onto the dining room table and fired up the coffeepot. After sorting through the heap, I continued my law-breaking spree and began opening J.J.'s mail.

The handful of items appearing to be personal correspondence drew my immediate attention. Two were hand-written invitations to political fundraisers, one a gracious "thank you" note from a freshman who appreciated Dr. Newell's helpful guidance, and the last a letter from a local real estate agent asking if J.J. had any interest in putting his house on the market. That was it.

Next, I examined bills, searching for the tiniest clue that might establish a trail. Nothing. His VISA statement carried a balance of less than $50, and the most recent expense was a month-old restaurant charge. The summary from American Express showed no activity during the same period.

I then opened his monthly bank statement, praying for a revelation. His checking account included six transactions, but my hopes were short-lived. All were of the automatic variety. Two were payroll deposits from UA Little Rock, and the remainder were routine deductions for water, electricity, insurance, and a mutual fund. No cash withdrawals had been made, leaving a balance in excess of $10,000.

Restacking the envelopes, I discovered one from Southwestern Bell that I had somehow overlooked despite a bold "Urgent" on the front. The statement contained a shut-off notice effective May 20, yesterday. The sole charges were the basic monthly fees plus the usual assortment of taxes. No long-distance calls at all.

I refilled my coffee cup and studied the rest of the mound. It was a collection you might expect from a professor's mailbox carrying a prosperous ZIP code: grocery store circulars, well over half a dozen magazines ranging from *The Economist* to *Sports Illustrated*, professional journals, clothing and home improvement catalogs, and solicitations from organizations representing an array of special causes—whales, rain forests, homeless children, and tall-grass prairies, among others. With four separate mailings, a national credit card company seemed intent on establishing an account for Dr. Newell. And, if the teasing messages on a pair of flashy wrappers were accurate, J.J. had won a couple of million dollars in sweepstakes.

There was one other thing at the bottom of the pile: an item from the Hillcrest Antique Gallery. I'd never been in the shop but recognized the name. Located in J.J.'s neighborhood, it occupied a small building a quarter of a mile or so from his house in a quaint commercial district along Kavanaugh Boulevard. I tore the envelope open, expecting a sales announcement. But I found a short hand-written note from the owner, one S. Goldman, reminding J.J. to pick up a piece of furniture he had purchased at an auction several weeks earlier.

I was staring at the mountain of paper when Leslie walked in. She stopped next to me and peered at the mess.

"J.J.'s mail," I said. "About 20 pounds altogether."

"How'd you get it?"

"You don't want to know."

"Anything useful?"

I shook my head. "Not a thing." I paused, then cleared my throat. "But I did make an interesting discovery at the post office. The signature on the order to hold his mail isn't J.J.'s. Not even close."

"Are you sure?" she asked, her eyes growing wide.

"J.J.'s always had sloppy handwriting and is a lefty to boot. The signature was neat and precise. And it slanted the wrong way."

"What about your other stops?"

As she drank a cup of coffee, I shared results of my trips to J.J.'s neighborhood and the university. "All in all, not a terribly productive morning," I said. "I also called Booker. He hasn't heard anything from J.J. either."

"Just one dead end after another," she muttered, refilling her cup.

"Tell me about your meeting with Ellen."

"It couldn't have gone better. She introduced me to her senior art director and his staff. They passed around my portfolio and I answered a lot of questions."

"Any possibilities?"

Her dimples flashed. "One of their national clients—a prominent paper company—is donating a huge tract of unique bottomland forest in southern Arkansas to a major conservation organization. They're planning a big publicity splash, and I've agreed to shoot photos for the media packets and then later at the official announcement."

"Sounds interesting."

"And it might lead to a lucrative annual report assignment."

"That's even better."

"Provided I take plenty of mosquito spray."

I fixed us a quick lunch of chicken salad and fresh fruit while Leslie talked on the phone with one of her stock agents. She bounced back into the kitchen.

"What's up?"

"The editors at *Audubon* have selected one of my photos for next year's calendar."

"Congratulations!" I pulled her close and gave her a big hug. "You now belong to quite an elite group."

She kissed me on the cheek. "The pay's not bad either."

The news of her sale to *Audubon* monopolized our lunch conversation. As I loaded the dishwasher, Leslie wrapped an arm around my waist.

"Maybe you should see the police about J.J.," she said. "It wouldn't hurt."

"I've been thinking the same thing. This situation is beginning to worry me."

"I still can't believe he simply vanished," she said. "Do things like that happen?"

"We could ask Jimmy Hoffa's family."

~ EIGHT ~

I followed Leslie's suggestion and added the Little Rock Police Department to my afternoon's schedule. Given the beautiful day, I chose to leave my truck at the office and walk the five blocks, figuring that exposure to fresh air might help clear my addled mind. The exercise wouldn't hurt, either.

Known for its eccentric characters, this part of the city didn't disappoint me. A cordial panhandler talked me out of five dollars, and a minute later I met an earnest young woman who offered a thick brochure, saying it could change my life. I accepted the free tract with a smile, rolling it into a tight cylinder as I continued my trek. While waiting for a traffic light to change, I opened the heavy pamphlet, groaning when *The Apocalypse and You* title appeared. Blaming the country's ills on Jews, Blacks, working women, the Trilateral Commission, the United Nations, and the Deep State (whatever that is), it gave me second thoughts regarding the First Amendment. I tossed it into a nearby trash bin.

A cluster of half a dozen round-the-clock bail bonding outfits and an equal number of unimpressive law offices indicated my journey was coming to an end. I was mulling over this curious symbiotic relationship when I strolled across a small flag-filled plaza and arrived at my destination—a low-slung, gray brick building with maroon awnings. Located a few blocks west of City Hall, the inauspicious LRPD headquarters won't be found on any architectural tours of the community. As I entered the tinted double-doors, I realized this was my first visit.

I walked across the lobby to a chest-high countertop situated below an Information sign. A stern, buxom woman in a wrinkled uniform sat behind the counter, seemingly oblivious to my presence. She mumbled something, but never looked up. Her eyes stared at a nail file flying back and forth across her short, thick fingers. The filing ceased, and she raised her head, brushing aside wayward strands of stringy hair. I lowered my gaze, letting it fall to the ID badge hanging crookedly on her shirt. Her name was Ramona.

She gave me a strange look, almost a double-take, like we'd crossed paths at some time in the past and had a history. "I'll give you another chance," she finally said, her voice low and sarcastic. "Can I help you?"

Still in a good mood, I didn't take the bait. "I need to file a missing person report."

"Your wife leave?" she asked. "Or maybe a girlfriend's skipped town?"

What is it about me and receptionists? I wondered. I shook my head, managed a deep breath, and tried to remain calm. "A friend. He's been gone close to a month."

Her large head bobbed up and down, the narrow, cruel lips forming an exaggerated circle. It was then I noticed she'd been rather careless with her tangerine-tinted lipstick. "Oh," she said. "A friend." As she glanced at my left hand, searching for my ring finger, I slipped it into a pocket. "How unfortunate." She returned to her manicure.

I wanted to slap some sense into her. Instead, I asked, "What's the procedure?"

"The procedure," she said, mocking my question, "is for you to take a seat over there." Using the nail file as a pointer, she gestured toward the opposite wall. "And then I'll see if we can find someone to collect details on your little tragedy." She fluttered her eyelids, then dropped the file to the desk. "Now go sit down like a real sweetie."

Mulling over my chances for probation on a first offense assault charge, I turned and marched to the bench, temples pounding.

Except for background noises of copiers, printers, and phones, the lobby remained quiet, much to my surprise. I suspected that most of the action took place in the back.

Ten long minutes after I'd arrived, a uniformed black man, carrying a notebook, emerged from behind a closed door and strode in my direction. In his mid-to-late-30s with a bodybuilder's physique, he wore the worried expression of a man with too much to do and not enough time.

I stood and extended my hand. "Randy Lassiter."

"Captain Billingsley," he replied, his grip firm. "What can I do for you?"

"I'd like to file a missing-person report."

Billingsley nodded. "Come on back." He glanced at his watch.

I trailed him around a corner and into a crowded office not much bigger than a patrol car. While he squeezed past a bulging file cabinet and slipped into the usual desk chair, I sat on a rickety wooden stool better suited to the repair room of an antique shop. As uncomfortable as it was old, it undoubtedly kept guests from overstaying their welcome.

The desk needed a disaster declaration. Scattered among heaps of paper and folders were plastic cups, soft drink cans, a cell phone charger, a couple of trashy paperbacks, and a half-full bottle of Tabasco sauce. A dead plant sat next to the telephone and a framed photograph leaned against its cracked terra cotta pot. Two blond, blue-eyed boys smiled at me through the smudged glass.

Noticing my gaze, Billingsley chuckled and then waved his hand across the top of the desk. "In case you're wondering, this is *not* my office," he said. "Jorgenson won't mind; he took his wife and kids to Florida this week."

"What's up with Ramona?" I asked.

"Is she in another one of her moods?"

"A little customer service training wouldn't be a bad idea."

"She's dealing with tough circumstances," he said. "Ramona has three children, one of whom has special needs. Her no-good womanizing husband has been brought in several times, once by yours truly, for domestic abuse." Billingsley then took a long look at me, shaking his head. "If I didn't know better, you could almost pass as his twin brother. What's that German word for—"

"Doppelgänger?" I offered.

"Yeah, that's it. Maybe that's why Ramona gave you some grief. You're a dead look-alike for the sorriest person she's ever met."

I felt some sort of reaction wouldn't be out of line, but didn't know what to say.

"No offense intended, of course." Billingsley opened his notebook and pulled out a form. "Now, who's the missing person?"

"James Joseph Newell," I said. "But he's known to everybody as J.J."

After I'd given him J.J.'s address, Billingsley asked for a complete physical description, raising his eyebrows when I answered "Six feet six" to the height question. "Any distinguishing scars, marks, jewelry, aliases?"

I shook my head. "Just a ring. A Phi Beta Kappa ring from college."

Billingsley marked the appropriate boxes. "His age?"

"Same as mine," I said. "Thirty-five."

"What's your relationship to Dr. Newell?"

"Close friends. We've known each other since our college days." Remembering the reaction from the receptionist, I felt some elaboration might be in order. "I'm getting married this fall, and he's agreed to be my best man."

"How long has Newell been missing?"

"Almost three weeks. I last saw him on May first."

He made an additional notation. "How do you know he's missing? Could Newell have taken a vacation?"

"J.J. enjoys traveling. But I don't think he's on a trip."

"What makes you say that?"

"I have a key to his house and let myself in yesterday. Some food in the refrigerator had spoiled, wet clothes had been left in the washer, and most of his tropical fish had died."

Billingsley rubbed his chin, staring hard into my eyes. "The place look okay? No forced doors, broken windows, signs of trespass?"

"The house was locked tight. Everything present and accounted for. Except J.J. and his car."

"Tell me about the vehicle."

I provided Billingsley with a description of the Jaguar.

"You don't happen to know the license?"

"It's a vanity tag. JJN."

"That should help." Billingsley's eyebrows arched once more as he entered the information. "I assume Dr. Newell lives alone."

"Right. And there's no family to speak of."

"What type doctor? GP?" He glanced again at his watch.

"The university sort. He teaches at UA Little Rock." I twisted on the stool, trying to accommodate an unhappy nerve.

He grunted. "The academic kind, huh. What department?"

"Biology."

"Any health problems?"

"None that I know of." I shrugged. "Why?"

"A man gets diagnosed with cancer, he might take the next flight to Mexico. The quack clinic routine."

I shook my head. "J.J.'s healthy as a horse."

"Can you think of anything else that's germane?"

Opening my mouth, I started to mention the situation with J.J.'s mail, realizing Billingsley ought to be aware of the fraudulent signature. Then I thought better of it, fearing that I might be arrested on the spot on a series of obscure federal charges. Stealing his mail had seemed like such a bright idea hours ago. Now I felt like kicking myself.

Billingsley shut his notebook, then slipped a piece of gum between his lips. I shook my head when he offered me the pack. "Your friend, Newell. What kind of man is he?" He leaned forward, his hands clasped.

"I'm not sure what you mean."

"Is he wild, prone to take chances, do things on a whim? Does he push the envelope?"

"Not likely," I said. "He's about as traditional as they come."

"Does he play the market, the ponies, the slots?"

"Trying a new restaurant is a big gamble for J.J."

"Lady problems?"

"Never married. During our last visit he mentioned he's seeing somebody, but I haven't yet met her."

When Billingsley stood, I did the same, eager to restore circulation to my aching back.

"We'll broadcast this information throughout the force. Your description of his car should be helpful."

"Then what?"

"Let's hope something turns up." After handing me his card, he stepped into the hall.

I followed him through the door. "Will this be a high priority in the department?"

Billingsley sighed, his eyes holding mine. "You look like a reasonable man, Mr. Lassiter."

"Depends on who you talk to. And when."

Giving me a faint smile, he flipped open his notebook and studied the page. "Our missing person is a healthy, affluent, well-educated, single male in the prime of his life. Plus, this individual is known to travel, and his semester's work at the university ended in recent weeks."

He let me draw my own conclusion, and my disappointment must have shown.

"I don't want to discourage you, Mr. Lassiter. But it's no crime to disappear."

Billingsley escorted me back to the lobby, shook my hand, and hurried away. As I neared the information desk, I saw Ramona eyeing me. I hesitated for a moment and then walked over to the counter.

"I had a good visit with Captain Billingsley," I said. "Thank you for putting me in touch with him."

She nodded and gave me a smile, not a big one but it looked sincere. "You're welcome. And I hope you find your missing friend."

~ NINE ~

I hadn't been back 20 minutes when my secretary slipped into the office, halfway closed the door behind her, and leaned over my desk. "There's a rather strange gentleman out front," she said, her voice low. "He's very insistent that you see him. Right away."

My initial thought was that an ambitious and remarkably efficient inspector from the U.S. Postal Service had somehow tracked me down with plans to make an immediate arrest. No doubt a fresh-faced federal lawyer with career aspirations to occupy the Office of the U.S. Attorney General. Not only would my apprehension hurt staff morale and bring unfavorable publicity to Lassiter & Associates, my absence—if prolonged—would put the firm at a severe competitive disadvantage. Another consideration, of course, was the intangible damage that imprisonment could do to my fragile self-esteem. And would Leslie post bond?

Before I could give my assistant any guidance, the office door swung open and a deep voice boomed through the entrance. "Mr. Lassiter?" Pulse racing, I peeked around my secretary and saw a white man, maybe in his early 60s, hobble into the room. The fact that I spotted no obvious badge hanging from his bright blue polyester sport coat made me feel a little better. He clutched a wooden cane in one hand and carried an old leather briefcase, thick and scarred, in the other. No drawn handgun, no visible warrant for my arrest, no armed associates, no eager TV crew at his heels. As my aide retreated to the safety of the reception area, the uninvited guest closed the office door with a firm push from his handsome walking stick.

I stood behind my desk and studied him as he turned and approached one small step at a time. Bald as the proverbial cue ball, he had a smooth head that glistened with a light coating of sweat. His widely spaced eyes were dark and beady, almost perched on the sides of his head under thin, almost invisible eyebrows. His nose was short and flat and pale as the rest of his face. A classic handlebar mustache stretched from one cheek to the other and, below that, a sociable grin.

He lowered the briefcase to the floor and extended his right hand. "Afternoon. My name's McCulloch. Catfish McCulloch."

"Randy Lassiter," I said, struggling not to chuckle as we shook hands. I'd never heard a nickname better suited to its owner. "Please have a seat."

Before McCulloch eased himself into a chair, he searched through a bulging wallet, located a business card, and handed it to me: *Catfish McCulloch—Capitalist/Entrepreneur/Consultant.* The address and telephone number were local. A mischievously smiling catfish, identical to one pinned on McCulloch's left lapel, occupied the lower right third of his card.

"You've got the bases covered." I placed his card on the desk and returned to my seat.

"Used to be a professional water-skier. Number two in North America back in the day. Got to work with the prettiest damn women in the whole country." He gazed out the window for a moment before slapping his right knee. "That is, 'til I ruint this leg going over a jump at Cypress Gardens in the summer of '89. That unfortunate accident forced me to reconsider my future and diversify."

"What brings you here?"

McCulloch removed a wrinkled handkerchief from the breast pocket of his distinctive coat and ran it over his shiny pate. As he folded the cloth, he nodded his head several times. "It seems we have a mutual friend: Rupert Exley."

"We've handled his advertising for years," I said. Exley's network of automobile dealerships, one of the largest in the state, ranked among the agency's major accounts. He'd asked me to represent his fledgling company only weeks after I'd opened Lassiter & Associates, and we've been his agency of record ever since.

"I reckon I've bought my last ten trucks from Rupert," he said. "Right outside your window is the latest."

I glanced through the window and saw a mammoth sport/utility vehicle parked at the curb. Fire-engine red with oversized tires, tinted windows, chrome running boards, and flashy striping, his top-of-the line rig featured at least three antennas angling skyward above the cab. Whatever McCulloch was doing, he appeared to be successful.

"That'll take you just about anywhere."

There was a long pause while he looked me hard in the eye. "Rupert tells me you're an honest man."

"In my business, relationships are everything. We treat our clients right."

McCulloch bent forward, retrieved the briefcase, and placed it on his lap. "That's what I wanted to hear." After loosening its tarnished buckles, he pried the case open and then stood and turned it upside down over my desk. Bundles and bundles and bundles of cash tumbled out, covering my phone, signature file, and in-box. He gave it a little shake and another half dozen spilled onto the pile. Stacks and stacks of currency were held together by rubber bands. I'd never seen so much money in my life.

I grabbed a bundle of twenties and flipped through the used bills. I didn't spot any dye or bloodstains, but wondered about traces of cocaine. Tossing it back with the rest, I said, "Mr. McCulloch—"

"Just call me Catfish."

"I'm not sure—"

"I've got a little project underway and need some help. Fast, reliable, professional help." He noticed my initial reaction and laughed. "Don't worry, son," he said. "I'm not gonna ask you to do anything illegal."

Breathing a bit easier, I swept an arm over the hoard of cash. "This is not the way we usually do business."

"I'm not your usual customer," Catfish said with a shrug. "I don't trust banks. The government either, for that matter."

Staring at the money, I wondered how much my desk was now worth. Catfish must have read my mind. "There's $30,000. Should be enough to promote the hell out of Arkansas's biggest gun-and-knife show."

So that's what this was: an unorthodox opportunity to add another account to the agency's list. I gazed at the mound of currency and tried to decide if I wanted to take on a challenge involving an eccentric and unpredictable client. Searching under the heap of bills, I found my legal pad and a pen. "Let's hear the details."

Over the next few minutes, Catfish explained that he'd booked the main exhibition hall of Little Rock's Statehouse Convention Center for a three-day "Mid-South Gun & Knife Expo" in late July. Promising his vendors that one-fourth of their fees would go to promote the show, he'd already signed up 400—at $300 each. What Catfish needed from Lassiter & Associates was attendance. "Huge crowds of eager buyers" was how he put it.

"Any suggestions on media? Or when you'd want the advertising to start?"

Squinting his dark eyes, Catfish gave me another long look. "You're the damn expert. Those are the questions for you to figure out."

This sounded better by the minute. "Tell me about your vendors."

"There'll be a handful of big dealers from around the region, but most are folks doing it as a hobby," he said. "The typical booth will be manned by a serious part-time collector trading sporting guns—chiefly firearms for deer, duck, and turkey hunters." Pausing for a moment, Catfish opened a pocketknife and began cleaning his fingernails with a long, pointed blade. "Some selling re-loading supplies, a few into specialty items like muzzleloaders, leather goods, or duck calls. There'll be a couple of blacksmiths with custom-made knives. Plus, the usual assortment of wackos, survivalists, that sort of thing."

I smiled at my guest before realizing Catfish wasn't joking.

He pocketed the knife and handed me a thin file folder. "Here's complete information on the show along with a list of my vendors. On top is a copy of my FFL."

"Your what?"

"My FFL," he said, shaking his head as if he couldn't believe what he'd just heard. "My damn federal firearms license. If there's one thing I've learned over the years, it's this: a man's got to stay on the good side of the feds."

I flipped through the material. He'd covered everything: a detailed schedule for vendor set-up and break-down, hours of operation, admission fees, security, insurance, parking, lodging, refreshments, and entertainment. I even found a logo, imperfect but passable, in the back of the packet. All he needed was a horde of warm bodies.

When I looked up, Catfish gave me a quick nod. "We got a deal?"

In some states, Catfish McCullough might be considered a politically incorrect client, but in Arkansas he was one-hundred-percent mainstream. Yet accepting his business proposition might upset several employees, not to mention irritating my liberal-leaning friends. But Catfish intrigued me, and the idea of doing something different carried a certain appeal. For one thing, it could help take my mind off J.J.'s disappearance. And a $30,000 campaign was nothing to sneeze at. Besides, in five or six weeks, the venture would be history.

"Yes, sir," I answered. "You have a deal." We shook hands over the heap of cash.

He winked as he reached for the empty briefcase. "I'm sure you're honest as the day is long, but why don't you go ahead and fix me a receipt? The damn IRS has made me sorta fussy about records."

It took fifteen minutes to count the bills. I scrawled out a makeshift receipt on a piece of letterhead and signed and dated it. I stepped outside to my assistant's desk and asked her to make a copy. When she returned, I gave the original to Catfish.

"I'll stop by every now and then to see how you're doing," he said. "Also, I've got some ideas about bringing in a celebrity or two. You know, to gin up some extra excitement."

"Sounds good," I said. "Keep me posted."

We shook hands again and he headed through the door, steadying himself with his cane. As I peered from my office window, Catfish McCulloch settled into his fancy new truck and merged into the Friday afternoon traffic. I snatched a heavy-duty garbage bag from the supply room, stuffed it with those interesting green bundles, and made a hurried trip to the bank.

~ TEN ~

I gave Leslie a kiss on the cheek early Monday morning before racing to the airport for Southwest Airline's 7:00 flight to Dallas's Love Field. We were in post-production on a series of television commercials for our biggest client—Merchants Bank of Arkansas. While my agency does most of its broadcast work in Little Rock, we employ a Dallas outfit for special projects requiring digital graphics or similar high-tech applications. I wanted to make sure there were no surprises.

Besides, Leslie and I needed a bit of space. We'd had our first real argument when I got home Friday afternoon and mentioned Catfish McCulloch's gun-and-knife show. "You didn't agree to handle it, did you?" Leslie had asked. When I admitted that I'd accepted his business, Leslie's chin dropped. "Aren't you worried about all these school kids and guns? Just yesterday a student in Michigan shot up his middle school, killing a teacher and two classmates. Don't you have a conscience?" I tried to explain that it would be a wholesome event, regulated by federal agents, but she slipped out the front door, tears streaming down her face.

Leslie returned an hour later, apologizing for her reaction. But I'd had enough time to reconsider and now realized that, at the least, I should have discussed the opportunity to promote the exposition with her before making a decision. We agreed on a compromise of sorts: Lassiter & Associates would assist McCulloch with this one event, and then end the account. No more gun shows. Ever.

While Leslie used most of Saturday morning to edit and organize her latest batch of images, I spent the time sitting on our patio with an unopened novel on my lap, watching mockingbirds defend their territories and trying once again to get a handle on where J.J. could have gone. I gazed across the backyard, eyeing the privacy fence J.J. had helped build and the pair of magnolia trees he'd helped transplant. And the picnic table he'd sat at only weeks ago. The epiphany never came. On Sunday morning, I drove a few miles outside the city to one of J.J.'s favorite places along the Arkansas River, hoping for an inspiration. Walking across the quiet sandbar, I spotted a pair of great blue herons and several wary turtles. Along the shore, I discovered an interesting assortment of tracks. But none of them led to J.J.

All in all, it was a pretty lousy weekend.

* * *

Ten minutes after leaving the house for the airport, I wheeled into Security Parking, a commercial lot half a mile from the terminal, and found an empty space against the fence on the west side. Grabbing my briefcase and travel bag, I stood behind the Toyota, waiting for the shuttle. One row over, the small bus headed my way. I glanced back to confirm that my lights were off—and my jaw fell open. Two slots beyond my pickup sat J.J.'s Jaguar convertible.

I felt the hair on my neck rise. Without question, I'd stumbled upon his car, the JJN license plate reflecting the morning sun into my disbelieving eyes.

An unexpected voice interrupted my confusion. "Sir, may I help you?" The shuttle driver peered from the open door, his face showing a trace of irritation. I guessed it wasn't his first effort to get my attention.

"Sorry," I stammered. "You caught me ... uh ... lost in thought." I handed him my bag, climbed into the van, and plopped into a vacant seat. Gazing at the Jaguar until it was out of sight, I felt like I'd uncovered another piece of the puzzle. But something about this piece didn't seem quite right.

The Southwest gate, of course, stood at the far end of the terminal. By the time I cleared the predictable TSA logjam, the attendants were herding the last of the stragglers through the covered jetway. I followed a family of four onto the Boeing 737, located an empty row near the rear of the plane, and took an aisle seat after stuffing my luggage into the overhead bin.

At 7:00 a.m. on the dot, the plane backed from the gate, and that's one reason I prefer Southwest. The airline tries hard to be on time and manages to do it most flights. At least that's what their ads claim. Also, I enjoy the irreverence and good humor of the staff.

As I daydreamed about acquiring Southwest's multi-million-dollar advertising account, an attractive flight attendant came down the aisle, checking seatbelts. She gave me a shy grin, made fleeting eye contact, and mouthed a short message. I didn't catch what she'd said but flashed my best smile. She soon passed by again, going the other direction, and touched my shoulder. When I looked up, she slipped a small, folded piece of paper into my hand. Clutching the note in my fist, I watched as she walked away on impossibly long legs, her full hips swaying from side to side in tight khaki shorts. Perhaps just a first name—maybe Dana or Mindy—and a phone number, I thought, although I fantasized for a moment that she'd penned an overt invitation to make my Dallas trip memorable. I'd have to pat her hand when I declined, stating I was engaged to an incredible woman. I chuckled, imagining Leslie's reaction when I described the flirtatious stewardess. After she disappeared from view, I opened the paper, catching a subtle whiff of perfume, and read the note. In elegant penmanship, her message was brief. No name, no number, not even a subject or verb. Just three letters: XYZ.

I sank into my seat, carnal thoughts washed away by a crimson blush invading my neck, and discreetly made the adjustment. The last time I'd suffered through an "examine your zipper" indignity had been over 20 years ago. In my eighth-grade civics class, to be exact, and the messenger had been the cute but gossipy Sarah

McAdams. When the Southwest attendants offered refreshments midway through the flight, I pretended to be asleep.

Half an hour after landing, I strolled into the lobby of VideoPro, the post-production house we'd used a couple of times a year for the past decade. No longer operating from a dreary warehouse in a suspect neighborhood, it now filled the first two floors of an ultramodern office building near the Southern Methodist University campus. Skylights, a huge aquarium, real plants, and chrome furniture indicated times had changed. So did the private rooms for clients' telephone calls, not to mention a complete kitchen stocked with coffee, hot teas, muffins, and bagels, along with a fine assortment of beers and liquors. No wonder the rates had risen.

I claimed one of the small conference rooms and made two quick calls. The first went to Booker.

"I need a favor."

"Splendid," he said, heavy on the sarcasm. The morning call no doubt had awakened him. "I shall enter yet another debit in my logbook. Whatever could it be this time?"

"J.J.'s car is parked at the Little Rock airport. Could you use your … er … special technical skills to determine if he had a ticket on an outbound flight?"

"Any particular period of time?" He sounded almost civil.

"Why don't you begin with the first two weeks of May."

"Actually, dear nephew, despite this inhuman hour, I'm rather pleased that you called," Booker said. "This past evening I finished writing code for a revolutionary program designed to infiltrate encrypted databases with nary a trace of my ingenious subterfuge. This task will provide a formidable but most welcome challenge."

I next called Leslie.

"How's it going?" she asked.

"I found J.J.'s car at the airport."

Leslie gasped. "You're sure?"

"I parked two spaces away."

"Could you tell if it'd been there long?"

"I had to jump on the shuttle and didn't have time to examine the car. I'll check tomorrow after my flight home."

The remainder of the day was excruciating. I sat fidgeting in a darkened room watching Abigail Ahart, my broadcast producer, and the VideoPro editor cut together a hodgepodge of shots we hoped would make sense as a dynamic 30-second message. Editing a television spot can be a slow and painful process, and about as glamorous as watching concrete set. Several times I swore my watch had stopped.

They had problems with the final edit on the first commercial. As Abbie and her editor debated options, I searched my briefcase for a bottle of aspirin. I'd been sitting in the same room for seven long hours, surrounded by an array of television monitors, staring at a troublesome series of three-second scenes for most of the afternoon. At 6:30 Abbie said we were done for the night.

I caught a taxi to the hotel, ate a tolerable room service Caesar salad, and then watched the latest Matt Damon movie. Once the lights were out, I had trouble going to sleep as my mind kept returning to J.J. and his disappearance. Tossing and turning until dawn, I arrived at the production house at 7:00 a.m. only to see the editing computer crash an hour later.

Remembering the kitchen and sunny garden atrium, I excused myself for a few minutes. If nothing else, the quiet would do me good. By the time I wandered back, Abbie and her hard-working colleague had solved the technical glitches. When I asked for details, Abbie forced a smile, patted me on the shoulder, and suggested another time might be more appropriate.

I decided to keep my scheduled mid-morning return flight and left them to wrestle with the two remaining commercials. I spent an hour working my way through the maze of metal detectors and federal friskers at Love Field before reaching the gate for Southwest's departure to Little Rock. I cringed, along with other passengers, at news that the plane was fully booked. Those of us holding boarding cards numbered 90 and above looked grim, realizing we'd be last on the crowded flight.

Eager to get back to Little Rock and check on J.J.'s car, I found the crew's usual antics rather childish and annoying. Maybe fatigue had something to do with my testy demeanor. I refused the offer of lemon lollipops as we stepped aboard, and struggled to keep my composure as another flight attendant made a lame effort at playing "The Eyes of Texas Are Upon You" on a kazoo. My long-legged correspondent wasn't to be seen, thank goodness, but I caught myself checking my zipper twice while shuffling down the narrow aisle.

We could have been a planeload of prosperous refugees, the overhead bins bulging with bags, boxes, and backpacks. I slid past an elderly woman occupying the aisle seat and settled in next to the window on the last row. Moments later, my shoulder gave way as a tall, lanky teenager wearing a UA Little Rock t-shirt squeezed into the middle seat.

Twenty minutes into our flight, I had my laptop open to review a proposed pitch for a potential client. Also busy with his computer, the young man next to me scrolled through page after page, deep in concentration. Trying not to be obvious, I stole an occasional glimpse at his screen. He appeared to be reading a medical research paper.

"Are you a student?" I asked.

"I'll be a junior next year at UA Little Rock," he said. "I'm majoring in biology, hoping to go to med school."

"One of my best friends heads up that department."

"You know Dr. Newell?" he asked. "He's been my advisor for two years now. He's also one hell of an instructor."

"He's a good man."

"I cannot imagine where I'd be without him."

I nodded, feeling the same.

* * *

Our approach came in over the Security lot for our noon landing in Little Rock. I tried to spot J.J.'s car from the plane but didn't have any luck. After a mad dash through the bustling terminal, I caught the shuttle just before it pulled from the curb. The three-minute ride to the parking area seemed to take forever. I didn't know what to expect.

But J.J.'s car had not been moved. I spent some time studying it, circling the classic convertible twice. Dirtier than I'd ever seen it, the Jaguar's deep green exterior lay hidden under a film of dust, grit, and pollen. Peeking inside, I saw nothing but his dog-eared Rand McNally road atlas in the passenger seat and a compact umbrella on the floorboard. Both doors and the trunk were locked.

I glanced at the tires. Small heaps of debris—residue from run-off flowing across the asphalt—were wedged against the base of each tire, indicating the Jaguar had been there for days. Or even weeks.

Tossing my gear into the Toyota, I rolled the windows down and sat for several minutes, my forehead pressed into the steering wheel. Something didn't fit … something about this situation didn't ring true. Whatever the discrepancy, I could not pin it down.

I slammed a fist against the dash in frustration, then started my truck and considered asking for the parking lot manager as I drove toward the exit. Remembering that supervisors are seldom helpful, I discarded the idea. As I neared the cashier's booth, I spotted one of the shuttle drivers sitting on an outside bench smoking a cigarette. I pulled to the side and walked over to the man, explaining that I needed to track down a friend, the owner of a green 1971 Jaguar convertible parked on the west end of the lot.

He nodded. "I know the car. We don't get many Jags here."

While he stared in the direction of the car, I noticed that his clothes were clean although worn. His shoes, however, didn't have many miles left, and a neat strip of duct tape held the frame of his eyeglasses together.

I stuck out a twenty. "I'd appreciate any help."

"That's not necessary," he said. But he took the cash. "I'll be right back." He stubbed out the cigarette, stepped into the office, and vanished. Even in the shade, it was sweltering. Loosening my tie, I rolled up my sleeves as rivulets of sweat trickled down my chest.

When he emerged five minutes later, my new friend wore the smile of a lottery winner. "I had to phone and check with Ray, one of our drivers. He logged the car in on May 8. He didn't remember much at first, but managed to recall a few details." He laughed, and then said, "Lucky for you, Ray's got a thing about Jaguars."

"Don't we all." I reached for my handkerchief and wiped it across my damp brow.

He referred to a notepad. "Ray remembered the car was driven by a woman. That sort of surprised him, plus the fact she wasn't dressed better." He scanned down the page. "Baggy clothes was what he said. And tall, sort of stocky. Couldn't place her age, though."

"A woman, huh?"

"And one more thing. Ray distinctly recalled that she had no luggage."

"None?"

"That's what he said. He dropped her off at the terminal, puzzled that she carried no bags."

That was an interesting tidbit. "Anything else?"

We gazed skyward as a Delta jet roared through our conversation and climbed into the clouds. Once the plane had flown from sight, the attendant looked back to me.

"Most folks don't leave their cars here this long," he said. "Any idea when your friend's returning?"

"I wish I knew."

~ ELEVEN ~

Leslie hadn't yet eaten when I called from the Security lot, and agreed to meet me for a late lunch at The Root, a popular restaurant on South Main known for a pleasant staff and reasonably healthy food. I'd ordered an appetizer of sweet potato fries when she arrived. After a peck on the cheek, she dropped into a chair beside me.

"Welcome back!" She gave my hand a squeeze as her look turned serious. "Tell me about J.J.'s car."

"It's been parked at the airport since May 8," I said. "A woman left it at the lot." I shared the rest of the information I'd acquired from the shuttle driver.

"A female, huh? And stocky. Perhaps it was J.J.'s new friend." Leslie sampled the tasty fries and then shook her head. "But no luggage? How unusual."

I nodded. "That's why he remembered her."

Once we'd made our selections from the menu, Leslie reached for her glass of water. "I'm almost dehydrated." She took another long swallow. "I forgot to take my cooler this morning."

"What were you shooting?"

"Central High."

My eyebrows went up.

"One of my agents said many foreign editors still associate Little Rock with the school's integration crisis. She wants me to send her a selection of my best shots."

78

"How'd it go?"

"The building is fabulous, and the principal went out of her way to help, even arranging for a group of students to serve as models."

Halfway through our meal of house salads, featuring locally grown organic produce, I felt my cell phone vibrate and stole a glance at the screen.

"Who is it?" Leslie asked.

"I don't recognize the number," I said with a shrug and set the phone aside. "If it's important, they'll leave a message."

After we ate and while we waited for the check, Leslie went to the restroom. I picked up my phone and found that Dr. Inez Ackerman had left a voicemail.

"Maybe some good news," I said when Leslie returned. "Dr. Ackerman, one of J.J.'s colleagues phoned. Perhaps I can schedule a time to see her."

"It's my turn to treat," Leslie said, handing the waiter a credit card. "Why don't you go ahead and call Dr. Ackerman. She might have some answers."

I stepped outside and gave the professor a ring. Much to my chagrin, it wasn't her direct line, but that of the gum-smacking receptionist. When she lost the connection, I counted to ten, redialed the number, and eventually got through to J.J.'s colleague.

Explaining that I had a few questions regarding the biology department, I asked for an appointment late in the afternoon. Dr. Ackerman agreed to see me, saying she would try to assist in any way possible.

* * *

While Leslie headed southwest on Interstate 30 for the small town of Hope to photograph Bill Clinton presidential sites for another frantic editor, I dropped by the office, where my beaming assistant delivered two encouraging reports. Not only had an exasperating client come through with an unexpected final payment on a long delinquent bill, the city's largest hospital had invited us to bid on its $2 million-a-year account. Health care was a field we were dying to enter.

I ran into Clifford, my talented but irritating copywriter, in the hall and made an unsuccessful attempt to avoid a conversation. He asked if I had read his latest e-mail. I promised to look at it and, as expected, the message requested my opinion regarding another proposed book title. This time it was *Machiavelli, Morality & Media: Messages for the Marauding Masses*. Muttering, I scrolled to the next item.

Four o'clock found me on the mid-town expressway heading to the university. Arriving late in the day, I located a vacant visitor's parking space near the Science Building. Given the 95° afternoon, I had a hunch my deodorant might be wearing thin.

The entire complex seemed deserted, but, sure enough, the same insipid receptionist loitered behind her computer screen. Today's bubbles, I noticed, matched her blue eye shadow and earrings.

"You're here to see Dr. Ackerman?"

Before I could reply, she lifted a skinny arm and pointed me down the hall and around the corner. A loud pop escorted me from the room.

Ackerman didn't meet my expectations. Short, a bit on the plump side, with rich gray hair, a quick smile, and blue eyes twinkling through thick horn-rimmed glasses, she could have been most anyone's grandmother. She wore a tailored blue pantsuit, a white silk blouse, and sensible shoes. A second glance confirmed that the unusual cloisonné brooch pinned to her left lapel was indeed a bejeweled frog.

Showing me to a chair, she sat behind a large, disordered desk. In biological terms, it wasn't even in the same family as the furniture in the dean's office. From another era, its style was what might be called Primitive Institutional Veneer.

Ackerman's office resembled a mini-museum. A hornet's nest the size of a basketball hung suspended high in one corner, and a couple of mounted skulls occupied the wall behind her. I wasn't sure what animals the skulls were from, but both carried antlers designed for business. A mottled snakeskin dangled from a three-drawer filing cabinet, touching the floor at both ends. Small specimen jars, easily a hundred or more altogether, lined the shelves of one bookcase. I sat in front of an even bigger bookcase, bulging with the predictable assortment of texts and journals. A tall, potted cactus bristling with toothpick-length spines blocked most of a narrow window.

She caught me inventorying her space and shrugged. "I should apologize for the mess," she said, "but this is my second home. Besides, a clean office is a sign of a sick mind."

"I feel the same. But I'm curious. What's in all those jars?"

"Frogs, for the most part."

That explains the brooch, I thought.

Anticipating my next question, Dr. Ackerman stated that many biologists, herself included, felt that frog populations serve as a valuable environmental barometer. Sort of a modern-day canary in the coal mine, she said. She'd been studying them for over 30 years, collecting samples from around the world.

"It must be fascinating."

She nodded. "Fascinating yes, but discouraging. We've seen severe declines in most species, and others have disappeared altogether."

Unwittingly, she provided the opening I needed.

"Do professors ever … disappear?"

Tilting her head, Ackerman gave me a strange look. "I'm afraid I don't understand, Mr. Lassiter."

"I've been searching for Dr. Newell for weeks. I can't find him anywhere."

She scooted her chair closer to the desk and propped her elbows amid the clutter.

"Now that you mention it, I haven't seen J.J. since the end of the spring term." Her eyes fixed on a point across the room, she rubbed her chin. "He's not teaching this summer, but even so, as a rule we'd find an excuse to talk every week or so."

"I'm worried about him," I said. "I've known J.J. half my life."

"You must be his former college roommate," Ackerman said with a slight smile. "He's often spoken fondly of those days." She paused and looked me in the eye. "I guess you've checked his house?"

"Vacant," I said. "Yesterday I found his car at the airport." I chose not to give her any additional details.

"I'm not aware of any travel he'd scheduled."

"Could he have taken a summer sabbatical?"

"He doesn't need 'em. J.J. enjoys his work too much. But I suspect you already knew that."

"I never heard him complain."

"He's not one to gripe. And J.J.'s not the disappearing type either." After a moment's hesitation, she reached for the telephone and pressed a button.

"Tiffany, would you unlock Dr. Newell's office?"

I watched as Dr. Ackerman shook her head. "No, dear. You have the spare key in your top desk drawer."

She turned to me as she covered the mouthpiece with her hand. "Our receptionist would test the patience of Job," she whispered. I grinned and gave her a knowing nod.

She listened for a few seconds, rubbing the bridge of her nose. "Yes, Tiffany. The key marked 312 is the one to Dr. Newell's office. We'll meet you there in a second."

I trailed Dr. Ackerman down the quiet hall.

"J.J.'s always been organized," she said. "Let's look at his calendar."

Tiffany stood at the door, fumbling with a key ring.

"It's not working, Dr. Ackerman."

"Are you sure that's the right one?"

Tiffany studied the keys for what seemed like an eternity before selecting another. It slipped into the lock and the door swung open.

"I guess that makes a difference," she said, her eyes blank.

"Thank you," Dr. Ackerman said. "I'll return the keys when I lock his office."

Down the hall a phone rang and Tiffany shuffled toward it. I heard the pop of another bubble.

As Ackerman had predicted, J.J.'s large office was shipshape, with a clean desk. Every drawer to his pair of filing cabinets displayed a neat label, and bound periodicals and proceedings filled two bookcases. Plaques and framed certificates covered the top half of one wall. Most were from academic groups, but in the center hung a handsome commendation from the Big Brothers Big Sisters organization. I remembered that J.J. had served as president of the local chapter a couple of years ago. Needing a printed program for an annual awards banquet, he'd asked Lassiter & Associates for some pro bono assistance. We'd been happy to oblige.

"Let's see what this tells us." She sat behind J.J.'s desk, with his month-at-a-glance calendar between her elbows. I peered over her shoulder and recognized his writing at once.

"He had a busy schedule through the end of finals," she said. Her fingers slid across the first week of May. He'd written the word "exam" within the square for each day, followed by cryptic abbreviations such as Herp., Vert. Zoo., and Ich. I assumed they were references to classes.

"Do all the faculty members carry this kind of teaching load?"

"Heavens no," she said, shaking her head. "J.J. is devoted to his students. He's the anonymous donor who for years has funded a scholarship program for minority undergraduates in the Biology Department."

"I had no idea." But J.J.'s generosity didn't surprise me.

"And he's our department chair, too."

"So, J.J. is also an administrator, reporting to ..."

"The dean of the College of Arts and Sciences."

"Any problems there?"

Dr. Ackerman shrugged. "He and Dr. Rankin Campbell seem cordial enough to one another. It might have something to do with the fact that both are LSU grads."

I thought back to my brief conversation with Dr. Campbell the previous week. I didn't remember catching any hints he and J.J. were friendly. Maybe my receptors weren't working at the time. Or perhaps Campbell was so eager to get on with his golf outing that he didn't appreciate my concern.

"What does being chairman entail?"

"Keeping the department on budget and submitting an ongoing series of required reports. And, of course, hiring, managing, and reviewing the staff." She paused a moment and looked back to the calendar. "I suspect that's the purpose of those meetings." She pointed to two notations during the same week as finals. One read "Saunders" and the other "Tillman." I noticed a slight change in her voice.

"Did you sit in on those meetings?" I asked.

"Goodness no. They were private."

Still standing behind Dr. Ackerman, I saw her pale neck turn crimson. There was something she wasn't telling me.

I walked around J.J.'s desk and sat in a chair facing the professor. She'd already flipped the calendar to June. "Not much else," she said. "His Kiwanis Club luncheons and a dental appointment." When she raised her head, her cheeks were still flushed.

"Those two confidential meetings, Dr. Ackerman. There's more to them than you've indicated."

She removed a tissue from her jacket and began wiping her eyeglasses. "They involved personnel matters," she said. "I'm not sure they're relevant to our discussion."

"I suspect you're correct. But right now, I'm grasping at straws."

She cleaned the right lens, the left, and resumed working on the right. Seconds passed. "I'm only telling you this because I know how close you and J.J. are," she said at last. "But it's not official and won't be until final approval by the university's administration. And you didn't hear it from me." Her voice dropped a level.

I nodded.

"As I understand, Dr. Norbert Saunders will be promoted to assistant professor. He's done everything expected of him. And more."

"Such as?"

"He's had half a dozen papers published in reputable journals, and several others accepted. In addition, he's very active in our

84

professional organizations. Thanks to him, the department has an exceptional website. And he's adored by his students."

She put her glasses on and flashed me a strained smile. "Much better." She began to rise from behind the desk. "Shall we go?"

"What about Tillman?"

Her smile evaporated and she sank back into the chair with a sigh. She clasped her wrinkled hands over J.J.'s calendar and reluctantly met my eyes.

"Yes, that brings us to Dr. Tillman." Biting her lip, she picked up a pen and began drumming it on J.J.'s desk. "Dr. Mackenzie Tillman returned to Little Rock eighteen months ago with a doctorate from Cornell."

"Returned?"

Ackerman nodded. "Mackie, as she's known, is the sole child of Benton Tillman."

I raised my eyebrows at this news. Benton Tillman, among the most powerful individuals in the state, had parlayed a small country grocery store into one of the region's biggest fortunes. Almost as controversial as he was rich, Tillman worked behind the political scenes, doling out large amounts of money to conservative candidates and conservative causes. But I'd never heard anything concerning a family.

"Her credentials are impeccable," Ackerman said. "Great school, degree with honors, dissertation research summarized in a leading journal."

"But?"

"It just isn't working."

"What do you mean?"

"When Dr. Tillman joined the faculty, she knew that all members were expected to produce and publish research."

"And she hasn't?"

"Not only that, her evaluations are awful. She can't relate to her students." Ackerman broke eye contact and shifted her gaze to the window. "Or her colleagues for that matter."

Was that frustration I heard? Or could she be jealous of Tillman's social standing?

"I'm unfamiliar with the academic way of life," I said with a shrug. "Does this mean she'll be placed on probation?"

"Worse." Dr. Ackerman shook her head. "Much worse. Her contract won't be renewed. Dr. Tillman will have to seek a position elsewhere."

"How's the job market?"

"Too many doctorates in biology. Not enough openings." She glanced at J.J.'s calendar, then grimaced.

"What's wrong?"

"I didn't see this earlier. It appears J.J. is scheduled to speak at the Ozark Society's annual summer meeting week after next." She made a note and stuck it in a pocket. "If he doesn't return soon, I may have to cover for him."

"Back to Dr. Tillman."

She nodded, but her scowl let me know our conversation would soon end.

"How did she take this news?"

"I haven't talked to either since their meeting."

"Any guess?"

She lifted her hands into the air. "I'm no mind reader. But I know J.J. dreaded the meeting."

"Nobody likes to deliver bad news."

"That was part of it. But Dr. Tillman …" Her voice trailed off.

"Yes?"

"Let's just say Mackie Tillman is not accustomed to rejection." Dr. Ackerman set her jaw and crossed her arms. "I've told you far more than I should, Mr. Lassiter."

"And I appreciate your insights," I said. "However, I'd like to talk to both Tillman and Saunders," I said. "Can you give me their telephone numbers?"

I thought I'd overplayed my hand, but after a stern look and a heavy sigh, Dr. Ackerman reached for a pen and notepad on J.J.'s desk. She then removed a cell phone from a jacket pocket and scrolled through her contacts, scribbling down a series of numbers. She pushed away from the desk and stood, giving me the small sheet of paper.

"One more thing," I said. "May I have a look at his calendar?"

She handed it to me, and I flipped it forward to October. What I saw made me smile. J.J. had circled the sixteenth and the words "WEDDING: LESLIE & RANDY"—scrawled across the square in his clumsy handwriting—were underlined twice followed by a pair of exclamation marks.

As I replaced the calendar, I noticed a clear plastic cube perched on the edge of J.J.'s desk and picked it up. Each of the six sides held a photograph, and two of them caught my eye. The first must have been 15 years old and showed J.J. and me canoeing on the Buffalo National River. The second, made earlier this spring according to the small corner inscription, pictured J.J. arm-in-arm with an attractive woman I didn't recognize. Both wore million-dollar grins. Could she be the woman J.J. had mentioned to Leslie and me? Puzzled, I replaced the cube on the desk.

Dr. Ackerman switched off the light as we stepped into the hall. We shook hands, and I gave her one of my business cards.

"Thanks for your time."

"I'm sorry I wasn't more help." She patted my shoulder. "You'd better find J.J. We need him." She pulled the door closed, its latch sliding into place with a solid snap.

Promising to call as soon as I'd learned anything, I turned to the elevator and almost collided with a petite woman carrying an armload of books. She pressed the button for the first floor.

"Excuse me," she said as I slipped into the elevator beside her. "Did I overhear that you're looking for Dr. Newell?"

Too surprised to speak, I nodded as the doors slid together. She was the woman in the photograph.

"Me, too."

The elevator lurched downward.

~ TWELVE ~

The elevator doors parted at the first floor, and I followed this mysterious woman into the empty lobby. After a brief hesitation, she turned and made eye contact, her free hand brushing aside a wayward strand of striking red hair. "Would you have time for coffee in the Student Union?"

My curiosity and her pleading eyes gave me no choice. "You'll have to lead the way."

As we walked, I studied my companion. A few inches above five feet, she looked to be older than the typical college student, maybe in her late twenties or early thirties. Consistent with the hair, she had a light complexion topped by a spray of freckles. Her eyes were a deep turquoise, emphasized by a subtle trace of liner. I noticed a cute nose, slightly upturned, and, below that, a reserved smile revealing braces on her upper teeth.

Other than the obligatory remarks on prospects for a hot weekend, we spoke little as we walked. Within five minutes we'd arrived at the Union and took our cups to a quiet corner. She shoved her books to one side of the table.

"I'm Summer Preston," she said, and we shook hands, her grip solid and firm. Her manicured fingernails were painted a deep red.

"Randy Lassiter."

Her face lit up. "I've heard so many things about you! You're one of J.J.'s best buddies."

"I'd like to think so," I said, still wary.

She dumped two sugars into her coffee and took her time stir-ring the mixture. When she glanced up, her eyes were moist.

"I'm not sure where to begin." She wiped away the tears and took a sip from her cup. After a deep breath, she forced a doubtful grin. "J.J. and I have been good friends—*very* good friends—for some time now." She paused as a blush crept across her face. "We started dating soon after the first of the year."

"Then I suspect you know him better than I do," I said, and she laughed. An honest laugh, it broke the tension.

It also broke the dam, and Summer spilled her story. I listened as she described a bitter divorce from a local stockbroker she had met through an online dating service. "I guess you might describe Brett as handsome," she said, "but all I remember now is the mean-ness, his manipulative personality, the mental games he played with me." I nodded, admitting that I'd been introduced to him a time or two at chamber of commerce functions. When their child-less marriage of three years ended last August, she decided to make a fresh start. First, she resumed use of her maiden name. Then, unhappy as an elementary school teacher, she applied to UA Little Rock's College of Business Administration for graduate work. Not only accepted into the program, she received an assistantship.

"What does an assistantship involve?"

"The primary responsibility is teaching a freshman class on the American economy." Summer waved a hand at the stack of books. "My tuition's covered and I get a small stipend. And a reserved parking space."

"Sounds like a good deal."

Her grin almost returned, but she partially covered her mouth before lowering her hand to the table. "I'm sorry. These braces are another part of my new beginning. Here I am—30 years old—and self-conscious about a temporary band of plastic on my teeth."

She blinked back tears and began twirling a lock of hair around a finger. Neither of us was in a hurry.

Summer took another swallow of coffee before setting the cup down. "While grading papers in the library at the beginning of the semester, I ran out of ink." I watched as she rubbed a finger across her chin, the faintest outline of a smile on an otherwise sad face. "J.J.—Professor Newell to me at the time—happened to be sitting at an adjacent table and overheard my mutterings. He loaned me a pen, and ... uh ... well, one thing led to another." She shrugged before adding, "Over a period of time, of course." Her face reddened again.

"I suspect you're the reason I didn't see J.J. much this spring," I said. Thinking back, I realized our visits over the past several months had been much less frequent. Smitten with Leslie, I hadn't been aware of it at the time. But I wasn't surprised that J.J. hadn't said anything about Summer until the May Day picnic. He'd always made a practice of keeping his social life private.

"We maintain our distance on campus. People might gossip about a relationship between a professor and a graduate student, even if we are in different programs." She sighed. "But we're two mature adults ..." She finished her coffee.

Four or five tall young men sauntered through the cafeteria, their plates piled high. I stared as they passed, realizing they must be on the school's basketball team. When I looked to Summer, a tear slid down her cheek.

"I just don't understand," she said, her voice trembling. "Where could he be?" She buried her face in her small hands.

I felt useless as she quietly sobbed. When a couple of students glanced our way, I tried to avoid their eyes.

Summer searched her purse, gave up, and dabbed her face with a napkin she pulled from a dispenser on the table. "I'm sorry. I've been so worried."

"Let me get refills," I said. "Another cup will help." By the time I returned, she had regained her composure, even managing a weak "thanks" as I placed our coffees on the table and left a pair of sugars near her cup.

"You may know J.J. and I have quite a history," I said. "Beginning with our freshman year in college."

"He's filled me in on some of your adventures."

"You're not serious!" I hoped J.J. had not violated our long-standing confidentiality pact.

She nodded with a slight smile. "My favorite was the time you two broke into the utility tunnels at the University of Arkansas in Fayetteville late one night and almost got caught sneaking into a girls' dorm."

I felt my face flush, recalling a successful effort the following weekend. Surely, he hadn't … "Did J.J. disclose that I once bailed him out of jail?" I asked, changing the subject.

"Jail!" Her chin dropped.

"He mouthed off to a rookie cop who'd blocked our driveway while investigating a fender-bender. J.J. got hauled in on an 'obstruction of justice' charge."

"Oh my gosh!"

"He spent a short time in lockup before I came to the rescue and bailed him out. The citation was dismissed the next day."

She chuckled and patted my hand. "Thanks, Randy. I'm feeling better."

I took a long sip of coffee, then cleared my throat. "The last time I saw J.J. was earlier this month. I'd invited him to a cookout to meet my fiancée who has moved to Little Rock."

"When was this?"

I put the cup down and massaged my temples. "Four weeks ago. May first, to be exact. Sometime during the afternoon, J.J. volunteered to lead us in pagan rituals."

Summer giggled, shaking her head. "That sounds like J.J."

"Leslie, my fiancée, later said we should have called his bluff, but I told her he probably wasn't joking." I thought back to that pleasant May Day afternoon that now seemed so long ago. "We're getting married in October, and I had asked J.J. to be my best man. When he drove off late in the day, he promised to call back and confirm the date. But I haven't seen him since." I swallowed the last of my coffee. "Right before he left, J.J. told us he had a special friend he wanted to introduce us to. He had to be referring to you."

"He'd asked me to accompany him to your cookout, but I'd already agreed to help with a friend's bridal shower." She brushed at a tear creeping down her cheek. Moments passed. I watched as Summer mindlessly folded an empty sugar packet into smaller and smaller squares. She pushed it aside. "Is Leslie a professional photographer?"

I answered with a slight nod.

"I'm a shutterbug of sorts, and J.J. mentioned that I needed to see Leslie's work, saying that I'd enjoy getting acquainted with her." She paused and looked at her hands, halfheartedly inspecting her manicure. "In fact, we haven't talked since."

"Do you remember the date?"

She opened her purse again and removed a pocket calendar. "A little more than three weeks ago. We'd gone out to dinner, but he seemed preoccupied. He claimed it was the stress that comes at the end of every semester. It was during our meal when he said he'd met someone who could critique my photography."

"And then what?"

"I tried calling him a few days afterward, but got no answer. At first, I didn't think anything of it. We'd made tentative plans for the weekend, and when that came and went without a word from J.J., I got concerned."

She stared over my shoulder, her troubled eyes focused on the past. Seconds ticked by as her gaze fell back to her hands, and I watched the restless fingers intertwine first one way then another, never satisfied.

"I guess you've been searching for him?"

"I've tried," she said. "But I'm working under a disadvantage. Since nobody else knew of our relationship, I don't have many doors to knock on. It's so frustrating."

"Any leads at all?"

"None. I've driven by his house half a dozen times, but it always appears vacant. I've stopped at the Biology Department on a couple of occasions before today, but the receptionist in the front office has the intellectual horsepower of a gerbil."

"You're being generous."

"And, of course, I've phoned his house many times." She hesitated for a moment before looking up sharply. "Somebody answered once, but it wasn't J.J. and I panicked and hung up."

"That was me," I said, remembering the unexpected call. "I have a key and let myself in one afternoon to check on things."

"Oh my God." Summer raised a hand to her mouth. "How are the fish?"

"The survivors seem okay."

"The angelfish are my favorites."

I shook my head. "They didn't make it," I said before thinking and instantly regretting it.

That news sent more tears trickling down her cheeks. She reached for another napkin and wiped her face. "Did you happen to spot a guitar in his house?"

"A Gibson," I said. "In the den. I was surprised to see it."

"I've played for years. For the last month or so before he disappeared, I'd been giving J.J. lessons. Although frustrated at first, he seems to be catching on. I think he has aspirations of being the next Stevie Ray Vaughan."

We watched the basketball players leave. One grinned and bobbed his head at Summer and she managed a weak smile in return.

"That's DeShawn Pitts," she said with a sniff. "Among the top freshman basketball players in the country, I'm told. He did well in my class."

Quiet returned to the cafeteria. All but a handful of students had gone.

"So, there's my report," Summer said. "What kind of luck have you had?"

I related my visit with J.J.'s neighbors, and the conversations with Dean Campbell and Professor Ackerman. I also noted my trip to the post office, but opted not to bring up the forged signature on the card. After describing J.J.'s assortment of mail, I shared the news about finding his car.

Summer's eyes narrowed and she leaned forward. "The airport? Are you sure? That's not like J.J. at all."

A jolt shot through my brain. "You're right! J.J. doesn't like fly-ing." In all the confusion, that fact had somehow slipped my mind. I shook my head, wondering how I could have forgotten his aver-sion to airplanes.

"Anytime he goes anywhere, he drives," she said. "When he has to attend conventions, he often uses them as excuses for field trips."

"And if my memory's right, he sometimes takes students along." I shut my eyes, recalling some of J.J.'s stories.

"He wants them to experience other parts of the country," she said. "During spring break, he took a vanload to a professional meeting in El Paso. But the highlight of the trip was their time at Big Bend National Park."

A set of double doors swung open and a young man emerged, pushing a mop bucket. One by one, the other customers took the cue and headed for the exits.

Summer glanced at her watch. "It must be closing time." She reached for the pile of books and got to her feet. I followed her through the door, tossing our cups into the trash bin as we went.

We found a bench in the shade at the base of a large fountain, and Summer commented on the late afternoon sun streaming through the pines towering above the campus. A flock of pigeons descended, eager to gauge their prospects. I shooed them away.

"Summer, was J.J. in any sort of trouble?"

"I've asked myself the same question a hundred times. But nothing comes to mind. Nothing."

I thought back to my conversation with Dr. Ackerman less than an hour ago. "Any problems here at the university?"

"The usual administrative hassles," she said. "But I can't think of anything out of the ordinary."

"Did he allude to any difficulties with his staff?"

"He didn't discuss his colleagues."

"Gambling issues?"

"We've gone to Tunica two or three times," she said, referring to the sprawling casino district across the Mississippi River from J.J.'s hometown of Helena-West Helena. "But always for entertainment. We'd each lose our 20 dollars on the slots and call it a day."

"I examined his bank statement," I said. "It doesn't appear he's in any sort of financial bind."

"He's a savvy money manager. After my divorce got finalized, I received a substantial cash settlement, and J.J. helped me select a handful of mutual funds that've done well."

"So, nothing was bothering him?"

She rubbed her chin. "I doubt if it's important, but I can remember one incident." She stopped and took a deep breath.

"What happened?"

"It was during that field trip to Big Bend that I mentioned. Something occurred and it worried him for a while, but I assumed it had blown over."

"Do you know any details?"

"J.J. took four or five students with him in a university van. One night while they camped, one of the men got drunk and made unwanted sexual advances to a female student. Repeatedly, I understand. First thing the next morning, J.J. hauled him to the nearest town and put him on a bus to Little Rock."

"Then what?"

Summer shrugged. "I'm not sure, but I think he left the biology program."

"Do you remember the guy's name?"

She thought for a moment and then shrugged. "Maybe I can recall it later."

One of the campus security officers waddled past, a short, pudgy man in his late fifties carrying a walkie-talkie on one hip and a nightstick on the other. He gave us a small wave before continuing on his rounds.

Too busy to notice, Summer scribbled on a piece of paper. "Here's my telephone number. Please call if you find anything." Her hand trembled.

I slipped it in a pocket and gave her a business card after writing both my home and cell numbers on the back. "The same goes for you."

A short walk brought us to the parking lot. I escorted Summer to her compact car, dodged a group of sweaty joggers, and hurried across the shimmering asphalt to my pickup. The cab felt like an oven.

On the way home I wheeled into the neighborhood liquor store. The clerk didn't know me by name, but remembered my typical purchase. "The usual?" he asked, reaching for a six-pack of my favorite local micro-brew.

"Let's make it a case."

~ THIRTEEN ~

Wednesday was ... well ... just one of those days. It began with the annual obligatory prayer breakfast hosted by the governor for over a thousand of his closest and dearest friends in the central Arkansas business community—at $100 a head. Held at the Statehouse Convention Center, this sanctimonious show of solidarity didn't deviate from its traditions of bland speakers and worse food. The sound system performed better than last year, but several at my table groused, preferring not to hear the vapid goings on. I smiled at the right people, avoided a couple of politicians no doubt looking for favors of the dubious sort, and passed on a third cup of cold coffee.

Following that blessed event, I went to Merchants Bank—thinking it wouldn't hurt to return some business to my biggest client—and spent an hour reviewing a proposed expansion of the agency's profit-sharing plan. I'd been considering the change for the past few months, firm in my belief that cash incentives help folks take their jobs more seriously. Bringing the entire staff into the arrangement seemed like the right thing to do. But finding a bright yellow parking ticket tucked under the Toyota's windshield wiper somewhat offset my positive attitude.

Swinging by the office, I returned half a dozen phone calls before checking e-mails. Clifford, of course, had sent another message regarding his "forthcoming international best seller," now titled *Machiavelli for Miscreants*. He assured me that the first chapter had already been composed "in my head," and that the volume would "transform the world's business establishment." I grumbled and hit the "delete" button.

Mid-morning found me at River City Studios, Little Rock's top video and film production facility, where I again sat in a small room surrounded by a bank of television monitors and within a minute had dribbled coffee down my white shirt. My presence had been requested by Megan, the account supervisor who handles Isla del Sol, the agency's Tunica casino and resort client. She gave a minute's worth of background before turning the meeting over to Abigail Ahart, our overworked but always smiling broadcast producer.

Abbie brought me up to speed on what they'd done and why. After weeks of planning—including focus group sessions in Jackson, Little Rock, and Memphis—they'd spent another three days filming on location in the casino.

"How much footage did you get?" I asked.

"A little over four hours."

As I calculated the costs, I tried not to cringe.

"I have two 30-second commercials for your approval," she said. "One's aimed at the blue-collar market and the other targets demographic groups a notch or two higher."

If my mental arithmetic was correct, Abbie had distilled over 14,000 seconds of film into two 30-second messages. No wonder her eyes were bloodshot.

"You'll see some differences," she promised as the lights dimmed.

The first version nearly wore me out with its pacing. Rapid-fire edits delivered a brilliant barrage of grinning faces, flashing lights, and breathtaking jackpots—all combined with the jerky camera work now in vogue and an energetic island beat.

"That's our blue-collar edition," Abbie said. "You may have noticed an emphasis on the slots."

I nodded. One-armed bandits—coupled with enticing payoff scenes—dominated the message.

"This next spot targets an older, more affluent audience."

A bit less frenetic than the first, it still moved at a brisk pace with music a tad more sedate. Rather than concentrating on slots, the spot gave equal billing to craps, roulette, and blackjack—with quick vignettes highlighting the resort's food, drink, lodging, and spa options. Sporting bright and colorful resort attire, the handsome and smiling talent conveyed a subliminal "You can be here, too" message. In all my visits to the casino, I'd never seen such an attractive clientele.

Despite that, my gut reaction was positive, but I kept it to myself. "Let's watch 'em again," I said. Abbie, too nervous to sit, fidgeted as she leaned against the wall.

On the second viewing, I noticed the subtle nuances that make the difference in a successful television commercial. The festive music meshed with the footage. The lighting was worthy of a Hollywood production and so were the camera angles—tight shots mixed with expansive, dynamic scenes. The props, the people, and the pacing were perfect.

As the lights came up, I glanced at Megan and Abbie. They stared at me, awaiting a reaction. I again wondered how many total hours had been devoted to those two spots. I'd find out soon enough when the final billing crossed my desk.

"I like them," I said, watching hesitant smiles creep across their faces. "A lot. But I've got one suggestion." The smiles wavered, and Abbie reached for her notebook. "The voice-over," I said. "It's the same for both, correct?"

"That's right," Abbie answered, biting her lip.

"Would it improve them if you used a more informal, folksy voice for the first, and maybe one a bit more sophisticated for the second?"

I could sense Abbie's relief. At least I hadn't asked her to re-shoot an elaborate scene or change the music, either of which would have been complicated and expensive.

"We can have it done by this time tomorrow," she said. "Will you want to view them again?"

Shaking my head, I'd started for the door when I stopped and—ignoring the stern "thou shalt not touch thy employees" edict of my lawsuit-conscious attorney—gave Abbie a brotherly hug. "Those are the best gambling commercials I've ever seen. You may single-handedly transform the Bible Belt."

"Just don't tell my dad," she said with an embarrassed grin.

As we left the studio, Megan stopped me in the parking lot, her scheduling calendar open. "Our Isla del Sol friends in Tunica are eager to see those spots," she said. "What about Friday?"

I glanced at the calendar on my phone and saw a single meeting, and it could be postponed. "You're on."

Disturbing news greeted me at the office. An editor from *Arkansas Business* had called for my reaction to an unconfirmed report that KACN, the state's top-rated country music radio station and a long-time Lassiter & Associates client, had been bought by a national media conglomerate. My heart racing, I re-read the phone message, deciding to return the call after I'd talked to the station manager. Fifteen minutes of one busy signal after another convinced me something had happened. I swallowed a couple of aspirin, then tried to gauge the effects of losing a $1.5 million-a-year account. It was not a pleasant thought. More than once I reminded myself that the sale—if indeed it had occurred—didn't mean that we'd be dropped as the agency of record. Right ... I again reached for the phone, but the line remained busy.

Noon plans called for me to meet Constance Engstrom at the exclusive Little Rock Club on the top floor of the Regions Bank Building. She'd called weeks ago to schedule lunch, and I felt sure it wasn't a social invitation. A little less than six months earlier Constance had been hired as executive director of the city zoo, and I had the uneasy feeling she wanted some free assistance.

Thirty-five floors up, Little Rock's geography sprang into view as I gazed out a floor-to-ceiling window in the reception area. Due west, and a mile away, stood the State Capitol, the gold atop its towering dome sparkling in the midday sun. In the streets far below, cars and trucks jerked from one stoplight to the next like colorful but spastic insects searching for food. From the northwest flowed the Arkansas River, snaking across the landscape toward the southeast. In the distance, I spotted Pinnacle Mountain poking through the horizon like a dormant volcano and, beyond it, the steep, narrow ridges that grew into the Ouachitas.

I felt a hand on my shoulder. "Randy, sorry I'm late."

Turning to face my lunch companion, I extended my hand. "I've been here all of two minutes," I said. "I never turn down a pretty view."

Constance, however, is not a very pretty view. Not unattractive, just plain. While I'd attended the Little Rock public schools, Constance had taken the Catholic route, including a three-year stint at Mount St. Mary Academy, and I always got the feeling she was using one of the aged sisters as her fashion consultant. But she had sparkling blue eyes and megawatts of enthusiasm, not to mention a rich and overbearing brother-in-law on the city's Board of Directors.

"Thanks!" She gave me a peck on the cheek. I think we both blushed.

As the maître d' led us into the dining area, I nodded at a handful of acquaintances, including the state's attorney general who held court at a long table with a collection of unsavory looking characters. I could tell by the expensive suits, flashy suspenders, big watches, loud voices, and occasional bow tie that he'd surrounded himself with other lawyers. I shuddered, and followed Constance into the next room.

Against the far wall at a solitary table sat Dr. Rankin Campbell, the UA Little Rock dean I'd visited with last week. Sitting across from Campbell was none other than Benton Tillman, Dr. Mackenzie Tillman's father and the Arkansas grocery magnate. They must not have been at the meal long, I realized. Their salads appeared intact.

Tillman was one of the most recognizable figures in the state. Tall and gaunt with saucer-like ears, he made a fascinating contrast with Campbell. While the dean covered the top end of the fashion spectrum, Tillman owned the other, wearing faded blue jeans, scuffed and muddy cowboy boots, and what might have been the original polo shirt of an indeterminate color. He wore his long gray hair in a ponytail, à la Willie Nelson. And like Willie, Tillman had experienced his share of problems with the Internal Revenue Service. I recalled a recent newspaper article in which he compared federal tax agents to Nazi storm troopers, no doubt endearing himself with the IRS leadership and putting him on the annual audit list for years to come.

I'd met Tillman two or three times over the course of my career, but we weren't close since our social circles didn't exactly overlap. Much to my chagrin, a large Atlanta agency had a lock on his multi-million-dollar advertising budget.

Leaning into each other and deep in serious conversation, neither Tillman nor Campbell paid us any attention. It looked like a sales job to me. But who was making the pitch? And what was it?

Constance and I were directed to a table for two on the opposite side of the room next to a window overlooking the river, with my back to Campbell and Tillman. Strange, I thought, that we'd get the choice seats while Tillman, who had enough money to buy the building many times over, occupied an economy spot.

"Perhaps you have an idea why I asked for this meeting," Constance said. A smile brightened her face.

"You're aware of my fondness for peanut butter pie." The Little Rock Club was famous for this culinary delight, despite its approximate 50,000 calories per slice.

Constance laughed a bit too loud, almost honked in fact, and a few wayward strands of hair fell across her face. "I need advertising help. You've gotten high recommendations."

"So, you've met my mom?"

She actually snorted this time, drawing the attention of nearby diners, and patted my hand. I made a mental note to tone down my humor.

"The glowing reference came from a key member of my advisory board," she said, flipping her hair back in place with a shake of her head. "Dr. J.J. Newell, a biology professor at UA Little Rock."

Nodding, I stared at Constance. As my pulse quickened, a cold sweat broke out over my body. Forcing myself to take short breaths, I prayed for encouraging news. "Did this happen recently?"

Constance held a tall glass of water to her mouth, and I've never seen anyone take such a long and slow and deliberate drink, seeming to savor each and every tiny, wet molecule. Oblivious to my pounding heart, she then wiped a napkin across her lips and gazed at me for several seconds. "I can't remember exactly when it was, Randy. Is it important?"

Nerves taut, I managed a small shrug. "J.J. and I are good friends, and I haven't talked to him in a while," I said, taking a shaky sip myself. "I thought you might have seen him in the past few days."

I could hardly believe it when Constance brought the water back to her lips. After another deep swallow worthy of a camel, she set the glass aside. "Oh, no. It must have been a month ago," she said. "I'm so far behind …"

My hopes dashed, I blocked out the rest of her sentence. She continued to talk, referring to a small notepad she'd pulled from a purse about the size of a diaper bag. Moments passed.

"… and like I said, we have so much to do with so little money." She smiled again and then resumed her rehearsed spiel.

Like a priest who's heard it all, I gave her a series of understanding nods at appropriate intervals, relieved when our waiter marched forward to recite the day's selections. As he took Constance's order, I shot a discreet glance across the room. Tillman and Dr. Campbell remained hunched over the table, their conversation animated.

"And for you, sir?"

Once the waiter departed, Constance and I busied ourselves with small talk until the meal arrived. She had asked for veal Parmigiana, while I opened my manhood up for question by ordering spinach quiche. My spirits somewhat reinvigorated by the food, I gave my lunch companion the attention she expected.

"How many hours of work a month would you need?" I asked. Whatever she answered, I knew to double it.

"Not more than ten."

Twenty hours times twelve months. Counting all costs, she had asked for an annual write-off to the tune of about $36,000. Plus, the chances were good we'd lose the KACN account within a matter of days. I took a gulp of iced tea. "What's in it for me?"

"All the exotic fertilizer you want."

She must have seen my lawn, I thought.

Our waiter returned. "Would you care for dessert?" It was a ridiculous question.

While I enjoyed my creamy peanut butter pie, and even let Constance experience a nibble, we discussed projects she had in mind. None seemed unreasonable, and a couple sounded quite exciting, including ambitious plans for a spacious new elephant compound. Before making any commitments, I needed to run her proposal past my colleagues. The contract with one of our current pro bono clients would be ending on June 30, still a few weeks away. Taking on the zoo might be a welcome change for the agency—and could bolster staff morale if we lost the radio station account.

After picking up the tab and promising Constance a prompt reply, I escorted her from the room. Tillman and Campbell, I noticed, had left, and their table was already cleared. I wondered what they'd been talking about.

~ FOURTEEN ~

Leslie pulled in seconds after I did and met me with a kiss on the porch. "I hope you're feeling sociable," she said. She lowered her camera bag onto the front porch.

"I am now." There was no sense worrying her with the KACN rumors. I'd share any news once the sale was confirmed. "What's up?"

"I ran into Ellen while getting shots of the sculpture garden downtown. She and Gib have invited us to meet them at the Arkansas Travelers' game tonight." She glanced at her watch. "I've already accepted. We're supposed to be there in half an hour."

"Just what the doctor ordered." I gave her a hug and then dashed inside to shed my coat and tie.

After storing her photo equipment, Leslie followed me up the stairs. "I'm clueless. Who are the Travelers?"

"A farm club for the California Angels. A Double A team."

Her puzzled look deepened. "Any particular sport?" Leslie was proud of the fact she'd gone a full decade without reading the sports pages of a newspaper. But I still loved her.

"Baseball, of course. The American pastime."

Her shoulders slumped and a rare frown emerged. "I was hoping for basketball. Or even soccer," she groaned. "But baseball …"

"These are real athletes. Minor leaguers, but still professionals. Maybe the next Hank Aaron or Mike Trout."

"Pros at scratching their crotches and spitting," Leslie said, shaking her head. "I didn't realize we were talking ... *baseball*. It's such a disgusting excuse for a sport."

"We'll have a great time. It's not an athletic contest as much as a social event. A unique outdoor drama."

Arms crossed, Leslie remained skeptical.

"There'll be lots of wonderful photographic opportunities."

Her frown retreated a notch. "Such as?"

"Kids, the crowd, all the pomp and ceremony that go with the game."

"I'll take the Leica," she grumbled. A small but classic German film camera, it was what she used when discretion was required. "At least it'll be fun to see Ellen and Gib again."

We met the Yarberrys at the main gate to Dickey-Stephens Park in North Little Rock, and Ellen led us through the throng to choice box seats down the third-base line. Well into her eighth month of pregnancy, my little sister seemed to enjoy cutting a wide swath. "I feel like an icebreaker in the Arctic," she said when we were seated.

"What's with this huge crowd?" I asked. Hundreds of kids milled around, although most, thank goodness, appeared to be somewhat supervised by adults.

"It might have something to do with the fact that my agency handles this account," Ellen said, batting her long lashes and giving me a large if insincere smile.

I'd forgotten about that. "So, I guess we can expect a gimmick," I answered with a wink. "Who is it this time? Captain Dynamite?" Promotion has always been her forte.

"We tried to get him," Ellen admitted. "And I even managed to reach the Captain over the phone. But he's blown himself up so many times, he's deaf. We couldn't carry on a conversation."

"Obviously, it's someone who appeals to kids," Leslie said.

Gib surveyed the spectators. "My guess is Pee-wee Herman."

Ellen gave his ear a gentle twist. "We've brought back an all-time favorite. The San Diego Chicken." She pointed at the Travelers' dugout. "There he is."

A tall, awkward mascot bearing a remote resemblance to a bedraggled bird cavorted with several players along the edge of the ball field. Dozens of children pressed against the fence, screaming at the strange creature. I began searching for the nearest beer vendor.

"Did Gib share his news?" Ellen asked.

"Give me a second," I said, rubbing my chin thoughtfully. "His charter membership in the Self-Improvement Book Club has been revoked?"

Ellen wagged a finger at me. "He's been elected to the board of the International Save the Puns Foundation."

While Gib struck his impression of an aristocratic pose, I grimaced. He'd been tormenting me with puns since our initial introduction. Sure, he's a good friend and my favorite (and only) brother-in-law, but I couldn't imagine Ellen's situation, living with him every day, just waiting for Gib to twist a word or phrase into something he thought clever.

"Congratulations," Leslie said, always diplomatic. "I guess this is recent?"

"The election results were reported last week," Gib said. "*Pun*ctual as usual."

I wanted to hit him.

"He's the first Arkansan on the board," said Ellen.

"The first from the South," said Gib. "The group's trying to be more inclusive. I suppose ..." and he paused for dramatic effect, "it's one of the club's *pun*damental beliefs."

Even Leslie rolled her eyes.

It was time to change the subject. "Who are we playing tonight?" I asked.

Gib glanced at his program. "The Midland Rockhounds," he said. "Based in Texas, they're part of the Oakland Athletics organization."

Bless her big and generous heart, Leslie tried to make sense of all this. "So, if a player does well here, he might advance to the major leagues?"

"Lots of players move up," I said. "Some of these men," and I gestured toward the field, "might play in a World Series within a few years."

Gib shook his head. "Maybe for the Travelers. But not from the Rockhounds. No way."

"What do you mean?" Ellen asked.

Gib smiled, and I dreaded what was coming. "The Midland players are not good, and they're not bad," he said with a shrug. "At best, they're … middlin'."

During the second or third inning, I glanced over my shoulder and saw the famed San Diego Chicken making its way in our direction. By now, much of the novelty had worn off and the mascot's followers had thinned to a handful of die-hards. Gib and I watched, spellbound, as a couple of cute but pudgy toddlers waddled over to inspect this feathered monstrosity.

Lifting her Leica, Leslie took a surreptitious shot.

Gib tapped her shoulder. "I've got a caption for you."

I tried to cover my ears.

"Chicken and dumplings," said Gib, slapping me on the back. "I love America."

Between innings, a child wearing a UA Little Rock jersey walked by, dribbling juice from his snow cone with every step. For the first time all evening, Gib appeared serious. "That reminds me. Any news from J.J.?"

"Not yet," I said. "I visited with the dean of the college, and he thinks J.J. may be traveling."

"What about the wedding?" Ellen asked. "Have you picked a date?"

"October," Leslie said with a smile. "The sixteenth."

"It's a Saturday," I said. "Keep it open."

Midway through the game Leslie and I wandered to the concession booths under the upper deck. We'd ordered hotdogs when I felt a hand on my shoulder. I turned and saw Catfish McCulloch, the newest client of Lassiter & Associates. After we exchanged greetings, I introduced him to Leslie.

"Pleased to meet you," he said. "I sure hope you can attend my show."

"I'm afraid not," she answered. "I have a big photo shoot lined up that weekend." My bride-to-be was a graceful and polite liar.

Catfish, clearly disappointed, turned to me. "How's our media campaign coming?"

"I've assigned one of my brightest staff members to it. A real outdoorsman. He's eager and will do a super job."

Promising to stay in touch, Catfish shambled away, melting into the masses.

"What an interesting face," Leslie said. "If we could get him out of that hideous sport coat, I'd enjoy taking his portrait."

We'd turned and headed for our seats when Leslie gasped. She grabbed my arm, almost causing me to drop our chili dogs. "Randy, look!" She pointed across the bustling concourse. "Is that J.J. buying a beer?"

Flicking past an ice cream vendor and a souvenir booth, my eyes stopped on a Budweiser stand some 75 feet away. His back to us, a tall man paid the clerk and, beer in hand, edged into the friendly mob.

"I think you may be right," I said, my heart racing. I shoved our food into Leslie's arms. "Let me check!"

I pushed through the horde, apologizing to one irritated fan after another while closing the gap. As the man angled into the stands above first base, I became convinced we'd found my long-lost friend. It had to be J.J.! The height was right. So were the walk and posture. He had J.J.'s build, not to mention his thick salt-and-pepper hair.

Closing to within ten feet, I was ready to shout "J.J.!" when the man stopped and halfway turned toward me, his fingers fumbling with a shirt pocket. As he brought a pinch of tobacco to his gap-toothed mouth, we made eye contact, staring at each other for a moment. I'm sure he wondered about the breathless stranger who then backtracked a few clumsy steps before lowering his head and slipping into the crowd.

I didn't have to say anything to Leslie when I returned to my seat; my expression told her the story. She gave me a kiss on the cheek and handed me a greasy wrapped hotdog and a stack of napkins. "Don't give up," she said, her fingers gripped around mine. "We *will* find J.J. That's a promise."

The Travelers jumped ahead as a result of several fielding errors by Midland's third baseman, a huge, broad-shouldered young man named DuPriest. Gib began razzing him unmercifully. Another grounder glanced off DuPriest's glove, squirting into left field, scoring a run. "Hey, kid!" he shouted. "Hey, DuPont! Is that a Teflon glove?" Every time one of the Travelers hit a ball anywhere near Midland's third baseman, Gib went through his "Teflon glove" routine. Two youngsters sitting behind us picked up the chant, taking turns screaming at the tops of their lungs. I left for another beer.

But DuPriest had the last laugh. In the top of the seventh, he hit a monstrous grand slam, a blast winning the game for the Rockhounds. As he trotted past third base, he shook a meaty fist at Gib.

My brother-in-law pretended to be reading the program.

The public-address system announced that the second half of the double-header would begin in 20 minutes. Ellen stood, her hands propping up her back. "I can't handle any more sitting."

Leslie gave me a slight nod, and I took the hint. "Same here. We're ready to go."

As we left, Ellen touched my arm. "Keep us posted if you make any progress on the search for J.J. He's our friend, too."

* * *

When we got home, I poured us each a glass of wine and we watched the late news. Afterward, I went upstairs to read while Leslie adjourned to a small room next to the kitchen we'd converted into her office. She said she had at least an hour's worth of correspondence to handle. I was surprised when she suddenly appeared at the bedroom door, breathing hard and her face ashen.

"What's the matter?" I asked.

"I saw a prowler in our backyard."

I reached for my cell phone. "Shouldn't we call the police?"

"He's gone," she said. "I caught a slight movement through the kitchen window while reading e-mails. Pretending I hadn't seen anything, I walked to the sink to fill a glass of water. I then flipped on the back light, catching him on the patio."

"Can you remember what he looked like?"

"I never saw a face, but it was definitely a man. I'm pretty sure it was an older man."

"What makes you say that?"

"His movements as he fled weren't those you'd expect from a young guy. Sort of stiff and jerky."

Before turning out the lights and going to sleep, we agreed that installing a home security system would be a good idea. I promised Leslie that I'd get on it first thing in the morning.

~ FIFTEEN ~

Thursday morning found me back in the office, asking my colleagues for advice on home security systems. When several recommended the same company, I called and scheduled a mid-afternoon appointment with a representative. I phoned Leslie and confirmed that she'd meet us at the house to go over estimates.

I spent most of the rest of the morning trying to make a living. Melissa, my creative director, shared a draft concept for a presentation to Baptist Hospital, the account we'd been invited to bid on—and one that I'd coveted for much of my career. With the KACN situation up in the air, this opportunity took on added importance. Unless, as I feared, the hospital administrators were doing nothing more than going through the motions.

"Is it worth pursuing?" I asked. "Going to all the expense and trouble?"

"A year ago, my inclination would have been to pass," she said. "But we have a real shot now."

If anything, Melissa tended toward understatement. Scooting my chair to the desk, I propped my chin on a fist. "You're sure?"

"I'm told it's going to be a legitimate review, on the up and up." She flashed me a conspiratorial wink. "Nothing's been greased."

Since the current advertising agency had serviced the account for most of my adult life, that bit of gossip grabbed my attention. "What happened?"

"The hospital's new CEO and the long-time account executive got off to a nasty start, and then things went downhill fast. From what I hear, a subtle chauvinistic remark mushroomed into a shouting match. They've tried to keep it quiet, but according to my niece, it's splitsville. Beyond repair."

An arrogant jerk, the man who'd mouthed off was long overdue for a severe comedown. I struggled but managed to conceal my elation. "Your niece," I said. "She's in a position to know?"

"Firsthand knowledge."

"What else can you tell me?"

Melissa leaned forward, her eyes sparkling with a competitive glint. "Those focus groups we held last night revealed a lot." She paused for a second. "We missed you."

Weeks earlier, I'd authorized Melissa to spend up to $5,000 on preliminary research for a Baptist Hospital bid. She'd budgeted most of it for two focus groups of potential customers in the greater Little Rock area. I had planned to sit behind the mirrored walls and observe both sessions, but forgot all about them and went to the baseball game instead. Could this be the onset of senility? "Something came up," I said lamely.

She slid a DVD of the recordings across the desk. "It's clear we need to target females," she said. "Women are frustrated with the local medical community—and are desperate for solutions."

"Such as?"

"Help with HMOs. Alternative treatments. A holistic approach to health." She glanced at her notebook. "A center dedicated to women got positive reactions across the board."

"Maybe combined with pediatrics?"

Melissa flung her hands up. "Excuse me," she said, not bothering to hide her exasperation, "but would you include pediatrics in a men's health center?"

I avoided making eye contact as she handed me a two-page proposal, and spent a few minutes skimming the plan. It was engaging and fast-paced, and would be far different from any hospital campaign I'd seen.

"What's the bottom line?" I asked.

"A full-blown dog and pony show will cost $30,000. Maybe more. We'll have to bring in some outside expertise."

My banker knew Lassiter & Associates had a strong balance sheet, so credit was no problem. Paying it back, however, meant we had to keep our billings up.

"So, if this were your money, you'd go for it?"

"It is my money." She smiled, but I noticed a certain firmness to it. "Remember our profit-sharing plan?"

Liking her answer, I nodded and waited.

"We can do it. All we need is your okay." She got up to leave. "Let me know what you think."

She'd reached the doorway when I stopped her. "Melissa, can you pull this off for $30,000 and not a penny more?"

A slight smile worked its way across her face. "Guaranteed."

"Let's do it."

"Thanks!" She flew down the hall.

I spent some time catching up on e-mail and wasn't surprised—or pleased—to find yet another missive from Clifford. "I'm having some misgivings regarding my idea for a Machiavellian book," he wrote. "What do you think about a non-fiction novel, something on the order of *The Adman Cometh?*" I started to ask him for clarification on the "non-fiction novel" term, since novels are by definition fiction—unless the author happens to be Truman Capote. I then decided against it, not wanting to encourage a conversation. My terse reply reminded him that his performance review cometh.

I then e-mailed the entire staff, describing Constance Engstrom's proposal for the agency to adopt the Little Rock Zoo as our next pro bono account. Asking them to give it some serious thought, I said the matter would be determined by popular vote, with responses due in a week. To stave off hallway chatter, I circulated another message stating that I'd share developments on the KACN status as soon as I learned of any.

Moments later the phone rang. Neal Stackhouse, KACN's general manager and an acquaintance since our college days, had returned my call. Maybe mental telepathy wasn't so far-fetched after all.

"I assume you've heard the latest?" he asked. He sounded weary.

"A strong rumor that the station's been sold."

"It's more than a rumor. We've been acquired by an aggressive outfit in Cleveland that's been buying a property a month."

"What's the scuttlebutt?" I asked.

"Let's just say we've all updated our résumés and have feelers out. Their typical M.O. is to bring in a new team."

"I guess it's premature to discuss account services."

"Lassiter & Associates has done great work," he said. "I'll put in a good word for you."

"Thanks—and good luck," I said as he signed off after promising to keep me posted. My gut told me a decision had already been made. Not many conglomerates from Cleveland or other large cities do business with Little Rock advertising agencies. They select national firms unfamiliar with local demographics. Within a year or two the accounts are a mess, market share's been lost, fingers are pointed, and a second round of managers is brought in. Oh well.

Gazing at an old, framed map of territorial Arkansas on my wall, I remembered J.J.'s correspondence from the Hillcrest Antique Gallery. I picked up the phone and dialed, expecting to explain the situation in a matter of moments. I should have known better. Once my call was answered, I found myself on hold three or four times while the person at the opposite end of the line dealt with other customers. When I got another chance to talk, I offered to drop by the shop over the lunch hour. A raspy but grateful voice said noon would be fine.

Before leaving, I reviewed mockups for the latest direct mail piece for our Hot Springs resort client, and suggested to the designer that she show more ethnic diversity in the photography. Next came a 20-minute conference call, after which I fled the phones, faxes, and finances. I ate my lunch, an apple I'd brought from home, in the truck.

* * *

Peering through its smudged display window, I realized the Hillcrest Antique Gallery carried far better items than the usual flea markets I visited on occasion while searching for vintage stuff. Other than a bell tinkling my arrival, the shop was quiet when I pushed open the door. I had just spotted an impressive Duncan Phyfe dining table with eight matching chairs when an overpowering stench of cigarette smoke almost knocked me back to the sidewalk.

"Hello." A gruff voice came from the back of the store. "I'll be right with you."

While I admired a striking oak library table, a short, older woman appeared from behind a French armoire. Heavyset and wearing an unattractive lavender smock that might have been the oldest thing in the building, she studied the table before taking a smoldering cigarette from her lips. I couldn't tell if her peroxide beehive was a wig or the real thing.

"Lovely, isn't it? I can make you a marvelous deal." She owned the deep, raspy voice.

"How good?" The tag read $675 *firm*.

She inspected the sticker, shut her eyes for a moment, and said, "Six hundred even. Local delivery included." She took another pull on her cigarette.

The price wasn't bad, but I already had a similar one. Yet this was better than mine, and we had a perfect place for it in the sun-room. I circled the piece once more and pulled out the drawer. The hardware appeared original, and the table was solid as a rock. But would Leslie like it? We'd compared ideas on many things over the past months, but tastes in furniture hadn't been among them.

"To tell you the truth, I'm here concerning a recent purchase by Dr. Newell. My name's Randy Lassiter. I'm a friend of J.J.'s." I extended my hand.

She looked at me hard through the smoky haze and took my hand. "Suzi Goldman." After crossing her arms over her chest, she nodded. "What can I do for you?"

116

"J.J.'s unavailable, and I'm keeping an eye on his house. I saw your note in his mail and figured I should stop by."

Ms. Goldman ground her cigarette butt in an overflowing ashtray, exhaled a stream of smoke off to one side, and pulled a pack of cigarettes from a dress pocket. She started to say something, but her strangled words evolved into a nasty, hacking cough. "That damn Stickley settle," she finally said, clearing her throat. "Nothing but trouble."

"I beg your pardon?"

"Several months ago, the executor of a local estate asked me to arrange an auction of a fabulous collection of Craftsman period furniture." She pointed to the library table. "Pieces in this style."

I nodded.

"Included were half a dozen Stickley originals."

"You've lost me."

"Gustav Stickley was the most famous of the Craftsman designers. His work dates from well over a century ago and commands a huge premium these days."

"Stickley stuff is in?"

She lit another smoke. "It's a media favorite now with Hollywood celebrities having discovered it."

"Like Barbra Streisand?" I vaguely recalled a magazine feature on the singer's interest in period American furniture.

"She has an exceptional collection, as do Brad Pitt and Jack Nicholson. Of course, J.J. began acquiring his pieces years ago, well in advance of the current trend." She waved her cigarette through the air. "His dining room furnishings alone are worth tens of thousands of dollars."

"What about the item he bought?"

"A magnificent settle."

My confusion must have been apparent.

"We'd call it a couch today. Let me show you."

Goldman led me through a maze of hand-stitched quilts, grandfather clocks, dusty chandeliers, and English wardrobes before coming to a stop next to a stuffed peacock near the back of her store.

"Here it is."

She pointed to a large, handsome piece of furniture, better than six feet long. Its frame was of deeply grained oak, and the cushions were rich, dark leather.

The bell tinkled again. "Look it over," she said as she trudged to the front door. "I'll be right back."

While Goldman tended to her new arrival, I examined the settle. Strong, sturdy, and simple, its beauty was in the details. The joints were crafted with precision, fitted together without a single nail, screw, or bracket as far as I could determine, and the wood's finish was a mellow golden brown. I'd taken a seat on the couch when Ms. Goldman returned.

"I don't know what this world's coming to," she grumbled. "That pushy young man had the nerve to fuss at me because I don't carry Beanie Babies. Whatever they are."

"Back to this ... uh ... settle."

"J.J. bought it some three weeks ago. Like I said, at an auction. He paid $25,000 for it."

I felt myself sink lower into the cushions. "How much?"

"You heard me," she said as she lit another cigarette. "Twenty-five. And he got a bargain."

I eased to my feet, and smoothed down the leather. "This thing should be in a museum."

"Some are. Not many individuals can afford these anymore. And the collector J.J. outbid is still seething."

My ears perked up. "Can you give me some details?"

"It'll have to be quick," she said following a hurried glance at her watch. "I've got a major appraisal scheduled later this afternoon."

While I leaned against a maple buffet, Goldman made herself at home on J.J.'s expensive couch, pulling the smock over her pale, knobby knees.

"The auction took place on Sunday, May second. I remember because it's my daughter's birthday."

And the day after I introduced Leslie and J.J., I thought.

"We must've had close to 25 people in the shop, but less than a dozen were serious bidders. An hour and a half after the auction began, we'd sold the entire lot. Sales totaled over a quarter of a million."

I whistled softly. "J.J.'s piece must have been the best of the lot."

"Right you are. We had five or six players interested in this settle, but most fell by the wayside within the first few minutes. J.J. and the collector from Stuttgart kept after it, and J.J. outlasted him."

"This Stuttgart man ... Is he the one you said was still angry?"

She nodded. "I don't know if he's mad at himself for not going higher, or upset at J.J. for buying it. But I ran into him at a show soon afterward in Memphis and he'd not forgotten it. His exact words were, 'That goddamn professor doesn't deserve that piece.'"

"Who is this person?"

I watched as her eyes darted past me, stopping on a mahogany nightstand. A folded newspaper lay across its top.

"Toss me that paper if you don't mind. My feet need a rest."

I handed it to her, noticing coffee stains on the edges.

She flipped to the first page of the second section. "Here's your man," she said, and pointed to a large photograph in the center of the page. "I'm saving this for him." She gave me the newspaper. "He's real serious about his collection."

The photograph had been taken weeks earlier in the Senate chamber of the State Capitol during an acrimonious budget hearing for the Arkansas Department of Higher Education. His fists clenched, State Senator Judson Claypool of Stuttgart railed against the "exorbitant salaries paid to our ivory tower imbeciles." Like many newspapers, the *Arkansas Democrat-Gazette* didn't mind running an unflattering photo, but this shot took the cake. Claypool resembled a madman, his eyes narrowed and lips locked in a malevolent sneer.

"Not a very good picture." I returned the newspaper.

Goldman studied the photo and shrugged. "That's pretty much the way he looks most of the time."

The telephone rang and she shuffled off to get it. While she handled the call, I again examined Claypool's portrait. Every hair of his pompadour was in place, but the veins in his sweaty temple and forehead had risen to the surface, standing out like ridges on a relief map. His momma would not have liked it.

Goldman reappeared and reminded me without any pretense of subtlety that she had an important appointment to keep. Escorting me toward the front of her shop, she asked, "When can you remove that settle? It's taking up valuable floor space."

"How 'bout late this afternoon? I've got a pickup." I smiled to myself when I realized the couch was worth three or four of my trucks.

"Be here before six."

We stopped at the library table while she searched her purse. After locating an enormous key ring, she ran her nicotine-stained fingers across the table's beautiful grain. "Five seventy-five. It's the best I can do."

I hesitated, then handed her a card. "I'm in the advertising business," I said, something I'm often reluctant to share with strangers. "Maybe we could work out a trade."

Goldman stepped back as if I had just confided I'd been diagnosed with terminal leprosy. "I don't think so," she said. She yanked a flyer from a pocket and shoved it at me. Printed on garish green paper, the handbill might have been designed—and I hesitate to even use that word—by an inept seventh-grader. Amateurish sketches crowded the page, too many typefaces fought for attention, and the word *coupon* had been misspelled. Twice.

"See this coupon?" She pointed at the bottom of the sheet.

"It caught my eye," I admitted.

"I've already redeemed over 20 of 'em this month. Want to guess who prepared this?"

I shook my head as I reached for the door. "An artist friend?" I ventured.

"Did it myself using a clip-art book. Want to guess what it cost?"

I thought of grabbing my handkerchief. I could wave it, indicating complete and utter defeat. As I slipped through the doorway, Goldman hung a "Closed" sign in the window. She followed me onto the sidewalk and locked the shop behind us.

"The book cost $12.95, plus tax," she continued, her spiel not yet over. "And getting 500 copies printed ran another $35.00 or so. Could you have done this job for that?"

Standing on the sidewalk, my shoulders slumped, I congratulated Goldman on her business promotion skills.

She turned, dropped the keys into her handbag, and gave me a perfunctory wave. "When you see him, pass along my regards to our professor friend."

I slunk to my truck and headed downtown.

~ SIXTEEN ~

The telephone rang as I entered my office. It was Booker.

"How's my favorite uncle?" The fact that I had no other uncles was not lost on Booker.

"When I find sufficient time, I shall lecture you on a subject unknown to your wasted and self-indulgent generation. Respect." He cleared his throat. "As for your earlier request regarding departures from Little Rock's National Airport during the first two weeks in May, I have experienced a bit of good fortune."

"I knew you could do it. You're my very favorite hacker." I tried my best to sound respectful.

"I must again beseech you to drop such a crude word from your pitiable and pathetic vocabulary. It is so ... vulgar ... and carries such disgusting and dreadful connotations." Booker paused for a moment. "Nevertheless, I appreciated the opportunity to access and peruse the varied databases. The airlines have upgraded their electronic security systems, and you know how I relish challenges. My new program is so proficient that I have taken to calling it the 'encryption prescription.'" He sighed. "It's lamentable I will not be able to capitalize on its vast commercial potential."

"Did you find any references to J.J.?"

"I have scoured manifests of five of the seven carriers serving our fair city and identified an even dozen Newells on various flights. But no J.J. thus far. When my surreptitious investigation of the remaining two airlines is completed, I shall give you another call."

After Uncle Booker signed off, I dialed Joan Pfeiffer, J.J.'s long-time friend, past lover, and occasional escort. A former UA Little Rock business professor, she'd parlayed her vibrant personality and quick wit into a flourishing career as a management consultant, a position that sent her from one coast to the other delivering motivational seminars to corporate climbers, including many in the Fortune 500 ranks. I host an annual retreat for the entire agency staff, and always invite Joan to conduct a training session for me and my colleagues. Her unique blend of enthusiastic pep talks and organizational insights has helped the Lassiter team land more than one account.

Joan surprised all of us a couple of years ago when she announced as a dark horse candidate for the state's House of Representatives. The combination of an aggressive door-to-door campaign—managed by one J.J. Newell—and an over-confident incumbent presented Joan and her supporters with a stunning election night victory. One of the local newspaper pundits dubbed her Joan of Ark, an appellation Ms. Pfeiffer has not appreciated. I seldom use it, and never if I'm within reach.

"Afternoon, Joan. It's Randy."

"What's on your mind? Female intuition tells me this is not a social call."

"Two things. First, have you seen J.J. in the past few weeks?"

The line was silent for a beat. "It's been a while. I guess the last time was in the neighborhood liquor store, and that must have been at least a month ago. Is something wrong?"

"I haven't run into J.J. in some time and have been trying to track him down." I felt guilty, but didn't want to share any details yet.

"If you can't find him, that worries me."

"You know J.J. He just finished another hectic semester and might have needed a break," I offered.

"Still, that doesn't sound like him."

It was time to change the subject. "What's the story on one of your fellow legislators—Senator Judson Claypool?"

"What do you want to know? He's the senior member of the Senate. Conservative as they come. Has a wife, no kids. Nice hair. And, of course, he's filthy rich."

"You sound like his PR puppet."

"If you want the real background, you'll have to buy me a drink. Maybe several."

"How about this evening?"

"Five-thirty? Capital Hotel bar?"

"Let's make it six. I've got to deliver a couch after work."

* * *

Beginning at 3:00, Leslie and I spent an hour with the home security expert. After touring the house and inspecting every downstairs door and window, he arrived at an estimate exceeding even my worst expectations.

"We'll do it," Leslie said, my mind still reeling. "When can you have it installed?"

"The crew will arrive first thing in the morning," he said. "We'll be finished before noon." When I handed him a check for the deposit, he scanned down his paperwork. "We recommend a four-digit security code. Shall I produce one we can randomly generate?"

I shook my head. "I already have one in mind." I wrote down a sequence of numbers and gave it to him.

After the technician left, Leslie rewarded me with a hug. "Thanks," she said. "This is important to me."

"And *you're* important to *me*."

"Is there any significance to that 0218 security code you gave him?"

"It's the month and date for J.J.'s birthday."

* * *

At 5:00, my part-time mail room clerk and I backed into the alley behind the Hillcrest Antique Gallery. Ms. Goldman opened the door at her loading dock, and Larry and I hoisted the settle into the bed of my truck. I had to drop the tailgate to make it fit.

"This thing sure doesn't look very comfortable," was all that he said. I didn't have the heart to tell him what my friend had paid for it.

We were in the cab, ready to drive off, when Goldman yelled. I killed the engine as she climbed down the steps.

"Can't be too careful these days. I need your signature."

She tossed her cigarette to the pavement and crushed it with a heel before thrusting a battered clipboard through my open window. I initialed the receipts, kept one, and handed her the other.

"Give me a call regarding that library table," she said as I let out the clutch. In the rearview mirror, I caught the flash of her lighter.

At a quarter to six, I dropped Larry off at the office with a quick thanks and a pair of twenty-dollar bills. We'd found J.J.'s house just as I'd last seen it. Quiet and empty. The lawn service company had been by a day or two earlier and at least the yard appeared decent. And I made a point of giving the fish several extra shakes of food.

Ten minutes later I strolled through the palatial lobby of the Capital Hotel, angling for the bar. Across the street from the city's convention center, the hotel is Little Rock's oldest and among the most storied in the South. Over the years it's provided accommodations for more than a handful of the rich and famous as far back as U.S. Grant. Its quaint and hospitable bar attracts both locals and travelers, and is preferred by visiting journalists seeking inside information on the latest political rumors and shenanigans.

This evening, though, the bar's clientele seemed to be regular folks. I nodded to a pair of fellow Rotarians, patted one of my unscrupulous competitors on the back since a knife wasn't handy, and found an empty table next to the window facing the busy Markham Street sidewalk. I watched a grungy skateboarder zip between a pair of self-important executives, interrupting their animated conversation.

"Lost in a fantasy world?"

I stood and gave Joan a hug. "Hardly. Just observing the ebb and flow of society."

She ordered a merlot while I asked the waiter for a draft pale ale from a local brewery.

"You look great," I said. A classic example of the word willowy, she had a drop-dead smile and rich, chestnut hair most women would die for. The ivory silk blouse over a colorful mid-calf-length skirt didn't hurt, either.

"Thanks! I feel good, too. My seminars are booked through the end of the summer, plus ..." she added with a wink, "I'm dating someone."

"Congratulations!"

She dismissed my response with a wave, although she was clearly pleased. "In fact," she said, glancing at her watch, "I'm supposed to meet him for dinner in an hour. But let's get down to business. What's going on with J.J.?"

"There's not much to say," I said, shrugging. "His house is empty, the mail's been stopped, and nobody seems to know where he is."

"I guess you checked with the university?"

"No luck. Same with his neighbors."

"Maybe our favorite professor went to the Yukon on a whim. He's fantasized about that excursion for years."

I, too, had heard J.J. describe his dream trip to northwestern Canada. He'd been collecting travel guides and maps since I had known him. "Do you think he might have done that?"

She took a sip of wine, eyeing me over the edge of her glass. "It's not beyond the realm of possibility. He's done stranger things."

"Like your trip through the Panama Canal?"

"Precisely," she said, shaking her head. Back when they enjoyed a much more serious relationship, J.J. had booked the two of them on a fourteen-day New Orleans to Los Angeles cruise, giving Joan little more than a day's notice. He later claimed he got the tickets for pennies on the dollar, filling berths that became available at the last minute. The return trip, a gut-wrenching flight from LAX, caused J.J. to swear off airplanes for good.

Joan placed her elbows on the table and edged closer. "What's with this unhealthy interest in Jud Claypool?" Her voice was little more than a whisper. While I sorted out a harmless reply, Joan leaned halfway over the table toward me. "Don't tell me you're going to handle the campaign of an opponent?" She had first-hand knowledge about the position of Lassiter & Associates on political races.

Soon after opening the agency, I had agreed to manage a distant relative's campaign for her local school board. Too busy sharing inflammatory comments with reporters to hear my advice, she lost by a landslide—and left me holding an empty bag for almost five thousand dollars in media buys I'd placed with her hometown newspaper and radio stations.

Following that disaster, the agency's political activity has been limited to encouraging the staff to vote. No doubt it's cost me a bundle of business over the years, but my sanity remains intact. As you may have heard, Arkansas politics are not for the faint of heart. Special prosecutors, subpoenas, and teams of FBI agents make me nervous.

Joan stared at me with wide, questioning eyes.

"No more campaigns," I said, laughing. "Never. I'm not that crazy."

She breathed a sigh of relief. "Thank God. Claypool's vicious."

"Tell me more."

"He served in the state House of Representatives until term limits forced him out and was then elected to the state Senate where he runs it like his personal fiefdom, controlling key committees such as budget himself and others through handpicked lackeys. I hear the governor has to get Claypool's consent before any major bills are introduced."

"How'd he acquire all that power?"

"Seniority, along with enough money to burn a wet elephant. The Claypool family estate covers 10,000 acres of the Grand Prairie," she said, alluding to the state's rich rice-growing district an hour east of Little Rock. "What they don't own, they've got their fingers in."

"Vices?"

She took a sip from her glass. "Greed, first and foremost, from what I hear. No rumors of hanky-panky. I think he's asexual."

"Joan!"

She blushed. "He gets off on control, orchestrating things behind the scenes. Much like the original Mayor Daley of Chicago, but at the state level."

"Any hobbies?"

"Maybe his hair," she said, smiling.

"Any talk about Claypool and antiques?"

"I'm told his hunting lodge is among the country's elite, but I wouldn't know since I've yet to receive an invitation for a visit. A testosterone thing, I guess," she said, rolling her eyes. "But now that you mention it, I've heard the place is a treasure-trove of heirlooms. His office in the State Capitol is crammed with antiques." She paused. "Why do you ask?"

"Claypool mouthed off to an acquaintance following an estate auction a few weeks ago," I said, telling her a portion of the truth if not the whole story. "She felt the threat was idle chatter, but later wondered if there could be any substance to it."

"Don't underestimate him. Some of it's good old boy swagger, but Jud Claypool always gets his way. Always. He will not accept anything less."

"Is he prone to violence?"

"No." She shook her head. "Not the senator. His hands are smooth and manicured." She finished the last of her wine, pushed her chair back, and stood, but her soft eyes never left mine. "He hires other people to take care of … things."

Joan leaned over, hugged me around the neck, and started for the exit, leaving a lingering hint of perfume in her wake. Conversations waned across the bar as most of the customers, male and female alike, eyed her graceful departure. I finished my beer, paid our tab, and departed soon afterward, my mind on State Senator Judson Claypool.

~ SEVENTEEN ~

Perched in front of her computer when I got home, Leslie scrolled through a batch of thumbnail-sized color photographs. She pressed a button and a new array of small images appeared on the screen before her. I ran my fingers through her hair, lifted it off her shoulders, and nuzzled the back of her perfect neck.

"What have we here?"

"Goosebumps," she said with a giggle. Leslie stood, circled her arms around my waist, and gave me a hug. I did my best to alleviate her chill.

"You're very friendly," she whispered. "Have you been seeing strange women again?"

"Just two."

She nibbled on my ear. "Tell me about them."

"I've got another idea."

"Such as?" She pulled me against her.

"I'd like to check out your … goosebumps."

"Later." She shoved me away with a laugh. "We have dinner plans."

"But my tux is at the cleaners." Which, of course, wasn't true since I'd never owned one.

Leslie punched my arm and glanced at her watch. "The lady you met at the university called not more than 15 minutes ago."

"Dr. Ackerman?"

"J.J.'s girlfriend," Leslie said. "Summer Preston, the grad student. She asked if she could drop by tonight. I suggested she come around eight, and said that we'd order pizza."

"Any idea what's on her mind?"

"She said she had some information to share." She shrugged, then turned back to the computer screen. "I've been reviewing the images I got at Central High." She opened the collection of small photos, highlighted one, and produced an enlarged version. "What do you think?"

She'd composed a vertical shot, with the imposing buff brick building filling most of the frame. Half a dozen attractive students, black and white, mingled in the foreground, carrying on what appeared to be an animated conversation. A deep blue sky punctuated with puffy white clouds provided the backdrop.

"It sure beats the hell out of those horrifying pictures from 1957."

"I'm hoping my editor feels the same." Leslie clicked the image away and closed the program. "Let's hear your story."

I recounted my visits with Suzi Goldman and Joan Pfeiffer.

"How serious was Senator Claypool's threat?" she asked.

"It's hard to say. Goldman didn't seem too worried over it, but Joan hinted that the senator isn't one to turn your back on."

She switched off her computer.

"One more thing," I said. "Uncle Booker called. He's had some success examining airline bookings for flights departing from Little Rock. But no sign of J.J. so far."

"Is Booker like those hackers we hear about on the news?"

"He claims he isn't."

"What's the difference?"

"Booker says it's simple: Only the ones who get caught make the news."

* * *

Leslie was upstairs changing and I'd just ordered pizza when the doorbell rang at 8:15. Summer Preston stood on the porch. She held a big bowl in one hand and a pair of kitchen tongs in the other.

"Hello, again," she said. "I felt guilty inviting myself for supper, so I brought a salad."

"Come in!" I said. Her sundress—a green print with crimson highlights—complemented her hair. She wore fashionable leather sandals, and I couldn't help but notice her candy-apple-red toenails.

Leslie bounced down the stairs with a warm smile. The white cotton tank top showed off her tan, and a sexy, wraparound skirt revealed an appealing glimpse of calf and thigh with every step. I caught her giving me a wink.

As I made introductions, both women snickered and pointed to the other's earrings. They were identical—stylized sunflowers with miniature bumblebees dangling below the lobes.

"This calls for a picture," Leslie said, handing me her cell phone. As they leaned together, I composed the shot and pressed the button, the flash blinding us all for a moment.

"Thanks for letting me stop by on such short notice," Summer said. "I appreciate your hospitality."

"Any friend of J.J.'s is a friend of ours," I said.

"That's why I'm here," she said. "I remembered the name of the man who caused the trouble at Big Bend. Max Alloway. He's listed in the student directory, so I've got a telephone number and address." Summer pulled a small piece of paper from a pocket.

Leslie gave Summer a questioning look. "Alloway is the jerk who hit on one of J.J.'s female students?"

"I figure he'd be more inclined to talk to Randy than to me," Summer said as she handed me the note. "My guess is he might feel uncomfortable if a woman asked him questions."

I tended to agree. I slipped the paper into my wallet while Leslie stepped into the kitchen.

"What can you tell me regarding this Alloway fellow?" I asked.

"Not a lot. I never met him. But I got the impression J.J. felt down deep that he wasn't a bad kid. That's why the situation worried him."

A few moments later Leslie joined us in the sunroom with cold beers for everyone. "Randy mentioned you're interested in photography," she said. "Any particular subject?"

"Scenics for the most part. Landscapes." Summer gazed at the wall. "Did you take these?" She gestured to a collection of Leslie's magazine covers I'd had framed as a surprise. Two *Audubons*, a *Southern Living*, and an *Outside* plus a handful of others made an impressive arrangement. Summer walked over and studied them, her eyes wide.

"Being in the right place at the right time is much of it," Leslie said. Modesty is among her many endearing qualities.

I rapped my beer bottle against a tabletop. "Ms. Carlisle is sometimes a bit too humble. The fact is, she worked her butt off for every one of those."

Leslie took a long swig from her bottle, and I suspected she was trying to hide a blush working its way across her face.

Summer eyed my favorite, a dramatic close-up of brilliant spring wildflowers with a sheer bluff in the distance. "Everything's in focus. Foreground. Background. How'd you do it?"

"The wide-angle lens was a big factor," Leslie said. "And a tripod made a very slow shutter speed possible, allowing me to close down the lens for better depth of field."

She'd already lost me, but Summer nodded. "Was this your only shot?"

"I wish," Leslie said with a laugh. "I spent a full hour on my belly, waiting for just the right lighting, and must have exposed close to a hundred images. It's the best of the lot."

While they talked photography, I set the table and then went outside to clip a bouquet of purple coneflowers for the centerpiece. I was beginning to appreciate the skills of a florist when Iriana's delivery van arrived with our supper.

I carried the pizza, salad, and flowers into the dining room. As Summer took her seat, I asked, "Is J.J. serious about playing the guitar?"

"I had my doubts at first," she said. "But after several sessions and a couple of weeks of practice, he bought that Gibson and claims he's hooked. He's made remarkable progress."

"I admire him," Leslie said. "Music's a great way to channel some energy."

"He's also supportive of my song-writing," Summer said. "With his encouragement, I've contacted an old friend in Nashville. Somebody who has insider connections."

"Speaking of insiders," I said, "has J.J. ever referred to a state senator by the name of Judson Claypool?"

She thought for a moment before shaking her head. "It doesn't ring a bell. Why?"

"I ran into an antiques dealer who claimed the good senator had threatened J.J. following a recent auction."

Her eyes narrowed. "Now I know who you're talking about. He and J.J. seem to enjoy their running feud. I believe J.J. calls him Senator Cesspool."

"From what Randy told me," Leslie said, "that name wouldn't be far from the truth."

"But you wouldn't put much stock in the threat?" I asked.

"That'd be my inclination," Summer said with a shrug. "As far as I know, J.J.'s never felt intimidated by anyone. He's big enough that most people won't mess with him. Maybe I misread the situation, but I don't recall him dwelling on Claypool. He thinks the senator is ... uh ... shall we say, amusing." She took a sip of her beer and turned to me. "Have you uncovered any other leads?"

"I forgot to mention it when we talked yesterday, but Dr. Ackerman—"

"Surely you don't believe she had anything to do with his disappearance?" Summer asked.

It never occurred to me a nice grandmotherly type like Dr. Inez Ackerman might be involved in J.J.'s vanishing act. But still, she'd not been eager to answer some of my questions. Also, she had failed to react when I told her that J.J.'s car had been left at the airport. And given her seniority and tenure, she was his heir apparent.

"No, or at least I don't think so. But she did tell me J.J. dreaded a meeting with one of his colleagues, Dr. Mackenzie Tillman." I stopped and waited for Summer's response.

She paused, a slice of pizza in her hand, and frowned. "I hadn't even thought of Dr. Tillman."

133

"How do she and J.J. get along?" Leslie asked.

"That's a tough one. They're pleasant to each other, at least on the surface. But I sensed an element of tension." Summer lowered the pizza to her plate. "I met her once, by accident, when we ran into her at the movies. J.J. introduced us, of course, but the conversation was awkward—and quite short. When I brought up her name later, J.J. sighed, made a fleeting reference to political penance, and changed the subject."

"Anything else?"

She looked at me, shaking her head. "J.J.'s always been professional when it comes to his staff. He doesn't gossip."

Summer passed me the pizza and I reached for a piece piled high with onions. And I got another serving of salad.

Leslie scooted her plate aside and propped her elbows on the table. "I'm going to Stuttgart soon to shoot rice fields for *Progressive Farmer* magazine," she said. "I'm sure I can make arrangements with Claypool to photograph his farm. Most entrepreneurs like the attention."

"And if he agrees, what will you do?" I asked.

"I'll stop by and introduce myself to the senator. When the timing's right, I'll mention that Dr. Newell and I are friends. See how he reacts when J.J.'s name is brought into the conversation."

"Then what?" Summer asked.

"I'll nose around and try to figure out what kind of relationship they had." Leslie paused and soon added, "But if I'm not back by dark, send a posse!"

She meant it as a joke, but the scenario made me uncomfortable. "Are you sure this is a good idea?" I asked.

After a sip of beer, Leslie nodded her head in my direction. "J.J. would do it for me."

"You're right about that," Summer said with a sad smile. Moisture filled the corners of her eyes.

"I'll check on Alloway," I said. "Maybe he'll talk. That incident at Big Bend happened several months ago, so he's had time to cool down."

"Which leaves Dr. Tillman to me," Summer said with a sniff. "I'll call her in the next day or two."

As we tidied the kitchen, Leslie gave my arm a pat. "Randy, why don't we go to J.J.'s house?"

"Now?" I peeked at my watch. It was almost ten o'clock.

"Men," she said, rolling her eyes at Summer. "Let's plan on meeting the day after tomorrow—Saturday morning. We can bring his plants here, and maybe Summer would be willing to keep the fish."

Summer's eyes lit up. "That'd be great. My apartment isn't large, but I've got room for a small aquarium. If we can find it, J.J. has a spare five-gallon tank that should be ideal."

"Given the few survivors," I said, "you won't need a lot of water." Summer's cringe and Leslie's sharp glance let me know I'd said the wrong thing. Tact has never been one of my strong suits. It seems to be lacking in the basic adman DNA.

"Before you go," Leslie said, "I want to loan you one of my favorite books on landscape photography. I think you'll enjoy it—and find it very helpful." She stepped into her office, returned with the volume, and handed it to Summer.

"You are so kind," Summer said, giving Leslie a hug. "Maybe you'll even let me accompany you on a shoot one of these days."

"Let's count on it," Leslie said.

As Leslie and I walked Summer to the sidewalk, we agreed to meet at J.J.'s house at eight o'clock Saturday morning. I promised to stop at Starbucks on the way and get coffees for all. After thanking us for dinner, Summer hopped into her car, leaving with a jaunty wave. Her taillights disappeared around the same corner where we'd last seen J.J. weeks earlier.

When we returned to the house, Leslie reached inside the front door and switched off the light. She grabbed me by the belt and steered me through the darkness to the end of the porch. Expecting a reprimand for my insensitive remarks on the fish, I instead felt Leslie's warm breath on my neck.

She kissed my ear and whispered, "You didn't tell me she was so pretty."

"Summer?"

"Who else?" She pinched my ribs. "She's beautiful and looked stunning in that dress."

"Not my type."

"What is your type?" She kissed my chin.

"A little taller. With a slender, athletic body."

"Any other characteristics?" She pushed me back, and I settled onto the porch swing.

"A ravishing brunette with creative tendencies."

She began unfastening my belt. "How creative?" The zipper was next.

"Extremely creative. Unbelievably creative." Soft and gentle, her hands knew where and how to touch.

"Have you ever made love in a swing?"

Before I could answer, Leslie lifted her skirt and carefully climbed aboard the seat, straddling me with her knees on the outside of my legs. She kissed me tenderly, her tongue tracing my lips as her fingers caressed my face. Running my hands under her skirt and then up her thighs and across her hips, I stroked her smooth, silky skin. And I soon realized the significance of her wink earlier in the evening.

"Have you been like this the entire night?"

"What do you mean?" She sounded so innocent.

"Without panties."

"Isn't this one of your fantasies?" she asked. She lowered herself onto me.

I answered by pushing the swing forward. Leslie gasped as the motion pressed our bodies together.

"And one of yours is to make love in a swing?" I asked as I nibbled on an earlobe.

We rocked back and surged forward again. Leslie moaned, then bit my neck.

"Swings," she whispered, "aren't just for children."

~ EIGHTEEN ~

The next day was Friday and it got off to an early start. I felt guilty about not searching for J.J., but I had to finish the week with a pair of unavoidable out-of-town appointments. Megan picked me up at the house at seven—just as the security system installers arrived—and we headed east into a bright sun for an eventual lunch meeting in Tunica. We'd be presenting a proposed media campaign to the Isla del Sol Casino & Resort management, including a small delegation of corporate bigwigs jetting in from Las Vegas. The drive takes around three hours, but we had allowed extra time for a stop in Pine Bluff, a community of about 50,000 some 45 miles southeast of Little Rock.

Home to several large industries, including one of the biggest paper mills in the South, Pine Bluff also claims the Arkansas Entertainers Hall of Fame. Following a recent expansion of the attraction in their convention center, city officials had invited us down for an informal discussion regarding promotional opportunities.

I'd been reviewing background materials in the car, but Megan insisted on briefing me as we neared the convention center. "They don't have much of a marketing budget, but the displays are first class," she said. "Lots of great memorabilia, along with exciting story lines perfect for kids. Your basic rags to riches scenarios."

"How well known are the artists?" I expected a collection of second-tier celebrities.

"Better than you might think. Charlie Rich, Al Green, Mary Steenburgen, Billy Bob Thornton, and Levon Helm, among others." She hesitated a moment and snapped her fingers. "And don't forget Johnny Cash."

I chuckled, remembering Jamie Emerson, my former neighbor and full-time Johnny Cash groupie. Maybe I'd finally be able to make her happy after all these years.

"His exhibit is the center of attention. It's a life-size animatronic—"

"A what?"

"One of those computerized mannequins. He talks, strums a guitar, winks, moves around a bit."

"But does he walk the line?"

She answered with an elbow to my ribs. Minutes later, I suffered another kind of assault, this time to my nose.

"The damn paper mill must be running at full capacity," I said, struggling to catch my breath.

"According to the locals," Megan said, "what you're smelling is the scent of money."

Those words sounded like a phrase a desperate copywriter would suggest, I thought. I was still gasping for air when she wheeled into the parking lot.

Compact but attractive, the Entertainers Hall of Fame exceeded my expectations, especially the lifelike Johnny Cash clone. I said as much to our host as she and her fellow board members gave us the VIP tour, concluding with a stop in a modest conference room where we drank tolerable coffee and munched on pastries and fresh fruit. She and her colleagues occupied three sides of a large table; Megan and I filled the fourth.

"What you've seen is the second of three phases," our host said. "Within five years, we plan on handling 100,000 guests annually."

It didn't sound like an unreasonable number, once the museum became a regular stop on the school group circuit. I nodded while my associate took notes. "Tell us about your marketing budget," I said, figuring we might as well cut to the chase.

Our host smiled, shook her head, and turned the tables. "Why don't you begin by describing Lassiter & Associates? Perhaps we can discuss the financial aspects afterward."

After almost choking on our coffees, Megan and I spent the next 15 minutes highlighting the firm's successes, emphasizing our tourism-related accounts in Hot Springs and Tunica. Always prepared, Megan had packed a portfolio to help make our case. When we finished, I felt we'd done a respectable job.

"We're not in the market for an advertising agency so much as we're seeking a partner," said one of the board members, a retired banker with a permanent scowl. I suspected the rotund gentleman had served on the bank's loan committee too long. His countenance suggested a slice of lemon had been implanted in each jowl. "We want somebody to stand with us through thick and thin." Staring at me, he took his time cleaning his glasses with a napkin.

I glanced at Megan, realizing we must have misjudged their financial situation, and sank into my seat. It appeared they had even fewer dollars to spend than our lowest estimate. While we insisted on giving every client a fair value, I didn't want to take on a destitute public agency, certainly not one run by a large group of do-gooder volunteers with too much time on their hands. Clearing my throat, I was composing a polite reply to that effect when our host spoke.

"Mr. Lassiter," she said, "We owe you an answer to your earlier question. Thanks to a generous corporate contribution that we've not yet made public, the board is prepared to spend $150,000 a year marketing the Hall of Fame."

Megan's eyes fluttered as I tried hard not to bolt upright. "First, let me congratulate you," I said. "But we'd hoped to bid on the account regardless of its budget. And, if Lassiter & Associates is selected, I can make you a promise no other agency can." I paused while every head in the room swiveled in my direction. "This talented young lady," I said, placing a hand on the shoulder of my colleague, "who will be your day-to-day contact, graduated with honors from Pine Bluff High half a dozen years ago."

Eyebrows edged upward and I detected a subtle but telling chorus of "ahs" as attention swung to Megan. In the tradition-rich South, such ties can be a deciding factor. "Eight, actually," she said as an embarrassed grin crept across her reddening face.

After another round of coffee and the obligatory closing comments, we said our goodbyes and climbed into Megan's car.

"Are we on time?" I asked as she steered us through the city and into the rural Arkansas countryside. The air quality improved with every mile as we headed east toward Tunica.

"We're half an hour ahead of schedule, maybe more."

"How'd we do back there?"

"I'm sure we'll be invited to bid, and I'd guess our chances are as good as anyone's."

"Hope you didn't mind me noting your stint at the local high school."

She gave me one of those looks that I'm certain is unique to irritated women. "Maybe you should've mentioned I was there only one year, my senior year. *After* my dad accepted a transfer to Pine Bluff."

"Details," I said. "Unnecessary details."

Darting around the occasional huge tractor lumbering along the highways, Megan drove steadily, slowing when we passed through Wabbaseka, DeWitt, St. Charles, and other small farming communities located on the pancake-flat Delta.

But my mind wasn't concerned with thoughts regarding Pine Bluff, Tunica, or the agricultural landscape. "Megan," I asked, "have you ever had a friend … uh … vanish?"

She considered my question for a while before turning to face me with a slight smile. "Two," she said. "The first was a former roommate who skipped town after she fell four months behind in her share of the rent. I've not seen her since. Thank God."

"And the other?"

"A worthless ex-boyfriend." She shook her head. "What a loser, a real scumbag. But I ran into him again two or three years later. The good-for-nothing degenerate had his skinny arm around some skanky teenage slut. Why?"

"I believe you've met J.J. Newell, my friend who teaches at UA Little Rock," I said. "He's stopped by the office a time or two."

"If I remember right, he's a tall, rather handsome man."

"J.J. has vanished without a trace," I said. "I checked with his neighbors and have been by the campus. I've even talked with the police. Right now, I'm at a loss over what to do."

A few seconds passed and then Megan turned to me with her eyebrows arched. "You could follow my little sister's example," she said. "Every month, she visits a local fortuneteller. I know the idea sounds crazy, but she swears by it. I went with her once, and it's pretty eerie."

"No doubt this soothsayer is a nasty crone wrapped in vintage shawls."

"Not quite. She's a young and beautiful Hispanic woman. I suspect you'd like her diaphanous caftans."

I forced a grin. "I may be asking you for details."

As we neared Helena-West Helena, Megan caught me taking a peek at my watch.

"We're well ahead of schedule," Megan said. "We have time for a break if you'd like."

"I have a good idea to fill some time," I said and reached for my cell phone. I tracked down a phone number for the mayor's office and placed the call.

After three rings, a woman picked up on the other end. "City Hall."

"Mayor Benoit, please."

"May I tell him who's calling?"

"Randy Lassiter, from Little Rock."

Megan shot me an inquisitive look. "A prospective client?"

"More likely a prospective convict. He's an old friend. I need to visit with him for a couple of minutes."

A moment later Buddy Benoit's voice boomed through the receiver. "Morning, hotshot. If this is a business call, you can forget it!" He laughed so loud that Megan gave the phone a curious glance.

I'd met him a decade ago when J.J. took me to Helena-West Helena, his hometown, for my first attempt to "get a deer"—and for reasons unknown to me I've been invited back every year. J.J., Buddy, and three or four of their high school chums belong to a small hunting club with a lease of several hundred acres of dense hardwood forest ten miles south of town. Located between the levee and the Mississippi River, the land is prime whitetail habitat, and each season one of the members brings in a trophy buck. Though none of us would admit it, we don't spend much time or effort in our roles as modern-day predators. We hire a wonderful local cook, as eating—and not always venison—is our top priority, followed by poker and horseshoes. Sitting around the campfire and telling lies is also a big part of our routine. The bar, said to be the best in Phillips County, doesn't open until five every afternoon. Safety may be the sole thing we take seriously.

"It's nice to know the city is in such capable hands."

"Speaking of hands, I hope to hell you've been to the shooting range." Another round of rude guffaws abused my ears.

After eight or nine pilgrimages to the deer woods with J.J., I still hadn't had any luck, and my dubious hunting skills had become something of a clubhouse joke. I'd come close a time or two, including last year when I'd had a clear shot at a magnificent buck not 25 yards away. But the combination of poor aim and shaking hands caused me to blow the bark off an oak tree a good five feet above his shoulder. The deer disappeared into a thicket, but my reputation grew.

"Fact is, your honor," and I paused for a sarcastic beat, "I'm outside of town and thought I might drop in for a bit."

"We'll have fresh coffee waiting."

* * *

Helena-West Helena is a small, time-forgotten Mississippi River town perched on Arkansas's eastern border. About two hours from Little Rock and an hour and a half south of Memphis, its major claim to fame is that it produced seven generals who fought in the

Civil War. All served on the losing side, and the community appears to have never recovered despite occupying, in Mark Twain's words, "one of the prettiest situations on the river." The tidy Confederate cemetery on the north side of town overlooking the Big Muddy is one of the few local attractions. With all the action these days occurring in the booming casino district across the river in Tunica, Mississippi, the town's future doesn't seem very promising. Given that half the buildings on Cherry Street, the main drag, are vacant, the present doesn't appear too good either, for that matter. Mayor Buddy Benoit may have the toughest job in Arkansas.

* * *

Megan parked within a block of the Helena-West Helena City Hall, agreeing to meet me at the car in a quarter of an hour. While I saw the mayor, she'd play tourist and visit the nearby Delta Cultural Center.

An unlit cigar dangling from his mouth, Buddy greeted me at the door. A couple of inches under six feet, he blocked the opening, his 350 pounds testing the seams of a natty seersucker suit.

"Welcome to the Delta!" he said, his hand swallowing mine in greeting. "Let me guess. You're gonna try to hit me up for free tickets to our King Biscuit Blues Festival."

That thought hadn't occurred to me, but it wasn't a bad idea. Leslie and I would enjoy the music, not to mention the spectacle of 15,000 folks juking to authentic Delta tunes, and she'd find the photo possibilities endless.

"Can you throw in a room?" I asked, knowing every hotel within 75 miles was booked months in advance of the September event.

"You can stay with the wife and me." He patted his immense belly. "As you can see, though, our cupboard's bare." He laughed and slapped me on the back. "Come on in, Randy. It's good to see you."

Mayor Benoit led me through the reception area toward his spacious corner office, handing me a cup of coffee along the way. I nodded to his secretary and a handful of other functionaries trying without much success to appear busy. After placing his cigar in a John Deere ashtray, he reached into a compact refrigerator behind his desk and pulled out a bottle of Coca-Cola. I watched as he funneled a small bag of roasted peanuts into the beverage before taking a hearty swig. The mayor caught me eyeing his concoction. "May I fix you one of these delicacies?" The snack had been among his morning rituals as long as I'd known him.

I shook my head, realizing it'd been at least twenty years since I'd enjoyed that classic combination. My stomach might not survive.

"Before we get to whatever's brought you to town, how's our mutual friend?" he asked, upending his bottle again.

"That's why I'm here. J.J. is missing."

"Missing." Mayor Benoit lowered his Coke. "Missing," he said again, and gave me a puzzled look. "What do you mean?"

I shrugged. "He's not at home and hasn't been seen on campus. Nobody seems to know where he is."

Benoit strummed his fleshy fingertips against the surface of his clean desk. "How long has J.J. been … missing?"

"What's today? The twenty-eighth?"

The mayor turned to face his wall calendar—another freebie from John Deere—and nodded.

"I last saw him four weeks ago tomorrow."

"Four weeks is not such a long time."

"Right. But his house is vacant. The mail's been stopped. And he owes me a phone call."

"Maybe J.J. went on that once-in-a-lifetime expedition he's always kept in the back of his mind." He finished his drink. "Someplace way up in Canada or Alaska."

"His dream of a trip to the Yukon has occurred to us. But I'm sure he wouldn't have left town without notifying somebody."

"Who's this 'us'?"

I told him about Leslie and how I'd met J.J.'s girlfriend, Summer Preston, on the university campus.

A faint smile crossed Benoit's face. "Earlier this spring he hinted that he had someone he wanted to bring by."

"But you haven't seen him in recent days?"

144

Benoit leaned back in his chair, his brow furrowed, and reached for his cigar. "Reckon the last time I saw J.J. was sometime in mid-April or thereabouts. Our conversation was brief, but I remember him mentioning that he hoped to introduce me to a special friend. He'd brought two or three students over to examine an unusual botanical site in the forest," he said, referring to the St. Francis National Forest north of town. "J.J. stayed long enough for his students to visit the restrooms before they left for their field trip. He seemed to be in good spirits."

"Have you spoken to him since?"

He shook his head. "We don't talk much by phone. Couple of calls a year, most often in the fall to organize our trip to the hunting club."

I glanced at my watch, then stood. "I've got to get going. If you have any ideas, please give me a call."

Benoit chewed on the cigar, his fingers intertwined on his desk. "You're worried about J.J., aren't you?" he asked.

"He's always been so predictable. This isn't like him."

As the mayor rose and escorted me from his office, his head swung from side to side. "What could have happened to him?" he asked. I'd never seen him so despondent.

"I don't know. I just don't know."

"Keep me posted."

I went out the front door, Benoit at my heels. As I got to the sidewalk, he whistled. "Lassiter, one more thing."

I stopped and turned to face him. "What's that?"

"Congratulations on your news. I'll expect an invitation."

Following a salute, I trotted down the sidewalk toward Megan's car. We arrived within seconds of each other, and soon were on the narrow bridge high over the swirling, muddy waters of the Mississippi River. To the south, a tug with a long string of barges rounded a bend in the river, fighting the heavy spring flow as it pushed upstream.

* * *

145

To be honest, I hadn't been very eager to bid on a Mississippi account. Like most folks, I carry my own biases, and the Magnolia State had never been among my favorites, chiefly because of a speed trap outside Clarksdale that I'd had the misfortune to experience while hurrying to Florida during a spring break many years earlier.

But Isla del Sol's $3 million annual advertising budget got my attention, and I examined things a little closer. It didn't take me long to realize that any state producing Elvis Presley, Archie Manning, William Faulkner, Eudora Welty, Brett Favre, and Oprah Winfrey—along with about every fourth or fifth Miss America—had something going for it. Plus, its residents are among the friendliest folks you'll ever meet and they don't have an accent, at least not to my ear.

* * *

Twenty minutes after passing the "Welcome to Mississippi" sign, we arrived in Tunica, a community that a few decades ago had been among the poorest in North America. There were no signs of poverty today as we joined the parade of cars and pickups heading into the casino district. Golf courses and high-rise hotels grew from what had been soybean fields in the not-too-distant past. While they looked out of place, it was the massive gambling halls themselves that appeared like mirages on the Mississippi Delta. I wondered what Mark Twain would think of these alleged riverboats lining the levee. With facades ranging from western saloons to the Taj Mahal, each one tried to outdo the others in gaudiness. Perhaps, I thought, we'd gotten what we deserved. And since Lassiter & Associates helped lure the masses to these very shores, I didn't have a lot of room to cast any dirt clods.

Our casino, as Megan and the rest of us referred to Isla del Sol, appeared a bit classier than the competition. At least that's what we told ourselves. The owners had invested tons of money establishing a Caribbean theme throughout the casino/hotel complex, including a lavish indoor swimming area complete with banana

146

plants, palm trees, and raucous parrots. The staff wears bright island garb, and calypso music is always playing in the background. As we entered Isla del Sol, I found myself humming along to a Harry Belafonte tune.

The bustling crowd, typical for Fridays, made me smile. Most every slot machine had captured a customer, and groups of anxious betters surrounded the gaming tables. Dozens of guests stood in lines at the ATMs scattered throughout the casino to replenish their cash. More than one seemed a little shell-shocked. I gazed over the throng, awed—as always—by the power of greed or hope.

We enjoyed a superb Jamaican jerk-chicken lunch with our hosts in the casino's private dining room and then got down to business. Giving us their full attention as we introduced the conceptual plan, our clients asked good questions that, of course, we answered intelligently and succinctly. They gave high marks to the proposed print ads, billboards, and Internet-based campaign, and even clapped when they saw the two television spots. After studying the recommended media schedule, they quizzed us on the reach and frequency of the broadcast buy. It's a bewildering subject, but Megan did a fine job explaining the need to penetrate each market and ensure that the client's message is heard and absorbed via repetition. We closed the presentation with a detailed analysis of our suggested social media program, using the time to stress the importance of maximizing the casino's exposure on Facebook, Twitter, and similar portals. When we returned to our seats, I felt it had gone well. My take on the meeting was confirmed when the group approved the proposal without a dissenting vote and then surprised us with an unexpected one-year extension on the contract.

As we left the meeting and strolled through the crowded casino, I stopped and handed Megan a $100 bill. "I'm feeling lucky. I'll meet you at the front door in half an hour."

Megan rewarded me with one of her winning grins and made a beeline for the blackjack tables. Never much of a gambler, I took the easy way out and opted for the quarter slots. Playing three credits at a time, I was almost through my ten-dollar stake when the gods of gaming—if indeed there are any—blessed my shiny little machine. I felt like a star in the commercials we'd just shown. Bells rang, lights flashed, and the credit indicator went up and up and up, topping out at two thousand. Five hundred dollars. Resisting the temptation to press my luck, I cashed out and slipped five crisp $100 bills into my wallet. Maybe it was time to forget about my old speeding ticket.

I beat Megan to the entrance. She arrived soon after, eyes sparkling and head held high, and handed me five twenties. "Thanks! Here's your money, and I won another $50 for me." As we walked to the car, I didn't have the heart to tell her my story.

~ NINETEEN ~

On Saturday morning, Summer pulled up just as Leslie and I arrived at J.J.'s house. She greeted us with a grin and eagerly took the cup of coffee we'd bought for her at Starbucks. Glancing over my shoulder, she pointed to a small window at the corner of the house. "Look! There's a light on in his kitchen." Summer slammed her car door and leaped to the curb, almost spilling the latte.

I reached for her elbow. "I left it on the other day," I said, "thinking it might help discourage would-be prowlers."

Summer's shoulders sagged and she leaned against Leslie.

"We have precious fish to rescue," Leslie said, leading her up the sidewalk. "And some plants to deal with. Let's go inside."

While the women walked toward the front porch, I went around to the back and let myself into the musty house and then opened the front door. Leslie and Summer entered quietly, tiptoeing across the hardwood floors as if they were visiting a museum. Summer flicked on a light switch in the den and we followed her to the aquarium. I sprinkled some flakes of fish food into the water.

"Why did the angelfish have to die? They were so beautiful ..." She grimaced and wrung her hands as a tear trickled down her cheek. While Leslie comforted her, I eased into the kitchen and again purged the refrigerator, robbing posterity of several emerging life forms.

Summer had finished her latte and was holding J.J.'s guitar in her arms when I returned and she played a few chords. "He was so excited when he got this guitar." Biting her lip, she set it aside and walked to the hall closet. "I know J.J. keeps a small aquarium some-where in the house," she said. "He uses it when he changes out the water in the big tank."

I heard her gasp and watched as she handed Leslie a carrying case.

"What is it?" I asked.

"I think it must be J.J.'s camera bag," Leslie said.

Summer stared at the case. "He never travels anywhere with-out it."

Leslie removed the classic 35mm Pentax camera J.J. had bought at a Fayetteville pawn shop for a graduation gift to himself. Over the years, he'd experimented with newer, fancier models but always came back to the Pentax. Compared to today's digital cameras, it was awkward and heavy, and the light meter hadn't worked in a decade, but it delivered good photos. That was enough for J.J.

After probing further into the case, Leslie directed a discour-aging look my way. She handed me a compact leather portfolio containing J.J.'s passport, ruling out Joan Pfeifer's theory of an impulsive trip to foreign lands. Summer reached for it, her face pale and drawn.

"Where could he be?" She clutched the passport in her fist. "Where could that wonderful man have gone?"

Leslie placed an arm around Summer's shoulders and held her tight. "We're going to help you find him."

True to my gender, I remained worthless in this situation. Shifting my weight from one foot to the other, I was trying to figure out what to do when Leslie got my attention and mouthed "hot tea." In a flash, I returned to the kitchen, searching for a kettle that I found the third place I checked. While the water heated, my lucky streak continued and I located J.J.'s cache of orange spice teabags. And I also discovered the spare fish tank in the bottom of the pantry near the kitchen sink.

By the time I'd prepared three mugs of tea, Summer and Leslie had moved to the living room and sat on the latest addition to J.J.'s collection of period furniture.

Summer wiped her nose with a tissue. "This is new," she said, twisting her neck as she studied the couch.

Between sips, I told her about my recent visit to Suzi Goldman's antique shop and the origin of the settle.

Summer patted its smooth leather surface. "So, this is what caused the squabble between J.J. and the notorious Senator Judson Claypool. You'd think it'd be more comfortable after all that trouble." She placed a pillow behind her back.

Leslie's eyes moved across the furnishings. "This room is beautiful. It could be a feature straight from the pages of *Architectural Digest*."

"J.J. told me his family had owned several Mission-style pieces when he was a boy," Summer said. "He spent years accumulating this stuff. It let him relive his childhood days." She shut her eyes, then took a deep breath. "There I go again, using the past tense." Another tear escaped and slid down her cheek.

Leslie's subtle nod told me it was my turn to do something.

I stood and rubbed my hands together. "I found the other aquarium. Let's get this mission of mercy underway."

Twenty minutes later the six surviving fish had been relocated to the smaller tank and transported to the rear floorboard of Summer's car. Likewise, a dozen or so potted plants now occupied the bed of my truck. J.J.'s house was now truly vacant.

As we gathered at the curb, Summer managed a weak smile and gave Leslie a kiss on the cheek. I had to settle for a hug. "I'll enjoy taking care of these little fellows," she said. "Thanks for the suggestion." She stepped to the driver's side of her car.

"Let's keep in touch," I said.

"I've got a photo shoot scheduled in a few weeks and may need an extra set of hands," Leslie said. "Any chance you'd be willing to help?"

"That sounds perfect," Summer said, her eyes showing a hint of sparkle. "Oh, there's one more thing." She reached across the car seat, grabbed a thin file folder, and handed it to me. "I couldn't sleep last night so I played with my computer."

"What is it?" I asked.

"It's a printout of the Biology Department's website. There's lots of interesting stuff, including biographical sketches of J.J.'s staff. You might find it useful." Summer gave us a quick wave, slipped behind the wheel, and pulled away, careful not to jostle her watery cargo.

~ TWENTY ~

Back home, I poured myself a glass of orange juice and grabbed the folder Summer had given us. Slipping out the front door and onto the porch, I got comfortable in my favorite sling chair and opened the file. I was midway through the first page when Leslie tousled my hair before bounding down the steps toward the driveway, hurrying to her Saturday aerobics class.

"I'll be back around one o'clock," she said, glancing over her shoulder. With a quick wave, she climbed into her car.

The folder contained two dozen or so sheets. The first few pages introduced UA Little Rock's Biology Department to prospective students and explained degree requirements, program options, and scholarship opportunities. The next six or eight listed and described every class offering in the curriculum, most of which had intimidating, polysyllabic titles. Classes like *Comparative Vertebrate Morphology*, *Vertebrate Histology*, *Ichthyology*, and so on. Reviewing the material, I remembered why a business degree had been so appealing. A section on the faculty followed, with one page devoted to each of the eight members.

Since J.J. was chairman, his was the first of the lot. Reading it, I realized how little I knew about his career. In the not-too-distant past, he'd served as president of the American Zoological Association and he continued to chair the organization's professional standards committee. J.J. sat on the editorial board of the *Zoological Review*, and he also served in an advisory capacity for both the St. Louis and Little Rock zoos. He'd produced an impressive collection of monographs over the years, his research appearing in major national and international journals. In addition, J.J. worked on several local causes, including a two-year stint heading up the Arkansas chapter of the Nature Conservancy. A single listing showed up under hobbies: Craftsman furniture.

I next skimmed the background sheet on Dr. Inez Ackerman. A native of Kansas City, she'd done her undergraduate work at the University of Missouri before obtaining her master's and doctorate from Texas A-&-M. She received the latter in 1990 and had been at UA Little Rock ever since. Like her department chair, she had authored a significant assortment of publications including a number, I noticed, on declining amphibian populations.

Of the remaining six faculty members, I was most interested in the two Dr. Ackerman had mentioned earlier: Dr. Norbert Saunders and Dr. Mackenzie Tillman. Saunders was before Tillman, but I skipped ahead, eager to gather additional details on Benton Tillman's sole child.

Some of it I remembered from my conversation with Dr. Ackerman. Mackenzie Tillman, a native of Little Rock, had left the state for her college work, getting a Ph.D. from Cornell with earlier degrees from Stephens College and Purdue. While publications were conspicuously absent, Tillman participated in a variety of campus and community associations. She belonged to the National Organization for Women, the League of Women Voters, and Partners for Pinnacle, a volunteer group working in behalf of nearby Pinnacle Mountain State Park. Hobbies included folk dancing and gardening.

I flipped back a page. Dr. Norbert Saunders had relocated a long way from Montreal, his home. Earning his doctorate from McGill University, he'd taught for a year at Michigan State before accepting the position with UA Little Rock. A product of the computer age, Dr. Saunders specialized in genetic modeling and zoological distribution, whatever those were. According to his biographical sketch, he had but one hobby: tennis, a sport he'd lettered in during his undergraduate days at McGill.

I played a little tennis myself, not at Saunders's level, but kept up enough to know that the second round of the French Open would be televised at noon. Acting on an impulse, I tracked down the slip of paper Dr. Ackerman had given me with the phone numbers for her associates and dialed Saunders, placing the note inside Summer's file folder. A male voice answered after the fourth ring.

"Dr. Saunders?"

"Is this another telemarketing call?" he asked. His voice carried more than a hint of irritation.

"I'm Randy Lassiter. A close friend of Dr. Newell." I decided this might not be the occasion to mention my ties to the advertising industry.

"Yes," he said, a bit more congenial.

"I'm looking for J.J.," I said. "Have you seen him in the past month?"

He hesitated a moment. "I can't state for certain the last time I saw him. I believe it was a Friday, during finals." After another pause, he said, "Maybe three weeks ago. Why?"

I sighed. "I'm worried about him. He seems to have fallen off the face of the earth." While Saunders mulled this over, I continued. "Any chance you could join me for lunch? My treat."

"Today?" His reply sounded as if I'd suggested a field trip to the local IRS office.

"Why don't we meet at the Athletic Club, the sports bar at the Embassy Suites, in half an hour?" I asked, referring to a prominent hotel located just off Little Rock's cross-town expressway. "We'll watch the French Open on a large-screen TV." I tried not to sound desperate.

"I don't know. My afternoon is pretty busy."

"An hour is all I'm asking."

"How do I know this is not a joke?"

"I've already visited with Dr. Inez Ackerman. Give her a call to check me out."

Seconds dragged by. "Okay," he said. "I'll meet you in 30 minutes. But I can't stay long."

"Which one of us will be wearing the pink corsage?"

"It's way too early in the day," Saunders said with a chuckle. "Look for a UA Little Rock logo on my shirt."

I scribbled a note to Leslie, slipped on a clean shirt and a pair of chinos, and caught I-630 westbound. Among the newer hotels in Little Rock, the 250-room Embassy Suites complex is located near the city's trendy western suburbs. Targeting affluent Gen Xers, its expansive sports bar includes half a dozen wide-screen TVs and one of the best beer selections in town, not to mention a wait staff that could have been assembled by a modeling agency. According to local buzz, the formula works. If my agency could only land the hotel's advertising account ...

I arrived five minutes ahead of time and hours in advance of the evening crowd. Selecting a location as far from the screens as possible, I slid into a booth, flipping its speaker switch to the tennis match.

A man I assumed to be Saunders walked in right on schedule, his eyes skipping across the room, but he didn't conform to my mental image of a university professor. My immediate reaction was relief we hadn't arranged a match; I knew at once he was a serious athlete and could cover a court with ease. In his early to mid-thirties and wearing white shorts, a navy polo shirt, and deck shoes without socks, he was tall and fit. A handsome man with short blond hair and a deep tan, he could have been a newscaster for one of the town's television stations. I suspected he'd set more than one coed's heart fluttering when he first walked into a classroom. Realizing he had a choice of an older couple, a family of six, or me, he strolled in my direction. I spotted the distinctive insignia on his shirt.

"Dr. Saunders?" I asked, standing and extending my hand. "Randy Lassiter."

"Please call me Bert," he said, his grip firm.

As he slipped into a seat opposite me, a waitress appeared, menus in hand. We ordered beers—his an Australian import and mine an English ale—and set the menus aside.

"Thanks for seeing me."

"I called Inez and confirmed you're on the up-and-up," he said, giving me a grin.

I already felt at ease around the man. "Did Dr. Ackerman give me a good reference?"

"Anything but," he said with a chuckle. "She claimed you're J.J.'s best friend."

"By the way, I like your department's website."

"So, that's how you made the tennis connection. I'm glad you used it. That website is one of my pet projects."

"I take it you're more adept with computers than J.J.?"

"That goes without saying," he said, sharing another smile. "J.J. has his strengths, and dealing with technology is not among them. Meanwhile, I use my computer to sort and analyze data, order books and movies, store photographs, and pay bills. When you telephoned, I answered the call on my home PC."

The waitress returned with our drinks and pulled out her order pad. "What's for lunch, gentlemen?"

"What do you recommend?" I asked. Neither Bert nor I had studied our menus.

"The teriyaki chicken sandwich is great. And lots of guys enjoy the jalapeño cheeseburgers."

We each opted for the marinated chicken sandwich.

"Has J.J. really disappeared?" Saunders asked.

"Strange as it may sound, that seems to be the case. Originally, I was tracking him down so my fiancée and I could confirm our wedding date. J.J.'s agreed to be my best man."

"Congratulations." He raised his frosty glass and I followed suit.

"But now I'm concerned," I said. "I can't find a trace of him anywhere. Things don't add up."

"You've checked his house, I guess."

"Vacant. His luggage, passport, and camera are all at his home."

"His car?"

"At the airport. I saw it there the other day."

Saunders narrowed his eyes. "That surprises me. J.J. hates flying." He knew his chairman. "What about the police?"

"They're not alarmed, reminding me that it's no crime to disappear."

Saunders, elbows on the table and staring at his beer, squeezed the bridge of his nose with one hand.

"Are you aware of any troubles that J.J. might have had?" I asked.

Saunders took another sip of beer and turned his attention to the big screen tuned to the French Open. A pair of annoying announcers chattered away, sharing their opinions on the day's pairings.

"J.J. and I aren't real close," he said, swinging his gaze back to me. "He's more old school while I'm viewed as a young upstart. The department's website illustrates our differences. He's given me all the resources I need to make it a top site, but doesn't spend much time there himself."

"He's always been conservative. A classic traditionalist."

"But we get along fine," Saunders said. "And we talk quite a bit, professional stuff for the most part, but I'd be stretching things to suggest I'm his confidant." While the waitress delivered our plates, he looked to the TV. The players blasted the yellow ball back and forth across the court. Saunders eyed his plate and grabbed a fry. "You asked if J.J. was having any sort of trouble," he said, waving the sliver of potato like a tiny baton in my direction.

I took a bite from my sandwich, awaiting his answer.

"J.J. is sometimes frustrated by the university bureaucracy, but no more so than the rest of us. I think he's a great departmental chair. I know he's held in high regard by his national peers."

"Does he get along with Dean Campbell?"

"Far as I know," he said, crunching another fry. "Of course, J.J.'s not a whiner." After a short pause, he reached for the ketchup. "J.J. has seemed rather content the past couple of months. I get the feeling he's seeing someone, but he keeps his personal life quiet."

I waited a few seconds, then changed the subject. "Were you granted tenure recently?"

He glanced up, surprise on his face, as he replaced the cap on the ketchup bottle. "I wish, but I haven't been here long enough. However, my contract is scheduled to be renewed."

"This university way of doing business is beyond me."

A burst of applause pulled our eyes to the big screen. The match ended, the number twelve seed having upset the fourth-ranked player.

"That kid is good," said Saunders. "Once she gets her back-hand equal to the rest of her game, watch out."

The waitress brought another round of drinks as the broadcast broke for commercials. I was amazed but pleased to see one of the new Isla del Sol spots that had been approved less than 24 hours earlier. Megan had worked fast.

"I'm on track for tenure," he said. "J.J. and I discussed it several weeks ago." He hesitated for a moment, rubbing his forehead. "In fact, I haven't seen him since that conversation. Even though he prefers traditional field work to computer modeling, J.J. is very supportive of my research, and said my papers would compare with any in the country." Apparently worried his comments might have sounded a bit egotistical, Saunders averted his eyes and gazed at his plate, eventually bringing the sandwich to his mouth.

"The same for Dr. Mackenzie Tillman?"

Stopping mid-bite, Saunders lowered his hands and made eye contact. "Excuse me?" He set the sandwich aside and drank a long swallow from his glass.

"I assume Dr. Tillman is making progress as well."

He smiled, a tight nervous smile, and leaned hard against the back of the booth, his hands placed behind his head. While I finished my ale, he eyed me thoughtfully.

"Have you talked to her?" he asked.

"Not yet."

He reached for his beer again. "I think that question should be addressed to Dr. Tillman herself." Saunders took a slow sip, then turned to the television as another onslaught of commercials flickered across the screen.

"She's on the list." I finished my sandwich and followed it with a couple of fries. When the waitress came by a moment later, I asked for the check, giving her a credit card.

Saunders ate the last of his meal and drained his beer. "Thanks for lunch."

We traded business cards, and he studied mine before slipping it into a pocket. "Advertising, huh? You don't practice any of that telemarketing nonsense, do you? I've had absolutely no luck signing up for the 'National Do Not Call Registry.'"

I shook my head and tried to look him in the eye. "We don't believe in the telemarketing approach," I said. I didn't mention that Lassiter & Associates had been a firm believer only months earlier. Thank God we'd dropped the aluminum siding company from our client roster. Its brash owner would have exchanged his firstborn for a hot list of telemarketing leads.

"Good." Bert gave me a warm smile. "Those SOBs are going to drive me crazy."

We scooted from the booth and stood. "I'm concerned about J.J.," I said as we shook hands. "Please call if you think of anything that might help. Anything."

"Guaranteed," he said. "And good luck with Dr. Tillman." With a nod, he headed for the exit.

~ TWENTY-ONE ~

Following my lunch with Saunders, I stopped by the office. I generally tried to avoid the place on Saturdays, but I'd fallen behind and needed to keep the paperwork moving. Especially the agency's billings. I unlocked the front door and found Booker parked at my assistant's desk, his eyes riveted to the computer screen. Today he wore black from head to toe. A matching fedora hung from a corner of the monitor.

"Good afternoon," he said, never even glancing my way. His tiny fingers danced across the keyboard.

His hair, a dark brown earlier in the week, had been transformed to a light, reddish blond with a hint of curls. It had amazing body, almost to the point of being puffy. I decided not to comment. But I couldn't ignore a peculiar aroma. "What's that strange smell?"

Booker scooted his chair to an adjacent credenza and lifted a dinner plate. "My own culinary creation. An incredible curried couscous and turnip casserole. Shall I prepare you a serving?"

"Thanks, but I'll pass." I've hated turnips my whole life.

"Should you be curious regarding this exercise, I'm gleaning the final bit of data relative to your earlier request." He studied the screen for a brief period, then tapped a key and the monitor went blank. "That exhausted our last option. J.J. Newell had not booked any commercial flight out of Little Rock in the interim you specified." He removed a thumb drive from the computer and slipped it into his pants pocket.

"Unless he used an alias."

"A rather far-fetched scenario given current security arrangements," Booker said as he got to his feet. Careful to place the fedora on his new hairdo at a precise angle, he retrieved the dish and stepped to the door with a fleeting nod.

I thanked him for his help and closeted myself in my office for an hour, reading and responding to an avalanche of e-mails. Clifford, my young copywriter and would-be author, had struck again. Noting the media's infatuation with cybersex, he proposed yet another book, *CyberCelibacy*. Clifford admitted that he had no idea where he'd go with it, but liked the title and wanted my reaction. My curt response suggested it was time for some cybersanity.

After replying to the last of the e-mails, I locked the office and drove home, again amazed at how much can be accomplished when the phones are silent.

Watering the flowerbeds, Leslie grinned and aimed a squirt at the windshield of my pickup as I pulled into the driveway.

"I got your note," she said. "Did you learn anything?"

"Saunders seems to be a nice guy, but our meeting wasn't very productive," I answered. "And he preferred not to discuss Dr. Mackie Tillman, suggesting I talk with her myself."

"We'll let Summer handle Dr. Tillman."

"Also, I ran into Booker at the office. He's confirmed that J.J. didn't take a scheduled flight out of the city, at least not under his own name."

After Leslie turned off the water, she pulled me close. "We need a diversion, Randy. Let's do something special this afternoon."

"Sounds good to me," I said, giving her a gentle pat on the butt.

"Not that, you pervert," she said with a laugh. "I'm a newcomer to Little Rock. Let's pretend we're tourists for an afternoon."

"What do you have in mind?"

"Something outdoors. I've heard great things about Pinnacle," she said, referring to the state park a few miles west of the city limits. "It's a perfect day for a hike."

"You're on," I said. "We'll have a picnic afterward."

162

We packed a hamper and left for the park. Rising like an extinct volcano, Pinnacle Mountain towers a thousand feet above the surrounding countryside, its steep, rocky slopes crisscrossed by a network of trails popular with central Arkansas residents. I'd climbed the peak often as a kid, but couldn't remember the last time I'd been to the top.

We somehow found an empty space in the crowded lot at the base of the mountain and parked my truck. Leslie strapped on a fanny pack and then locked her door.

"Didn't you bring your camera gear?"

"This girl needs a break," she said, raising her arms in a graceful stretch. "I'm here to relax."

A perfect Saturday afternoon will not get you a wilderness experience at Pinnacle during Memorial Day weekend. It seemed like half the folks in Little Rock jammed the twisting, narrow trail to the summit. After passing a group of nuns with hiking boots peeking from beneath their habits, Leslie shook her head with regret. "What a photograph that would've been."

We fell in behind several teenaged couples, the young men eager to give their dates boosts as they climbed up and around the boulders. Muttering under my breath, I questioned their chivalry, much to Leslie's amusement. We hurried to the side of the trail as a troop of Cub Scouts raced downhill, moving en masse like a human luge ricocheting off the rocks. We heard a weary scoutmaster shouting for them in the distance.

Two-thirds of the way to the crest, we paused to catch our wind. Leslie looked over her shoulder and gasped. "That's beautiful!"

To the west and far below, Lake Maumelle glimmered in the afternoon light. At least 25 to 30 sailboats were grouped at the near end of the long lake, each with its bright sail billowing in the breeze.

"There's a regatta most spring weekends."

"I can't believe you let me make this hike without my camera." She punched my shoulder.

"And we're not even to the top."

The rocky summit looked like a small convention of outdoor enthusiasts. Two dozen or so hikers and three or four happy but tired dogs occupied the narrow crest when we arrived. Breathing hard, Leslie and I collapsed against each other.

"I've got water when you want it," she said, tossing me an apple from her pack.

In the distance, more sailboats resembled bright confetti tossed onto the lake's deep blue surface, and beyond, the Ouachita Mountains gave the horizon an interesting and uneven edge. A light wind from the southwest cooled our sweaty, red faces.

"Where's the city?"

I pointed behind us. Tops of the downtown skyscrapers peeked above the ridges to the east.

"And that's the Arkansas River?" Leslie gazed down at a wide ribbon of water a mile to the north. Spring rains had caused the river to spill out of its banks onto adjacent farmlands. A towboat with a string of barges inched upstream while a pair of bass boats sped in the opposite direction toward Little Rock, sunlight glinting in their long V-shaped wakes.

"Follow it far enough west and you'll hit the Rockies. Or the Mississippi if you go downstream."

Leslie rolled her eyes, not impressed with my geographical trivia.

"This would be perfect for a sunrise or sunset shot," she said. "Is the park open early or late?"

"I'll ask Janetta next time I see her."

Leslie arched an eyebrow.

"Janetta Strickland," I continued. "She's the park superintendent."

"Are you buddies?"

"I met her when she became the park naturalist eight or ten years ago. At the time she also ran the Partners for Pinnacle program, a group of volunteers who build trails, plant trees, raise money."

"And you volunteered?"

164

"The whole agency did. We adopted the park as our first pro bono account and worked with Janetta for several years promoting festivals and other special events."

Leslie ducked as a Frisbee glided over her head.

"We had to resign the account when the load got too heavy. But also because of politics."

"Politics? You're kidding!"

"Some of the other ad agencies in town were jealous. In addition to Pinnacle receiving lots of public exposure, our creative campaigns won two or three national awards."

"Who's handling the account now?"

I shrugged. "I'm not sure. To keep things peaceful, Janetta rotates the work among the local firms."

"Maybe you can introduce us."

"You'll love her. She's sharp, hard-working, and devoted to this park. I wouldn't be surprised to see her named director of the entire state park system before she's done." I took another bite from my apple.

The crowd had thinned by half. I followed Leslie's upward gaze and saw a small squadron of turkey vultures circling high above, making the most of the afternoon thermals.

"Let me tell you a story about Janetta," I said. "She was a star athlete in high school and attended college on a track scholarship. Her older brother had nicknamed her Flash during her childhood, and it stuck. But when Janetta came to Pinnacle and started appearing in the newspaper and on TV, a few of her lazier colleagues resented the attention—and gave her another nickname: Flashbulb."

"That's mean."

"Janetta's strong. She doesn't let much bother her."

One of the nearby kids pointed to a C-130 flying low over the landscape. Three others followed closely behind, returning to Little Rock Air Force Base after another training flight. It's not often I can peer down on a convoy of airplanes.

"I'm getting hungry," Leslie said, once the noisy planes had passed. "How far to our picnic basket?"

I led her to the edge of the rocky outcrop and pointed to the parking lot far below. "Look carefully and you can pick out the truck. It's on the opposite side of the lot near the playground." The Toyota appeared no bigger than a Matchbox toy.

"Whoa!" Leslie grabbed my elbow and eased back from the rim. "Let's descend via the traditional route."

Thirty minutes later we reached the base of the mountain, and soon after, we spread our picnic across a shady table. I'd just bitten into a smoked turkey and Swiss cheese sandwich when I heard a shout. "Randy! Randy Lassiter!"

Leslie and I turned to see a slender African-American woman striding to us. Wearing a pressed drab brown uniform, she had a wide smile lighting up her pretty face.

"Randy Lassiter!"

I jumped to my feet in time to catch a big hug. Almost matching my height, she held me tight and gave me a nice smack on the cheek.

"You're looking great, Flash," I said, my arm draped across her shoulders.

"For an old white man, you're not doing too bad yourself."

By now, Leslie had risen and watched the commotion with a slight smile.

"Superintendent Janetta Strickland, I'd like you to meet Ms. Leslie Carlisle. My fiancée."

Janetta's mouth dropped as she shook Leslie's hand. "Are you serious?"

Leslie nodded as a blush crept up her neck.

"Congratulations, girl!" Janetta then turned to me. "Truth is, I should be congratulating my favorite advertising executive. He has outdone himself!" She slapped me on the back.

"Will you join us?" Leslie asked. "There's plenty of food."

Janetta glanced at her watch. "I can stay for a couple of minutes. But I better not eat, though. Some self-righteous taxpayer will write the governor and complain that I'm abusing my position."

166

She laughed, but I knew there were a handful of low-life rednecks in the community who would like nothing more than to make Superintendent Strickland's life miserable.

"I thought you had weekends off," I said.

"I am your personal tax dollar at work. On call twenty-four hours a day, seven days a week." She winked at Leslie. "And given that the assistant superintendent called in sick, I thought this might be a good occasion to mingle with my people."

"How goes the park business?" I asked.

"Similar to yours. Too much to do. Not enough time or money. Folks second-guessing your every decision. Your basic career," she said with a chuckle, but then studied Leslie with a hint of a frown. "Don't tell me you're in advertising, too."

Leslie shook her head and grinned. "Photography. Which reminds me. Do you let photographers shoot sunrises and sunsets from the summit?"

"We'll allow it, provided you make provisions to climb in the dark. What we don't like is hauling dead people off this mountain. There are nasty messes to clean up, overtime to deal with, grieving families, reporters badgering you, and paperwork like you wouldn't believe," she said, halfway serious. "And, of course, it hurts our image."

"Speaking of image, how's the Partners group?" I asked.

Janetta shrugged. "It seems to have lost some momentum. Is Lassiter & Associates ready for another run at it?"

"Maybe later." And then I remembered Tillman. "Flash, I'd like some details on one of your volunteers."

She fixed her eyes on me. "Who?"

"A professor named Tillman. Dr. Mackenzie Tillman."

Janetta whistled. "That Mackie … She's one strange woman."

"What do you mean?"

"Dependable enough, but as cold as they come. I've given up trying to get acquainted. She stays in her own special world. What's your interest with her?"

"Tillman works with another friend of mine at UA Little Rock," I said. "I noticed that she had listed Partners for Pinnacle on her biographical sketch. That got my curiosity up."

"I guess you know she's a neighbor."

"I don't understand."

"Her daddy, the world-class tycoon, used to own a lot of land out here," Janetta said. "He sold most of it over the years, including some to us at inflated prices. But he kept a pretty forty-acre tract on our south boundary and gave it to Dr. Tillman when she returned to Little Rock."

"Does she get to it often?" Leslie asked.

"You could say that," Janetta said. "She lives there."

For some reason, this news caused my pulse to quicken. "What's her place like?" I asked. "No doubt it's fancy."

Janetta snorted. "Don't ask me. I tried a couple of times to drop by. You know, playing the role of a dutiful bureaucrat, meeting my neighbors. But the property has a gate that a military base would be proud of, not to mention **No Trespassing** signs posted every 50 feet on a heavy-duty fence." She glanced at her watch, stood, and brushed the back of her trousers. "I hate to leave, but it's time for me to make a loop through the park."

"It's great to see you again," I said, giving her another hug.

"Don't wait so long next time." She shook hands with Leslie. "And good luck to you."

"Thanks," Leslie said. "I'll give you a ring about after-hours work from the summit."

"I'll be expecting your call," Janetta said. She turned and began walking, her long strides quickly carrying her away. She'd gone some 50 feet when she stopped and faced us with a smile. "When's the big date?"

"October 16," Leslie said.

"Mark your calendar," I added.

With a hearty wave, the park superintendent resumed her rounds.

168

~ TWENTY-TWO ~

We slept late Sunday, ran a few errands, and piddled the afternoon away doing odd jobs in the yard. My least favorite neighbor, a retired know-it-all army colonel who'd settled next door a few months earlier, was experiencing the joys of home ownership for the first time. He'd purchased every lawn tool known to modern manufacturing, including an industrial-strength, ear-piercing leaf blower. For the past hour he'd been "sweeping" his driveway, porch, and sidewalks with the irritating machine. I've considered running for the state legislature, the sole plank of my platform a vow to make possession of those God-awful blowers a third-degree felony. Now and then the calls of robins, mockingbirds, blue jays, and squirrels broke through the urban cacophony.

While I mumbled to myself, digging a hole for an expensive sugar maple I'd bought during an impulsive stop at a local garden center earlier in the day, Leslie pulled weeds and the last of our drooping winter pansies from a flowerbed out front. She examined a handful of yellowish leaves before tossing them into a bucket.

"Have you had the soil tested?"

"Something needs to be done," I said. "The spring daffodils didn't flower much either."

"My grandmother owned the original green thumb," said Leslie. "She used bone meal to cure a variety of garden ailments. Let's get a bag next time we're out."

"Bone meal," I said. "That sounds gruesome."

Leslie shrugged. "She swore by it."

I wiped the sweat from my brow, dug out another grapefruit-sized rock with the shovel, and slid the maple's root-ball into the shallow hole. It was a tight fit. "Did your grandmother have any advice about transplanting trees?" I asked.

"As a matter of fact, she did," Leslie said with a mischievous smile. "Here's one of her favorite sayings: 'Don't plant a $10 tree in a $5 hole.'"

Giving my fiancée a halfway serious glare, I carefully removed the tree and reached once again for my shovel. "I'm not sure my back can afford a $75 hole," I said, and returned to work.

Later in the afternoon, after the maple had been set in place and watered, I took a long run around the neighborhood while Leslie showered. I thought back to the May Day picnic Leslie and I had shared with J.J. and how much fun we'd had teasing back and forth. I remembered how J.J.'s eyes had brightened when I'd asked him to be my best man. I recalled the big hug he'd given Leslie and the firm handshake we'd exchanged moments before he climbed into his car and drove away. And I realized again how much I missed his calls, his friendship, and his involvement in my life.

* * *

That evening Leslie and I went to the premiere of a play at the Arkansas Repertory Theatre, where we ran into Gib and Ellen in the lobby. A few weeks away from delivering their first child, Ellen guaranteed no more public appearances before the birth.

"I'm as big as a house," my sister said, hands resting on her extended belly.

I thought she looked great and said so.

Leslie agreed and then nodded at Gib. "How goes the pun society?"

I tried to escape but found myself hemmed in by the crowd.

Gib placed a hand on my shoulder. "Randy," he said. "You've got to loosen up."

"But your puns are terrible," I said. "They stink."

At first, I thought I'd hurt his feelings, especially when Leslie flashed me a sour glance. "They don't really stink, do they?" he said with a sniff. "I thought they were merely ..." and he paused, a smile breaking across his face, "*pungent*." He hooted, which I felt was rather undignified for one of the city's top surgeons, causing a couple of questioning faces to turn our way.

Leslie made a game effort to steer the conversation in another direction. "Have you selected a name for the baby?"

Ellen shook her head. "But my doctor said we could concentrate our search on boys' names."

"I'd already picked one out for a girl," said Gib. "*Punelope*."

I shoved a program under his nose. "Here's some reading material."

While Gib thumbed through the booklet, Ellen asked Leslie about handling another photo shoot before, as she put it, "things go bonkers." The lights flickered as they worked out details, and the four of us began hunting for our seats.

Gib tossed me the program. "There's an intriguing production scheduled for August," he said. We stared at him skeptically. "A classic," he said. "*The Prodigal Pun*."

As luck would have it, we sat in different sections and avoided further verbal beatings. I expected the worst at intermission, but the Yarberrys bade us a quick good-bye. Ellen found the prolonged sitting too uncomfortable. They promised to keep us informed as her due date approached.

While Leslie and I mingled in the crowd during the break, I saw a vaguely familiar face. Standing a bit less than six feet tall and thick bodied, the man caught my gaze and gave me a subtle nod of recognition before joining the throng at the bar.

When he emerged a few minutes later, I nudged Leslie. "See the guy in the navy sport coat? The one carrying two glasses of wine?"

She turned little by little, discreetly eyeing the individual in question, and kept her head moving as he stopped beside a curvy, long-legged blonde and delivered a drink. Young enough to be his daughter, the man's companion wore a tight, provocative gown suggesting it was the sole garment on her extraordinary body.

"The one hovering around that brazen hussy?" Leslie asked with a giggle.

"I can't remember his name, but I'm pretty sure he's Summer Preston's former husband."

She exhaled a low whistle. "Let's not mention this to our friend."

* * *

Monday was Memorial Day, and I had special plans. Coaxing Leslie into the truck, I promised a memorable breakfast stop within the hour. Once we crossed the foggy Arkansas River, we drove east on Interstate 40, leaving town a little after eight o'clock. At nine, we took the Brinkley exit and passed the predictable cluster of chain restaurants in favor of a small, nondescript establishment surrounded by pickups. All my Toyota lacked to fit in was a gun rack in the rear window. And a muddy exterior.

"Something tells me to forget a croissant," Leslie said, surveying the lot.

"And don't ask for an espresso, either."

What we got was exceptional service, fresh-perked coffee, home-made biscuits, and the biggest omelets either of us could remember. While we ate, four men in overalls sitting in the booth behind ours groused over the high cost of herbicides; at the table beside us, two older women traded stories and photographs of their grandchildren. In the back corner, a pair of kids competed for the next selection from a jukebox that, so far, had produced nothing but country tunes. The decor ranged from a menagerie of taxidermied waterfowl to an array of Arkansas Razorback football schedules for the past 30 years.

"How 'bout another refill?" Not bothering to wait for an answer, our young waitress smiled and topped off both cups.

Leslie's gaze took in the entire room. "This is the real America, isn't it?"

I was digesting her comment and chewing the last of my omelet when the door opened and two large men stepped inside. Pausing

172

as they inspected the surroundings, they slid sunglasses into their vests and wiped their faces with bright red bandannas. Hair askew and faces unshaven, they wore identical leather outfits, with Harley-Davidson logos prominent on their lapels.

"Now there's the real America," I said.

Leslie studied the pair. "At least they appear clean," she mumbled.

I made eye contact with the men and they waved as they took their seats.

Her mouth fell open. "You know them?"

"They're brothers from Little Rock. One's a high-flying venture capitalist and the other's said to be the best divorce lawyer in the state."

"Either way," she said with a clever grin, "they'll get your money."

Leaving the cafe, we passed a group of teenage boys admiring two gleaming motorcycles and climbed into the truck. We passed through West Memphis a little before eleven and approached the Mississippi River bridge. The skyline of Memphis towered above the waterfront, its architecturally underachieving Pyramid reflecting the morning sun.

Leslie leaned forward, her eyes bright. "In all my travels, I've never been to Memphis."

"That's why we're here. First, we'll check out locations made famous by John Grisham. Places like the Peabody Hotel and Front Street, including a lunch stop for barbecue at the Rendezvous."

Leslie—who has all of Grisham's novels in hardback, including several signed first editions—gave my hand a squeeze.

"Later, we'll stay as long as you want at Graceland."

She gasped, leaned across the seat, and planted a big, wet kiss on my cheek. I learned early in our relationship that Ms. Carlisle had owned an Elvis collection since her college days. In fact, I'd given her one of its most cherished items—a moving portrait of Elvis, complete with teardrop, on a velvet background—mere days after we'd met. It now hangs in a place of honor above our washing machine. Last time I noticed, one of Leslie's bras dangled from the frame, drip-drying over his shoulder.

We arrived at the Peabody in time to observe the famous march of the mallards from the elevator to the elaborate fountain in the hotel's bustling grand lobby. Escorted by a uniformed keeper, a small flock of ducks waddled down a bright red carpet before plopping into the water. A crowd of over a hundred tourists, a third of them Asian, watched the short parade under a stroboscopic barrage of electronic flashes. When Leslie threw a look of confused disbelief my way, I shrugged and guided her to the exit.

"What's so great about those ducks?" she asked.

"Classic thinking-outside-the-box marketing," I offered. "One of the most ingenious promotional gimmicks in the lodging industry." At least that was the general consensus in the strange world of advertising. How could I argue with that?

Next, we took the Main Street Trolley a short distance north and strolled a block west to Front Street, passing by historic Cotton Row. A paddle wheeler cruised far below us and beyond it we saw the Mud Island Monorail. Farther upstream, the I-40 bridge leapfrogged the mile-wide Mississippi, its steel superstructure dwarfing an endless convoy of cars and trucks.

Leslie eyed the river as a tow pushed a dozen barges against the current before shifting her gaze to the old brick buildings. "Straight out of a Grisham book," she said, and then subtly gestured down the sidewalk to three well-dressed older men huddled near an ornate doorway. "They could be some of his shady characters concocting another scheme," she added with a wink. At that moment a limousine rounded the corner and came to a quick stop near the trio, its tires squealing. With a wary glance in our direction, the men disappeared into the shiny, black vehicle, the last taking a final drag on a cigarette before flipping it to the curb. As the car accelerated past us, I stared into its tinted windows and saw nothing but a fleeting reflection of two wide-eyed tourists who seemed familiar.

"Maybe so," I said, clutching her hand. "Maybe so."

174

We walked back to Main Street and rode the trolley south to the Beale Street Historic District. The clubs hadn't yet opened, but we enjoyed seeing the landmarks and visiting the specialty shops, including a music store where I bought a Robert Lockwood, Junior, CD. I'm partial to Arkansas musicians, Delta bluesmen in particular.

We then spotted an antique emporium and walked to it. Featuring everything from primitive duck decoys to barrister bookcases, the window display did its job, luring us through the open double doors. A salesman approached as I studied a handsome library table. When I got to the price tag, my cursory review came to a close.

"Most of our oak is in back if you'd care to see it," he said.

Leslie grabbed my elbow. "Sure," she said, and he led us to the rear of the store. Mission-style furniture filled an entire room.

"Searching for anything in particular?"

"Just browsing," Leslie said. "A good friend collects similar pieces." She put her hands on her hips and cast an appraising eye at a buffet that cost no telling how much. "This is magnificent," she said. I watched with a twinge of apprehension as she stepped back to admire it from another angle.

"Our entire Craftsman inventory is 25 percent off," the salesman said.

"I'm not sure it would fit in the truck," I said. I knew it wouldn't fit in our budget, even with the discount.

"We offer free delivery," he said, smiling.

He was close to getting on my nerves. "Not to Little Rock, I suspect," I countered.

The clerk's eyes lit up. "Are y'all from Little Rock?"

I nodded while Leslie continued her inspection of the large sideboard. She examined the hardware, ran a hand over the top, and pulled out a drawer.

"I've got a couple of good customers over there," he said. "One's a professor at the local university."

After Leslie glanced at me, we swung our eyes to the shopkeeper.

"Dr. Newell, by any chance?" I asked.

He broke into a big grin. "You know J.J.? He's one of our favorite clients."

Feeling weak, I leaned hard against an armoire and stared at the floor.

Leslie took a step closer to our host. "Have you seen him in recent weeks?"

"Our biggest show occurs every spring as part of the Memphis in May festival," he said. "J.J.'s always been a fixture, at least 'til this year."

"He didn't attend?" I asked.

"Far as I know, nobody saw him."

We thanked him for his time and began moving toward the exit. "Give me a call if you decide that buffet will work," he said, handing Leslie a card. "And please tell J.J. to stop by. I've got an assortment of new pieces he needs to see."

Back on the sidewalk, Leslie slipped her arm in mine and pulled me close. "It's a small world."

Our spirits rose at the end of the block, where we pulled even with a tiny tattoo parlor, its narrow storefront display showcasing hundreds of possibilities. Faces inches from the plate glass, we took turns suggesting designs for the other, the more lurid and bizarre the better. With a wink, Leslie said she might consider the *Bad Girl* pattern that caught my eye, "depending on its anatomical location." We scooted aside when a boisterous group of potential customers, Germans from their accents, crowded around the window, pointing out first one tattoo option then another.

She needed no persuasion when I mentioned lunch. Fingers intertwined, we took our time walking to the Rendezvous. Her grip tightened as I led us into an alley and past overflowing dumpsters before heading down a darkened stairway and into the smoky dive. Arriving well after the noon rush, we found a table near the back and ordered ribs and a pitcher of beer. Black-and-white portraits of celebrities who'd sampled the menu over the years covered the walls, including autographed photos of Willie Nelson, Cybill

Shepherd, and Liberace above our seats. I gave up trying to understand the significance of this grouping, but my eyes kept wandering back to Liberace's tasseled and sequined suit. He must have had a lot of guts to wear it, I thought.

"I see why Grisham included this place in his books," Leslie said, interrupting my strange reverie. She peered through the thick blue haze. "It's unique, with a lot of authentic character. I like it."

She also liked her lunch, using the bread to sop the last morsels from her plate. "What's next?"

"You might consider wiping the barbecue sauce from your chin," I suggested. She grinned ever so sweetly before applying the toe of her sandal to my shin.

* * *

Half an hour later found us in line at Graceland behind an excited group of a dozen European teenagers. We enlisted for the "Platinum Tour" and spent two hours at the King's shrine, beginning at the mansion with meaningful stops in the "Jungle Room" and at the gravesite. Following an inspection of Presley's two jets, we visited the auto museum, where we had our second Harley-Davidson experience of the day. The man had acquired some very nice toys.

We then spent 30 minutes in the sprawling souvenir shop, amazed at the range of items. After exploring every aisle at least twice, Leslie selected a semi-tasteful snow globe and an oversized rhinestone comb for her Elvis collection. She gasped when the customer ahead of us rang up purchases of over $200—and almost keeled over when the woman handed the cashier a credit card bearing a likeness of Elvis.

Leaving Memphis in late afternoon, we crossed the Big Muddy again, driving under the large blue sign reading, "Welcome to Arkansas—The Natural State." Surrounded by semi-trailers as we passed through West Memphis, I pointed out the exit to Jonesboro.

"Your buddy Grisham's hometown."

Leslie gave me a skeptical look. "*The* John Grisham?"

"He spent his formative years in northeast Arkansas."

She peeked at her watch. "How far?"

"Let's wait 'til they build a museum," I said, chuckling. "Or at least erect a monument."

Traveling west on I-40, Leslie and I instinctively ducked as a bright yellow biplane came out of nowhere, screaming across all four lanes of the highway. Wheels mere feet above the ground, it shot across a field, discharging a fine spray over endless rows of soybeans. Several cars had stopped on the shoulder to watch, and at least one spectator recorded the aircraft with a camera, taping the pilot's aerial acrobatics.

"Good God! That plane scared me to death."

"Your basic crop duster," I said.

"You'll never catch me in one of those things."

An hour later Leslie had fallen asleep, her head leaning against my shoulder.

~ TWENTY-THREE ~

In the office by seven o'clock the following morning, I discovered that Clifford had sent me a flurry of irritating e-mails over the long holiday weekend. He'd titled his latest book idea *The Caraoke Cousins*, a proposed coming-of-age novel featuring a pair of orphaned but precocious youngsters making their way across America in search of a rich, nomadic great-aunt. Surviving by their wits, juvenile charm, and singing ability, they would perform "at a country club soiree one day and at a bar mitzvah the next." Clifford wrote that he hoped to soon determine their names ("something alluringly alliterative"), zodiac signs, and personality quirks. Pointing out in my reply that he'd misspelled karaoke at every opportunity gave me some satisfaction.

I got a couple of hours of work done before the routine Monday morning staff meeting. Copies of the new direct mail piece for our Hot Springs client were passed around by the designer, and my creative director shared a progress report on the proposal her team had under development for the Baptist Hospital bid. When I brought up the last item on the agenda, our media campaign for Catfish McCulloch's gun-and-knife show, at least one of my colleagues groaned aloud. I pretended not to hear.

As the meeting ended, Neal Stackhouse, KACN's general manager, phoned and gave me the name of his contact at the Cleveland conglomerate. The one other piece of information he had was that the sale was expected to be finalized within two, perhaps three, months. When I called Cleveland, the person I wanted was unavailable, of course, so I left a message asking her to give me a ring. I was not expecting good news.

The next appointment was with a self-centered magazine rep from Chicago. I thought his fifteen-minute presentation on marketing opportunities within Generation X would never end. He finally left, presenting me with a cheap collapsible umbrella—the fifth such bribe I'd received in the past year. I figured it'd be good for maybe one thunderstorm.

Twenty minutes late to Rotary, I arrived just in time to catch every uninspiring word of a lengthy PowerPoint presentation on the state's tire recycling efforts. I'd joined the club a decade earlier, hoping to make valuable contacts in the business community and to keep my conscience clear with the occasional good deed. While I enjoyed the camaraderie, the cost often included marginal programs and submarginal food. At least the coffee was good. And we'd quit singing those goofy songs years ago.

My Tuesday afternoon was open, and I took advantage of it. I drove to southwest Little Rock, pulling in at the local farmers' cooperative. Leslie wanted half a dozen bags of mulch for the flowerbeds plus 20 pounds of bone meal, and I needed fertilizer for the yard. On impulse, I also bought a squirrel-proof bird feeder and a sturdy wheelbarrow. Thank God for pickups.

Reaching into my wallet at the cashier's counter, I discovered a slip of paper tucked between two credit cards. A name and address were written on the folded note. Following several seconds of total bewilderment, I recognized it as the information Summer Preston had given me a few days ago. If her facts were right, Max Alloway, the UA Little Rock student kicked off the Big Bend field trip earlier in the spring by J.J., lived in this part of town. I decided to pay him a visit.

After driving through a haphazard assortment of residences, quasi-commercial properties, overgrown lots, and abandoned buildings that would drive a city planner crazy, I passed a busy salvage yard. A block farther down the road stood a battered mailbox displaying Alloway's address.

As I pulled into the rutted driveway, steering around a series of muddy potholes, I noticed a discarded Christmas tree all but hidden in the brush, its branches draped with clumps of tarnished tinsel. A doublewide sat at the rear of the lot against a chain-link fence, and parked below its improbable bay window was a metallic blue Chevrolet pickup. A customized low-rider, its tinted windows were the color of molasses. From 50 feet away, a decal on the rear bumper delivered a clear message: "Protected by Smith & Wesson." Off to one side, a rusting Ford Pinto rested on concrete blocks, and next to it stood a hulking satellite dish, the black bowl aimed at the heavens. Grayish-blue smoke billowed from a nearby burn barrel, its acrid aroma drifting into my truck. It was not a Norman Rockwell scene.

A scrawny German shepherd crawled from beneath the mobile home. Ears back and tail low, he trotted through the weeds toward my truck with the quick, short steps of a dog on a mission. I had serious doubts about his motives.

I'd already shifted into reverse when the front door opened and a young woman appeared on the rickety porch. Approximately Leslie's height, she was attractive, her blonde hair pulled back in a bouncy ponytail. Wearing tight, skimpy shorts and a thin, abbreviated top, she snapped her fingers. "Come here, Prince." The dog eyed me a second longer before changing course and slinking under the steps.

The woman turned to me. "Are you here regarding a classified ad?"

I climbed from the truck, keeping a wary eye out for her canine companion. "I'm looking for Max Alloway."

She tilted her head at the door. "He's sleeping right now."

As I neared the porch, I forgot the dog and worked hard to maintain eye contact, forcing myself to ignore the series of discolorations on the woman's thighs, calves, and arms. I noticed a deep shadow below her right eye that wasn't the result of sleepless nights. She also had a puffy lower lip. Either she'd been in a car wreck or had come out on the wrong end of a fight. My money was on the latter.

Given her tall, slender body and high cheekbones, with a little help, she had real possibilities as a model, I thought. But even clever lighting and a soft-focus lens can't hide a barrage of bruises.

"I'm Randy Lassiter."

"Beth Anthony." When she bent over the railing to shake hands, an unexpected glimpse confirmed she wasn't wearing a bra. I saw nothing wrong with her breasts. "What's your interest with Max?" she asked.

I didn't have a ready answer. Buying time, I searched my wallet and found a business card to give her. "I'd like to visit with him on a matter relating to UA Little Rock. Could you ask Max to give me a call?"

After studying the card for a moment, she somehow slipped it into a rear pocket.

Something crashed inside the trailer. A man shouted, "Beth! Goddamn it, Beth, where are you?"

The front door flew open and a young man in need of a shave stumbled onto the porch, a beer can in one hand, his eyes but narrow slits in the bright daylight. Slicked back, his thick, dark hair glistened in the sun, and his sideburns reached almost to his jaws. Barefooted and powerfully built, he wore an orange muscle shirt several sizes too small and a pair of wrinkled blue gym shorts. Stopping behind his girlfriend, Alloway ran his free hand over her flat stomach and slid it upward while nuzzling her neck. As it neared her breast, she clasped his hand with one of her own. "Max," she said. "We have a guest."

His head pivoting, Alloway squinted in my direction, bringing me into focus. A small golden ring dangled from his right ear. "You're the one who phoned concerning those radar detectors, aren't you?" he asked, and the instant, brilliant smile of a television evangelist flashed across his face. "They're in my workshop." He pointed to a small, padlocked storage building beyond the end of the porch as he took a sip of beer. "I'm ready to make you the deal of the year." When his grin ratcheted up a notch, he could have been auditioning for a toothpaste commercial.

I shook my head, mesmerized by the transformation. "No, I—"

Alloway never missed a beat. "Must be the night vision goggles then. I've had a lot of calls about 'em. An incredible high-tech product straight from the Russian army. They're amazing, absolutely awesome."

"Sorry," I said, "but I'm here on another matter."

The smile vanished as his chin jutted upward, and I felt the full force of his cold, unblinking eyes. "Who the hell are you then? And what do you want?"

"My name's Randy Lassiter."

"He'd like to talk with you about UA Little Rock," Beth said. She bit her lower lip.

He shoved her to the side and leaned hard against the railing. Draining the last of his beer, he crushed the can and flung it at the burn barrel. Missing the mark by ten feet, it tumbled to a stop in the dirt. "Yeah?" Following a loud burp, he wiped a forearm across his mouth. It was then that I spotted a voluptuous mermaid covering much of his left shoulder. "This better be good." He stared, waiting, challenging me to respond.

I hesitated, unsure what to say or how to say it.

Alloway took the initiative. "If you're here representing that damn Dr. J.J. Newell, you can kiss my ass!"

When I flinched, a sneer crawled across his face. His nose, I noticed, had been broken at least once.

"You can tell that butthole he's going to regret ever having met me."

I didn't doubt it, but I was curious. "Why's that?"

"Because I'm going to sue him to hell and back." He waved his arms in a wide arc. "I'll take him for everything he's got. Every damn penny."

"You're sure a lawsuit's necessary?" I didn't know what else to ask.

"Goddamn right!" He turned to Beth. "Get me another beer, darlin'." She eased into the trailer.

"That sorry son of a bitch ruined my reputation," he said, slamming his fist against the top rail. As the porch shook, the dog crawled from between a pair of posts and darted past a cast-off water heater into the backyard, tail tucked between his legs.

"You're serious? About suing Newell?"

"Serious as shit. I've already retained a lawyer. A guy named Newcastle."

"Jeremy Newcastle?" We had belonged to the same Rotary Club for years. In fact, we'd eaten lunch together earlier in the day.

"That's him. A real hard ass. Your friend Newell better get ready to bend over," Alloway said with a cackle. Beth gave him the beer and slipped back inside.

"Newcastle's tough," I agreed. He'd developed a reputation as a formidable litigator, winning several of the largest judgments ever awarded in the South.

"I know." A mile-wide smirk crossed his face. "I did my research."

As Alloway upended his beer, I turned and started to walk back to my truck.

"Hey, buddy, one more thing. You never told me what you wanted," he said, rubbing his chin. "I reckon you're here to check out the possibility of a settlement." He paused and shot me a nasty smile as his eyes darkened. "Not interested."

I stopped and shrugged. "I did have another question."

He tilted the can again. "What's that?"

"Have you seen Dr. Newell since the Big Bend trip?"

Alloway snorted. "Are you kidding? He abandoned me in some pissant town in west Texas and I haven't laid eyes on him since." He finished his beer. "But I'll see him soon. In court." He flipped the empty can high over his shoulder, and it joined a collection on the roof of the mobile home with a hollow clunk. "As for you, don't come back." His unwavering glare told me it wasn't an idle threat.

As I returned to the truck, Alloway slung open the front door and disappeared into his trailer.

~ TWENTY-FOUR ~

When I returned home mid-afternoon, I found a disturbing note from Leslie on the kitchen counter. A morning photo shoot had been postponed, freeing her day, and she'd called Senator Judson Claypool in Stuttgart, explaining her magazine assignment. According to her note, Claypool relished the idea of publicity and promised her a personal tour. She'd left at once to photograph his rice fields. Although the message ended with her guarantee to be back by supper, the situation made me uneasy.

I phoned the office, telling my assistant I'd be spending the rest of the day at home and could be reached at the house should any problems arise. Next, I scrolled through the directory on my phone and then called Jeremy Newcastle's law firm. After a short wait, his receptionist connected me.

"Afternoon, Jeremy. It's Randy Lassiter."

"So, you survived today's Rotary presentation? Isn't it time we made you program chairman?"

"Not interested," I said. "Been there, done that."

"But you could bring back Dr. Libido, or whatever she called herself."

"I'm not sure she's ready for a return trip to Little Rock." A few years earlier, I had volunteered to fill in when our program chairman became ill. Among the speakers I recruited was a national radio talk show host specializing in adult relationships. An attractive and vivacious woman, she gave a humorous but frank spiel on differences between the sexes. The stimulating question-and-answer session following her remarks carried us well past our traditional one o'clock adjournment, and she sold and autographed books and posed for photos for another hour. Two or three members resigned in disgust, but the club gained another dozen or so when word of the session filtered through the business community.

"Speaking of that sort of thing, I understand congratulations are in order," he said.

"I'm eager for you to meet her."

"If you're looking for a prenuptial agreement, I'll have to refer you to someone else," Jeremy said with a laugh.

"Actually, this is a business call. Sort of."

"Great! Let me flip on the meter."

"I've got a friend—" I began.

"And his girl's in trouble," Jeremy interrupted.

"Almost," I chuckled. "Seriously, a close friend of mine disappeared a month ago."

Jeremy's tone changed. "Foul play?"

"I don't know what to think. But this friend, a UA Little Rock professor and my former college roommate, has vanished, and I'm trying to find him."

"I assume the police have chosen not to get involved."

"Not until they're convinced a crime has occurred."

"I can recommend a private detective if that's what you're after."

"Maybe later," I said. "But right now, I want to ask about one of your clients, provided we can talk without violating … um … whatever you call it."

"Client-attorney confidentiality?"

"My professor friend had a run-in with Max Alloway." I hesitated, waiting for the name to register. "I believe he's hired you."

"Tell me what you've heard."

I gave him an account of the Big Bend incident, or at least what I'd been told regarding J.J.'s trip to southwest Texas with his students.

186

"So, you're concerned that this student—or former student—might have a motive for harming his professor?"

"Who knows why people do what they do?" I answered. "But I met Alloway earlier today, and he's got a lot of anger directed at Dr. Newell. That's how I learned that he'd engaged you as his attorney."

"Hang on for a moment while I close my door." Returning to the phone seconds later, Jeremy said, "First, Mr. Alloway is not my client." After a pause, he continued, "Since I will not be representing him, I can share certain things with you—if I have your word this conversation will go no farther."

"You've got it."

I heard Jeremy's sigh through the receiver. "About a month ago, one of the firm's paralegals asked if she could have a few minutes of my time. When we visited, she said that her younger brother had been forced to drop out of school and wanted to sue the university. I said I'd meet with him."

"Max Alloway?"

"Right. He came by the office that afternoon. After he and I'd talked ten or fifteen minutes, I agreed to look into the situation. I'm acquainted with UA Little Rock's legal counsel and called her a week or so later. She knew all about the incident and said the university halfway expected a complaint. She faxed me a lengthy report with Dr. Newell's statement, the statement of the woman involved, plus sworn statements from everyone else on the trip. Everybody but Alloway, that is. Taken together, the accounts present a thorough narrative of the evening, almost minute by minute."

"That seems rather unusual."

"Virtually every organization fears discrimination and harassment suits these days," Jeremy said. "Educational institutions, in particular. When something like this incident occurs, they act at once to minimize their exposure."

"But why no statement from Alloway?"

"Good question. They tried on more than one occasion. But he wouldn't cooperate."

"Do I get the impression Alloway doesn't have much of a case?"

After a brief pause, he said, "That's a fair conclusion. I can tell you I won't be handling it. My letter to Alloway went out this morning."

"Let me ask you something else, Jeremy. I got the feeling Alloway hates Newell so bad he can almost taste it. Did you have the same reaction?"

"Alloway is a bitter young man. Very bitter. In his mind, there's an account to settle."

"Do you think there's any chance—even remote—that Alloway could be involved in Dr. Newell's disappearance?"

Again, Jeremy took a few seconds to respond. "In this line of work, I see all kinds of folks. Most are decent, hardworking people who've been wronged in one fashion or another," he said. "But Max Alloway … I don't know what to think. He's smart—his sister claims he has the IQ of a genius—although something about him makes me uneasy."

"Would you consider him stable?"

"That's just it. I've been in this business 15 long years and can almost always tell the con artist from the real thing. Yet after watching his body language and listening to him …" There was a pause followed by another sigh. "I wouldn't be a bit surprised if Alloway isn't suffering from some sort of serious personality disorder."

"Looks like he's not above roughing up his girlfriend."

"Don't underestimate him, Randy. I suspect he's bad news."

"I'll be careful. And thanks for your help."

"Give some thought to our Rotary programs," Newcastle said, signing off.

After changing clothes, I spent the next hour spreading fertilizer. I had just hung the new bird feeder from the front porch when a shiny SUV pulled next to the curb. I'd seen it once before.

~ TWENTY-FIVE ~

While Catfish McCulloch climbed from the driver's side of the vehicle, a man unknown to me—wearing a rakish black beret—emerged from the opposite door.

"Howdy!" Catfish hobbled along the sidewalk, leaning hard against his cane. "Your office guaranteed you'd be here." Since he wore the same unattractive sport coat I'd seen on the previous occasions when we'd met, I figured it was his unofficial uniform.

"Come on up in the shade," I said from the porch. "I'll find something cold to drink."

Struggling as he climbed the steps, Catfish paused when he drew even with me. "I've got somebody I want to introduce." He gestured to his tall, muscular companion who trailed a few paces behind. "Randy Lassiter, meet DuChamps."

Catfish's friend closed the gap and I stuck out my hand. "Pleased to meet you, Mr. DuChamps." Large and rough and calloused, his hand gripped my fingers like a bear trap. Somewhere in his mid-to-late 50s, he had the broad shoulders and narrow waist of an athlete half his age. He struck me as the kind of man who might throw himself to the ground and do 20 one-armed push-ups to make a point.

Catfish chuckled. "No need to call him mister. He goes by DuChamps. Nothing more, nothing less."

"Sort of like Liberace," I said, and regretted it at once. I'd spouted off the first one-name wonder who came to mind, perhaps a bit of subliminal residue from the recent trip to the Rendezvous in Memphis. Feeling his grip tighten, I wished I'd hesitated just a moment, long enough to have thought of another example. Something manly like Ulysses. Spartacus. Rambo. Or even Michelangelo.

The powerful chap in possession of my right arm stared into my eyes, his expression yet to change. Behind his tanned and leathery acne-scarred face was a cold, blank look.

Catfish saved me. "Liberace!" he hooted. "I told you he had a great sense of humor." I put on my warmest adman smile and threw in a small snort for good measure.

The vise rearranging the bone structure of my fingers opened and my hand fell limply toward the floor of the porch. "My pleasure," said DuChamps, his low and raspy voice hiding most of a French accent.

When I returned with three glasses of iced tea, Catfish and his colleague had made themselves at home in a pair of sling chairs. I plopped down on the porch swing and took a long swig. While my visitors did likewise, I managed a surreptitious glance at Catfish's strange friend. His camouflage cargo pants, olive drab T-shirt, and sleeveless khaki vest screamed ex-military. The dog tags dangling from his thick neck and the gleaming combat boots supported that theory. As did a deep scar extending from the lobe of his right ear to his throat. Not to mention the beret.

"You're probably wondering why we're here," Catfish said.

"That has crossed my mind," I admitted, flexing my throbbing hand.

"DuChamps here is the world's foremost expert on personal security. What with all those terrorists on the loose and the public skittish, I figured he'd be a great addition for my show's lineup. You know, a genuine celebrity appearance."

I looked to DuChamps, who stared across the yard, his impenetrable eyes locked onto something he alone could see.

"He's going to sell autographed copies of his latest book throughout the show. Isn't that right, old buddy?" DuChamps's expression never changed, but that didn't bother Catfish. "You may have noticed he's not much of a talker. He'll chime in once he gets to know you."

While DuChamps gazed into space, I filled Catfish in on our progress on generating a big crowd for his gun-and-knife extravaganza. I explained how the agency had already booked radio buys with every country-and-western station in the region and had arranged for remote broadcasts from the site Friday evening and throughout Saturday. I didn't mention that our business relationship would soon be history.

"What about television?"

"Still working out details," I said. "I can pretty much guarantee we'll get one of the local weathermen to do his five and six o'clock reports from the main stage."

Catfish slapped his hands together. "Hot damn! How'd you do that?"

"Money talks," I said. "We're telling the stations we've budgeted $15,000 for TV spots—and the best deal gets it all."

Out of the corner of my eye, I saw DuChamps's head make a slight turn. "Playing one against the other?" He almost grinned. "I like it."

"Anything else?" Catfish asked, toying with one end of his handlebar mustache.

"We'll drop quarter-page ads in the sports section of the *Arkansas Democrat-Gazette* every Sunday between now and the show. The paper's outdoor writer promised to give us several prominent plugs in his columns."

Catfish had pulled a small pad from his breast pocket and took notes.

"Also," I said, "we're still recruiting sponsors. All the major sporting goods stores in the area have agreed to distribute discounted admission tickets beginning ten days out." I took another sip of tea. "And we've rented 10 or so billboards in prime locations, along the interstates in central Arkansas for the most part. Things are falling into place."

After scribbling a final item, Catfish tucked the notepad away and gave me a satisfied nod before waving a hand at his colleague. "What about DuChamps? He'd be willing to do some television interviews, wouldn't you, partner?"

His gaze still locked somewhere well beyond the porch, DuChamps reached inside his vest and extracted a cigar the size of a small club. He lit it and swung his dark, empty eyes to Catfish. "My face is better suited for radio."

He had a point. I hesitated a moment, not wanting to agree too quickly. "Radio's a wonderful idea," I said after what I hoped was an appropriate pause. "There's a local talk show host with a big following. He's a self-described liberal and would love to take you on."

For the first time, I saw a glint of life in DuChamps's shadowy eyes. "Let's do it." He blew a plume of smoke into a strand of honeysuckle wrapped around a porch railing. I halfway expected the blossoms to wilt.

"I'll need some background material," I said. "Do you have a biographical sketch, something with details about your career?"

Without a word, DuChamps rose and walked to the truck as Catfish's head bobbed. "The man's prepared," Catfish said. "Always prepared. You could call him an adult Boy Scout."

I wondered about that.

Taking the porch steps two at a time with the grace of a leopard, DuChamps returned with a manila envelope and a small book. He presented them to me without comment, then settled back into his chair. The envelope contained a three-page summary of his career, full of cryptic military acronyms and abbreviations that appeared impressive.

A former officer in the French Foreign Legion, he'd served tours of duty in Asia and Africa before settling in the U.S. and offering his services as a security consultant. Involved in a handful of paramilitary organizations, he spent a good deal of time on the international lecture circuit. He'd also written a couple of books, the latest of which rested on my knee.

The cover of the slim paperbound volume was barely big enough to accommodate the title—*Defending Your Future: A Safety & Security Guide for American Patriots*—floating in big type over an Old Glory background. The back cover featured half a dozen glowing quotes from reviewers, most ending in double or triple exclamation points. Other than *Soldier of Fortune*, I'd never heard of any of the publications. A one-paragraph blurb on DuChamps accompanied a small, stark photograph of the author leaning against a streetlight in a dark and apparently dangerous neighborhood.

When I looked up, DuChamps had resumed his vacant gaze. Catfish, however, nodded with gusto. "Great stuff, huh?"

"We won't have any trouble scheduling that radio show." Whether or not the host could goad the celebrated author and expert into talking would not be my problem. Flipping the book open, I stopped at the table of contents. With chapters ranging from schoolyard safety to avoiding carjackers, DuChamps had covered the bases. My erratic mind made a disjointed jump to J.J.'s disappearance.

"DuChamps," I said. "You're an authority on preventing crime, right?"

Still staring across the lawn, he gave his head a slight dip.

"Have you written anything from … uh … the other end of the spectrum?"

His head swiveled until our eyes met. "As I matter of fact, I have," he said, eyeing me with unexpected interest. "A confidential piece for, shall we say, an elite military unit that must remain nameless." He flicked half an inch of cigar ashes over the railing. "Not for public consumption."

It must be a favorite subject, I thought; DuChamps was on the verge of becoming loquacious.

"Advertising business not lucrative enough?" Catfish asked with a laugh. "Is my buddy Lassiter planning on the big score?"

"Not quite," I said. "I have a friend who's missing, and I hope he's just traveling. But this book made me realize there are … maybe you'd call them rules or whatever, for the perfect crime."

DuChamps took another sip from his glass and placed it on the porch railing. Shifting in his chair, he leaned forward, closing the gap between us. "When you say 'perfect crime,' I assume that you mean what civilians call murder?" He asked the question as if we were discussing the weather.

"Yeah," I said. "Murder. Theoretically, of course." My throat felt dry and I reached for my iced tea.

Stretching his sinewy arms, DuChamps bent one finger back at a time, cracking his knuckles. He then tilted his head with a twist and popped his neck.

"In general terms," he said, "I adhere to three essential principles."

I got the distinct impression DuChamps wasn't speaking from theory but from actual experience. Sort of like Nick Saban talking about football. Or maybe Madonna discussing men.

Catfish glanced at me, his eyes huge. "Most clients would pay big bucks for this information." Like a bookie getting the tip of his life, he yanked out his notepad.

DuChamps ignored him. "The first, of course, is to never do anything stupid. Like leaving the tiniest bit of incriminating evidence."

Pushing a stroller, one of my neighbors passed by on the sidewalk, saw us on the porch, and smiled and waved. Her reaction might have been different, I thought, had she been able to hear details of our conversation. Catfish and I waved back.

"The second rule is to do everything yourself. Never involve anybody else." He examined his watch, then stood. "Never."

"And third?" Catfish asked, beating me to the question.

"The most obvious of all." DuChamps shrugged like an impatient teacher. "You get rid of the body. Without a corpse, everything else is circumstantial." He started down the steps.

As Catfish struggled to his feet, he shot me a wry grin. "Are you lucky or what! I've never heard him speak this much with anyone."

They hadn't been gone five minutes when Leslie returned, startling me with a quick toot of her horn.

194

~ TWENTY-SIX ~

While Leslie grabbed her camera bag, I retrieved the tripod and a small duffel from the trunk. I followed her up the steps and into the house, hoping she wouldn't notice the lingering stench from DuChamps's cigar as we crossed the porch.

"Whew," she said, collapsing on a rocker in the sunroom. "What a day." Red-faced and streaked with perspiration, she appeared as if she'd run a marathon.

"Thanks for leaving the note, but you had me worried."

"Sorry." She gave me a sweaty kiss. "When Dillard's canceled my shoot at the last minute, I called Senator Judson Claypool on a lark. I was surprised to get him, and still more amazed when he invited me to Stuttgart."

"How'd it go?"

"I now understand his political success. He's charismatic, makes good eye contact, and is a great listener. To top it off, he's quite handsome."

"Even with that big hair?"

She grinned. "Remember, I'm from Texas."

"Did you mention J.J.?"

Leslie nodded. "But I waited until I'd already spent much of the day with the senator. Claypool owns an immense farming operation, and we must have seen every acre." She bent over and untied her muddy boots. I pried them from her feet.

"Any good photos?"

Leslie looked up, her eyes sparkling. "I never would have expected it, but I got some outstanding shots."

My eyebrows arched. "In that flat country?"

"The rice fields are so lush and green," she said, "with levees meandering across the land just begging to be photographed."

"Too bad you didn't get to see them from the air."

"But I did! Once I'd spent the morning shooting his fields from the ground, he took me to his private airstrip and told the pilot to do whatever I wanted."

"Are you kidding? After what you said the other day?"

Wearing a dimple-to-dimple smile, Leslie shook her head. "I spent two hours strapped inside a crop duster. Other than throwing up twice, it's among the best afternoons I've ever had. Professionally, that is," she said, patting my knee.

"Why don't I fix supper and you can fill in the details."

Leslie stretched and twisted her body from side to side, her arms extended. "What I need is a hot bath."

"Let me help." I pulled her from the chair and led the way upstairs. While Leslie undressed in the bedroom, I started the water, remembering to add her favorite vanilla-scented bubble bath.

When I returned with a bottle of Champagne and a pair of flutes, Leslie lay in the tub, her eyes shut, with the foamy water lapping at her breasts. We'd dated for well over half a year and lived together for better than a month, but I still found myself mesmerized by her body—and the self-assured way she moved with and without her clothes. Maybe it was the artist in her. Or, as she put it, the pervert in me.

Her eyes peeked open. "Is this standard room service?"

"You've had a busy day," I said, handing her a flute. "Let's hear the full story." I plopped down on the mat beside the tub.

"God, this water feels good." She took a sip of Champagne and nodded. "I arrived at Claypool's headquarters in downtown Stuttgart at ten o'clock. His office could pass for an interior decorator's showroom, bursting with antiques."

"Did you ask about them?"

196

"Not 'til much later. We spent a couple of hours in his truck touring the property, and I recorded enough shots to fill two memory sticks." She reached for her flute and took another drink of Champagne. "We then went to a ramshackle old general store out in the middle of nowhere for lunch."

"Let me guess. Fried catfish."

"With French fries, hush puppies, onion rings, and, of course, fried green tomatoes. Oh, and there were fried peach pies for dessert."

"No wonder you got sick."

"It was the flying. Claypool's pilot handled his plane like an airborne sports car. Made all those Disney rides seem tame."

"How old was he?"

"Young, and real cute," she said with a wink. "Maybe twenty-five."

"That sounds about right. You never meet an old crop-duster."

Leslie splashed some water at me. "After I got aerials of the rice fields, he flew us over enormous fish farms, an awesome swamp filled with cypress trees, and towering grain elevators. I can't wait to begin downloading the images."

I refilled our flutes. "Back to the esteemed Senator Claypool. What did you learn?"

"The pilot drove me to the senator's office following the flight. After a bit of small talk, I spent a few minutes examining a piece or two of Claypool's furniture and, at some point, said a friend of mine in Little Rock collects similar items. That got his attention."

She sipped her Champagne and leaned forward, the top half of her body emerging from the bubbles as she added hot water to the tub.

"Have I mentioned how beautiful you are?"

She reached for my hand and pulled it against her warm, damp breast. I felt her heartbeat, and then her nipple hardening under my touch as she bent toward me and our lips met.

"You make me feel pretty," she said, lifting my hand and kissing my palm. "Now, where were we?"

"Claypool, I think."

"When I dropped J.J.'s name, Claypool's eyes widened and he clapped his hands like a kid. He said, and this is a quote, 'I've known your lazy-assed professor friend for years,' and next recited their history."

"He claims they're friends?"

Leslie's head bobbed up and down. "When I told him I figured they might be rivals, Claypool slapped his knee and cackled."

"Was he putting you on?"

"I thought so, at first. But the good senator marched to a bank of beautiful antique filing cabinets and rummaged around for a moment before pulling out a folder."

"Paperwork?"

"Claypool said he and J.J. have been exchanging letters for years, and he's saved a copy of them all."

"That sounds weird. Is he a pack rat?"

"My initial reaction, too. But according to Claypool, he's kept a complete record of every piece of correspondence since his very first political campaign. At some point, he hopes to donate his 'papers,' as he called them, to a university archive."

"Has he earned a place in history?"

"The senator told me in no uncertain terms he plans to seek higher office. His political career, at least in his mind, is nowhere near its peak."

That news made me shiver. "That file you noted earlier. Could it have been bogus?"

"Why don't you take a peek at it? It's downstairs in my duffel."

My chin dropped. "He let you take it?"

"Why not?" Leslie batted her eyelids at me. "We're close friends now."

My chin remained on my chest.

"Actually, I didn't bring the originals. He had his secretary make me a copy of the entire file."

Half a minute later, I returned with the manila folder, leafing through the half-inch-thick stack of papers. The correspondence had been arranged in sequence, with the most recent items on top. I glanced at the first piece. Dated May 7, it was a response from Claypool to a May 3 letter from J.J.

"Have you examined this?"

"I didn't have time," she said. "But Claypool acknowledged that he'd written J.J. a few weeks ago. It seems J.J. accused the good senator of unfairly bidding up the price on an antique couch."

Typed on his official Senate stationery, Claypool's full-page reply made me chuckle, its caustic comments including a reference to J.J.'s "professorial poverty" and an offer to purchase his Jaguar should J.J. suffer any more "auction atrocities." At first, I wondered why I hadn't seen it in J.J.'s mail, but then noticed it had been sent to his campus address.

Watching me read J.J.'s original letter with amusement, Leslie demanded I share it aloud. Equally inflammatory, it pronounced Claypool as premier of the state's Pompadourian Party, and, apparently referring to the same newspaper photograph I'd seen at the Hillcrest Antique Gallery, blamed Claypool's bulging veins on excessive exposure to hairspray.

"These are great," I said. "Competitive insults."

"Claypool claimed that they're good buddies, even trading antiques on occasion."

"What about that auction?"

"He laughed and admitted to having had some fun at J.J.'s expense, describing it as repayment for a similar stunt pulled by our professor friend," Leslie said. "Claypool showed me a piece that, according to him, is a better example than the one J.J. bought."

I leafed through the file. The letters from J.J. appeared genuine, their sloppy signatures consistent with ones I'd seen in the past.

"What's your opinion?" Leslie asked.

"I'm surprised. But this," I said, lifting the file, "seems authentic, and it's not too far-fetched to envision J.J. and Claypool having this kind of friendship." I paused for a moment, and then asked, "Did you tell him J.J. is missing?"

Leslie shook her head. "I didn't feel comfortable doing that. But I promised to pass along his regards next time I saw J.J."

"So, where does this leave us?"

Leslie gave me a quick inspection. "It looks like you need to bathe."

Having spent a sweltering afternoon pushing the fertilizer spreader, I couldn't argue with her. "I'll hit the shower," I said, rising to my feet.

"There's room here." She scooted to one end of the tub. "If you don't mind sharing my water."

I didn't mind at all.

~ TWENTY-SEVEN ~

When we finally got around to having dinner, I told Leslie of my conversations earlier in the day with Max Alloway and Jeremy Newcastle. However, I opted to avoid any reference to the unexpected visit by Catfish McCulloch and his strange associate.

"Alloway sounds like a pig," was her initial reaction, and I didn't try to dissuade her. "I wish you hadn't mentioned his girlfriend. I'll worry about her now."

I shared Leslie's concern, but didn't know what we could do. "My guess is that Alloway is not involved in J.J.'s disappearance," I said. "Unless I'm badly mistaken, he's still looking for revenge. Why else would he have gone to the trouble of asking for Newcastle's help?"

"It could be that he's several moves ahead of us, much like a grandmaster in a chess match," Leslie said, reaching for the salad. "Maybe Alloway is establishing a line of defense to keep himself off any list of suspects."

I remembered Newcastle's comment regarding Alloway's intelligence. And his suggestion that we not underestimate him. I swallowed hard.

"Back to Claypool," Leslie said. "I think we can rule him out. He seemed genuine to me. Or else he's an awfully good actor."

"But isn't that a requirement for any successful politician?"

We cleared the table, then adjourned to our favorite sofa, where Leslie stretched out, her head in my lap. I ran my fingers through her hair, massaging her neck.

"Today is the first of June," she said. "We last saw J.J. one month ago. What do we do now?"

I still couldn't believe our carefree cookout in the backyard had occurred just weeks earlier. I felt as if my life had been turned upside-down in the interim.

"Maybe Summer's had luck with Dr. Tillman," I said. "Have you heard anything from her?"

"Tried calling over the weekend, but had no luck. I left a message on her phone."

Moments later, the telephone rang. Leslie hopped from the couch and answered it in the kitchen.

"It's for you. A woman, but I didn't recognize the voice. She sounds pretty young," she added with a wink.

I lifted the receiver, expecting a voice from the office. "This is Randy."

"Mr. Lassiter. This is Beth Anthony." After a brief pause, she continued, "We met at Max Alloway's home earlier today."

"Hello again," I said. "What can I do for you?" Maybe she had some secrets to share, I thought, as my pulse quickened.

"First, I want to apologize. Max treated you rudely."

"Thanks, but there's no need to apologize. I arrived unannounced, and he had a right to be testy." I tried hard to be kind.

"I hope you'll forgive him. It's just he has this terrible temper and …" Her voice trailed off. "That's the way Max is. Unfortunately."

"It's nice of you to call," I said. I hoped there'd be more to it than an apology. Seconds passed.

"As for the lawsuit he threatened, I wouldn't spend much time worrying over it."

"Why's that?"

"Max talks big, but seldom follows through. In the last few months, he's mentioned plans to sue a fast-food place over hot coffee, a car dealer for warranty problems, and so on. His older sister is a paralegal, and Max has a fixation on suing folks, always dreaming of a windfall."

"So, you think this deal involving Dr. Newell will blow over?"

202

"He hadn't said anything about it for days. Not until you showed up."

"Maybe he'll let it drop," I said, wondering how he'd react to the letter from Newcastle. Or maybe Alloway had accomplished exactly what he had set out to do.

"I've got to go. Max will be returning soon."

"Ms. Anthony, there's one more thing."

"Yes?" She sounded hesitant.

"Have you ever considered working as a model?"

The line was silent for a couple of seconds. "Is this a joke?"

"We hire models all the time and so do the other advertising agencies in town. I think you should give it a try. It's interesting work and it pays well."

She sighed. "I wouldn't know how to get started."

"First thing tomorrow, give this lady a call." I gave her the name and phone number of the owner of Little Rock's leading talent agency. "She'll treat you right."

There was a moment's pause. "I'm just not sure—"

"I work with her on a regular basis," I said, interrupting. "I'll let her know you'll be in touch."

There was another pause, this one a bit longer. "Okay," she said. "I'll do it."

"This might be just what you need to get out on your own." I knew it was meddling, but said it anyway. At least I'd feel better.

After a quick "Thanks," the line went dead.

"Alloway's girlfriend," I said, returning to my spot on the couch. "She called to apologize for his brutish behavior."

"It sounds like she's much better than he deserves."

"But aren't you all?" I bent over and kissed her cheek. "She also said Alloway often talks big and she doubted if he'd follow through with the lawsuit."

Leslie's eyes met mine, and then she glanced at her watch. "Speaking of following through, why don't I try Summer again?" She swung her legs to the floor before giving me a peck on the lips. "I'll be right back."

A short time later she returned, shrugging her shoulders. "Still no answer. Maybe she's taking an extended weekend. Yesterday, after all, was a holiday."

* * *

In the kitchen the next morning, I emulated Leslie's spartan breakfast routine, eating a toasted bagel without cream cheese or any topping. Muttering over this sacrifice, I opened the iPad to read the *Arkansas Democrat-Gazette*. On the front page, beneath the fold, ran a headline grabbing my attention: "Grocery Tycoon Makes UA Little Rock Donation." The subhead read, "Benton Tillman Gives \$25 Million to Build Center for Excellence." A large color photo showed Tillman, the governor, and the university chancellor displaying one of those oversized checks prepared for such occasions. Tillman, true to form, was tieless but wore an ill-fitting sport coat someone had probably loaned him seconds before the picture was snapped. The photographer had arranged the shot so Tillman's long gray ponytail couldn't be seen.

Padding around in a short, thin robe that excelled at diverting my attention, Leslie saw me studying the article. "What's up?"

"Interesting news. Dr. Tillman's father has contributed a ton of money to build a think tank on the UA Little Rock campus."

She stood behind me, rubbing my shoulders. "Any reference to her?" Leslie's hands were like magic.

I flipped the paper to page 4A where the story continued. "Near the end," I said. "It notes that his daughter is on the faculty in the Biology Department."

About to close the paper, I glanced back to the article's last paragraph. According to reliable sources, Dr. Rankin Campbell, dean of the College of Arts and Sciences, had first broached the idea to Tillman several years earlier and was the odds-on favorite to be named director of the new center. Despite Leslie's efforts, I felt my muscles tighten.

~ TWENTY-EIGHT ~

Leslie phoned me at the office mid-morning. "Randy, I'm worried. I've had no luck contacting Summer."

"Have you tried calling her again?"

"That's just it. When I've dialed the number, Summer has never answered. Her voice mailbox was full so I couldn't leave a message."

I thought about it for a moment. "I'm not sure about our next step."

"Let's run by her apartment."

"Do you know where she lives?" I asked.

"Somewhere on the city's west side. I thought you had her address."

"All she gave me was a slip of paper with her phone number." I had left it hanging near the phone on the refrigerator, held up by a Razorback magnet.

"That may be a problem."

"Let me work on this a bit, and I'll call you back," I said. "I guess you're at home?"

"I'm going to take a CD by the camera shop and print some enlargements from the Stuttgart trip to send to Senator Claypool. Later, I'll shoot some scenes downtown in the River District. I should be home by noon."

While signing a stack of work orders, I had an inspiration. Shoving the paperwork aside, I called Vaughn Gregory, another fellow Rotarian and longtime Southwestern Bell employee. Director of the company's human resources division, he had contacts not just in his organization but throughout the telecommunications field.

"Morning, Vaughn. It's Randy Lassiter."

"Can you believe how awful yesterday's speaker was?" he asked. "Why don't you bring back that lovologist or whatever she was? Now, that was a *fine* Rotary program."

"I might consider it, if you can do me a small favor."

"Your timing is bad," he said, a hint of weariness in his voice. "I'm leaving town in a couple of hours for the rest of the week, but I'll give it a shot. What do you need?"

"I've misplaced the mailing address for a woman named Summer Preston. She's done some work for me and I need to drop her a note." It wasn't far from the truth.

"This is on the up-and-up, right? No tricks, nothing unethical?"

"You can trust me. Remember, I'm in advertising."

Vaughn mumbled something unintelligible but called back ten minutes later. "7400 Green Mountain Drive," he said in a rush. "And you need to consider taking over our Rotary programs."

Once the work order pile had disappeared, I drafted a couple of letters, then spent half an hour responding to three dozen e-mails. One, marked "urgent," came from Clifford, and I debated opening it. But curiosity won out. I scrolled through it, learning that he had given up—for the time being, at least—on the idea of writing a book. Planning to concentrate on a script for a "spell-binding screenplay revolving around displaced trapeze artists," he promised to keep me posted. "Just imagine the sets!" he had written. I hit the delete button.

Close to twelve, I gave Leslie a call.

"Any luck?" she asked.

"I've got an address. Why don't we grab a bite to eat, and then check it out?"

After picking up Leslie at the house, I drove us to the city's western suburbs, muttering as we snaked through the thick noon hour traffic. The city resembled Dallas more each day. We'd stopped at a red light when Leslie pointed out my window. "I believe that young man is trying to get your attention."

I glanced through the glass to my left. Max Alloway straddled a huge motorcycle in the adjacent lane, sitting behind one of the biggest, dirtiest men I'd ever seen. Not six feet away, he mouthed something I didn't understand. When I failed to respond, Alloway sneered and then flipped me off with a defiant wave of his right hand. The light changed and the cycle surged ahead, its roar rattling the cab of my truck.

"Close friend?" Leslie asked.

"Max Alloway."

"I wouldn't want to meet his driver in a dark alley."

I'd thought the same thing, thanking the gods that his buddy hadn't been at the mobile home yesterday.

A few blocks later we arrived at Whole Foods Market, a combination organic deli/grocery. While we munched on veggie sushi and fresh blueberries, Leslie filled me in on her morning, excited that the first batch of her rice field shots looked good. The magazine had bumped the Stuttgart story up an issue, and her agent was champing at the bit for photos.

"Back to the Alloway character," she said.

"J.J. should have left him under a rock in west Texas."

"He frightens me. Something about his eyes isn't right."

I nodded, again remembering Jeremy Newcastle's closing comments regarding his would-be client.

Following lunch, we found Green Mountain Drive. As we searched for Summer's address, we passed one uninspiring apartment complex after another, the monotonous string interrupted by the occasional convenience store, tanning salon, or liquor store. Strip development at its best. Or worst.

"Here it is," Leslie said, pointing to a sign reading: *Green Ridge Apartments, 7400 Green Mountain Drive*. I turned into the entrance. "What's the apartment number?" she asked.

"Damn! Vaughn didn't say." From the looks of things, we'd entered a massive compound, easily containing several hundred units.

"Can you give him another call?"

I shook my head. "He's on his way out of town."

Leslie was in no mood to concede defeat. "Let's find the manager. He'll know where she lives."

When we walked into the office, an older man sat behind the counter, his glassy eyes glued to a TV mounted on the opposite wall. I looked at the screen and saw a couple of folks in hospital garb groping one another. Without even glancing at us, he said, "Sorry. No vacancies."

"We're looking for Summer Preston," I said. "One of your tenants."

"What's the number?"

Leslie hadn't finished with her "I can't remember—" when the man said, "I'm not allowed to give out personal information." He almost made an effort at eye contact. "It's a legal thing, you know. Privacy." His head swiveled back to the television. One of the doctors ripped off his lab coat, exposing a hairy chest, as the show broke—thankfully—for a commercial.

Grumbling, I turned toward the door, but Leslie slammed her fist on the countertop. "Look here," she said, her voice icy. "I haven't been able to reach my sister for days and it's worrying me to death. I drove all the way from Hot Springs and I'm not leaving until you get off your lazy butt and help us. What's your name? I'm going to write the owners." She opened her purse and found a pen and notepad.

The old man muted the soap opera and sprang to his feet. "No need to get all fired up," he said, then spat a stream of tobacco into a nasty paper cup. "Who are you looking for again?" *P. Boykin* was stitched above his shirt pocket. I hid a smile as Leslie wrote his name in large letters across her paper, eyeing the embroidery on his shirt a time or two to make her point.

"Summer Preston," she said, underlining her writing.

The manager flipped through a large ledger and worked his fingers down the page. "I'll need proof you're related," he said, glancing back to Leslie.

208

I expected another tirade, but she surprised me. "Here's my driver's license," she said, her voice light and cheery. "As you might expect, we have different last names." While Boykin studied her license, Leslie again reached into her purse and scrolled through her cell phone. "Here's a picture of Summer and me from my birthday party." She showed him the photo I'd taken at our house last week when they'd worn matching earrings. I hadn't given it any thought, but supposed they could pass for sisters. Well, maybe stepsisters.

"That'll do," he said, returning his eyes to the ledger. "Ms. Preston's in Building C, apartment 16. But she's behind in her rent. It was due yesterday. On the first." His "Got-cha" expression annoyed me.

"How much does she owe?" I asked.

"Rent's $1,000 a month." He spat into his cup.

I searched through my wallet and found the cash I'd won at Tunica a few days earlier. "Here's $500," I said. "That'll cover the next two weeks." I handed it to him, and Leslie and I rocked on our heels while he filled out his paperwork.

"I haven't heard from her in days, and she hasn't returned my calls," Leslie said with a sniff. "I got so flustered I couldn't even remember her apartment number."

The old-timer gave me a receipt, then grabbed his key ring. "Let's go check on sis." We trailed him out the door to the curb, where he settled into a golf cart sporting a faded *Green Ridge Apartments* decal. "You'll have to follow," he said. "Another one of those lawyer matters."

We climbed into the pickup and fell in behind the cart as it crept up a steep incline. If there ever had been a green ridge on the property, it was either covered by asphalt or buried under an ugly edifice.

"You displayed a lot of patience back there," I said. "I figured you were ready to slug him."

"I remembered some advice my grandmother passed along to Mom years ago. 'Never smack a man who's chewing tobacco.'"

We parked at the base of Building C. Apartment 16 was on the second floor, with a handful of flyers scattered at bottom of the door.

"Looks like she's out of town," said our escort. He knocked, waited a short time, then rapped again before slipping his passkey into the lock and twisting the knob. "Anybody home?" he asked, pushing the door open.

Other than the steady hum of the air conditioner, the place was quiet. Boykin and I waited in the cozy living room while Leslie made a quick tour of the apartment.

"She's not here." Leslie dropped her purse on the couch, then faced the manager, her lower lip quivering. "Thanks," she said, touching him on the shoulder and subtly directing him toward the door. She sniffed again, then dabbed her eyes with a tissue. "I need a couple of minutes to freshen up. We'll lock her apartment when we leave."

Boykin hesitated for a moment before giving her a nod and a gentle pat on the back. "Maybe she's taking a long weekend." He shuffled down the stairs, then stepped into the cart, eager to return to his televised melodrama.

"What other hidden talents do you possess?"

"Did I overdo it?"

"Not at all. You're just a sensitive young woman concerned about her missing sibling."

We spent half an hour examining every nook and cranny of Summer's apartment. With the exception of a small tuna steak that I flushed down the disposal, the food in the refrigerator seemed fresh, no big surprise since we'd seen her not quite a week earlier. J.J.'s surviving fish swam around vigorously, darting in and out for the flakes I crumbled over the small aquarium. And her plants on the balcony appeared healthy, several displaying robust new shoots.

Summer's bed was made, and her bedroom closet bulged with outfits and shoes. Two guitar cases leaned against the wall. Leslie opened the dresser drawers and found what she expected—the usual assortment of jewelry, socks, scarves, and undies. A bookcase held biographies and best sellers and a CD player with a good selection of discs. A collection of sheet music covered the top shelf.

In the spare bedroom, a laptop sat on a large desk, its starburst screensaver exploding across the monitor in a random pattern. When Leslie tapped the "enter" button, a recipe for broiled tuna sprang to the screen. That explains the fish, I thought. Leslie closed the program, then opened the computer's main menu. A quick scroll through Summer's word-processing directory revealed no obvious red flags, and her electronic calendar showed nothing out of the ordinary, at least not to our eyes.

"Too bad Uncle Booker's not here," I said. "He might find something useful in her files."

Three or four textbooks were stacked at the edge of the desk along with a pile of manila folders, no doubt materials for her college classes. The single desk drawer yielded canceled checks, current bills, stationery, and a key.

"Looks like a spare for the apartment," Leslie said, tossing it to me. "Booker may be able to help after all."

The room's closet held Summer's winter clothes, jackets and sweaters for the most part, plus a matched set of luggage. A camera bag, two jigsaw puzzles, and a Parcheesi game sat on the top shelf.

Leslie gasped as she entered the bathroom. "There must be $2,000 worth of cosmetics in here." Peering over her shoulder, I saw bottle after bottle of skin cream, dozens of eye shadows, and at least ten tubes of mascara. Opening a drawer of the vanity, Leslie discovered Summer's stash of nail polish, every shade imaginable. I watched from the hall as she searched the medicine cabinet. It held no surprises, just routine over-the-counter remedies and a single prescription, apparently an allergy treatment. Leslie grabbed a small plastic container. "This is interesting," she said. "Her contact lens case. And it's empty." I heard a low whistle, then Leslie said, "Bingo. Birth control pills." She gave me an anxious look. "She wouldn't have left these if she went on a trip."

When we returned to the living room, I examined a framed photograph of J.J. and Summer. Standing in front of the dock at

Gaston's White River Resort, they displayed huge smiles, holding a stringer of rainbow trout that would have made Izaak Walton proud. A small heap of similar photos, including one taken at Oaklawn, the thoroughbred track and casino complex in Hot Springs, lay on the coffee table.

"What's missing?" I asked. "Besides Summer?"

"Her purse, for one thing. I haven't seen a wallet or checkbook."

I spotted a small notepad on the kitchen counter next to a cell phone charger. What appeared to be a telephone number had been written on the top sheet. I tore it from the pad and handed it to Leslie.

"It might be worth checking out," I said.

While Leslie tested the spare key and then locked Summer's door, I stepped across the landing and knocked on the door for Apartment 15. No one answered.

As we walked to the truck, Leslie glanced over the parking lot. "I don't see her car. And except for the spare to her apartment, there weren't any keys upstairs."

We left Summer's neighborhood, if that suburban hodgepodge could be called one, and drove toward our house via the cross-town expressway. When I flipped on the turn signal for our usual exit, Leslie touched my elbow. "Let's keep going," she said.

"Any particular destination?"

Leslie lifted her eyebrows. "The airport."

"Are you thinking her car might be near J.J.'s?"

"My grandmother had another saying. 'When times are crazy,' she said, 'go with your intuition.'"

Ten minutes later, we took the airport exit.

"This is a long shot. All I remember is that she drives a compact."

"A Honda Civic," Leslie said. "Sort of silver."

"It'll have UA Little Rock parking stickers. Probably not more than 75 of them in the city."

"With brand-new Pirelli tires?"

I wheeled into the entrance to Security Parking, then looked to my companion. "And how do you know that?"

She gave me a tired smile. "I think you were dealing with the pizza guy the other evening when Summer told me she'd spent her vacation money on a set of tires. She couldn't afford to go to Europe, so she bought Italian tires."

We began at the back of the lot. J.J.'s Jaguar sat at the same place, dustier than ever. Searching row by row, we spent the next few minutes looking for Civics. We must have seen 15 or so resembling Summer's. After a couple of false alarms, we made the final turn. Another 10 or 12 vehicles and we'd be done.

And then Leslie gasped. Tucked between a Chevrolet Suburban and a top-heavy customized van sat a small silver Honda Civic. I stopped the truck, and we walked toward the car slowly and quietly, as if it might be sleeping. With UA Little Rock parking permits adorning both bumpers and the trendy imported tires still showing a bluish tint on the whitewalls, it seemed to be Summer Preston's car.

Leslie squeezed my shoulder. "Look in the back," she whispered.

In the middle of the rear seat was the photo book Leslie had loaned our new friend.

~ TWENTY-NINE ~

When we returned home, Leslie stepped from the truck, walked around to my open window, and bent toward me. Her face mere inches away, she looked deep into my eyes. "I'm glad we did this," she said. "But this puzzle just seems to get more confusing by the day."

"We'll find some answers." I reached out and ran my fingers through her hair. "Sooner or later, we'll get to the bottom of J.J.'s disappearance."

She leaned forward and planted a lingering kiss on my lips. When we broke apart, her eyes were moist. "You're not going to vanish, too, are you?"

"I have honeymoon duties yet to fulfill," I said with a wink.

She pinched my cheek and then blew me another kiss as she walked to the front porch. I waved, slipped the pickup into gear, and returned to work as the first large drops of an afternoon thunderstorm pelted the windshield.

I'd been away from the office less than three hours, but things had gone to hell. Lightning had struck a nearby electrical transformer, knocking the fax machine out of commission. To make matters worse, every terminal in our computer network refused to respond, each static screen indicating server problems. Booker had already been summoned, and he strolled in moments after I arrived.

He stuck his small blond head into my office. "Regarding those pecuniary benefits we were negotiating—"

214

"Get us back in operation within the hour and they're yours."

"Retroactive?"

"To the first of last month."

"Thank you, oh great benevolent one." He started to genuflect, but I motioned him into the room.

"J.J.'s girlfriend has a laptop in her apartment," I said, handing him the key and a slip of paper with Summer's complete address. "Would you see if it contains anything useful?"

His lips pursed, Booker took his time slipping the key into a pocket of his tight canary yellow linen slacks. I wondered over the significance of the new color. Maybe it had something to do with his hair. "Are you prepared to handle the repercussions?" he asked.

"I'm not sure I follow."

"Breaking and entering commands a rather sizable bond, I dare say. Not to mention the negative publicity Lassiter & Associates would accrue upon my arrest."

Now I understood. "Ms. Preston seems to have vanished, too," I said, shrugging. "Just like J.J. You might as well check to see if she'd booked an outbound flight."

He ran a silk handkerchief across his pale brow. "What a ghastly contagion."

"And while you're at it, see what you can uncover on a local character named Max Alloway."

"Any particular starting point?"

"Why don't you begin with the police department."

As Booker left, my assistant handed me a wad of phone messages, three of them marked "urgent." The first two, one from my insurance agent and the other from a pesky magazine representative, didn't generate any excitement, but the third message, a call from Catfish McCulloch, raised my eyebrows. I recognized it as his cellular number and gave him a ring.

"Afternoon, Catfish. Randy Lassiter returning your call."

"Sorry for the bother," he said, "but DuChamps has phoned me a couple of times regarding the radio show. Have you confirmed it yet?"

"I've got a verbal commitment and should have a written agreement with complete details before the week's done."

"Great! DuChamps will be all smiles."

I had my doubts about that. "Tell him it'll be on a Friday morning, the first day of your show, during what we call 'drive time.' I'll send more information soon."

Seconds after I hung up, the telephone rang. It was Leslie.

"The other day Summer mentioned she has a sister. Maybe we should try contacting her. The real one," she added with a nervous laugh.

That would be easier said than done. We didn't even know where she lived. And how do you tell a woman that her sister is missing, I asked myself.

"Are you still there, Randy?"

"Just lost in thought," I said, "wondering how we'll track her down. Maybe Summer's ex-husband will help. I'll try phoning him." I couldn't remember his name, only recalling that he was a stockbroker. And the city seemed to be full of them.

"Let me know what you discover," she said, signing off.

My efficient assistant, who'd parked herself near the door, darted in and dropped a stack of folders on the desk. "These have to be signed and placed in today's mail," she said, glancing at her watch. I got the message and grabbed my pen.

Toward the end of the day, once the New York markets had closed, I phoned my broker. "I'm trying to recall the name of a guy I met several years ago," I said. "He's in the securities business, belongs to the chamber, is in his late thirties, and got divorced within the past year."

Wyatt, my broker friend, laughed. "You could be describing nearly any of us."

"Right now, he's seeing a sweet young thing."

"Not much help."

"I can't guarantee this, but his first name may be Bart or Brett or something like that," I said, trying to recall the initial conversation I'd had with Summer days ago.

216

"I think I know your man," Wyatt said. "Hang on a bit while I think." The pause continued for ten, maybe twenty seconds. "He used to work for Schwab." There was another short delay. "His name's Etheridge. Brett Etheridge. I don't know where he's based now."

"Thanks. I can take it from there."

"Tyson took a dip today. I think it'll bounce back. Interested?"

Caught once before between rising grain prices and a massive product recall, I kept my distance from poultry stocks. "How'd Apple do?"

"Up another point and a half. You should've bought a month ago." That's what I had proposed at the time, but Wyatt had talked me out of it.

I mumbled a hurried good-bye and called the Arkansas Securities Commission. Within minutes I had Brett Etheridge's business number.

He answered with a stern, no nonsense voice. "Etheridge here." He sounded breathless, like I'd caught him dashing from his office. If he had another date with the young lady that we'd seen him with at the Arkansas Rep a few days earlier, I could understand.

"Brett," I said, "Randy Lassiter. We've met a time or two at chamber events."

There was a moment's hesitation, and I could visualize him trying to place my name. "Yeah, Randy, I remember. You're in advertising. What can I do for you?"

"This is a long story and I suspect you don't want to hear it. I need to talk with Summer's sister and thought you might be able to help."

"Shit." His voice hardened. "Why don't you call her? The bitch."

"It's an emergency, and Summer's not around."

"Her kid sister is Libby. She and her worthless husband Alex live in Spokane. Last name's Janzaruk." He spelled it for me and hung up, not waiting for thanks and not interested in details. I suspected Summer had no regrets about splitting the sheets.

I phoned Leslie and shared what I'd learned during my unpleasant exchange with Etheridge.

"We haven't even considered him," she said after a pause. "Do you think he could be involved in whatever's going on? Maybe he blamed their split on J.J."

Leslie had a point; Etheridge radiated intense hostility over the phone. "Although Summer described it as a nasty separation and divorce," I said, "she never implied Etheridge was still lurking in the background. But she did say her former husband had a volatile temper. And she mentioned that the financial settlement she received had upset him. I believe apoplectic was the word she used."

"First things first," Leslie said with a sigh. "I'll call Spokane and check with Summer's sister."

* * *

When I got home from work, Leslie met me at the door, shaking her head. "Summer's sister wasn't much help. She said they aren't close, sometimes going months between conversations."

"So, she's not worried that we can't find Summer?"

"Not at all. It seems Summer's gone to Cancun, the Florida Keys, and Canada without telling Libby until later. Usually much later."

"Another dead end," I muttered.

"But we did get this in today's mail." Leslie handed me a small white envelope, our names and address handwritten in fine but unfamiliar penmanship.

On embossed stationery, the message read:

Saturday, May 29

Dear Leslie & Randy —
Thanks for sharing your evening with me. I really enjoyed our visit, and hope we can get together again soon. And Leslie, if you ever need someone to lug camera gear around, give me a call!
Summer
p.s. — I've been invited to Dr. Tillman's house this afternoon. I'll keep you posted. And good luck with Alloway and Claypool.

218

"Damn!" I re-read the note.

"What's our next move?"

"Maybe it's time to pay Dr. Mackie Tillman a visit."

Following a quiet supper, we played an uninspired game of Scrabble. Leslie drubbed me, using the last of her letters to spell ZERO, across a **TRIPLE WORD SCORE** no less, while I got stuck with the Q and K tiles. Before going to bed, we watched the late news. Benton Tillman's $25 million donation to UA Little Rock was the lead story on all three stations. I'm not sure I ever went to sleep.

~ THIRTY ~

While I read the newspaper over breakfast, Leslie nibbled on a blueberry muffin and reviewed the file I'd assembled on UA Little Rock's Biology Department. It included information that I'd downloaded from the Internet, the material Summer had left with us, and the two telephone numbers Dr. Ackerman had given me.

"Here's something I hadn't noticed," she said.

I set the sports section aside and looked up.

"Dr. Mackenzie Tillman is on the board of the Arkansas Country Dance Society. Perhaps this organization would present the perfect opportunity for me to make some new friends, to include a certain university professor."

Leslie had taken dance lessons from her toddler days through college, a practice no doubt contributing to her elegant posture and grace. She'd hinted earlier that her weekly aerobics classes weren't providing enough exercise.

"It's worth a try," I said as I carried our dishes to the kitchen. "You think she's involved?"

"Right now, I don't have any better ideas."

Refilling my coffee, I heard Leslie gasp. "Randy! Can you bring me my purse? It's on the counter."

After tearing through her handbag, she found the piece of paper we'd retrieved from Summer's apartment. She then fumbled through the material in her lap and showed me the telephone number Dr. Ackerman had provided for Mackie Tillman. "That number we discovered on the notepad in Summer's kitchen. It's Tillman's," she said, her eyes wide. "Summer must have placed a call to Dr. Mackenzie Tillman's house."

My pulse quickened, and not because of the coffee. "Are you sure?"

Leslie held both pieces of paper in front of me. The numbers were identical.

* * *

I spent the first half hour at the office parked in front of my computer keyboard. Prior to dealing with my e-mail inbox, I sent Booker an e-mail and asked him to set his electronic sleuths on Dr. Mackenzie Tillman in UA Little Rock's Biology Department. I mentioned it could be important.

Next, I reviewed a long list of incoming messages. The two from Clifford I ignored. Most of the rest were replies to last week's poll regarding the proposal to take on the Little Rock Zoo as the agency's newest pro bono account. The vast majority of the staff supported the idea, and several with youngsters at home were enthusiastic with their reactions. Only two offered negative comments. One, a veteran but lazy media buyer, felt we'd be unable to give the account proper attention. The second objection came from Uncle Booker, who aired his vehement opposition to cages and confinements of any sort. He sent a lengthy but eloquent response, quoting Chinese philosophers, American transcendentalists, and three or four contemporary but obscure authorities. I penned a kind reply, suggesting that if animals had to be confined in a zoo, perhaps our fundraising efforts would make them more comfortable.

After reporting the poll results via return e-mail, I wrote a letter to Constance Engstrom and invited her to suggest some dates so we could sign a formal agreement between Lassiter & Associates and the Little Rock Zoo. I asked my assistant to draft a media release describing the new partnership. Everybody needs a periodic pat on the back, even if you have to apply it yourself.

I'd reserved the next hour for Abigail Ahart, my broadcast producer. For well over a year, she'd lobbied for a fully equipped audio-visual conference suite, stressing its potential for presentations and client consultations. Following her latest subtle reminder, I'd asked Abbie to prepare ballpark figures on the costs.

"Congratulations on those Merchants Bank spots," I said as she pulled a chair near my desk. The bank's marketing director had approved all three television commercials, and had then asked us to produce another series in the same vein for a fall campaign.

"Thanks for coming to Dallas," she said. "Your support means a lot."

"How many hours did you spend in the editing room?"

She smiled and patted me on the shoulder. "You don't want to know."

I suspected she was right. "Fill me in on this conference center idea. Can we afford it?"

Always organized, Abbie opened a thick file and handed me a packet. She suggested that we convert two seldom used offices into a 20-by-30 foot "war room," with a large high-definition television monitor, state-of-the-art sound system, and video-conferencing capability, along with an assortment of related equipment and furnishings. Working through the proposal point by point, she made a strong case. Moving walls and putting in new carpet and installing canned lights in an acoustic ceiling would be relatively inexpensive, she said. The real cost would be the electronic gadgetry.

"How much?"

"Close to $150,000 altogether." I grimaced, but she never missed a beat, handing me another sheet of paper. "It'll pay for itself in five years max," she said. "My guess is three. Booker helped with these estimates."

I examined their figures, shocked at how much we'd spent in recent years on room and equipment rentals. She'd also projected expenses 18 months into the future. The combined total was staggering.

"We build this," she said, "and I'll guarantee one new major client a year. No other agency in town has similar capabilities." She clenched her jaw.

"How soon can we get an architect?"

Peeking at her watch, Abbie broke into a big grin. "It'll take an hour at least."

The lawyer from the Cleveland broadcast conglomerate had phoned during my meeting with Abbie. We'd been playing telephone tag for what seemed like a week. When I dialed her number, I learned that she'd left for the day. A court appearance, her assistant said. Convinced it had something to do with closing on the KACN property, I searched my desk for the diminishing supply of Rolaids.

Leslie called a little after eleven. "The rice field images turned out great," she said. "I sent an electronic file to *Progressive Farmer* and also forwarded a selection to my stock agency in New York. And I got the prints for Senator Claypool in the mail."

"Shall I spring for lunch to celebrate?"

"Sure," she said. "And I'll share some other interesting news."

We agreed to meet at Doe's Eat Place, a popular dining establishment a few blocks from my office. Located midway between the State Capitol and downtown, it occupies the bottom floor of a long, skinny two-story brick building dating from the 1920s. The interior is a bit more contemporary, mid-to-late 1940s, although the faded prints and pictures hanging from the discolored walls can't be pinned to any particular period. With its smoke-stained ceiling, chipped black-and-white tile floors, and antiquated restrooms, Doe's is a throwback to another era. The same holds true for its menu. Specializing in carnivore cuisine, the cooks prepare thick, juicy burgers and tamales during the lunch hour and slab-size steaks—sold by the pound—in the evening.

Doe's was almost full when I arrived a little after twelve. The mayor and her noisy City Hall entourage surrounded the large circular table near the entrance, while smaller clusters of state legislators huddled with lobbyists toward the rear. I exchanged greetings with several acquaintances before laying claim to a freshly vacated table under an autographed poster of Tonya Harding. I had my doubts regarding the bold signature, given that its red ink matched her drawn-on mustache and goatee.

Leslie walked through the door, spotted my waving arm, and greeted me with a kiss to the cheek. She sat across the table from me and picked up her menu.

"I'm starving!"

Moments later, our orders for cheeseburgers and fries were in the kitchen. We'd decided one burger a month wouldn't kill us.

"What's the news?" I asked.

"The public library's reference desk had a telephone number for the Arkansas Country Dance Society."

"Any luck?"

She nodded. "The timing's incredible. There's a board meeting late this afternoon, and I've been invited to attend." When I raised my eyebrows, she shrugged. "They've been seeking some help with photography and I volunteered."

"You didn't talk to Tillman, did you?"

"No," she said. "Some older guy. But there's more. This weekend the group's having a big dance in Hot Springs. It's sort of a semi-annual event. I've already made us reservations at the Arlington Hotel."

"Have I mentioned how awful I am at dancing?"

"I recall a memorable slow dance on the banks of the Buffalo River."

I, too, smiled, remembering our impromptu dance around a campfire months ago, soon after we'd met. A chorus of frogs and crickets had provided the music, with lighting courtesy of a full moon.

"Besides, they have lessons for beginners. We'll do fine."

"Only if you promise to lead," I said as our plates arrived.

* * *

I spent much of the afternoon with Abigail and an architect she'd located who specialized in meeting rooms and conference centers. As we toured the offices slated for remodeling, he asked a ton of questions and took at least a dozen digital photographs. By the time he left, he had filled a notepad with sketches, measurements, and comments. He promised an estimate within a week.

The designer had been gone all of five minutes before Abbie walked into my office with a large cardboard box in her hands. "I found this buried in a closet of one of the rooms we'll be converting," she said and placed it on my desk. The cell phone in her rear pocket rang and she backtracked into the hall.

Sealed with packing tape, the box didn't look familiar. But across the top were the words *Lassiter—Personal* in black marker. I recognized the crude handwriting as mine. I grabbed a pocketknife and popped open the lid, not sure what I'd discover.

On top of the pile was a page torn from an old Little Rock telephone directory. In the middle of that thin, brittle yellow sheet was the first advertisement for Lassiter & Associates, a one-by-two-inch display ad that had strained my budget at the time. I set it aside and dug deeper. I uncovered a handful of rude and obnoxious birthday cards I'd been given in younger years, newspaper clippings on accounts the agency had won in its formative days, a couple of personal letters signed by President Bill Clinton, and musty yearbooks from my stint at the University of Arkansas. Most of the remainder was a collection of advertising awards and certificates of one sort or another.

In the very bottom of the box, I found a discolored, unmarked envelope. It contained a hand-written letter that J.J. had sent me on the first anniversary of Lassiter & Associates. "Congratulations!" he had written. "I knew you could do it." I bit my lip, closed the box, and slid it under my desk.

* * *

When I got home a little after six, Leslie had already left for her meeting with the dance group. I changed clothes, selected a locally brewed ale from the refrigerator, and then tossed a handful of pine cones at a potbellied squirrel perched atop our new squirrel-proof birdfeeder before reaching for the day's mail. While I studied the latest Victoria's Secret catalog for helpful advertising concepts, the phone rang. It was Leslie.

"This meeting's going to adjourn soon," she said. "Dr. Tillman is here, and I thought it might be interesting if we followed our suspect afterward. Mostly to see what happens."

"I'll be right there," I said, and she gave me directions to a branch bank in the western part of the city that had made its community room available to the organization. I heaved several more pine cones at the cocky squirrel while killing the last of my beer.

Grabbing the binoculars as I left the house, I parked near Leslie's car a quarter of an hour after her call. She trotted from the bank to my truck within a few minutes.

"That's Tillman." Leslie gestured over the pavement to a tall, big-boned woman climbing into a Toyota pickup similar to mine. Her dark hair cut short, she wore a sleeveless cranberry top with black slacks.

"What's she like?" I asked.

"Pleasant enough. Quiet, but enthusiastic about the Hot Springs dance."

Tillman pulled from the bank and drove west on Arkansas 10. Once the traffic cleared, I aimed my truck into the setting sun and kept a reasonable distance behind her pickup. A mile later she wheeled into a sprawling Kroger complex. I drove to the next entrance, turning into the big lot at the opposite end, and parked a couple of rows away from Tillman's spot. Handbag hanging from her shoulder, she walked into the store, never glancing our way.

"I need a snack," I said.

Leslie stayed in the truck while I made a beeline for the express lane. I chose a candy bar, changed my mind, and instead selected a packet of teriyaki beef jerky. After paying for my purchase, I hurried across the scorching asphalt.

When I offered to share my treat, Leslie stared at the package for a moment and then shook her head. "I don't believe I'll ever be that hungry," she said.

"How did the meeting go?"

"It's a nice group of people," she said. "All ages, all shapes. Folks who enjoy a good time. And they made me feel right at home." Leslie paused a second and added, "There's one more thing."

"What's that?"

"Remember the card we got from Summer?"

I nodded.

"I'm not sure Summer ever saw Dr. Tillman."

"Oh?"

"I overheard Tillman as she talked to one of her friends before the meeting started. She said something about a memorable two-week vacation."

"Maybe Tillman spent the time here."

"It sounded like she'd returned from a trip to Italy with a cousin within the past day or two."

I remained skeptical. "She could be laying the foundation for an alibi."

"Maybe so," Leslie said. "But Tillman's friend thanked her for a postcard from Siena."

I was trying to make sense of this new information when Dr. Mackie Tillman emerged from the store. She placed a sack of groceries on the passenger side, walked around the truck, and settled into her seat. While we trailed her from a discreet distance, she continued west for several miles on Highway 10 before turning north on Highway 300.

"Isn't this the way to Pinnacle Mountain State Park?" Leslie asked.

"It appears she's heading home." I bit off another chunk of jerky.

We'd gone about a mile when Tillman suddenly hit the brakes and swerved her truck onto the shoulder, dust flying as she came to a hurried stop. A hundred yards back, I had no choice but to drive past, gazing straight ahead while Leslie ducked from sight.

"What the hell's going on?" I asked.

Leslie reached for the binoculars and twisted around in the seat so she could watch through the rear window. "She's getting out of her truck."

A convenience store was half a block away, and I edged onto the lot while Leslie continued her play-by-play.

"She's carrying a shovel, and what looks like a black plastic garbage bag."

I squinted toward Tillman's truck, but couldn't discern any details. "A shovel?"

"But not the usual kind. The blade is squared off, sort of like a snow shovel."

This was getting stranger by the minute. I took another bite of jerky.

"I don't believe it … I'm not really seeing this." Her voice low, Leslie sounded disgusted.

"What's going on?"

"Yuck! Dr. Tillman just scraped a dead animal from the center of the road." Leslie lowered the binoculars and turned to stare at me, her eyes wide. "She dropped the roadkill into the bag and placed everything in the bed of her truck."

Thinking back, I remembered straddling a flattened opossum while passing Tillman's pickup. The jerky lost its flavor.

~ THIRTY-ONE ~

A quarter of a mile beyond the C-store, we discreetly followed Tillman as she turned off the highway and angled east on a narrow asphalt road. About 200 yards of pavement and a Volvo station wagon full of kids separated our pickups. To the north, Pinnacle Mountain loomed over the valley, its steep rocky face glowing in the evening light. Half a dozen turkey vultures circled far above, soaring on the summer updrafts and perhaps wondering about the strange human who'd taken what by all rights should have been theirs.

"Why would anyone want a dead opossum?" I asked. Or a live one for that matter.

"She's a biologist," Leslie reminded me. "Maybe it's for research. Or perhaps she's an angler and uses the fur for flies." Neither explanation sounded very plausible, but I couldn't generate a better one.

Ahead, Tillman slowed and pulled onto a wide graveled driveway on the left side of the road. We continued our course, trailing the Volvo, while Tillman stopped short of an imposing gate. State Park Superintendent Janetta Strickland hadn't exaggerated in her description of Tillman's fortress-like security arrangements, the fence and gate worthy of a government installation. As we passed Tillman's drive, she reached through the open window of her truck and entered a combination on an electronic keypad. In my rearview mirror I watched the gate swing open, and then something else caught my eye.

Leslie whistled. "She must like privacy."

I turned around at the first chance and drove past Tillman's entrance once more, coming to a stop on the shoulder of the road next to her mailbox. Her truck had disappeared down the long curving driveway beyond the closed gate, and no other vehicles were in sight.

"What are you doing?" Leslie's voice had an edge to it.

"I'll be right back." Leaving the engine running, I darted from the cab and picked up a heavy white plastic sack at the base of Tillman's mailbox, heaving it into the bed of the truck. Ten seconds later we had resumed our journey toward Highway 300.

"Are you crazy?" Leslie's eyes were wide. "Did you just steal her garbage?"

"I suspect it's the week's recycling. I'm thinking the contents of that bag might help us better understand the strange and mysterious Dr. Mackenzie Tillman."

Leslie was still muttering when I dropped her off at the branch bank so she could reclaim her car. I followed her home, opened our gate, and lugged the plastic sack onto the deck overlooking the backyard patio.

"Don't you dare bring that inside," she said. "No telling what's in there. It could contain another highway scraping."

Before inspecting the bag's contents, I yielded to another request from Leslie and reviewed ensembles for tomorrow night's dance. Earlier in the afternoon, she'd combed through the local costume shops for suitable attire. For me, she'd chosen loose cotton pants with a drawstring and a billowing, bright red shirt from the Three Musketeers' era. While I tried them on, she undressed and slipped into an outfit. Wearing a white peasant blouse paired with a black, ankle-length full skirt, she seemed to have captured the medieval flavor. But Leslie wasn't satisfied. "Something's not quite right," she said, studying her reflection in a mirror at the bottom of the stairs. "I'm trying for an upscale wench look." She looped a heavy, golden chain around her neck and unfastened a couple of buttons on her blouse, mumbling under her breath.

While she fussed with her costume, I returned to the deck and began examining my dubious acquisition from the Tillman compound. As I'd expected, the bag contained items she'd put out for the county's recycling program: newspapers, tin cans, plastic bottles, scrap paper, and some 10 pounds of magazines ranging from *Cosmopolitan* to *The Nation*. If nothing else, Dr. Mackie Tillman was a voracious and eclectic reader.

Leslie stepped onto the porch. "Is this any better?" She'd switched to a navy gathered skirt, extending just below her knees.

"Give it a twirl."

As she performed a graceful pirouette, the skirt lifted, exposing several inches of smooth, muscular thighs. "I like it," I said, giving her a frisky leer. She swung a foot my way before stomping into the house.

Sifting through the remaining papers in the sack, I made an interesting discovery. "Leslie, got a second?"

She soon reappeared on the porch, hands on her hips. "I'm still not happy with this." Yet another skirt hung midway down her calves. Glancing at the piles surrounding me, she wrinkled her nose and asked, "What'd you find?"

I handed her a piece of stationery. "It appears our Dr. Tillman has applied for faculty positions on other college campuses."

She read the correspondence, a letter from the biology department at Texas Tech University. The chair thanked Tillman for her interest, but reported that she had no vacancies. Perhaps Tillman got some satisfaction that it wasn't a form letter.

"J.J. must have had his talk with her."

"It sure appears to be the case," I said and gave Leslie another letter. "Here's a similar note from Rhodes College in Memphis. And there are three or four others."

She flipped through the papers, shaking her head. "This situation continues to get crazier and crazier."

Leslie went into the house and I cleaned off the deck, adding Tillman's recycling to ours, saving nothing but the series of letters. When I came inside, Leslie stood in front of the mirror, frowning as she examined her reflection. "Maybe it's the shoes." She scooted out of a pair of lightweight clogs and into ballet slippers.

"You'll be the prettiest in all the land."

"Tell me," she said, a flicker of amusement returning to her eyes, "when did you last have your way with a wench?"

"It's been days, maybe weeks," I said, sidestepping another playful kick.

Leslie wenched me up the stairs and into bed.

* * *

At ten the next morning, Leslie phoned me at the office, but I was stuck in the middle of a conference call. My assistant recorded her message, taking great pleasure in delivering it while a handful of colleagues lingered near the coffee pot outside my office.

"Randy, you're to meet a Ms. Leslie Carlisle in Dillard's lingerie department at twelve sharp," she announced, her tone quite serious. She handed me the note, stifled most of a giggle, and marched back to her desk.

Leaving the building sounded like an excellent idea. My mid-morning conference call had been the long-awaited conversation with representatives from the media group buying KACN. While it had gone better than anticipated, I was still disappointed. Rather than summarily firing Lassiter & Associates, the Cleveland office gave us six months to close down the current campaign and submit our final billing. In the interim, I felt, we could land a new client or two, perhaps even the Baptist Hospital business. But I dreaded sharing the news with my KACN team. The account executive, in particular, would be devastated. He'd devoted most of his short career to building the station's audience, working weekends and holidays on one promotion after another. Grousing to myself, I grabbed my suit coat and drove to the Park Plaza Mall.

Befuddled by Dillard's layout, I asked a saleswoman for directions. During her description of departments I'd pass along the route, I peered beyond her shoulder and spotted a familiar figure searching through racks of evening dresses. Unaware of my presence, Booker examined a fuchsia gown, caressing the fabric between his fingers. I went the other way.

Arriving in the lingerie section at noon, I found Leslie holding a pair of silken brassieres. She selected another, gave it a cursory examination before adding it to the collection, and smiled, reaching for my hand. When the clerk turned to deal with another customer, Leslie hurried me into a changing room. "I've figured it out," she said. "My outfit needs a push-up bra. Every wench has one." She latched the door.

It was a first for me. I leaned against the wall, hands tucked in my pockets, as Leslie removed her blouse and sorted through the candidates.

"I've never worn one of these," she grumbled, trying on the first of the lot. "No doubt they're designed by a secret society of sadistic perverts somewhere in Paris. Or maybe southern California. Fanatics fulfilling their own sexual fantasies." She worked with the straps for a moment, leaned forward, and adjusted the cups before righting herself with an exaggerated sigh. "What do you think?"

In my opinion, Leslie's breasts were perfect, and I'd said so on numerous occasions. But this little bra provided an interesting effect. I shrugged. "It's pretty."

Leslie gave me one of those glances before trying on the next. "Hmmm," she said. "This isn't as uncomfortable as I expected. Any comment?"

It looked wonderful, incredible, marvelous. "Not bad," I stammered.

Leslie twisted first one way, then another, examining herself in the floor-to-ceiling mirror. "I could get used to it. Not for all day, but on special occasions." She gave me a wink.

The third one had the least fabric of all. Edged with delicate lace and all but sheer, it left most of her breasts delightfully uncovered. "This is what they call a demi bra. Do you like it?"

Shoving my hands deeper into my pockets, I nodded, trying hard to act as if this was an everyday occurrence.

"One of these might be ideal for my wedding gown," she said. "What's your favorite?"

I extracted a hand, found my wallet, and gave her my American Express card, hoping she wouldn't notice my trembling fingers. "Let's get them all."

* * *

At three we left for Hot Springs, arriving in the historic spa city an hour later. The Arlington Hotel, one of the state's largest with some 500 rooms, is known by regulars for its ancient elevators— the slowest in the South according to one well-traveled friend— and for having hosted Al Capone during his gangster heyday.

When we approached our suite, Leslie rolled her eyes, the elevators having performed as predicted. I promised to show her the door to the mobster's hideaway before we left. The bellman knocked within a few minutes, his cart stacked high with our bags, several of them bulging with Leslie's photo equipment. He agreed to return at seven and haul her gear to the banquet room.

After unpacking, we adjourned to the deck, enjoying the pool, hot tub, and outdoor bar. At six, we abandoned our temporary escape into hedonism and went to our suite to prepare for the evening's festivities. When Leslie emerged from the bathroom, she was a new woman. She'd plaited her hair and fastened the braids to the top of her head in an Old-World European style. Her costume was perfect, and the push-up bra, combined with a low-cut blouse, added another dimension of interest.

"Is this too much?"

"It's wonderful!" I kissed her cute little nose. "And if you're concerned with … shall we say … overexposure, you can always button up."

Her fears were unfounded. Most of the other women wore similar outfits, many displaying far more flesh than Leslie. I wondered why we hadn't discovered this group earlier.

Soon after our arrival, Leslie subtly gestured across the room. "There's Mackie Tillman," she said. Like most of the women, Dr.

Tillman wore the full, sweeping skirt and a peasant-type blouse. She would never be mistaken for a ballerina, I thought. Not fat or heavy, but solid and broad in the shoulders, reminding me of the more or less female athletes East Germany used to send to the Olympics.

Following the first series of dances, I helped Leslie position her electronic strobes, reflective umbrellas, and backdrop in a corner of the room. For an hour, she stood behind her tripod, taking photos of everyone. Time and again she demonstrated a knack for getting even the shyest or most sullen to smile.

"I didn't know you did this sort of work."

Leslie flashed me a questionable grin while swapping batteries. "I hate it," she said, her voice low. She stepped to the next couple, patted the man on the shoulder like she'd known him her entire life, and straightened his collar before adjusting his partner's scarf and necklace. "Give me a big smile," she said, and the strobes popped. "It's just focus and fire," she mumbled once the happy pair rejoined the crowd. "No talent required." I squeezed her hand and then brought her another glass of wine.

A few minutes had passed when she introduced me to Dr. Mackie Tillman. Maybe an inch taller than Leslie, she had a firm handshake, pleasant smile, and dark, penetrating eyes. But the red rose pinned behind her ear didn't quite seem to fit.

"Why don't you two join me for dinner?" she asked. "We'll be eating after another song or two."

Apparently without a date, Tillman grabbed my arm and escorted me to the dance floor as the music resumed. She was used to leading, which was okay by me, and we circled the room without disaster. "Thanks," she said, out of breath. "Make sure you and Leslie sit at my table."

Walking toward the bar, I felt another hand on my elbow. "Not so fast." It was Leslie. Standing on tiptoe, she whispered into my ear, "What's it like to dance with our primary suspect?" Before I could respond, the musicians started again and Leslie spun us around the hall, laughing as I tried to keep pace. When the band quit, Leslie gave me a kiss. "I've worked up an appetite," she said. "Let's eat."

We joined Tillman at her table for eight, and she introduced us to the others, all of whose names I failed to register. Seated between Leslie and Tillman, I listened as they compared their dancing experiences. Halfway through the meal, Tillman changed the direction of the conversation. "I know Leslie's a photographer," she said, turning her gaze to me. "Do you also work in the arts?"

"A closely allied field," I said, eagerly bobbing my head. "Advertising."

She gave me a polite smile as a thin glaze settled over her eyes. Exercising tremendous self-control, I shelved my usual spirited spiel on the wonders of my chosen profession. "What about yourself?" I asked.

"I'm an instructor at the University of Arkansas Little Rock. In the Biology Department."

The door had been opened. "What a small world," I said, feigning surprise. "My former college roommate teaches in the same program."

She thought for a moment, sorting through the possibilities. It didn't take long, given the small staff. "You must mean Dr. Newell, chairman of our department."

I nodded, watching for a nervous twitch, a change in her voice, a furtive look, a reckless break for the exit—all the dead giveaways you notice in Hollywood productions. Nothing.

"We haven't seen much of J.J. in recent weeks," Leslie said. "I'm sure you talk to him often."

Tillman shook her head. "I'm not teaching the first summer term." She took a sip of wine. "In fact, I assume he's still out of town."

"Oh?" Under the tablecloth, Leslie squeezed my knee. Pulse quickening, I cleared my throat. "Is he on a field trip?"

"I don't know," she answered with a shrug. "But at J.J.'s request, I left his car at the airport several weeks ago."

Before I could pry my chin from my chest, the chairman of the event, a heavyset man in his 70s who had danced nonstop with the grace of a gazelle throughout the evening, stepped to the table and whispered into Tillman's ear.

236

"I've got to help with installation of the new officers," she said, scooting her chair away from the table. "Please excuse me." She stood and patted Leslie on the shoulder. "See you later."

~ THIRTY-TWO ~

We didn't get another chance to talk with Dr. Mackenzie Tillman that evening, and by the time we were coherent enough to call her room the next morning, Mackie had already left the hotel. Leslie told me not to worry, promising that we'd soon find time to quiz Dr. Tillman. I hoped she'd be right.

Following her shower, Leslie strolled from the bathroom, wrapped in a thick towel. She stopped and surveyed the room. "Have you noticed all the mirrors?"

Between last night's rush and this morning's grogginess, I hadn't paid much attention to our surroundings. Half the walls were mirrored, including a full-length version opposite the bed.

Leslie let her towel drop to the carpet. "You may think me strange," she began, but I didn't let her finish the sentence.

Afterward, we played tourists for a day in America's oldest national park, beginning with mineral baths and semi-masochistic massages in the hotel's quintessential spa. Next, we visited the fourth floor, creeping along the dark, quiet hallway and eyeballing the door to Suite 443, Capone's headquarters in the Arlington three-quarters of a century earlier. Imagining a burst of ragtime music or maybe a gangster gunfight, I jumped as an ice machine behind us rattled to life.

We then took a stroll down Bathhouse Row, stopping to inspect several art galleries along Central Avenue. The sidewalks teemed with people, many of them in line to ride those peculiar

238

World War II amphibious vehicles—dubbed "ducks" by their promoters—offering land and water tours of the area. We instead opted for a "chicken" experience by challenging a handsome white hen in tic-tac-toe at one of the lowbrow tourist haunts. I lost two games—the damn chicken *always* goes first—but Leslie, laughing so hard that tears coursed down her cheeks, played the vicious beast to a tie.

Checking out from the Arlington before noon, we enjoyed a tasty barbecue lunch at McClard's. Leslie ordered pork, but I insisted on pit-broiled chicken, of course. Above our booth hung an autographed photo of President Bill Clinton dining at the same place. Stuffed, we aimed the truck toward Little Rock.

* * *

Back home in the Capital City, we relaxed on our porch swing, cooling off with fresh-brewed beer from Vino's. Leslie sat sideways, draping her long legs across my thighs, and I rubbed her calves.

"What's your reading on Tillman?" I asked.

Leslie took another swig from her mug and sighed. "Maybe I'm wrong, but I didn't get the impression she was trying to hide anything. If Mackie Tillman has a problem with J.J., she kept her emotions in check."

"Still, I think we ought to pay her a visit," I said. "We have to learn why she drove J.J.'s car to the airport. But what excuse can we use to appear at Fort Tillman and get past her damn gate?"

Silent for a few moments, Leslie snapped her fingers. "Those photos from the dance in Hot Springs will be our passport into the Tillman compound. I'll call Dr. Tillman and offer to drop by with a set of prints."

The jangling of my cell phone telephone interrupted our conversation. It was Catfish McCulloch. "I'll be over in ten minutes," he said. "We're going to Conway."

"I'm not sure—" I said, then realized the line was dead.

"Who was that?" Leslie asked.

"Catfish McCullough. He's taking me to Conway."

"Why?"

"I have no idea."

* * *

Nine minutes later I climbed into the passenger seat of Catfish's enormous SUV. He pulled from the curb before I'd fastened my seatbelt.

"Afternoon," he said. "Glad you could make it."

I didn't realize I had a choice. "What's going on in Conway?" One of Little Rock's suburban communities, it lies 25 miles to the northwest.

"A pretty good gun-and-knife show. I figured you need to experience one firsthand."

"I've been to boat shows."

Catfish snorted. "Ain't the same, son. Just ain't the same."

My host parked among a throng of pickups and SUVs at the Conway Expo & Event Center. After slipping into his signature sport coat, he led me to a large metal building, his cane grating on the loose gravel of the parking lot. A hand-lettered sign at the entrance read: "Admission—$10." I reached for my wallet, but Catfish waved my hand away. "Don't you worry 'bout that."

A thin man wearing an orange hunting vest stood at the door, a wad of bills in one hand. Spotting my guide, he flashed a big grin our way. "Hot damn, Catfish. I haven't seen you in a coon's age."

"You're looking good, Howard," Catfish said. He nodded in my direction. "I want you to meet a friend of mine. Randy Lassiter."

We shook hands.

"You boys come on in and enjoy yourselves. It's on the house."

As we wandered through the congested aisles, Catfish greeted most of the dealers by name, chiding two or three for not having signed on for his upcoming show. When a beefy Faulkner County deputy sheriff steered him away for a private conversation, I bought a lukewarm hot dog from an acned vendor and gazed across the loud, bustling scene.

The building held enough guns and ammo to launch a small war. But it was a congenial crowd, with lots of backslapping and good-natured jostling. Ninety-five percent of the horde were men, most wearing one form of camouflage or another. The handful of women stood out like guys at a cosmetics counter. And then I spotted a familiar female face on the far side of the room.

Catfish tapped my shoulder. "What do you think?"

"Fascinating. And what a diverse group."

"We've got 'em all," Catfish said. "Strippers to stockbrokers."

"I think I recognized a university professor."

"You must mean Dr. Mackenzie Tillman."

"Is she a gun nut?"

A couple of large men standing nearby spun around and glared. Catfish grabbed me by the elbow and moved us to a quiet corner. "Those are not words we like to hear," he said. "Think of Dr. Tillman as a ... patriot."

I tried to nod with conviction.

"Truth is, Dr. Tillman got mugged in Houston not too many years ago. She purchased her first pistol soon after and has become an excellent shot."

"Her first gun? How many does she own?"

Catfish shrugged. "I've seen her buy at least three. All of 'em choice pieces."

* * *

On Sunday, Leslie and I took it easy, reading the *New York Times* over a brunch of coffee and croissants at Community Bakery. She tackled the crossword puzzle and I read the business section, making note of the latest Madison Avenue activities and shaking my head at the size of the national advertising accounts up for review. I wondered what it would be like to win a $50 million contract. Or to lose one.

Leslie interrupted my research. "What's a seven-letter word for lawyer?"

"Deviant?"

We left the bakery on that note, arriving home in time to catch the telephone. It was Booker. "I have compiled a progress report for you. Three summaries, all told."

I gestured to Leslie, mouthed "Booker," and activated the speaker-phone. "Good afternoon, Uncle Booker," she said.

"Salutations to you, Ms. Carlisle. I trust you're continuing to enjoy the transition to Little Rock?"

"I'll be happier if you have encouraging news."

"Ms. Preston's computer did not yield a great deal," he said. "But she had assembled a file of sorts on Dr. Mackenzie Tillman."

"On Dr. Tillman?" My pulse quickened.

"Don't elevate your aspirations, dear nephew. It's a rambling list of phrases like 'aggressive personality,' 'dominating family,' 'only child,' and so on. A stream-of-consciousness type thing. Nothing for a grand jury, I dare say. I left a sealed copy on your desk along with the key to her apartment."

"Anything else of interest on her computer?" Leslie asked.

Booker cleared his throat. "There was another item, and I hesitate to mention it. However, Ms. Preston—who's quite the accomplished lyricist—has written an emotive musical composition dedicated to Dr. Newell. A work for the guitar, I surmised." He cleared his throat again. "I chose not to reproduce this very personal expression."

For a moment I recalled Summer's faraway gaze when she held J.J.'s guitar days earlier. "Tell us your other news," I asked.

"My latest program is astounding," he said. "Amazing, in fact. Beyond my wildest expectations. If its functions were not ... uh ... prohibited, I'd apply for a patent at once. In a matter of seconds—mere seconds, mind you—it enabled me to scan the entirety of Dr. Tillman's electronic correspondence."

"A smoking gun?" Leslie asked.

"Not per se. But she had transmitted several vitriolic messages to a confidant at Cornell University. Perhaps a mentor or former professor."

I remembered Tillman had received her doctorate from Cornell. "How bad are they?"

242

"She was furious with J.J., feeling he had not given her sufficient time to satisfy what she felt were unreasonable demands."

"Anything beyond that?"

"Briefest of all, Dr. Tillman's last communication concluded with, 'I've got to do something soon.' Her exact words. You'll find a complete printout in your office."

"Did you say you had three reports?"

"Ah, yes," said Booker. "In England, the Alloway character might be described as one of those serious soccer thugs—hooligans, I believe they're called. In addition to a handful of disorderly conduct incidents, his dossier includes two arrests for assault plus a grand larceny charge that was dropped." He paused for a moment. "Outside of a terroristic threatening complaint, he's been rather quiet the past six months."

Leslie and I exchanged glances, thanked Booker for his electronic prowess, and replaced the phone's receiver. Curiosity getting the better of us, we drove to my office and retrieved the items he had left. Leslie studied the files as I impulsively steered us to Summer's apartment. We let ourselves in, picking up a handful of circulars that had been left at her door as we entered. The place looked the same as we'd last seen it, with no sign of Ms. Preston. Leslie checked the plants while I tended to the tropical fish.

As I locked Summer's apartment, Leslie rapped on the neighbor's door and stepped back. It opened at once, and a fat calico cat bounded out and brushed against my leg. A young black woman dressed in exercise gear trailed the feline. She stood in the doorway, cell phone pressed to her ear, and held up an index finger. "Just a minute," she whispered. The conversation soon ended and she gave us a nice smile. "Yes?"

Leslie introduced us. "We're searching for Summer Preston," she said. "Maybe you've seen her?"

Summer's neighbor thought for a moment before shaking her head. "I can't remember the last time I saw that girl, but we need to visit. She babysits Nefertiti on those days I'm traveling." Hearing her name, the cat gave us the silent meow treatment, flung her tail high, and paraded back and forth, rubbing against Leslie's bare shins. Muttering "damn cat" all the way to the truck, she erupted in a sneezing fit before I got the engine started.

That evening we took in a movie, the latest in the never-ending series of James Bond adventures. Another predictable combination of pulchritude and politics, it occupied our minds for two hours.

~ THIRTY-THREE ~

Monday morning served as one more reminder that life is not fair. While I toiled away in the office dealing with clients and Clifford, Leslie photographed fly-fishermen on the Little Red River, a premier trout stream not much more than an hour north of the city. I helped haul her gear inside when she returned near dark and made salads as she showered. She soon strolled into the kitchen.

"How'd it go?" I asked.

Hair still damp, Leslie wore one of my old dress shirts, sleeves rolled up to her elbows, and apparently not much else. She smiled, crossing her fingers. "If I didn't get some good shots today, I'll turn in my tripod. Perfect skies, and I found a classic S-curve in the river with both banks draped in lush foliage. And standing in the middle of the rocky shoals were two men, each a master at casting."

"They didn't mind you taking photos?"

"The guys were eager to help, signing releases and asking for nothing but a pair of prints as payment. And that reminds me. I dropped off the CDs from Friday's dance this morning. The pictures should be ready tomorrow."

"You want to call Tillman after supper and schedule a visit?"

"Might as well," she said. "What do we have to lose?" That very question had been on my mind all afternoon.

After we finished dinner, I loaded the dishwasher as Leslie searched for the folder with Tillman's telephone number. Finishing our tasks at the same time, I edged close to Leslie as she dialed,

245

listening to her half of the conversation. Once the obligatory opening pleasantries had been exchanged, she got down to business. "The photographs from the dance in Hot Springs will be ready tomorrow," she said. "If you're agreeable, Randy and I thought we might drop by late tomorrow afternoon so you can see them."

I could hear Tillman's voice, but was unable to pick up her words.

"No," Leslie said. "It won't be any trouble at all. I think I got some good shots, and am eager to share them with you."

Slowly nodding as Tillman spoke, Leslie winked at me.

"Yes, I'm familiar with Pinnacle Mountain State Park. In fact, Randy took me there just a few days ago. The view from the summit is incredible."

Again, I was unable to comprehend Tillman's response, but Leslie gave me a big grin.

"You're saying that we probably saw your house from the top?"

As the conversation continued, Leslie flashed me the A-OK with her free hand.

"I'm ready for your address," Leslie said, and then repeated it back to her. "After I plug this into my GPS, we shouldn't have any trouble getting there."

After another long pause, Leslie shook her head. "Your telephone number? I … uh … can't remember exactly who it was, but I ran into one of your fellow board members in the lobby of the Arlington Hotel the morning after the dance and he gave it to me."

She nodded again. "Good. We'll see you at six thirty." She ended the call with a breath of relief.

"What's wrong?"

"Mackie asked how I got her phone number."

"You handled it nicely," I said. "But I am a bit alarmed at how easily you can fabricate things."

"This coming from the consummate adman?" Leslie said, giving me a light punch on the shoulder. "Anyway, we're on for tomorrow evening. Let's hope she likes the pictures."

246

Shortly after I returned home from work the next day, we left for Tillman's house in Leslie's car. I wanted to make certain our host didn't recognize my truck from last week. Tillman awaited our arrival, leaning against the fence. Wearing a white pith helmet and a sleeveless denim blouse with canvas shorts and work boots, she could have passed for an archaeologist at a dig. She gave us a smile before waving us through the gate like a traffic cop. The gate closed on its own.

"Hello, again. Mind if I have a ride?" After sliding into the backseat, she said, "Follow the drive."

The road twisted and turned for a good quarter of a mile before ending at a large, two-story stone house. With Pinnacle Mountain looming in the background beyond the red-tiled roof, I felt as if we'd been transported to the European countryside. Thick rock walls marked the edges of the front lawn, a green expanse spotted with flowering plants and fruit trees almost as far as the eye could see.

Leslie gasped. "This is incredible."

"The property's been in the family for four generations," Tillman said. "It had been neglected for a decade, and I've spent the past few years restoring the place."

She'd done a masterful job. I halfway expected to see a group of foxhunters cantering into view any second.

"Let's go inside to look at your photos," she said. "Afterward, I'll give you a tour. It's too nice an evening to stay indoors."

Hanging her headgear on an antique oak hall tree near the front door, she led us through a spacious foyer and into a comfortable living room, its large picture window framing the cone-shaped mountain to the north. Tillman handed me a photo album. "You might enjoy this," she said. "Before and after pictures."

While she and Leslie examined the stack of photographs from the dance, I flipped through Tillman's collection, marveling at the progress she had made in such a short time. In the not-too-distant past, the house had been all but invisible behind a dense thicket of kudzu. Where a small fishpond now reflected the early evening sun, a trio of abandoned cars had also been overtaken by the aggressive vines. The interior of the house had been in shambles, with broken windows and water damage throughout. In one photo, wasp nests as big as dinner plates dangled from what was left of the ceiling in this very room, and another showed a nasty rat's nest occupying the fireplace in front of me.

"Leslie, your shots are perfect," Tillman said, studying one of the portraits taken at the dance. "No one's done this before."

"I enjoyed it." Leslie, I noticed, was practicing her lying skills again.

Tillman brought a hand to her chin, seemingly embarrassed. "I'm not much of a hostess. Would you care for something to drink?"

She went to the kitchen to prepare iced tea for everybody and I handed the album to Leslie. "You won't believe the transformation."

I walked to the big window, startling a plump rabbit nibbling on tender shoots of clover beyond the glass. It darted into the yard, spooking another one hidden in the grass. They hopped from view, and I swung my eyes to the lawn stretching toward Pinnacle. As large as a football field, it—like the front lawn—was bordered by striking stone walls that must have taken months—maybe years—to build. Off to one side I saw what appeared to be a vegetable garden.

Tillman stuck her head into the room. "Sweetened or unsweetened?"

After following Leslie's healthy example and requesting the latter, I spotted a framed photo on an end table near the couch and examined the picture. It appeared to be a recent shot taken on a cruise ship, an image of Tillman and a man, their arms interlocked. Her companion seemed familiar, but I couldn't place him, the opaque sunglasses hiding much of his frowning sun-burned face. I propped it on the table as she brought a tray of beverages into the room. We each took a glass.

"You've worked a miracle," Leslie said, returning the album to Tillman. "How'd you pull it off?"

"Dumpsters," Tillman said with a laugh. "Hauling off half a dozen dumpsters of debris will do wonders. Ready for the grand tour?" She started for the hall.

Leslie reached out and touched Tillman's arm. "Could we first ask you a couple of questions about J.J.?"

Tillman shrugged and sat on the couch beside Leslie. With a puzzled look, she said, "I'm not sure I understand."

I dropped into an easy chair, a rustic coffee table separating us.

"I'll cut to the heart of the matter," Leslie said. "J.J.'s going to be Randy's best man when he and I get married this fall."

Tillman's eyes brightened. "Congratulations." It sounded genuine.

"But J.J. seems to have fallen off the face of the earth," I said. "We've been trying to find him for the past month."

"During our conversation the other evening in Hot Springs you mentioned something about moving his car," Leslie said. "We thought you might be able to fill in some gaps."

Tillman narrowed her eyes and took a sip of tea. "It's a long story. I'm not certain where to begin."

~ THIRTY-FOUR ~

"**I**'m resigning from the university faculty," Tillman said, her eyes fixed on some point across the room. "The letter's upstairs in my study. I'll drop it in tomorrow's mail."

"So, is J.J. aware of this?" I asked.

"No," she said, shaking her head, "but it won't really surprise him. I've not been happy as an instructor. Miserable is more like it. J.J. and I discussed this at length a little more than a month ago, and he suggested—with great tact, of course—that I might consider seeking employment elsewhere." Tillman took another long gulp of tea. "I was stunned at first, angry to be quite honest, and came close to saying some things I would've regretted later. But once I'd thought it through, I realized he was right."

"What do you mean?" Leslie asked.

"I'm a good clinician, probably the best in the lab among the Biology Department staff," she said without sounding boastful. "But I'm awful—beyond awful—in the classroom. My people skills are lousy, plus I'm impatient. J.J. said I have a lot of options, but I'm not destined to be a teacher. In time I came around to agreeing with him." Tillman forced a weak smile. "I joined the dance group a little over a year ago to improve my social know-how."

"What are you going to do?" I asked, ignoring the fact it wasn't any of my business.

"The day after J.J. and I had our long talk, I mailed a bunch of résumés to other colleges and universities," she said. "But I've had time to reconsider, and I now plan to establish a consulting firm, working as a contract biologist. I'll concentrate on things like environmental impact statements for highway relocations, utility corridors, and even state park projects."

"You're making a bold step," Leslie said. "It's like when I resigned from *Texas Monthly* and started my own freelance business. It's scary."

Tillman nodded. "But exciting, too. A couple of solid leads have already turned up."

I had no doubts about that. With a few telephone calls, her father could steer enough business Tillman's way to keep her occupied for years.

Tillman sighed, then said, "And, I won't have to move. I've got too much invested in the old family homestead."

A break in the conversation gave me an opportunity to quiz Tillman on a key point that still had me baffled. "You mentioned the other evening that you'd driven J.J.'s car to the airport. Did he ask you to do this?"

She shook her head. "Not exactly. Following our talk, I felt we had bridged some gaps in our relationship, so I wasn't too surprised to find a note from J.J. in my mail slot at the departmental office. According to the message, he'd been called out of town on an emergency, and had just enough time to catch a ride from one of his graduate assistants to the airport terminal."

"You drove his car to the airport on that same day?"

"That's right," she said. "His car keys were attached to the note, and it asked me to drive the Jaguar from his reserved spot near the Science Building to the Security Parking lot at the airport, hiding the key ring under the floor mat." She hesitated a moment. "I assume he's carrying a spare set."

"Anything else?" Leslie asked.

"He'd also placed a twenty-dollar bill in the envelope. His instructions suggested that I take the shuttle from the parking lot to the terminal and return to campus via a cab." Tillman shared a sly grin. "Actually, I used Uber, an option no doubt unfamiliar to J.J."

Leslie gave me a subtle nod. She realized Tillman's account jibed with the report I'd gotten from the parking lot attendant.

"Your note from J.J.," I asked. "Was it handwritten?"

"It was typed on a plain sheet of paper, thank goodness. J.J.'s handwriting is awful."

"Do you remember if it was signed?" Leslie asked, and I felt my pulse quicken.

Tillman rubbed her forehead, her eyes closed. "I can't recall," she said. "Is it important?"

"I don't know. I just don't know."

"Did you also drive Summer Preston's car to the airport?" Leslie asked.

Looking first to Leslie and then to me, Tillman lifted her hands, palms up. "I'm not following you," she said. "Who is Summer Preston?"

"J.J.'s girlfriend," I said.

Tillman stared at the floor for several seconds before raising her head and meeting my gaze. "Earlier this spring J.J. introduced a woman to me, and that name sounds sort of familiar. But I've not seen her since. Nor did I deliver another car to the airport." Her eyes were steady, her voice unwavering. She took a sip of her tea with a relaxed hand. "What's going on?"

"Ms. Preston seems to be missing, too," I said. "It's a big puzzle, and we're searching for pieces."

Leslie stood, our empty glasses in her hands. "Let me put these in the kitchen and we'll be ready for your tour."

* * *

Perhaps the late afternoon light streaming through the landscape had something to do with it, but I'd never seen a more beautiful residential setting. Casting ever-lengthening shadows across the lawn, we followed Tillman from one highlight to another as she pointed to ancient roses, gurgling fountains, and handsome fieldstone pathways. A trio of rabbits watched us warily, and at the far edge of the grass two deer grazed, never taking their eyes from us for more than a few seconds.

"Promise me I can come back with my camera," Leslie said. "This would be a perfect photo-essay for a magazine."

"You'll need to do it soon," Tillman said. "Once the summer heat sets in, the place begins to wilt."

Tillman led us to a small, unpainted wooden building off to the side of her house. When she said, "Here's my private mental hospital," I glanced at Leslie as she raised her eyebrows a notch.

A cheery homemade sign tacked above the door read, **Mackie's Potting Shed**. We followed Tillman inside, pausing as she fumbled for a switch. I blinked in amazement when the lights came on, thinking I'd stepped onto the set of a photo shoot for an upscale gardening catalog.

A wheelbarrow and an assortment of big tools—shovels, rakes, hoes, saws, several varieties of each—leaned against one wall, all clean and neat and organized. Next to them hung half a dozen hoses, coiled and suspended from large spikes. Another wall, the top half covered with pegboard, held every kind of small gardening tool imaginable: pruners, shears, clippers, trowels, spades, dibbles. Stacked below were trays, buckets, pots, and watering cans. Sacks of peat moss, mulch, and potting soil filled the end of the shed. In the center of the room, on the spotless concrete floor, sat a worn potting table, at least eight feet long and half as wide. Constructed of massive wooden planks, it must have weighed 500 pounds.

Walking to the table, Tillman gestured to an ancient mechanical contraption perched on its opposite side. "There's my pride and joy. It belonged to my great-grandfather."

I had no idea what we were looking at, but it appeared to be something belonging in a museum. The large device, bolted to the table, resembled an overgrown sausage grinder, its smooth wooden handle attached to a heavy metal flywheel a good foot and a half across. I stared at Leslie, my mouth gaping, and she also seemed to be at a loss.

"What is it?" she asked.

"A bone grinder," Tillman said. "Sometimes called a bone mill. These were quite common in Victorian England. Folks would drop by the butcher shop, take home a sack of bones, and grind them into meal for their vegetable gardens."

"Yuck." Leslie grimaced. "That sounds disgusting."

"On the contrary," Tillman said. "The meal is a great source of phosphorus. It's worked wonders on my roses."

"Wouldn't it be easier to buy a bag at a garden shop?" I asked, remembering my recent purchase for Leslie.

Tillman scowled and gave me a dismissive wave. "That over-processed commercial stuff is often contaminated with nasty by-products." She reached under the table and scooted a large bucket in front of us. "This, on the other hand, is nature's perfect fertilizer. One hundred percent organic."

She scooped a hand into the grayish mixture, letting the particles sift through her fingers like coarse dirty sand. A puzzled expression crossed her face and she peered under the table, mumbling to herself. She caught me watching and managed a small grin. "I didn't realize my inventory was this large," she said.

I peeked beneath the table and saw a row of five-gallon plastic buckets. Three altogether, counting the one at our feet, and each filled to the brim with bone meal.

"Is it easy to make?" Leslie asked.

"Let me show you." Tillman searched under the table again, bringing out a wicker basket full of what appeared to be small bones. She grabbed a couple from the top, both curved examples not much bigger than short, misshapen pencils, and studied them for a moment. "A raccoon's rib," she said, showing us the first. "And this one's from a skunk."

They appeared identical to me. "How can you tell them apart?" I asked.

Tillman arched her eyebrows. "Years of practice. Bones are my specialty. I'm wrapping up a research project on bone mass."

I recalled a reference to something called skeletal modeling on her Biology Department biographical sketch.

She grasped the handle and began cranking it, adding speed with each revolution. Using her other hand, she dropped the bones into a wide opening at the top of the grinder. They vanished at once, sounding like a handful of tortilla chips getting crushed, and two or three tablespoons of meal dribbled onto a tray at the base of the machine. Tillman released the handle and the heavy flywheel coasted to a stop.

Leslie's eyes opened wide. "Wow!"

"Big bones take longer, of course," Tillman said. "But this thing will grind the femur of a cow."

My ignorance of basic anatomy must have been apparent.

"It's the biggest bone in the leg," Tillman said, glancing at her watch.

Leslie took the hint. "It's time for us to go."

"I wish we could visit longer, but I've got to pack," Tillman said, leading us from the shed. "I'm leaving town for a short time."

"Let me guess," I said. "You're traveling to Europe to buy costumes for the dance society." Maybe my effort at prying wasn't too obvious.

"I wish! Some girlfriends and I depart in the morning for Eureka Springs. We're going to take a long weekend in the Ozarks and enjoy the annual jazz festival. And maybe do a bit of shopping, too."

"Sounds fun," Leslie said. "And thank you for the tour."

"My pleasure," Tillman said. "And your photos are wonderful. Thanks so much."

"If I leave them, can you see that they get to the right people?"

"Certainly!"

The three of us walked from the potting shed to our car. As Leslie and I started to drive away, Tillman gestured for us to stop. She trotted to Leslie's open window. "I forgot to tell you," she said. "The gate opens on its own as you near it and will close once you're through."

The security system performed on cue, and Leslie soon had us on the paved road, returning to Little Rock.

"What an interesting afternoon," she said. "Very interesting."

"But I still have questions."

"Like where does she get those bones?"

"It'd take a heck of a lot of roadkill to produce all the bone meal stockpiled under that table."

"You saw more than one bucket?"

"Three of 'em," I said. "Fifteen gallons."

"How does she get the flesh off the bones?"

I hadn't even thought of that.

As we neared the junction with Highway 300, the sun dropped through the clouds, painting the horizon with a full palette of colors. Leslie turned to me, a quizzical look occupying her sunlit face. "You seemed rather interested in that framed photo you examined," she said. "The one on her end table."

"I think the picture was taken on a cruise ship. Tillman with a man I've seen somewhere, but I can't place his face." I was still pondering that nagging question when Leslie touched my arm.

"I forgot to tell you," she said, her eyes wide. "Something I discovered on her kitchen windowsill."

"A small handgun? A Bowie knife?"

"A prescription bottle. A drug called Lavorcet."

"Let me guess. A truth serum?"

Leslie sighed patiently. "My cousin takes it to regulate her thyroid." She paused for a beat. "But I believe its primary use is to control violent mood swings."

I was digesting the implications of that discovery when she added, "The bottle was empty."

~ THIRTY-FIVE ~

"I think we need to inspect the rest of Tillman's property."

Leslie crossed the centerline to give a trio of spandex-clad bicyclists plenty of room. "But she's leaving town."

"That's my point."

She turned to me, surprised. "You can't be serious."

"It's the perfect opportunity," I said. "What could go wrong?"

"You're sure this is a good idea?" was her delayed response. Not a good sign.

When we arrived home, Leslie excused herself to edit her recent trout fishing shots from the Little Red River. I searched the contact list on my cell phone, found a listing for a J. Strickland, superintendent of Pinnacle Mountain State Park, and dialed the number. She picked up at once.

"Is this Janetta Strickland?" I asked. "The best state park superintendent in the entire nation?"

There was a short pause. "Lassiter?"

"Also known as president of the Flash Fan Club."

"You're not calling at this hour to be sociable," she said, chuckling. "What do you want?"

"I need a favor. A small one."

"Those are often the worst kind."

"Leslie and I got a quickie tour of the Tillman compound earlier this evening."

Janetta whistled. "You got past her gate?"

"Dr. Mackenzie Tillman herself showed us around."

"What's it like? Any slaves?" Janetta asked with a laugh.

Flustered, I mumbled some vague comment on the landscaping.

"What do you need from me?" Her voice had lost its light touch.

"We're hoping you might take us on a private nature hike, perhaps to the southern edge of Pinnacle Mountain State Park where—"

"Where it butts up against the Tillman tract?" she asked, interrupting.

"While Leslie and I continue our harmless and innocent exploration, you can return to more pressing business. Matters of state. State parks, that is."

Janetta ignored my feeble attempt at cleverness. She took her time replying, clearing her throat several times. "So, I lead you in, then disappear?"

"Right."

"How's your friend Tillman going to react when she nabs a pair of familiar faces trespassing on her precious estate?"

"Dr. Tillman will be vacationing in the Ozarks for the weekend."

The line was silent for what seemed like a full minute, and I felt my old adman premonition of a lost sale. "I'll do it, but not tomorrow," Janetta said at last, causing a momentary blip in my synapse circuitry. "I'm scheduled to attend another mandatory training session that'll blow the entire day. Some bureaucratic blueprint for multi-culturalism, whatever the heck that is," she said with a laugh.

"Let's make it Thursday. Will 5:30 work?"

"How about 4:30?" Janetta countered. "There won't be so many people in the park in the late afternoon. Fewer potential witnesses."

Leslie was still busy at her desk when I stepped in to share the news. She leaned forward, not bothering to look at me, and placed her chin in her hands. Seconds crept by. "Okay," was all she said.

* * *

In the office by seven o'clock the next morning, I walked straight to the small kitchen, ready to begin the day's coffee ritual. But a welcome aroma drifting through the hall told me that a fresh pot awaited. Abbie handed me a steaming mug and refilled her cup.

"What brings you in at this hour?" I asked.

"Expense reports. If I don't submit one soon, I'll get a dunning letter from American Express."

I remembered one or two addressed to me in years past. "How's work going?"

"Frantic. But the TV spots for Exley are falling into place," she said, referring to the automobile dealer whose account we'd held for a decade. "That reminds me. A new model asked me to say 'Hello.' Beth somebody."

That was great news, I thought. Maybe Ms. Anthony would gain confidence and strike out on her own, dumping that disreputable Alloway creature. "How'd she do?"

"A bit nervous at first, but she settled down and sailed through her part. She was impressive, a natural in front of the camera."

"Did she require much makeup?"

Lowering her mug, Abbie arched her eyebrows. "I don't believe so. Why?"

"Last time I saw her, I noticed some bruises." I shrugged. "Er … maybe a bicycle crash."

"She looked good. Real good."

A phone rang somewhere in the office, and as she raced to get it, I adjourned to my desk and switched on the computer. Two dozen e-mails, including one from Clifford. I should have known better, but I read it first. "I have abandoned the screenplay idea," he wrote. "I believe it's my destiny to write a best-seller, something mainstream. Titles I'm considering are *Confessions of a Fruitcake Addict* (non-fiction, heavily illustrated) and *The Taxidermist's Son-In-Law* (fiction)." I hit the delete key.

Thirty minutes later my assistant escorted two young men into my office, explaining that they had each completed their junior year in college and would be employed as our new summer interns. During the next half hour, I discovered one to be bright and enthusiastic and the other—I'll be blunt—a plodding and insufferable mouth-breather whose father held a prominent position in state government. I assigned the former to Abbie. Clifford got the chucklehead.

Meetings filled the remainder of the morning, including yet another conference on telephone service contracts. We seemed to have one every six months. An hour into the presentation, I wished for the good old days of Ma Bell when we didn't have to choose from so many confusing and conflicting options.

Lunch was a two-hour planning session with a Chamber of Commerce committee. We'd been assigned the daunting task of raising $3 million so the Chamber could expand its building over-looking the Arkansas River near the Main Street Bridge. Earlier meetings had been non-productive or worse, derailed by clashing egos and an indecisive chairman. I'd offered to provide lunch and had arranged for a catered affair from a nearby Chinese eatery whose owner was among my favorite clients. Unknown to the group, I'd worked with the chef to serve customized fortune cookies carrying a special message: *Chinese say best way to eat elephant is one small bite at a time.* I can't say for certain the cookies made a difference, but following the meal our committee started to click. Maybe we'd see the new facilities in my lifetime.

With the dreaded Chamber committee meeting out of the way, I slipped into the office at two and spent three miserable hours deal-ing with a backlog of correspondence and performance reviews. Seconds after a blinding flash of lightning, the lights flickered a time or two and went out. I watched from the window as another spec-tacular thunderstorm—complete with marble-sized hail—lashed the city, grinding everything to a halt. Booker would have a busy evening, I thought as I locked the building. With soggy shoes and an inside-out mini-umbrella (the worthless swag from that media rep I'd seen a few days earlier), I slopped into the house, dripping every inch of the way. It was just as well Leslie and I had postponed our return trip to the Tillman compound until Thursday.

After dinner we cuddled on the couch in front of the television, watching an alleged situation comedy with an annoying laugh-track. The best part of the half hour was a pair of Isla del Sol Casino & Resort commercials produced by Lassiter & Associates. We went to bed once the late news had aired.

* * *

Half a dozen times on Thursday I shook my watch, certain the battery had died. I enjoyed a lunch appointment with a pair of representatives from the Miss Arkansas pageant where we discussed the possibility of Lassiter & Associates handling their promotions, but anticipation of the afternoon's unauthorized tour of the Tillman property occupied my mind. I pulled into the driveway to meet Leslie at 3:30, feeling nervous—much like the pre-presentation jitters I get before making pitches to potential clients. Sweaty-palmed and giddy, I took her advice and, after changing into boots, blue jeans, and a denim work shirt, sat on the porch swing to steady my nerves. Filling her daypack with two water bottles, insect repellant, binoculars, her cell phone, the Leica, and extra film, Leslie remained her calm, confident self. She could have been preparing for a bird-watching expedition.

Arriving at Pinnacle's day use area, we found Janetta on her knees near her drab state park pickup, talking to a pair of young kids. One held a box turtle in her tiny hands. Its long neck extended, the turtle kicked all four legs through the air, searching for a toehold. "Now do like you promised," Janetta said, "and let him go in the grassy area by the playground."

"Yes, ma'am," they said in unison, and scurried to the designated turtle release zone.

Janetta gave Leslie and me each a hug before glancing at her watch. "You're sure you want to take this hike?"

"We just love Mother Nature," I gushed.

Not amused, Janetta swung her gaze to Leslie. "It's not too late to reconsider marrying this smart ass."

Leslie grinned. "I like challenges."

Janetta's glare softened after I handed her a $500 check drawn on my personal account. "A donation for your Partners program."

We shared a can of bug spray, drenching our arms, pant legs, ankles, and waists, exterminating everything but ourselves within a six-foot circle. Coughing our way clear of the chemical cloud, Leslie and I followed Janetta to a marked trail more or less paralleling the Little Maumelle River, a small stream meandering through the park's southern reaches. We'd hiked a couple hundred yards when our guide left the worn path.

"We'll bushwhack from here," she said, leading us into the brush and assuming the role of park naturalist. "This," she said, pointing to an evil stalk covered with wicked spines, "is a devil's walking stick. And those pretty green vines surrounding Randy's feet are poison ivy."

We fought briars and honeysuckle thickets for another 50 yards before coming to the riverbank. Janetta studied the lush riparian landscape, first looking upstream and then down. "I believe we need to go downstream a bit farther."

A short time later, she stopped beside a huge tree trunk. Positioned three feet above the water, the ancient cypress log spanned the stream, stretching from one muddy bank to the other. "Here's where we cross," she said, climbing atop the massive natural bridge. Never faltering, she pranced to the other side like a drum majorette on parade, jumped to the ground, and faced us, hands on her hips. "Next."

"Ladies first," I said.

Leslie mumbled something unfeminine regarding my masculinity before nimbly scampering the 25 feet or so to the opposite shore. I clambered onto the trunk and started across, surprised at the slipperiness of the log. It must still be damp from yesterday's rain, I told myself, and inched forward. I was midway over the channel when Janetta said, "The large snake under Randy's feet is a water moccasin." Her voice hadn't changed a bit. "They're one of the few venomous reptiles in Arkansas."

I laughed, enjoying her sense of humor, and lifted a foot to take another tentative step. A slight movement below the log caught my eye, and I glanced at the sluggish water. Janetta wasn't kidding. The monstrous snake—four feet long and thick as my arm—swam lazily, its long, sinuous body gliding beneath the surface.

"Not a good time to fall," Leslie offered.

"He'd be okay," Janetta said. "The water's not much more than knee deep."

Perched precariously on the slick log, I swung an arm through the air, hoping the snake would sense a threat and flee. Instead, it stopped. Holding its position against the slight current, the reptile then lifted its broad triangular head another six inches above the water. Staring at me with dull black eyes, the moccasin swam closer, flicking its tongue and raising its fist-sized head even higher like a poisonous periscope.

"These big ones are vicious," Janetta said. "They're very territorial and extremely aggressive."

I stumbled forward and leaped for the bank, landing on all fours and scrambling up the muddy slope.

"You asked for a nature hike," Janetta said, patting me on the shoulder. "I'm delivering."

We followed her through tangled thickets as the land rose. Stopping, she pointed into the brush. Leslie and I gazed beyond her extended arm. I saw nothing to warrant my attention. Seconds passed before an armadillo emerged from behind a tree, its long snout skimming the ground like a vacuum cleaner as it rustled through the fallen leaves. We kept still, and the small, armored beast nosed between Leslie and Janetta, oblivious to our presence as it searched for grubs. It vanished into the undergrowth behind us.

"What we have here is a rare variety of armadillo," Janetta said. "A non-flattened, three-dimensional specimen."

I lobbed a pine cone her way, but she side-stepped my toss with a grin.

"We're getting close," Janetta said. Within five minutes we reached an imposing barbed-wire fence, its heavy metal posts anchored in concrete footings. **No Trespassing** signs hung from the strands every 50 feet.

"This is as far as I go," our guide said. "I hope you've enjoyed today's Arkansas State Park experience." She smiled again and presented us with a sharp salute.

"In case something happens, could we have your number?" Leslie asked. "I brought my cell phone."

Janetta removed a business card from a breast pocket and started to hand it to Leslie. She stopped in mid-motion and slipped the card back into her uniform, giving us a wink. "This adventure is beginning to remind me of Watergate. Rather than you getting arrested with my card in your possession, why don't you memorize my number?"

"I've got a better idea," Leslie said. She searched through her day-pack and found her phone. "I'll place your number in my directory."

Janetta repeated it a couple of times and Leslie returned the phone to her pack.

After a round of handshakes, Janetta gave us a nod and said, "Good luck." She turned and, like the armadillo, soon disappeared into the foliage.

Spreading the strands, Leslie and I slipped between the nasty barbs and onto Tillman's property. We walked for five minutes through open woods, going more or less south, before spotting a break in the trees. As we neared the edge of the forest, Leslie hesitated a moment and pointed to a mound of ashes at least three feet across. "It appears somebody built a cozy little fire," she said, and walked around the debris.

Thinking it was an unusual place for a campfire, I bent down for a closer examination and noticed a strange pattern in the ashes. "I don't believe this was a routine marshmallow roast."

Leslie paused and peered over her shoulder. "What do you mean?"

I poked a stick through the cinders and lifted a slender, charred item above the pile. Leslie backtracked and squatted at my side for a better view. "Is that a zipper?"

"That's sure what it looks like," I said, dropping it to the side. I dug further into the pile and uncovered a chunk of melted plastic.

264

I scooted it clear of the ashes. "I can't guarantee it, but I believe that's what remains of a cell phone."

Leslie studied the ground. "Something's not right about this."

She stood, took my hand, and led me to the edge of the clearing. A hundred yards in the distance, we saw the rear of Tillman's house and started toward it, each lost in our own thoughts. After clambering across a stone wall, we almost panicked when a human figure in a nearby garden sprang into view.

"It's only a scarecrow," Leslie whispered. We walked to it. The mannequin wore a billowing white gown topped by a purple pillbox hat and matching sash and gloves. It looked like an outfit Booker might have selected. My heart continued to pound as we neared the house.

As expected, we saw no sign of Tillman's truck. The place was quiet, the silence interrupted by a pair of wind chimes jingling in a crepe myrtle. We walked straight to the potting shed, Leslie flipping the lights on as we entered.

Dropping her pack to the floor, she leaned into the handle of the bone grinder, its worn gears rumbling to life. "I've got to give this a try." She found Tillman's basket of bones under the table and selected what might have been the remains of a chicken leg. Cranking the flywheel until the table vibrated, she dropped it into the mouth of the grinder. The powerful machine pulverized the bone, spitting dabs of meal onto the collecting tray. Her eyes large, Leslie released the handle, and the antique contraption coasted to a stop. "Unbelievable" was all she said.

I circled the table to give it a whirl, but the slamming of a car door put an end to that idea.

~ THIRTY-SIX ~

As I snapped off the light, Leslie peeked through the open doorway. "I don't see anything," she whispered. I slipped through the door behind her, and we tiptoed across the gravel to the corner of the potting shed.

We saw an elegant Mercedes S-class sedan parked in front of Tillman's house. The shiny black car had a sales sticker glued to the right rear window and a temporary license hanging above the rear bumper. An older man, dressed in a white poplin suit and bright bow tie, stepped to the front porch, a frisky rottweiler at his heels. He didn't knock, but let himself into the house with a key, the dog following.

"That's the man in the photo with Tillman." I leaned hard against the wall, trying to make sense of what I'd just seen. "The picture taken on the cruise ship."

"Who is he?"

"Dr. Rankin Campbell. The UA Little Rock dean." What was the connection between Campbell and Tillman?

"We'll talk later," Leslie said, noticing my apparent confusion and squeezing my shoulder.

I pushed myself away from the wall. "It's time to go."

"We can't leave the same way we came in," she said. "There's too much open ground to cover."

I pointed to the opposite side of the lawn. "This shed will screen us until we get to the stone wall. We can then slip behind it, crouch down, and work our way back to the river and the park."

Halfway to the wall, Leslie skidded to a stop, disgust written across her face. "I forgot my darn daypack," she muttered. Before I could say anything, she returned to the shed, disappearing behind the door. The seconds dragged by. I expected to hear Campbell coming any moment. Leslie finally emerged, the pack hanging from one shoulder, and we jogged toward the wall.

"Sorry it took so long," she said. "But I thought I'd better clean up the mess I'd made on the potting table."

Keeping the shed between us and Tillman's house, we came to the stone fence and scrambled over it, dropping to the ground on the other side. Crawling on all fours, we moved east, aiming for state park property. We'd gone less than 50 backbreaking yards when a sharp whistle caused us to pause. Peeking above the top course of rocks, we saw Campbell sitting on the porch, tying his boots. He'd changed into work clothes. As the large dog trotted to his side, Leslie raised her camera and snapped a frame.

"I'd like to stay and see what happens," I said, glancing at my watch. "But I don't want to get caught out here in the dark."

"And I sure don't want to get caught by that rottweiler."

After another 100 yards of arduous scrambling, we reached the point where the fence turned the corner at the edge of the forest. Leslie and I were eager to vanish into the trees, but a faint trail caught my eye. Beginning at a small wooden gate where the south and east walls of the fence converged, the path led into the woods. I looked back, gazed at the house, and saw no movement.

"Let's see where this goes," I said. "These tracks are fresh." The prints in the dirt were made by a human. Adult boots.

"Okay," she said, "but let's make it quick."

Leslie stopped after we'd jogged a short distance and extended an arm across my chest. "What's that?"

In a small clearing sat a concrete structure, the path leading straight to it. About four feet tall, five feet wide, and maybe eight feet long, it appeared out of place. "I think it's a septic tank," I said. "But they're usually buried." A small stepladder leaned against the nearest side, and next to it stood a long pry bar.

Checking behind us, we saw no sign of Campbell or his dog, so we trotted toward the tank. Leslie staggered to a stop and wrinkled her entire face. "My God! What's that smell?"

It hit my nose like a brick wall. I tried clearing my throat. Worse than any other stench I'd ever encountered, it made me wish for the smell from Pine Bluff's paper mill. The horrid fumes sucked my breath away, the rank, putrid aroma burning my eyes. Gagging, we backed off. Nearby limbs stirred and a breeze moved through the clearing, bringing fresh air to our aching lungs.

I edged closer and saw a heavy lid fashioned from two-by-fours and plywood covering the tank. About to backtrack, I noticed a subtle movement in a large break along the tank's base near the ground. Taking another hesitant step forward, I stared at dozens of small, dark bugs scurrying in and out of the crevice.

"Do you have an empty film canister?" I asked, praying for another breeze.

"I don't want to know why," Leslie said. My eyes still fixated on the swarming insects, I heard a zipper. "Here you go."

I turned, caught her toss, then took a big gulp of air. Darting to the crack in the concrete, I scooped several bugs into the container, snapping the lid shut while Leslie said "smile" and exposed a couple of frames. As I dashed to her side, the rottweiler barked in the distance.

"I assume there's a method to your madness?"

"These insects might be a clue," I said, giving her a nudge. "Let's go." Another bark. Closer.

"That dog's beginning to worry me."

We sprinted through the brush, aiming for the spot Janetta had led us to earlier. When I ducked under an overhanging branch, my foot caught on a root. I sprawled headfirst into the undergrowth, the canister shooting from my hand.

"Are you okay?"

I scrambled to my knees, searching through the leaves. "I lost the bugs." As Leslie dropped to the ground, we heard another bark, much nearer than before.

"Here it is!" Leslie flipped the little container to me, and I jammed it into my pocket. We raced toward the park.

"I see the fence!" Leslie shouted. Moments later, I yanked the strands apart and she slipped through. Behind us, I heard the dog crashing through the bushes, his excited barking growing louder and closer. I lunged between the wires, the sharp barbs tearing at my shirt.

Ahead, Leslie waved to get my attention. "Hurry! Here's our trail!"

Ripping fabric, I forced my way through the fence and followed Leslie at a dead run. By the time I arrived at the tree trunk spanning the stream, Leslie stood on the other side, a wry grin on her face.

"I've already checked," she said. "No snakes."

I bounded across the log, leaping onto the muddy shore at her side. In the distance, we again heard Campbell's dog.

"It sounds like he stopped at the fence."

Hand-in-hand, we trudged to the marked path and walked to the truck. As we approached the parking lot, the playground sounds of laughing children seemed light years away from our experience on Tillman's property.

Leslie brushed leaves and twigs from my shirt, stepped away, and gave me an unsolicited inspection. "You look awful. A skinned elbow, torn sleeve, plus a hole in your jeans."

I wanted to respond with a snappy reply but wasn't able to do it. Other than a few wayward strands of hair, Leslie looked great. Cheeks rosy, eyes sparkling, and bouncing with energy, she could have been a model on an outdoor photo shoot.

As we neared the Toyota, Leslie pointed to the windshield. "I think somebody left us a message."

"Let's hope it's not a ticket."

It was a note from Janetta, written on the back of her business card, apologizing for not leaving it with us earlier. She'd also included her personal cell phone number, asking that Leslie give her a call when she was ready to shoot from Pinnacle's summit. Leslie slipped the card into her pocket.

"Janetta's got the instincts of a survivor," I said. "I'd be cautious, too, in her position."

"We did okay," Leslie said. "Now, hand me the keys. You're too tired to drive."

Halfway home, she wheeled into the drive-thru of a Taco Bell. We devoured our supper before we got to the house.

"What kind of relationship do Tillman and Campbell have going?" she asked. "Besides being colleagues on a professional basis."

That same question had been bouncing around in my mind off and on for the past hour. "For one thing, he has a key to her house."

"And knows the combination to her gate."

"Maybe they're good friends and he'd been asked to check on things as a favor since she's out of town. Or perhaps he brings his dog to her place for its exercise."

Leslie turned and gave me a slight grin. "It could be that Tillman and Campbell are lovers. They apparently went on a cruise together."

"But why wasn't he with her in Hot Springs?"

"It could be that he doesn't dance," Leslie said. After a pause, she added, "Or maybe he had something else to do."

We arrived home and I made a beeline for the shower. Leslie angled for her laptop, saying she needed to check on messages. Rinsing shampoo a few minutes later, I felt a gentle pat on my butt.

"Mind if I join you?"

I didn't, of course, and searched her body for ticks and she examined mine. She came up empty-handed, but I found two, neither attached. One hid in the soft spot behind a knee and another crawled above her right hip. I offered to conduct a more thorough follow-up inspection, just in case I'd somehow overlooked one of the pesky parasites, but Leslie swatted me with the washcloth. "It's time for bed," she said. "I've got a busy day on tap for tomorrow."

"Oh?" I handed her a towel.

"My agent sent an urgent e-mail. An editor needs shots ASAP of the Ozark Folk Center, wherever that is."

"Mountain View. A couple of hours north of here."

"She's already made all the arrangements. I'll spend the morning and afternoon shooting craft demonstrations before photographing the cloggers and musicians during their evening performance."

"A full day is right. You'll be lucky to be home by midnight."

Leslie wrapped the towel around her hair. "But the pay's good."

I found my state highway map and showed her the quickest route to Mountain View. "Your GPS may not work in those deep valleys."

She muttered something about my "old school tendencies," reluctantly dropped the map on top of the pile of gear she'd stacked in the hall for an early departure, and led me to bed.

"I'd never dream of telling you what to do." She tossed her towel aside, reached for the nightstand, and switched off the light.

"Okay," I answered, wondering where this conversation was headed.

"But I want you to promise me that you won't do anything foolish tomorrow while I'm gone."

"You've got it." I scooted next to her warm body. As my fingers played with her hair, she stroked my chest, moving her hand downward.

"I've just changed my mind," she said, pulling me on top of her. "I am going to tell you what do to. Unless, of course, you're too sore."

Propped on my elbows, her bare skin beneath me, I chuckled. "Your every wish is my command."

"Kiss me," she said.

~ THIRTY-SEVEN ~

With a steaming cup of coffee in hand, Leslie left the house at 6:30 for Mountain View, and I followed her out the door, heading for the office. Forty-five minutes later, I'd worked through a tall stack of folders and also handled over 30 e-mails, pleased that a message from Clifford wasn't in the mix for once. The ringing of my cell telephone startled me.

"Good morning, Randy. It's Ellen."

"Still carrying that baby around?"

She moaned. "That's why I'm calling, big brother. Gib and I wanted to let you and Leslie know that if he doesn't arrive in the next 48 hours, we'll induce delivery."

"Nursery complete?"

"The paint's still tacky," she said with a laugh. "Gib finished at midnight."

"Anything we can do?"

"Bring a bottle of Champagne by in a couple of days. I'm craving adult beverages."

"Consider it done."

She signed off, handing the phone to her husband. "I haven't talked to you in days," Gib said. "Any news on J.J.?"

"Nothing yet. But that reminds me. Are you familiar with a drug called Lavorcet?" I spelled it for him.

"I've got a pharmaceutical directory in the next room. Let me check." Seconds later I heard him thumbing through a book.

"Lavorcet ... The medication has several secondary applications, but its primary use is for patients exhibiting bipolar symptoms."

"Which means?"

"Your basic manic-depressive."

"Do people afflicted with this disorder ever snap?"

He hesitated a moment. "That's not a usual medical term. What do you mean?"

"Under certain conditions, could a manic-depressive—let's say one who had ceased taking medication—become violent?"

"Remember, I'm a plastic surgeon. We're talking psychiatry, and that's an altogether different world. But I suppose it could happen. I can find out, if it's important." After a pause, he asked, "Does this have anything to do with J.J.'s disappearance?"

"I'm not sure," I said. "It just might."

My brother-in-law promised to call back before noon with an answer.

* * *

Clifford walked in, pulling the door shut behind him, and took a seat. This couldn't be good news, I thought. Unless, of course, he'd stepped in to announce his immediate resignation. Hoping that might be the case, I gave him my full attention.

"Randy," he said, "I'm so excited about a new idea that I couldn't sleep last night."

"Which client are you talking about?"

"Not for a client," he said. "It's my latest inspiration for a book."

Stifling a groan, I glanced at my watch. "I've got a meeting in five minutes. Make it quick."

"Are you familiar with the French writer Georges Perec?"

I shook my head. "Sorry, but I've never heard of him."

"He wrote a book called *A Void* back in the late 1960s. It's a classic lipogrammatic—"

"A what?" I asked.

"A lipogrammatic novel, meaning that the book is written entirely without one letter. Perec chose to eliminate the letter *e*."

I just looked at him.

"My novel will lack the letter *a*."

"Why would you do that?"

"My full name is Clifford Young McCuen. An *a* is the only vowel that's missing."

"I mean, why would you even consider writing a book, leaving out one letter of the alphabet?"

"Think of the creative challenges," he said, his eyes wide. "Producing this novel will put my writing talents to the ultimate test. You know, picking out precisely the right words, seeking those perfect synonyms, crafting each and every sentence with the utmost care."

I continued to stare, slowly shaking my head.

"I've done the research," he said. "A typical novel of 100,000 words contains about 450,000 characters, and about 8% are the letter *a*. So, I'll have to replace about 36,000 characters."

I wondered if the time had come to replace my copywriter.

"It won't be as difficult as Perec's book, leaving out every *e*," he said. "In the average novel, the letter *e* makes up about 12% of the character count."

He had crossed the dreaded threshold, giving me far too much information. I stood, hoping Clifford would get the hint. He did. For the first time, I noticed tattoos on each of his arms as he walked out the door. Not images, but words. A few days earlier my assistant had informed me that Clifford had decided to have a collection of the world's most memorable advertising slogans permanently placed on his body, starting with "Think Different" and "Just Do It."

"Copywriters are an unusual breed, aren't they?" she had asked. She had that right.

* * *

At nine, Abbie showed me rough edits of the television commercials for the Exley account, our lone car dealership. I liked them, Exley would love them, and he'd continue to sell a lot of cars. And, I hoped, keep us as his agency of record. I told her to proceed with final production and I'd schedule a meeting with the client next week.

"The camera likes our new model," I said, referring to Beth Anthony's impressive debut.

"So does the cameraman," she said with a giggle. "Gossip has it they're already an item." I smiled at the news, feeling a little smug with my successful meddling.

Returning to my office, I spotted the film canister perched on a corner of my desk. Its lid now punctured with tiny air holes, the small container held those mysterious bugs Leslie and I had captured on Tillman's property the previous afternoon. I'd brought them with me this morning, thinking it might be worthwhile to get them identified. Given the absence of other leads, I felt we had nothing to lose.

But who could do it? The Biology Department at UA Little Rock was not an option, and the local high schools had closed for the summer weeks earlier. And then I remembered that the Cooperative Extension Service had assisted me a few years ago when unknown pests had attacked my roses. A helpful staff entomologist diagnosed the problem as aphids and prescribed a treatment producing prompt results.

I got online and found the homepage and telephone number for the Extension Service. Moments later my call was answered by a cordial receptionist, and I asked her to connect me to an insect specialist.

"Which one?" she asked. "We have two entomologists."

"Whoever's handiest."

"Let me transfer you to Dr. Lapinsky. Dr. Lyndal Lapinsky."

After hearing my request to have some insects identified, Dr. Lapinsky invited me to his office in the Extension Service complex located a few blocks north of the UA Little Rock campus on South University Avenue. I promised to be there within a quarter of an hour.

Mid-morning traffic was light, and I got lucky and parked 20 yards from the main entrance. Directed to the second floor, I found

Lapinsky hunched over his computer, typing furiously. Spotting me hovering at the door, he invited me in with a nod, while pounding the keyboard with long, bony fingers.

"Damn reports," he grumbled before rising and stepping from behind his desk. He stuck out his hand. "Lyn Lapinsky."

"Randy Lassiter."

"I like *Awkansas*, but this transition to the bureaucracy is driving me crazy," he said. I placed his accent somewhere north of Boston. If he was having trouble fitting in with state government, I had serious doubts about its adjustments to him. Tall and thin as a rail with a face to match, he wore wire-rim glasses, with a bright red rubber band confining his shoulder-length hair to a short ponytail. He had on a faded chambray shirt over blue jeans, with an unusual tie—a praying mantis motif—loosely knotted around his narrow neck. Thick, once-white socks and an old pair of Birkenstocks completed his ensemble.

"New to the state?"

"Second week on the job." He rubbed his hands impatiently. "What did you bring me?"

"Not sure," I said, tossing him the container. "I found a mess of these yesterday afternoon and am curious about them."

Lapinsky pried open the top and emptied the canister into a stainless-steel tray resting on a credenza near his desk. While he bent over and peered at the trio of bugs scurrying across the shiny surface, I glanced at the diplomas hanging from the wall. He'd earned his Ph.D. from Rutgers last year, with previous degrees from Amherst and Yale. Even with the advanced education, I thought, it might take him years to overcome his speech disorder.

Decorating his new office must have been a high priority. Prints, posters, and photographs of insects covered most of the available wall space. I found myself wondering what this serious bugman did on his vacations.

"These are dermestids," he said. "A kind of beetle."

"Is that good or bad?"

His expression indicated it wasn't a very good question. He turned back to the bugs. "Did you find these in your *godden*?"

"Out in the country. Near a meadow."

Lapinsky walked to his window and gazed at the parking lot. "Do you have any idea how many different species of beetles exist? Thousands, tens of thousands. Beetles make up one-fourth of the animal species on earth. One-fourth." He glanced at me, as if to see if I was paying attention.

I put on my most earnest look. "That many?"

"Fireflies are beetles. Same goes for what are known as lady-bugs." He took a couple of long steps to a tall storage cabinet and opened a door, exposing a collection of large, flat boxes. Running a finger down the labels, he pulled one out, holding it with care. "Beetles are so diverse. Let me show you."

He placed the container on his desk, motioning for me to join him. Covered by a clear plastic lid, it held a fascinating array of beautiful and bizarre bugs mounted against the bottom of the box.

I pointed to one at least six inches long. "I hope he's not local."

"That's a Hercules beetle," Lapinsky said. "Collected him in Panama." His use of the word *collect* reminded me of the way my hunting buddies have adopted the verb *harvest*. Nobody kills things anymore.

"And that one?" Almost as long as the Hercules, it possessed what seemed to be fearsome pincers.

"A long-horned beetle from French Guiana."

I nodded, figuring my curiosity regarding his vacation destinations had been answered.

"It's not as vicious as you might think," Lapinsky continued. "Its diet is mainly liquids."

"That smaller one in the corner appears pretty harmless." Grayish with a long snout, it was less than half an inch long.

He snorted, shaking his head. "That little rascal transformed the South."

I took another look at the bug and then turned my gaze to Lapinsky.

"The notorious boll weevil. Collected him in a cotton field in northeastern *Awkansas*."

Somebody needed to have a serious talk with him concerning the pronunciation of his new state.

"What about them?" I asked, tilting my head toward the creatures I'd brought.

"Those fine specimens are useful to science. They've saved countless hours of gruesome work."

He gestured to a chair and I sat, unsure what I'd gotten myself into.

"Your beetles, and especially their larvae, feed on dead flesh." He smiled when my body flinched. "In fact, I like to think of dermestids as the piranhas of the insect world."

I felt the hair on my neck rise. "What do you mean?"

"It's a fascinating process. As you know, many biologists spend a lot of time studying skeletons of their specimens. All that dead, nasty flesh would get in the way, wouldn't it?"

"I ... uh ... imagine so." Actually, I didn't want to imagine it at all.

"It's not unusual for large laboratories, such as the Field Museum in Chicago, to have entire rooms devoted to dermestid colonies. They place a carcass in the bug-room, wait a period of time, and—presto—the flesh is gone, leaving nothing but bones." He frowned, then shrugged. "And a rather disagreeable odor."

That answered another question. "You've done this yourself?"

"Many times," Lapinsky said. "Back in undergraduate days, I housed my dermestids in a five-gallon bucket." He scratched his head. "I believe the largest animal I worked with was a rabbit. Nothing big."

"But can they ... uh ... dispose of larger animals?"

"Most definitely," he said, waving his bony hands through the air. "A good, healthy colony could consume a dead cow in a couple of weeks. Maybe less."

"What makes for a—?"

"Good, healthy colony?" he interrupted. "The larvae need to be in a tight-fitting container, but well-ventilated. They must be fed, of course."

"Fed?"

"When the colony is not cleaning a carcass, it still requires nourishment. Some people add dried dog food. Others use roadkill."

That answered another question, I thought, remembering Dr. Mackie Tillman's unexpected stop on the highway near Pinnacle. "What about heat, humidity, that sort of thing?"

"An *Awkansas* summer provides the perfect environment. Warm and humid. A dermestid's dream." He paused for a moment, marched to a nearby cabinet, and opened a drawer. "Somewhere I have a handout on getting a colony established."

While Lapinsky searched his files, I reached for the tray and placed it across my knees. Oval and about the size of raisins, the brownish-black bugs skittered back and forth, relentless in their search for food.

My organized host soon returned, waving a sheet of paper. He handed it to me. "Here's a good introduction to these particular beetles."

"So, the larvae of these little creatures will eat everything but the bones?"

"They're marvels of efficiency."

"Is this ... er ... scientific technique used here in Arkansas?"

Lapinsky shrugged. "I don't know for certain since I've been here such a short time." Staring at the floor, he paused, running a hand through his ponytail. "I believe there's at least one practitioner. Earlier this week, my colleague mentioned a local biology professor—Timmons, Tisdale, or something similar—who maintains an active colony."

"There's a Dr. Mackenzie Tillman at UA Little Rock."

He snapped his fingers. "That's it. Tillman. If you know her, maybe you could introduce us."

"I've met her a time or two, but we're not close." I motioned at the tray in my lap. "Would you like these?"

"They're very robust," he said, retrieving the beetles. "I'm sure we can find a use for them."

When I stood to leave, Lapinsky held out his free hand. "Thanks for stopping by. I hope I've been of some assistance."

"You've been most helpful," I said as we exchanged a handshake. "And welcome to *Arkansas*." The devil made me stress the R.

~ THIRTY-EIGHT ~

As I stepped into my office, the telephone rang. It was Gib.

"Anything to report?" I asked.

"I talked to a pair of local psychiatric experts, folks I know and trust. Both agreed it would be unusual for someone with bipolar disorder to resort to violence." He hesitated a moment. "But it's been known to happen. In those cases, the scenes weren't pretty."

"Care to elaborate?"

"Murder and mayhem. You may recall that triple slaying in Hot Springs earlier this year?"

"A love triangle, or something like that?"

"An extreme bipolar case," Gib said. "Gruesome stuff. More than a few of the notorious mass murderers over the years have been tied to bipolar disorders."

"Anything else?"

"Ellen's still patiently waiting for her contractions to begin."

"Good luck!"

"One more thing," he said. "Did you notice the article in today's paper about the deceased woman in Cabot? The one who left her estate to a pair of poodles?"

I vaguely recalled the crazy story. "Something over half a million dollars, I believe."

"Right," said Gib. "I guess the bank now has what you'd call ... a Fidociary responsibility."

He cackled as I slammed the receiver into place. I took another couple of calls and refilled my coffee. For 45 minutes I tried to concentrate on the latest pile of paperwork but couldn't stay focused. My mind wandered, bouncing from bones to bugs and back. I had a strong urge to return to that disturbing corner on Tillman's property. But I had promised Leslie that I'd do nothing foolish.

Perhaps, I thought, I could hedge my bet. I dialed UA Little Rock's College of Arts and Sciences. "Dr. Rankin Campbell, please." If he picked up, I'd end the call.

"I'm sorry," a woman's voice replied, "but Dr. Campbell is on the other side of campus meeting with the chancellor."

"Should I call back following lunch?"

"One moment, please." I heard her rustling papers. "It appears Dr. Campbell won't be returning to the office today. He's scheduled to be in Pine Bluff all afternoon. May I take a message?"

"Thank you," I said, "but I'll try again at a later date." I hung up and pumped my fist into the air. I'd just been given a green light.

Tossing my sport coat over a shoulder, I told my assistant that I'd be taking the rest of the day off. Getting a jump start on the weekend, I explained. I went to the house, inhaled a fat bologna and sliced onion sandwich for lunch, and changed into grubby jeans, an old t-shirt, and work boots. I decided to leave Leslie a note, writing it on the back of the handout Lapinsky had given me. Even though I was 99% sure that I'd be home prior to her return, there was always the remote chance she could finish her assignment in Mountain View ahead of schedule.

I next reached for the phone and dialed Booker's number. He didn't answer, but I left a message asking him to do a bit of electronic snooping on Dr. Rankin Campbell, UA Little Rock's Dean of Arts & Sciences. A speedy reply would be appreciated, I said.

After placing my cell phone and a flashlight into a small daypack, I went to the kitchen pantry and grabbed a bottle of water. I spotted a box of facemasks left over from the COVID-19 pandemic of 2020/2021 and added a pair to my pack. Climbing into the truck, I drove west on Highway 10, making a five-minute stop at a hardware store for a pair of leather work gloves.

The picnic grounds at Pinnacle Mountain State Park were busy, no surprise given the beautiful Friday afternoon. I parked the truck, slipped on my pack, and started down the same trail Janetta had introduced Leslie and me to a day earlier. Within minutes I'd left the marked path, bushwhacking toward the river. I didn't bother to look for snakes, but bounded across a familiar cypress log and angled through the woods to Tillman's property line. I crawled through the fence and made a beeline for the septic tank and its mysterious beetles. A pair of crows rose from the meadow and flew into the woods, mocking me with harsh caws as they departed.

As before, a stepladder and pry bar leaned against the tank. I'm not sure why, but I snapped a couple of pictures with my cell phone and then donned a mask and approached the concrete structure. My eyes sought out the crack along its base. If anything, the beetle population had swelled overnight as dozens—maybe hundreds—swarmed in and around the break.

Taking another step forward, I pulled the gloves over my shaking, sweating palms. The horrific smell gave me an instant headache, but the facemask seemed to eliminate at least a little of the indescribable stink. I glanced at the ground and saw what appeared to be small bone fragments scattered in the grass. They hadn't been there yesterday.

I climbed to the top of the stepladder, nearly overcome by the stench, and shoved against the heavy plywood lid. It failed to budge. I lowered my shoulder and tried again with the same result.

Eyes burning and gagging from the acrid aroma, I clambered down the ladder, swallowing hard to keep bile from welling up in my dry throat. Stumbling to a stop 30 feet away, I doubled over, catching my breath and spitting onto the ground. I found my pack and slipped a second mask over the first, hoping an extra layer might help. When I looked back to the tank, my eyes stopped on the pry bar. After staring at it for seconds, I shook my head. As I returned to the tank, I wondered if the vile odor had affected my mental acuity.

Grabbing the hefty steel bar in one hand, I again climbed the ladder. Ramming its tapered end between the top and wall of the tank, I shoved my arms forward. The heavy wooden cap opened eight to ten inches as it scraped against the concrete. Fighting an overpowering urge to retch, I again jammed the point in the narrow slot and pressed my weight against the bar, forcing the lid to yield another foot. One more time I repeated the exercise before leaping from the ladder, choking back the vomit.

Standing in the thick, humid air, my entire body heaving, I wondered if I was losing my sanity. Surely to God the tank didn't hold the remains of J.J. and Summer. I shuddered, wondering if Dr. Mackie Tillman could have gone berserk, killing in a fit of rage. Was Dr. Rankin Campbell capable of murder? Could they have acted together? What would be the motive? Tenure for Tillman? And how did Benton Tillman's donation to UA Little Rock fit in, if at all? As these troubling thoughts filled my mind, I remembered DuChamps's final rule for the perfect crime: you get rid of the body.

I let the pry bar fall to the ground. Flashlight clutched in a trembling hand, I swallowed a fresh gulp of air and trotted to the ladder, bouncing up the steps. Shining the slender beam into the dark opening, I saw nothing at first. Accustomed to the brilliant sunlight streaming through the trees, my eyes had trouble adjusting to the black bowels of the odious tank.

And then, over the course of a few agonizing, horrible seconds, my worst nightmare came into focus. Three feet below the top of the tank, a writhing, seething mass of bones and beetles appeared under the weak cone of light. I wanted to scream, but couldn't, sure that I'd throw up instead.

I leaned further over the tank for a better look, and my cell phone slid out of my shirt pocket, disappearing into dark and nasty muck. I cursed my bad luck, but never even thought of reaching for it.

Bones were everywhere, big ones and little ones jumbled together like a giant heap of pick-up sticks straight from hell, beetles clinging to every one. Looking closer into the pile, I saw strange grub-like creatures, thousands upon thousands of them. The dermestid larvae, I thought, recalling photographs from Lapinsky's handout. About half an inch long and bigger than the beetles, the hairy, brown larvae were fulfilling the ancient Biblical charge of ashes to ashes, dust to dust. Their small, subtle movements made the decaying mound almost seem like a large, living beast at rest.

Feeling faint, I swung the beam into a far corner of the tank, and my hand froze. Until then, the bones could have come from any number of sources. But staring back under my unsteady light were the empty eye sockets of a human skull.

Jerking my head from the horror, I heard a loud snarl at my feet. Poised to spring at any second, Campbell's rottweiler crouched at the base of the stepladder. Ears down, lips curled back, and teeth bared, the big dog had the look of death in his eyes.

~ THIRTY-NINE ~

I stared at the massive brute, petrified, desperate to hide my fear. Weighing a good 120 pounds, the dog looked no more than two, maybe three, years old. His open mouth glistened with teeth, all shiny and sharp, and there wasn't a single grayish hair around his snout. Thick-chested with powerful shoulder muscles bulging under his black hide, the rottweiler pranced around the base of the stepladder. I knew it was only a matter of time before he attacked, snapping his powerful jaws shut on some unfortunate part of my anatomy.

I caught a movement out of the corner of my eye and glanced toward Tillman's house. Dr. Rankin Campbell walked through the gate between the walls, pushing a wheelbarrow. His trip to Pine Bluff must have been a ruse. The dog, realizing my attention had shifted elsewhere, leaped at me with a savage snarl, his shark-like teeth slashing at my left knee. I yanked my leg back, slamming my calf and thigh into the concrete wall of the tank, as the rottweiler ripped the denim in my jeans all the way to the cuff.

A sharp whistle pierced the air. "Conan! Come here." The dog bounded to Campbell, who now stood ten yards away. Stepping from behind the wheelbarrow, he gave the dog a rough pat on his back, said "Sit," and turned his gaze to me. Hands on his hips, Campbell radiated hostility. "Can't you sons of bitches read?" He didn't give me time for an answer. "We've posted two dozen goddamned **No Trespassing** signs, and here you are, vandalizing private property."

A wave of nausea roiled upward from my aching gut. I managed to stagger down the stepladder and jerk both facemasks aside before losing both my lunch and breakfast in the weeds. I'd never been so sick in my life.

"Goddamned redneck," he said. "What are you doing here anyway? Searching for catfish bait?"

When I managed to stand upright, wiping a sleeve across my mouth, Campbell looked at me and then did a double take before advancing a couple of deliberate steps in my direction. A sadistic smile emerged on his face. "Well, if it isn't Mr. Randy Lassiter." His voice had changed. "I've had a recurring vision that we might run into each other again." He paused, staring into me with cold, empty eyes, his jaw muscles working overtime. "You and your damn search for Dr. Newell."

"Did I find him?" It was the wrong thing to ask, but I was angry and lightheaded.

Campbell answered by reaching around to his back, his hand reappearing with a small pistol he must have stashed in the waistband of his trousers. "It's just a .22. My snake gun. But don't try anything stupid, okay?"

I nodded, remembering my promise to Leslie.

Campbell muttered under his breath, gave me a wicked glance, and began pacing back and forth like a caged animal, his face growing redder by the second. He soon stopped, his chest heaving and a heavy gold chain bouncing around his neck, and waved the pistol at me. Spittle clung to the corners of his mouth. "You seem to have an uncanny ability to screw things up, don't you?" Low and raspy, his voice dripped with venom.

"You want me to leave?" It was worth a try.

Campbell snorted. "I believe you'll come with me." He motioned the barrel of his gun toward the open gate. Still unsteady, I shuffled along the path and into the large meadow behind Tillman's home, Campbell and his dog trailing. My head throbbed with every stride. When I slowed down to catch my breath, Campbell jabbed the pistol into my back, knocking me forward.

He's probably using one of Mackie's gun show purchases, I told myself, and this was my reward.

"To the left," Campbell said as we neared the house after the long walk. "The little building off to the side."

Entering the potting shed, I felt another sharp push against my spine. "Now, drop to the floor, facedown. Do as I say and you might live a few more hours." He snapped his fingers, pointing at my head, and the dog positioned himself inches above my neck, close enough that I felt his hot, rancid breath swirling over my skin.

I heard Campbell searching the shed, opening doors and shoving things around. He grunted with satisfaction. "Give me your hands," he ordered, and bound them behind my back with duct tape and repeated the procedure with my feet. "Roll over." I didn't move quickly enough, and a swift kick to my ribs reminded me to do better next time. After covering my mouth with the tape, he finished the roll, securing my ankles to a leg of the immense potting table.

"It's too late to be a hero, you dumb piece of shit." He gave me another kick for good measure. "I've got a job to finish. I'll deal with you afterward." He snapped his fingers again. "Let's go, Conan."

Once the door shut behind them, I tested my restraints. Flopping around like a carp tossed onto a sandbar, I managed to scoot the heavy table a fraction of an inch, but that was it. I wasn't going anywhere soon. Not only had Campbell done a thorough job immobilizing me, I remained weak and dehydrated after all that vomiting. My throat ached from thirst.

Twenty minutes or so lapsed before I heard noises outside the shed. Moments later, Campbell burst into the room, pushing the wheelbarrow, with Conan bouncing in at his heels. His face beet red, Campbell had sweated through his shirt. Breathing hard, he shot me a grim smirk and dug a gloved hand into the bed of the wheelbarrow. He pulled out a long, curved bone—a rib from the looks of it—and grabbed the handle of the grinder, setting it in motion. Within seconds the bone had disappeared, and Campbell wasted no time selecting the next. Bound to the table, my body shook with the constant vibrations as he shoved one bone after another through the grinder.

I watched his face. He appeared to be whistling as he attacked the pile, but I couldn't make out the tune over the unrelenting rumble of the antique contraption. When Campbell finished the load, he marched out the door with the wheelbarrow, Conan leading the way. It was then that I was able to discern the melody. I shuddered, recognizing the song from *Snow White and the Seven Dwarfs*. Campbell marched to his repository of bones whistling, "Heigh Ho, Heigh Ho, It's Off to Work I Go."

He'd left the door cracked, and an unexpected sunbeam angled across the gloomy room. Like plankton drifting in the Gulf Stream, countless dust particles danced in and out of the light. I stared at the swirling motes, realizing the tiny, lifeless specks were bits of bones. Bones that in the not-too-distant past had been living, breathing creatures. Humans? I closed my eyes.

After another half hour or so had passed, Campbell reappeared, sweat dripping from his brow, and again parked his stinking load of freight next to the potting table. He started with what must have been a leg bone, given its length, and spent several minutes reducing it to dust.

Without any warning, he began to talk. "Things were going so well," he said, taking a break but never glancing my way. "After I'd labored months and months fine-tuning my proposal, Benton Tillman finally agreed to fund the project. A spectacular $25 million showcase. Equal to any in the nation. In the world, for that matter. My hand-picked team would tackle and defeat global problems. All under my direction. And, at long last, a chance for me to be paid what I'm worth." He selected a small bone and pushed it through the grinder in seconds. "And then your friend Newell decides Dr. Mackenzie Tillman is not good enough for his precious Biology Department. That her contract would not be renewed." He slammed his fist onto the table, his eyes wide.

Twisting my neck, I watched as Campbell emptied the tray, piled high with meal, into another five-gallon bucket. "I took care of that problem, and my plan was back on track." He shook his head and ran a handful of small bones through the machine before letting it coast to a stop. "Out of the blue, a young woman calls here one Saturday morning. I believe it was a Ms. Preston. She asks if she can come by and talk about Professor Newell." He laughed—a strange, high-pitched, repulsive laugh—and shrugged his shoulders. "How could I say no?"

Working like a madman, Campbell finished the rest of the load in ten minutes. Wiping his hands on his pants, he turned and glared at me, a quiet, maniacal rage in his eyes. "After you barged into my office quizzing me about Newell, I had to do something to discourage your meddling. That was me, of course, who spooked your lovely fiancée late one evening," he said, grasping the handles of the wheelbarrow. "Poor thing. She's going to be so lonely." He and Conan disappeared through the door, returning to their boneyard.

I couldn't see my watch, but guessed it was late afternoon when they reappeared. Campbell seemed exhausted. Working less frantically than before, he continued his routine, sometimes speaking between sessions at the grinder, although seldom making eye contact. "Mackie has no idea I'm feeding her nasty little bugs," he said, a twisted smile on his gaunt face. "She assumes her colony is having an exceptional spring." He cackled and grabbed the next chunk of calcium. "But she's so naive. She thinks I care for her, the spoiled bitch. Thought I enjoyed that goddamned cruise." He hooted and beat the table with the long bone. "She's crazy, you know." After mopping his brow with a grimy handkerchief, he leaned once more into the grinder.

I noticed him taking short breaks, rubbing his left shoulder. "I'm getting too old for this," he muttered. "My arm keeps going numb." He waggled an index finger my way, his eyebrows arched. "Maybe I should let you give this handy little machine a spin. Put your fine young muscles to work one last time." But he discarded that idea, sparing me untold agony, and reached into the wheelbarrow.

290

My eyes shut, I worried about Leslie. What would she do when she found my note? I prayed she wouldn't end up flat on her back, tied to the same table, watching Campbell convert my skeletal remains into a mound of meal.

The room grew silent, and the seconds dragged by. I opened my eyelids a crack as Campbell snorted. "Ah, this is special," he said. In his right hand he held a human skull, turning it one way and then another. Realizing it was J.J.'s or Summer's, I felt my chest heave. But there was nothing left to vomit.

Campbell examined the skull for a few more moments before placing it at the table's edge. Raising my head as high as possible, I squinted, staring with disbelieving eyes, and spotted plastic braces stretching over its upper teeth. My God, I thought—Summer. Her rich red hair, turquoise eyes, and shy smile flashed through my mind … the gentle woman who'd written a love song for J.J. and who had taught him to play the guitar. Just as I started to gag, Campbell shattered the skull with a hammer, blasting fragments throughout the room. "I found out earlier these are too big for my machine." He grunted and tossed the hammer to the floor.

After pulverizing several smaller pieces, Campbell lifted a thick section of skull from the table, dropping it with a violent shake of his hand. "Goddamned maggots!" He swept the tabletop with his arm, showering me with debris. I didn't think much of it until I felt something inching across the thin fabric of my t-shirt. Lurching to one side, I must have flipped the larva to the floor; the crawling ceased.

Spinning the handle like a man possessed, Campbell attacked these last pieces. As the grinder spat out the bone meal, he looked to me and sighed. "One more load. And that will open a special vacancy reserved for you."

But he wasn't the same man. The color had drained from his face, giving him a ghostly cast. Smudged and smeared with bone dust, his glasses rested halfway down his nose. His eyes, still sinister, had sunken further into his face and his cheekbones seemed more prominent. As Conan leaped outside through the door, Campbell followed, pushing the wheelbarrow, his shoulders slumped as if carrying the weight of the world. He was too tired to whistle.

Dusk arrived, and neither Campbell nor his dog had returned. The only parts of my body not aching were those already numb. Rocking back and forth on the concrete floor, I tried to restore circulation in my arms and feet. My throat and mouth felt like I'd swallowed a quart of sand. In the distance, I heard a freight train rumbling on its tracks near the Arkansas River, and closer, a pair of blue jays squabbled over territorial rights.

As darkness descended on the Tillman compound, I figured Campbell had gone inside Mackie's house to rest, maybe to prepare himself dinner. When he finished with his last load, it would be my turn in the tank. DuChamps, I thought, would have been impressed with Campbell's system. I imagined myself, mortally wounded by a shot from Campbell's pistol but still conscious, sinking into the morass of that dark hellhole, slowly enveloped by the voracious larvae. One tiny bite at a time, my body would disappear. I flinched as a cold sweat drenched my skin.

The minutes dragged into hours, and still no sign of Campbell. A squadron of mosquitoes feasted on my face and neck, while others took perverse pleasure droning in and out of my ears like tiny kamikaze pilots in training. At some point well into the evening, I felt sure a mouse crawled across my legs, but it scampered away before I could react. I shook myself a time or two before collapsing into a troubled slumber. I dreamed that Clifford, my young copywriter, was directing a movie à la Hitchcock. He had titled it *The Bugs*, and I'd been given a starring role.

A slight noise outside the shed awakened me. Lifting my head from the concrete floor, I heard something rustle in the leaves and enter the shed on padded feet. I tilted my ears toward the door, but it was so dark I couldn't tell if my eyes were open. Without warning, one of the tools on the opposite side crashed to the floor, bringing down three or four others with it. A loud yelp erupted, and a large animal, I later assumed to be a raccoon, bounced against my chest like a defibrillator as it raced to the exit. My

292

shouts muffled by the tape, I lay still while the adrenalin level in my bloodstream returned to normal.

I began counting, adding the seconds one by one. I'd reached 3,514 when I heard another noise outside, louder than before. Campbell, I thought. Doubtless awakened from an unscheduled nap and eager to complete his task. If he'd now killed two people, what difference would one more make?

Holding my breath as quiet footsteps approached, I saw the rays of a flashlight sweep in from the open door across the threshold. The beam bounced around the room, lingered on the table-top for a few seconds, and soon flickered back to the entrance. The door began to close.

Yanking my legs with every ounce of strength I could muster, I jerked the table enough to create a scraping noise. As I did it again, the narrow cone of light shot back into the shed. My grunt was followed by a gasp at the door. The light swung to the floor, landed on my knees, and moved up, stopping on my face with a blinding brilliance.

~ FORTY ~

"Janetta!" The shriek accompanying the flashlight was Leslie's. "He's here in the shed!"

The beam ricocheted through the air to my side. "Randy! Are you okay?"

I struggled to nod.

Placing her light on the concrete floor next to my shoulder, Leslie reached behind my head and grabbed an end of the duct tape. "This may sting," she said before ripping it from my face. I figured I wouldn't have to shave for a week.

"Are you hurt?"

"Just a bit stiff." I rolled to the side so she could free my wrists.

Janetta trotted in with another flashlight, aiming it at my arms while Leslie peeled away the bindings. "You had us concerned, chief." I noticed a serious handgun hanging from a holster on her right hip. She shifted the beam to my ankles and Leslie made me a free man.

With her help, I staggered to my feet, using the potting table to steady myself. I felt like I'd just crawled from a car wreck.

"So, how was Mountain View?" I asked, rubbing my burning cheeks.

Tears streaming down her face, Leslie wrapped her arms around my sore and aching body and pulled me tight. "You had me so worried."

Janetta shined her light on my chest. "Leslie, I'm not sure this man—any man for that matter—is worth the trouble," she said. "If it's not one thing, it's something else. Bad news all the way around."

Leslie's hand grasped one of mine. She sniffed and took a step back. "Did Campbell tie you up?"

"Hours ago."

"Where is he?" Janetta asked.

I tried shrugging, but my muscles wouldn't respond. "He must have left after I dozed off."

"Wrong. His car's parked in front of the house."

"Could he be in the house?"

"I don't think so," Leslie said. "The lights are off and the front door's wide open. We didn't see any signs of life."

"And no trace of that monster dog Leslie mentioned," Janetta said.

"He might still be at the boneyard," I said.

"Boneyard?" Leslie asked. "What do you mean?"

"That out-of-place septic tank you and I discovered at the rear of the property. It's where Campbell disposed of the bodies."

Leslie gasped. Janetta swung her flashlight to my face. "Bodies? Like in homicides?"

I picked Leslie's light up from the floor and shined it on the newest batch of bone meal. "Campbell spent most of the afternoon trying to complete the perfect crime. Those beetles in the tank consumed the bodies, and Campbell made sure the bones disappeared. He mumbled something about spreading these buckets of meal in the meadow. No bodies, no evidence, no crimes."

"J.J. and Summer, both dead?" Leslie's voice was but a whisper. "I read the article on the other side of your note. But I didn't want to believe ..."

I placed an arm on her shoulders.

"You're saying this Dr. Campbell could still be on the property?" Janetta asked.

"Maybe we should check the tank," I said. "But he's carrying a pistol."

"I'm a licensed law enforcement officer," Janetta said, patting the holster on her hip. "I'm not afraid to use this."

Each supporting an arm, they led me from the shed into the cool night air. I glanced at my watch, its glow-in-the-dark dial reading 2:20. I then realized how dry my throat was. "Anybody got any water?"

Leslie pulled a bottle from her fanny pack and handed it to me. I took a long swig, caught my breath, and then drank another deep swallow. I'd never tasted anything better. "Don't you think we should bring in reinforcements?" I asked, wiping a forearm across my chapped lips.

"We tried," Leslie said. "This is outside the city limits, so the Little Rock Police Department has no jurisdiction."

"What about the county sheriff's office?"

"I gave them a ring after I found your truck in the parking lot," Janetta said. "Leslie called me around midnight, asking me to check."

"No luck?" I asked.

"Their dispatcher was frantic," Janetta said. "It's a Friday night, and all hell had broken loose. A couple of nasty car crashes, a major brawl at a tavern, and two drug raids, not to mention the usual assortment of domestic disturbances. All the officers were working incidents."

"I'm not out to be a hero," Leslie said. "But I don't want Campbell to get away."

"Damn right," I said. "He has a debt to pay."

"Let's go," Janetta said. "Quietly. And kill the lights."

We spread apart, a quarter moon overhead, and walked slowly as our eyes adjusted to the darkness. The grass, blanketed in dew, soaked our shoes and lower pant legs before we'd gone 20 yards. Halfway across the meadow, we stopped. Behind us, Mackie Tillman's house sat empty and dark. Ahead, the forest looked like a black void, broken only by the occasional firefly.

"How did you get here?" I whispered.

"When Janetta called back to let me know she'd discovered your truck, we agreed to meet at the Visitor's Center," Leslie said.

"We then drove to Tillman's gate, climbed over the fence, and here we are," Janetta said. "Nothing to it." She touched my arm. "Now, show me where we're going."

"The corner where the south and east stone walls converge," I said, pointing toward the general area. "It's still a hundred yards away."

We approached with caution, the stone walls gradually coming into view. The sounds of frogs and crickets filled the night air, and deep in the woods an owl hooted.

"How much farther?" Janetta whispered.

"There's a gate in an opening some 20 yards beyond us, and the tank itself sits another 30 yards or so past that."

We reached the corner, dropping behind the rock fence. As if on cue, the chorus of frogs and crickets ended, and a curtain of quiet descended upon us. For several minutes we squatted motionless, waiting for a sound, a movement, some sign of activity.

On her knees, Leslie peeked over the wall, gazing in the direction of the tank. "I can't see anything," she said, her voice low.

Janetta unsnapped her holster, holding the pistol in her right hand. "I'll go down the middle of the trail," she said. "Nice and easy. I want you two to stay well back of me, one on each side. And don't do anything foolish."

I'd heard that before.

As we stepped through the gate and under the canopy of trees, the darkness enveloped us, a black so thick I felt as if I'd entered a cave. Fifteen yards away, the septic tank remained indefinite, a shadowy outline whose presence was given away only by its hellish smell. The stench stopped us in our tracks.

"This is the police," Janetta called out, her voice loud and clear. "Anybody here?"

For moments there was no reply, and then a low, guttural growl broke the silence.

"That's Conan," I whispered. "Campbell's dog."

The rottweiler snarled again, but remained invisible, his black coat blending into the night.

"This is the police," Janetta repeated. "Anyone here?" She took another couple of steps forward, and Leslie and I did the same.

Conan provided the sole reaction, a sharp bark somewhere ahead.

Janetta switched on her flashlight and Leslie followed suit, their beams pinpointing the dog. Lying at the base of the tank, Conan looked at us warily, but made no aggressive moves. The stepladder was on one side of the dog and the wheelbarrow on the other. We saw no sign of Campbell.

Janetta swept her light over the area. She paused and then retraced the path of its beam. "What's that?" A small canvas object at the edge of the trail had drawn her attention.

"My daypack," I said. "I left it here earlier." I started to retrieve the bag.

"Oh my God," Leslie said. "I think I've found him."

I wheeled around and saw Leslie gripping the flashlight with both hands, her arms extended. She aimed it above the stepladder at the top of the tank. The plywood cap had been pushed aside, leaving a gaping hole. Leslie's light wavered, but left no doubt about the scene. Protruding from the opening were the feet and lower legs of a human.

~ FORTY-ONE ~

"Shit!" Janetta took a tentative step toward the body in the tank, but Conan sprang to his feet, head down and ears flat. As he curled his lips, again displaying a fine set of sharp teeth, a low growl rumbled through his thick chest. A quick study, Janetta jumped backward, stumbling against Leslie in her haste to appease the rottweiler. "Easy, boy," she whispered. "Nice and easy. I can see just fine from here. Just fine." The dog dropped to the ground and Janetta directed her light back to the tank.

I knew the body was Campbell's. After spending hour after hour flat on my back staring at Campbell's feet and legs while he ran bone after bone through the grinder, I recognized the boots and what I could see of the pants as if they were my own.

"What happened?" asked Leslie.

"Maybe a stroke," Janetta said. "Or a heart attack."

"Or perhaps," I offered, "an act of a vengeful God."

Seconds passed as we stared at the gruesome scene, the flash-lights fixed on Campbell's feet and legs.

"The last time I saw him, Campbell looked awful," I said, remembering his haggard visage. "Like he was on the verge of collapse."

Janetta pointed her flashlight at the feet and worked the beam past his socks and to the cuffs of his trousers. As the light swept over the few inches of exposed, pale skin, I saw something stir.

Leslie must have seen it, too. "What was that?" she asked. She swung her light to the spot, and Janetta's followed. There was a small movement along a sock and another on the sole of his left boot.

"Dermestids," I said. "The beetles."

One appeared on Campbell's pasty shin before scurrying into his pants leg and out of sight. Another dangled from a shoelace, spinning in a lazy circle before dropping to the ground.

As Leslie switched her flashlight off, she cleared her throat. "I've seen enough." She turned and began walking away from the tank.

"Could I borrow your light?" I asked. After she handed it to me, I aimed it at the wheelbarrow. A pile of bones filled its bed, bones that once lived in the bodies of J.J. and Summer. I shuddered and fell in place a few paces behind Leslie.

Janetta brought up the rear, opening the cell phone she'd carried on her belt. "I believe it's time to try the sheriff's office again," she said.

While we stopped at the gap between the walls, leaning against the cool rocks of the fence, Janetta dialed a number. "This is Superintendent Janetta Strickland of Pinnacle Mountain State Park. We have an emergency situation." She paused a moment. "No, I'm not in the park." She was silent for several seconds before giving directions to Tillman's property. "My truck's parked at the gate," she said. "We'll meet your people there." She nodded. "The situation? It's hard to say, but looks like we have a double homicide along with a natural death." There was a short hesitation. "Yes, that's right. A double homicide and one natural death." She listened for a few seconds. "Right. Call the coroner. And bring lots of gloves and facemasks, plus something to sedate a dog." She nodded her head again. "I'm serious. A real big dog."

We made the long walk across the meadow, past Tillman's house, the shed, and Campbell's car, and down the drive. Rather than climbing the imposing fence, we stayed inside the gate. Within ten minutes a patrol car stopped beside Janetta's pickup, and a deputy got out. Introducing himself, the deputy said we might as well wait on the others before going to the scene. Still standing outside the gate, he pulled a notepad from a hip pocket and asked for our names, addresses, and telephone numbers, beginning with the women. As I began providing my information, I pointed to Leslie, and said, "I can be reached on her cell phone."

Leslie gave me a confused look.

"My phone," I said, "fell out of my shirt pocket and is somewhere in the depths of that septic tank."

"So, that's the explanation of why you never answered my calls." She then wrinkled her nose and grimaced.

By 3:30 a.m., a small crowd had gathered at the entrance to Tillman's property. The three of us remained inside the fence while the others milled around outside, most enjoying fresh doughnuts someone had brought. The county coroner and his assistants arrived in a shiny black Suburban, followed by a film crew from Channel 5, the local "blood and guts" television station. Its news director, if rumors could be believed, kept a police scanner in every room of his house.

The Pulaski County sheriff appeared a short while later. His starched uniform would look good on the news, I thought. As he stuck his arm through the iron bars of the gate and shook Janetta's hand, he leaned forward, allowing them to talk in private for a short time. When she pointed to Leslie and me, he nodded and glanced our way. Once their conversation was complete, he issued instructions to his staff.

While a couple of deputies tried without success to jimmy the gate open, the rest of the group used a worn rope ladder that an officer had pulled from his trunk and climbed the fence one at a time. When everyone was over, we began the long trek past Tillman's house to the opposite end of her property. With the exception of the sheriff, the law enforcement agents were loaded with gear. We moved en masse, flashlights flickering across the dark, dewy field. Leslie wrapped her cold fingers around my hand.

As we walked, I attempted an abbreviated explanation of the sequence of events to the sheriff. Several times he came to a stop, looking hard into my eyes, and asked for additional details. Janetta and Leslie corroborated my account when appropriate.

Had they not been along, I had the feeling I might have been wearing handcuffs by now.

One of the cops, a fresh-faced young man who couldn't have been more than 25, kept trying to shove a search warrant into my hands. Placing them in my pockets, I had to tell him twice I didn't own the property, didn't live on it, and wasn't related to the owner. He then tried the same act on both Leslie and Janetta.

The sheriff paused to light a cigarette. "Then whose property is it?" He blew a cloud of smoke through his nose.

"Dr. Mackenzie Tillman's," I said. "A UA Little Rock professor."

"And," Janetta added, "Benton Tillman's daughter."

I saw a member of the Channel 5 news team reach for her cell phone.

The sheriff flung his cigarette to the ground and snuffed it with heel of his boot. "Goddamn it!" he muttered. "Why can't things be simple?" He gestured to his chief deputy. "Track down Benton Tillman's lawyer," he said. "Give him a heads-up but keep it vague. Tell him we'll provide details as soon as we know what the hell's happened. Shit!" He gave me another hard look. "Don't tell me things are going to get worse." As he resumed walking across the field, the group fell in behind him.

"There is one other matter," I said as we neared the tank.

The sheriff stopped to face me once more. "What's that?"

"There's a dangerous dog back here," I said, loud enough for everyone to hear. "Somebody will need to tranquilize him."

A huge hand slapped my back. "Don't you worry about that. I'm good with pups." A deputy who looked like a veteran of the pro wrestling circuit was the self-described canine counselor. "All you got to do is look 'em straight in the eye and establish who's boss. It works every time."

Janetta started to say something but changed her mind. We soon arrived at the break in the stone fence and heard Conan's familiar growl. Everyone came to a stop but the brawny deputy. He kept going as every light swung to the dog. Advancing one step at a time and talking in a soothing tone, he closed the gap, his right hand extended with its palm up. "Easy does it, boy. Easy does it." Conan stood his ground but didn't look as menacing as earlier. Ears erect and mouth closed, he let the man get within five feet before growling again. "Good boy," the deputy whispered. "You're a good boy." He took another step and had started to crouch when the dog lashed forward with a vicious snarl, snapping at the deputy's massive hand. Screaming in pain, the would-be hero toppled onto his back, clutching his bloody fingers, as Conan spun around and resumed guard duty.

A couple of other deputies had drawn their pistols but the sheriff waved them off. He laughed and searched his shirt pocket for another cigarette. "Somebody find a tourniquet for Leroy," he said. "And I want the dog sedated. Right now." Conan, I thought, would already be a dead dog had the media not been present.

As his associates sprang into action, the sheriff looked over his shoulder to us. "Where are those bodies? And what's that goddamn smell?"

Janetta and Leslie swept their flashlights through the air like synchronized beacons, stopping on the legs at the top of the tank.

"There's one of them," I said.

"Good God Almighty," the sheriff muttered. A restless murmur passed through the group as a dozen beams fell on Campbell's feet and legs.

Leslie turned her light to the wheelbarrow. "Here's what's left of the others."

The sheriff nodded and rubbed a hand across his chin. "I think I've got the smell figured out."

Several minutes later, a dart to the shoulder subdued Conan. Two deputies carried his heavy, limp body to the edge of the meadow and tied him to a tree with a stout rope. Following the dog's removal, other officers cordoned off the area, stretching yellow **Crime Scene** tape in a 25-yard radius around the septic tank. Channel 5's crew stayed busy.

The men working on Tillman's entry gate must have been successful. A squad car, the Pulaski County coroner's Suburban, and

two official Jeeps appeared in the meadow with additional equipment, including a pair of generators that soon powered portable
lighting units. The coroner and an assistant climbed into bright
orange jumpsuits and shuffled toward the tank, adding an even
more surreal element to an already bizarre scene. They had gone
less than ten yards when they stopped and shouted for face masks.

Leslie and Janetta excused themselves, claiming an interest in
Conan's welfare. Not sure I wanted to watch the next stage of the
work at the tank, I tapped the sheriff on his shoulder. "There's a
nearby site you might need to see," I said. I then led him and two
deputies to the northeast corner of Tillman's property and aimed
a flashlight at the pile of ashes Leslie and I had stumbled across.
The sheriff dropped to one knee and studied the piece of scorched,
melted plastic we'd found earlier. "Definitely a cell phone," he said,
and then dipped his fountain pen into the debris, uncovering the
zipper. He had one officer encircle the area with reflective tape
while the other sifted through the cinders, depositing charred items
into small plastic bags.

"Anything else?" he asked.

I started to shake my head, but had another thought. "You'll
need to examine the potting shed."

"Where is it?"

"Near Tillman's house."

"Take me there. And then we'll get statements from you and
the two women."

From a distance, the busy scene across the meadow resembled
a festive outdoor party. Bright lights and plenty of people milling
about. But there was no music, laughter, or loud voices, nothing
but the low hum of generators.

When we neared the tank, the sheriff motioned to two more
officers and got the attention of Leslie and Janetta. "Let's get away
from this madhouse." He didn't have to ask twice. We began the
long walk to the potting shed.

The sheriff spent a few minutes inspecting the room, running
his pen through a bucket of bone meal and studying the ancient

grinder, careful not to touch it. He pointed at the scraps of duct tape strewn across the concrete floor and looked to me. "This is where you were held captive?"

As I thought back to the image of Campbell toiling away at the grinder and remembered the indelible sense of helplessness, a sharp tightness gripped my throat. I coughed and gave him a slight nod.

After instructing one deputy to document the scene with photographs before collecting any physical evidence, the sheriff led the rest of us to the house. "I believe you said nobody's home."

"Far as we know," said Janetta.

Marching up the front steps and through the open doorway, the sheriff switched on lights as he went. While he checked the ground floor, his colleague looked upstairs. Once it was determined we had the place to ourselves, the five of us convened in Tillman's kitchen. The deputy searched through his large satchel and pulled out a tall thermos and a stack of plastic cups.

"Coffee anyone?" he asked. The sheriff and Janetta joined the deputy in having a cup.

"What we'll do next is take statements," said the sheriff, settling onto a stool at the counter. "Deputy Johnson and I will talk with you one at a time. The other two can wait in the big room with the fireplace and bookcases." He got nods from the three of us while Johnson fished a tape recorder and notepad from his bag. "Who's first?" the sheriff asked, lighting another cigarette.

Leslie and Janetta looked at me. "I believe you're it," he said. I collapsed into a chair as the women left the room.

By 6:00 a.m. our statements had been taken and signed, and we were free to go. As we trudged down the long driveway to Janetta's truck, still parked beside the open gate to Tillman's property, a helicopter hovered low over the house. At first, I assumed it was a law enforcement chopper, but then the logo for Channel 5 came into view. When the aircraft swung around, we saw the silhouette of a cameraman perched at the door. It must be ratings month, I thought.

"Got some advice for you, Flash," I said.

Janetta cocked her head, giving me a tired look. "What's that?"

"You might want to slip into a clean uniform. Touch up your lipstick."

"Maybe you should check a mirror yourself, sport."

"But I have this crazy feeling it's you we're going to see on television tonight."

~ FORTY-TWO ~

Leslie and I squeezed into the cab of Janetta's state-issued truck and rode with her to Pinnacle's Visitor's Center where Leslie had left her car. A quiet trip, it ended with tearful hugs and promises to stay in touch. Leslie then dropped me off at the park's day use area, where I crawled into my pickup and followed her home.

After a quick shower, I slipped into bed next to Leslie as the neighborhood came to life. I tossed and turned under the sheet for an hour, unable to sleep, as my mind replayed scenes that would never go away. While Leslie dozed, I eased down the stairs and switched on the computer, figuring that a review of my office e-mails would provide a welcome diversion. An announcement from Clifford provided the biggest surprise. He'd been accepted into the Iowa Writers' Workshop at the University of Iowa and gave me his two-week notice. I penned a short if insincere congratulatory reply, wishing him the best of luck with his lipogrammatic novel, and hit the "Send" button.

I then wandered onto the front porch, reading the Saturday morning newspaper on the iPad. The quarter-page ad in the sports section for Catfish McCulloch's upcoming gun-and-knife show caught my attention for a moment, but the thought of a yet-to-be-written front-page story in tomorrow's edition caused my head to throb.

I was about to set the iPad aside when my eyes stopped at a short article in the local news section. Below a "Man Arrested on

Stalking Charges" headline, a two-paragraph piece reported that Max Alloway, age 26, had been taken into custody by the Little Rock Police Department for allegedly harassing Beth Anthony, 24. According to a police spokesman, Alloway had been under a court order to stay away from Ms. Anthony. Due to an outstanding warrant for aggravated assault, Alloway remained in jail.

When Leslie awoke and stepped outside after noon, she found me on the porch swing with the day's mail in my lap, still unopened. She gave me a sleepy kiss that was interrupted by the jangle of her telephone. She dashed inside to answer the call, rejoining me 10 minutes later, her jaw tight. "That was Mackie on the phone. She just saw the midday news."

I grimaced. "We should have tracked her down."

"I said the same thing, but Mackie claimed that we'd never have found her. She and her friends are staying in a resort near Eureka Springs, and one of her friends had rented the cabin."

"How's she taking it?"

"The news about J.J. shocked her, causing her to cry. She said more than once that he was one of the most decent men she'd ever met. But she sounded strong and claimed her relationship with Dr. Campbell had ended weeks ago. I think she's hurt by the way he used her. And she's upset with herself for never insisting on the return of her house key or changing the combination to the front gate."

"Did she have any idea what Campbell was doing?" I asked.

"Clueless was how Mackie described herself. She now assumes Campbell must have spent a lot of time at her place, performing his dastardly deeds, while she vacationed in Europe."

"Anything we can do?"

"She's already called the sheriff's office, and plans to drive home this evening to give her statement and answer questions."

We went inside for a light lunch, the first food I'd eaten in 24 hours. But I had no appetite and ate less than half of my sandwich. When her telephone rang again, Leslie spoke for a moment before handing me the phone. "It's for you."

A man who identified himself as the Pulaski County coroner was on the other end of the line. "Mr. Lassiter," he said. "I hate to impose, but we've got a problem."

"*We* do?"

"Let me explain. I need help. Dr. Rankin Campbell, whose body we presumably recovered earlier this morning, has no close kin. It's a Saturday and I've been unable to locate any university officials." After clearing his throat, he continued. "According to the sheriff's office, his ... uh ... colleague, Dr. Mackenzie Tillman, is out of town and won't be available for hours."

I had an uneasy feeling where this conversation was headed. "What do you need from me?"

"A positive identification of the body."

"Now?"

"The sooner the better."

I wanted to say no, but couldn't think of a reasonable excuse. "Where do I go?"

"The body's at the State Crime Lab off West Markham Street. I'll meet you there. But let me warn you," he said and paused for a beat, "it won't be a pretty sight."

As he gave me directions, I interrupted, asking him to repeat the address. My disbelieving ears had heard correctly. There must be a thousand streets in the city, and the state morgue is located at 3 Natural Resources Drive. The very concept of stockpiling corpses on Natural Resources Drive struck me as ... well ... macabre, something straight out of those unnerving dystopian scenes in *Soylent Green*, a movie that had always given me the creeps. Shaking my head, I slipped on a pair of shoes and walked out the front door.

Leslie sat on the porch swing, lost in thought, her eyes moist. When she looked up, I explained about the coroner's request. "Please hurry back," she said. "I don't want to be alone." I kissed her cheek, plodded down the steps, and climbed into my truck.

I wheeled into the visitor parking lot of the State Crime Lab 15 minutes later, surprised by the campus-like setting. A forest of towering pines surrounded the stark, three-story white concrete building. I walked past a pair of police cars parked near the entrance and signed in with a pleasant receptionist who put her knitting aside to give me an ID badge. I was #8. While awaiting my escort, I realized the closest I'd ever been to a morgue were several vicarious visits courtesy of novelist Patricia Cornwell.

Within a few minutes a man wearing a light blue lab coat entered the room, his hand extended.

"I'm Jerry Jeffries," he said. "Pulaski County coroner." As I introduced myself, I recognized him from much earlier in the day. Jeffries led me around a corner to an elevator station, where he pushed the button marked "Basement."

"I guess you determined the cause of death?" I asked.

"Myocardial infarction. A classic heart attack."

"Did he—"

"Suffer?" Jeffries interrupted. Overestimating my character, he mistook my interest for sympathy. I hoped Dr. Rankin Campbell had been conscious for a time, that he had felt the dermestid beetles and larvae crawling over his skin, into his shirt, and through his hair.

"Death came quickly, if that's what you're asking," Jeffries said as the elevator doors slid open. "My theory is that he experienced the attack while on the stepladder and then slumped forward into the concrete tank. Even if he'd been fully prepped and on an operating table inside the Mayo Clinic, there would have been no chance of survival."

I nodded, thinking perhaps Campbell had indeed been aware of the tiny feet skittering across his face. Ashamed for a moment, I got over it.

Jeffries guided me down a quiet sterile hall, greeting half a dozen colleagues before shoving open a pair of swinging stainless-steel doors and showing me into a bright and spacious tiled room. Despite all the lights, the room was cold. "I'll be back in a jiffy," he said, disappearing through another set of double doors. A hint of what I'd smelled yesterday hung in the air, mixed with new and discomforting aromas. I realized that even Cornwell's descriptive passages hadn't prepared me for the odors, the coldness of the place, and its sense of finality.

I wondered what kind of person it took to handle the duties of a coroner. "That was a pretty awful scene last night," I said as Jeffries returned. He carried a clipboard in one hand.

Jeffries shrugged. "At least he wasn't a floater."

"A floater?"

"Somebody who drowns, then rises to the surface weeks after the incident. Those are the ones we dread. The hot summer months are the worst. There's nothing quite like dealing with a bloated, decomposing body on a one-hundred-degree day in late August."

The doors opposite us opened and a young woman in a white polypropylene jumpsuit pulled a shiny gurney into the room. A corpse, Campbell's I assumed, lay under a white sheet with nothing visible but a pair of bluish feet. A red tag not much bigger than an index card dangled from the big toe of the left foot. Jeffries nodded to his assistant and she left the room.

"This won't be pleasant," he said. "Those bugs had a couple of hours to do their work." As Jeffries reached for the top of the sheet, I noticed that he'd set his jaw. Using both hands, he pulled the cloth away, exposing the body to its mid-section.

I took a clumsy step backwards, stumbling against a stool. I wanted to look away, to shut my eyes, to do anything but stare at the cadaver before me. But my gaze was beyond control, anchored to what less than a day earlier had been human.

"Too bad he collapsed face-first into the tank," said Jeffries. "They did a job on him."

The eyes were all but gone, along with much of the nose, particularly the soft tissue surrounding the nostrils. His lips were in tatters, although the cheeks and chin were partially intact. I couldn't see the right ear from my vantage point, but the one closest to me had been reduced by a quarter. Not wanting to, but doing it anyway, I edged closer, peering at the rest of a face. Even the gums had been attacked.

"I guess you removed his tongue in the autopsy?" I blamed my question on morbid curiosity.

"It was already gone when we recovered the body."

My stomach churned as my eyes studied the torso. A major Y-shaped incision couldn't be ignored. Running from his shoulders to his abdomen, it had been sewn together with thick twine, the dark stitches similar to those on a baseball. Most of the balance of the body appeared unblemished, although the fingertips had been mutilated and one elbow showed damage. I glanced again at the face. Or what remained of it. Feeling as if I might faint, I turned away and lurched to the other side of the room, slumping into a metal chair next to a water cooler.

Jeffries tugged the sheet back into place, sat on a nearby stool, and studied his clipboard. "Mr. Lassiter, can you make a positive identification of this body?"

I searched for my handkerchief, buying a little time to let my stomach settle. After blowing my nose, I took a deep breath before replacing the handkerchief in a pocket. "It's the right size, and the hair looks like his, I guess, but I cannot say for absolute certain that is Dr. Rankin Campbell. I remember a dimple in his chin, but …" That part of the face had been severely disfigured. I filled a paper cup and took a long drink of cold water. "He had a heavy gold chain hanging from his neck last time I saw him," I added, attempting to be helpful.

Jeffries studied the clipboard for a few seconds. "There's a gold necklace listed in the personal effects." He stood, sliding his pen into a pocket. "It was worth a try. Thanks for your time."

"What are you going to do?"

"Since fingerprints are out of the question, we'll use dental records," he said. "We had hoped to close this case today, but it'll wait until Monday when his dentist's office is open." He led me through the hall to the elevator.

"You're not going to bring Dr. Tillman here?"

He shook his head. "Comparing teeth to dental x-rays is our next option. It should lead to a positive ID."

"What about the dog?"

Jeffries gave me a strange look and shrugged as we stepped into the elevator. "I guess he's been placed with the Humane Society."

"I mean for identification. The fact that his rottweiler stood guard over the body should be proof enough that you'd found Campbell."

"I hadn't thought of that," he said. "But to the best of my knowledge, there's no precedent for using that kind of … canine … to make an ID." He shot me a sly grin, clearly pleased with his pun.

* * *

When I got home, Leslie and I took a long stroll through the quiet neighborhood, arms wrapped around each other's waists. Lost in our own thoughts, we walked for blocks, pausing only to let traffic pass.

"I still can't accept that J.J.'s dead," I finally said. "Maybe Campbell in his madness concocted portions of his story. Maybe …" I couldn't finish the sentence.

Leslie pulled me closer. Rounding the very corner where we had last glimpsed J.J. Newell's smiling face weeks earlier, we saw a Pulaski County sheriff's car parked at the curb in front of our house.

"Is this ever going to end?" she asked, clasping my hand. Deputy Johnson, the same man who had assisted with our statements hours ago, emerged from the driver's side as we approached his sedan.

"Hello again," he said. "The sheriff directed me to drop by and visit with y'all for a bit."

A pair of neighborhood children on bicycles skidded to a stop on the sidewalk, joining our small group. "Are you going to be arrested, Mr. Lassiter?" one of them asked. A precocious ten-year-old and the child of attorneys, she lived with her parents on the opposite side of the street. "Want me to get my mom?" Her young eyes brimmed with excitement.

"Thanks, Courtney," I said, "but that won't be necessary. This officer needs to talk with us for a minute."

Leslie squeezed my fingers. "Let's go to the porch," she said. Leslie and I sat on the swing while the deputy occupied a nearby deck chair. The children rode back and forth on the sidewalk like pre-pubescent paparazzi, casting wide-eyed glances in our direction every ten seconds. Gliding across the lawn, a mockingbird landed in a nearby magnolia and started through its repertoire.

"We recovered several items from the crime scene," the deputy said. "The sheriff thought you might help in their identification." He removed two small plastic bags from his briefcase, handing the first to Leslie.

She gasped, and then bit her lower lip as tears trickled down her cheeks. "Her earrings," she said. "Summer's earrings." Sobbing, she touched her right ear and lifted her hair to the side. "I'm wearing mine today." As I placed my arm on Leslie's shoulder and leaned against her, I felt her body trembling.

The deputy pulled a pen from a shirt pocket. "Ms. Carlisle, am I correct in understanding that you've identified these earrings as a pair owned by Ms. Summer Preston?"

While Leslie nodded, he made a notation on his pad before replacing the earrings in his briefcase. He next picked up the other bag and gave it to me. It held a ring, a large one, big enough for a man's hand. I removed it from the bag, surprised at its heft, and let my fingers investigate the worn, nicked surface. The words *Phi Beta Kappa—University of Arkansas* encircled a deep red stone. "This is J.J.'s," I said. "His initials are engraved inside the band." I reached for my handkerchief.

"And you, Mr. Lassiter, can identify this ring as one owned by Dr. James Joseph Newell?"

I returned the piece of jewelry to the bag and handed it to the deputy. "I went to the jewelry store with him the day he got it." When informed that he'd been elected to the honorary fraternity, J.J. had saved tips from his part-time bartending job at the VFW club in Fayetteville to purchase the ring. For six months, he added to his private cache in a cigar box, its total gaining ground ever so slowly. He never knew that I'd slipped in a pair of twenties.

"We also uncovered a cell phone from that tank," he said, again reaching for his briefcase.

Before he could continue, I said, "That's mine, and I have no interest in it." I couldn't imagine holding that device anywhere near my face.

"I'm sorry for the intrusion," the deputy said. He closed his briefcase, stood, and gave his head a slight dip. "I appreciate your help." He walked to his patrol car, shaking hands with the kids on the sidewalk before he drove away.

Leslie, who had gone inside to get a tissue, met me at the door. "Your Uncle Booker must have called while we were gone. He left a message on my cell phone."

I didn't recognize his voice at first. "Dear Ms. Carlisle," he said, out of breath. "Given that I have been unable to reach my nephew, I hope you can pass this message along to him. I fear Dr. Rankin Campbell is an evil being, the devil incarnate. He has recorded an electronic diary of barbaric, horrendous deeds. He may be responsible for the deaths of both J.J. and Ms. Preston. I shall summon the authorities at once." His tone grew sharper. "I beseech you both to be careful."

After returning the phone to Leslie, I trudged up the stairs and fell into bed, totally fatigued, where I slept two or three hours. It was late afternoon when I joined Leslie on the porch. She'd fixed us each a bourbon and water when her phone rang. It was Gib.

"Yes, he's here. Randy had ...uh ... a mishap with his phone," she said, and handed me her cell.

"We just heard the terrible news about J.J.," he said. "Ellen and I are stunned by his death. J.J. was such a great guy, one of a kind."

"Leslie and I are equally shocked," I said. "It still hasn't really sunk in that he's gone."

"There is at least one ray of light on this dark day," he said. "Ellen gave birth less than an hour ago. You're now an uncle."

I had completely forgotten about their baby.

"Eight pounds, twelve ounces," Gib said. "The cutest little boy I've ever seen."

"Congratulations! How's she doing?"

"Your sister is exhausted, but otherwise doing fine. Can you and Leslie stop by the hospital later tonight?"

"We'll sneak in a bottle of Champagne."

"One more thing," he said. "We've named him Jimmy."

"You've picked a good, solid all-American name. I like it."

There was a pause on the other end of the line. "His full name is … James Joseph Yarberry." Gib's voice broke as he ended the call.

Leslie provided the shoulder, and the cry that I had put off for weeks felt right.

The End

ABOUT THE AUTHOR

A former partner in a canoe-outfitting business on the Buffalo River, Joe David Rice spent a good deal of time roaming the Ozarks during his younger days. And as Arkansas's tourism director for over 30 years, he gained an unequaled familiarity with the state, its people, and Arkansas's intriguing nuances. A prize-winner in the Ozark Creative Writers Conference, he's also the author of the two-volume *Arkansas Backstories: Quirks, Characters, and Curiosities of the Natural State*. He and his wife, Tracey, enjoy their cabin, which backs up to the Buffalo National River's Ponca Wilderness in Newton County.

A Nasty Way to Die is the second novel in the Randy Lassiter/Leslie Carlisle series. They meet in the first book, *An Undercurrent of Murder*. Randy and Dr. Gib Yarberry, his brother-in-law, are on a hiking getaway in the Buffalo River country and stumble into Leslie, a professional photographer in the area on an assignment, during their October trek. A chance encounter with a group of desperate drug-runners soon has them fleeing for their lives, battling both Mother Nature and some very bad dudes.

The final book in the trilogy, *A Piece of Paradise*, will find Leslie and Randy in the Commonwealth of the Bahamas, searching for a missing friend while a Category 4 hurricane is bearing down on the islands. The novel will be available in the near future.

Made in the USA
Coppell, TX
10 August 2021

60274174R00177